EVIDENCE OF THINGS UNSEEN

The second volume of
The Zoë Journals Series

by

BEVERLY BUSH

WORD PUBLISHING
Dallas•London•Vancouver•Melbourne

PUBLISHED BY WORD PUBLISHING, DALLAS, TEXAS

LIBRARY OF CONGRESS CATALOGING-IN-PUBLICATION DATA:
Bush, Beverly.
    Evidence of things unseen / by Beverly Bush
        p.   cm.—(The second volume of the Zoë journals series)
    ISBN 0-8499-4040-0
    I. Title.   II. Series: Bush, Beverly, 1927–   Zoë journals series; 2nd v.
Ps3569.M5114E75   1997
813'.54—DC21   95-10953
                                                                       CIP

7 8 9 0 1 2 3 4 QKP 9 8 7 6 5 4 3 2 1

PRINTED IN THE UNITED STATES OF AMERICA

To the three loving Zoës in my life:

My mother, Zoë Marguerite,

My sister, Zoë Patricia,

My niece, Zoë Anne

Acknowledgments

Thank you Lord, for:

Ernie Owen, my advocate and cheerleader,
and his partner in encouragement, Pauline.

Nancy Norris, essential strand of that threefold cord:
The Lord, editor, and author.

Patty Bradbury and her courageous sharing
from her personal pain.

Carol, my trusting and affirming "sister,"
whose servant's heart enriches my life and writing.

Diane, whose prayers shine with her gifts of
discernment and sensitivity.

Linda, Elaine, Hank, Eileen, and Mary, critique-ers
extraordinaire.

Barbara, who shared her computer expertise and proofread,
together with Clara, Kim, and Wilma.

Kay Arthur and Precept Ministries who introduced me
to the "high tower" of God's name in their *Lord, I Want to
Know You* study.

My steadfast and forbearing Bob!

PROLOGUE

ॐ

RISING FROM THE CHILL NIGHTIME DEPTHS of the Pacific, the surf broke white, foaming along the narrow strand of sand in Malibu. Just beyond the beach, across Pacific Coast Highway, the mountains rose, looming black against a star-bright sky.

Just after midnight, the headlights of a single car, turning off Pacific Coast Highway, violated the darkness of Seabreeze Drive.

Like the luminous eyes of a snake, they twisted slowly up the mountainside, now to the right, then left, negotiating the hairpin turns. Higher and higher they mounted, passing houses notched into the hill or perched on landscaped buttes or sheer cliff—all overlooking the ocean.

The headlights stopped only when they reached the end of the paving. Here, on the crest of a knoll, where a wild garden of red-berried toyon grew, two driveways branched off from the road. One led to a white stucco home, while the driveway on the left led to a rustic cedar ranch home. The headlights blinked off, but through the billowing clouds of exhaust, the taillights glowed like hot coals. Then they, too, went black.

꒰꒱

Inside the cedar house, a terrified shriek pierced Andrea Lang's deep, dreamless sleep. She lifted her head groggily, listening to the prescient silence. The time shone from the clock: 12:30. From the next room, the wail rose again, even louder.

"Not tonight, not before such a big day," she groaned, grabbing her robe from the foot of the bed to hurry through the darkness to her daughter.

By the glow of the night-light, she could see the small figure in blue pajamas against the wall at the head of the bed. "Joy, it's OK. It's OK," Andrea soothed. As she scooped her daughter into her arms, Joy locked her sturdy arms around her neck. Then, as she carried her to the white rocker by the window, Joy pulled back, shrieking still louder.

Andrea looked up as Peter came into the room, concern in his heavy-lidded brown eyes. "Hey, what's all this noise about?" he asked gently.

Joy took a shuddering breath and pointed at the window. "S-somebody looking inna window," she managed. Her cries rose again as she clung to her mother.

1

From Zoë's Prayer Journal:

January 2: Dear Lord, You seemed to waken me from the soundest sleep, and I know that's usually a call to prayer. What comes to mind immediately is my Malibu family. Is it because for some time I've been concerned over Andrea's priorities? It's not that I'm opposed to her working. But I wonder if she's giving my grandchildren all they need. My angel, Joy, is still so little—just three-and-a-half. And my buddy, Tim, may be eleven, but he still needs his mom. (OK, I admit I wonder, too, if this isn't hard on Peter!) Is there anything I can do without being a meddling mother-in-law? I ask You, my sovereign Lord, to please help Andrea see the importance of time with those precious kids. I thank You that You love them, want the best for them even more than I do! In Jesus' name, amen.

SHOVING THE DISHWASHER DOOR SHUT with her foot, Andrea balanced the breakfast dishes on one arm. With her free hand, she grabbed the milk from the refrigerator, closing the door with a quick thrust of her hip.

"The one-woman band," Peter laughed, taking the dishes from her and setting the table. "All five-feet-two of you!" He looked up as Joy and Tim clambered into the room. "Morning, guys," he said, helping Joy into her booster chair.

As they sat down, Andrea looked across the breakfast table at her slender son. *A good kid. Solid, dependable, like his dad,* she thought. Her focus shifted to Joy, whose smile seemed to light up the whole kitchen. She stared for a moment at Joy's burnished blond hair and the heart-shaped face, so like her own. *Cuter than the kid our client uses in that cereal commercial,* she decided.

Joy turned to Peter, cheeks dimpling. "Daddy, Daddy?"

"Mm?"

"How much do you love me?" She held her chubby hands a few inches apart. "This much?"

Peter grinned. "No. More than that."

"This much?" She moved her hands farther apart.

"Oh, no. More than that."

They continued their routine till Joy could reach out no farther. "Then, *this* much?" she demanded.

"No, no, no!" Peter exclaimed, holding his own hands at arms length. "This much—and more!"

"Yea!" Joy clapped her hands. She slipped down from her booster chair and held out her arms to him. As he scooped her onto his lap, she snuggled against him and declared, "You're a good daddy. You rocked me last night and made me feel better."

"Good." Peter hugged her, and Andrea thought how protected she looked, nestled against his solid 190 pounds.

"Well, you sure made enough noise last night." Tim pointed his cereal spoon at Joy.

Andrea shot him a frown. "She had a nightmare. That's all."

"Somebody at my window." Joy nodded emphatically.

"Yeah, sure!" Tim scoffed.

"Now, honey, we've been through all that," Andrea said. "Remember, Daddy turned on all the outside lights?"

"And what did you see?" Peter prompted.

"A bug!" Joy laughed.

"Ri-i-ight!" Andrea said. She turned to Peter. "Did you give Joy her medication?"

He nodded.

"Good." She didn't want a repeat of Joy's episode with convulsions five months ago when she'd run a high fever.

Joy reached up and tugged at Peter's necktie. "You goin' to work?"

Peter nodded. "Yep, Christmas vacation's over for your mom and me. It's back to work we go."

"Hi-ho, hi-ho," Tim began the dwarfs' song from *Snow White*.

"It's offta work we go," Joy joined in. Her sweet little voice, slightly off-key, was beguiling.

"No, *they* go," Tim corrected, pushing back a wave of chocolate brown hair that immediately fell over his forehead again. "Ha ha! But I don't gotta go back to school till next week."

"'Don't gotta?'" Andrea recoiled in mock horror. "Maybe you'd better go *this* week! Oh," she remembered, "but one thing you do need to do is get a birthday present for your cousin, Scott. Esther'll take you."

"Check." Tim looked across the road at the contemporary white house. "I wish the Coopers were here. That Brant looks cool."

"Maybe you can see him when they get back from skiing," Andrea said.

Peter stood and gently set Joy on the floor. "Your mom's got a big day today. Super important presentation."

"She can do it," Tim said confidently.

"Thank you, darling." She crossed her fingers. "I really, really want this account. It'd be the plum of my career." She turned to Peter. "Any parting advice?"

He thought a moment. "Don't rush it."

"Moi?" Andrea pointed at herself, eyes all innocence. "When did you ever see me hurry?"

Peter looked at his watch. "About two minutes ago, whipping across the kitchen, using every available appendage."

"Yeah, Mom. You're always running or doing a bunch of things at once," Tim said.

"Well." She lifted her head defensively. "That's how things get done."

∽

After Peter left for work, Andrea headed for the bedroom, anxious—no, she decided, *eager*—to get on with her day. She opened the closet door.

"S'prise!" Joy giggled, a broad grin dimpling her face as she popped out from behind the dresses.

"Oh!" cried Andrea, feigning shock. She laughed and rumpled her daughter's hair. "You going to help me dress?"

"Yep."

Andrea groaned inwardly. This morning, she really could do without the "help."

"Bring your shoes?" Joy asked.

"Great. Dark blue pumps, please."

Obediently, Joy found the shoes on the rack and placed them carefully beside the bed.

"Mom?" came Tim's voice at her doorway, "Esther's here and I'm going outside."

She turned toward him. "Fine, Tim,"

He pulled the corners of his mouth down with his fingers. "Poor Mom. Back to work."

"We had a great holiday together, didn't we?" She smiled at the memory. "First Christmas in this house. Holly from the hills to deck the halls."

Tim's eyes twinkled. "Even if you didn't find the outdoor Christmas lights."

"Details, details!" Glancing at the clock, she put her hand on Joy's shoulder. "Want to go outside with Tim?"

"Come on," he urged his sister.

She sighed with relief as Joy followed her brother. She loved her daughter, but this morning, she didn't need the distraction.

Ten minutes later, she stood before the mirrored closet door, buttoning her silk print blouse. She put on her suit jacket—well tailored, but not too severe, her best shade of soft blue. Slipping on her pumps, she took a final look. "You look like something out of your *Dress to Win* video," she told her reflection. "Well, whatever it takes!" She grabbed her briefcase and looked at her watch. Five minutes for the kids, and she'd be on her way. Excitement mounting, she hurried down the hall, calling out her greeting to Esther.

Esther emerged from the kitchen, her twiggy body clad in a clean but slightly large rust-colored dress that she'd pulled together at the waist with a braided belt. She shook her head, and her drab blond hair swung across her face. "I see your vacation didn't slow you down. Now, don't worry about a thing. I remember about getting the birthday present."

"Good. And no Christmas candy for the kids during the day, OK? Thanks, Esther. Have a good day." She opened the double doors and stepped outside. The air smelled of sage and a hundred other plants she hadn't yet identified, all growing wild in the green, unspoiled hills behind their house. How good to be away from the precisely squared yards and row-on-row houses of the city.

By the entryway, a sea of iceplant bloomed in a dayglow orange that almost hurt her eyes as the morning sun reflected from droplets of dew. Detouring toward the play yard, she called, "Joy? Tim?"

With a ring-ring of her red Christmas tricycle bell, Joy pedaled toward her. Her jaunty smile faded as she saw Andrea's briefcase. "Don't want you to go."

"Honey, you know I have a big day at the office." She glanced at her watch, feeling the time slipping by. "Tell you what. Let's play 'owl.'"

She squatted down, hoping her pantyhose wouldn't run, and put her nose and forehead against Joy's.

"Close your eyes and don't peek," Joy ordered.

"Okay," Andrea said. "One—two—three—OWL!" They both opened their eyes and laughed at the sight of the two big close-together "owl eyes." She held her daughter close and kissed her. "You be good with Esther today, darling." Standing, she glanced toward the kitchen window and waved at the housekeeper, grateful for her warm, watchful care.

"Leaving now, Mom?"

Andrea stood as Tim rounded the corner from the play yard. "Yes, and I need a hug before I go. Can you help me out?"

He grinned. "Yeah. I guess so."

She bent down for his feel-how-strong-I'm-getting bear hug. "Now I can get through the day," she sighed.

"You see the minivan's all ready for you?" Tim asked. "Dad and I checked the tires and oil, and I washed the windshield."

"My car-maintenance specialists! Thanks, Tim. Okay, now,

remember, Esther's taking you to the toy store later to buy a present for Scott's birthday."

As she started toward her white minivan, she heard Joy begin to cry. Oh, no. What was this, a new clingy stage? She'd have to get out her child-development book.

She turned to see Tim pick up Joy, trying not to stagger with her weight. "Come on, Joy, let's go back to the swing. Mom'll be back soon. Let's wave at her now."

Good old Tim, she thought, blowing a grateful kiss to him as she climbed in the car and put the window down. Just before she started the engine, she heard him say, "Don't worry, Joy. Your big bro's gonna take care of you."

2

ANDREA BACKED HER MINIVAN down the driveway. "Love you! See you guys around five."

She breathed a sigh of relief as she entered the winding road down the Malibu hillside. *It's hard to do it all—balance home and career,* she admitted. *But I love my work, and I'm good at it.*

Looking down on the rooftops below and a powder-blue expanse of sea blending perfectly into the sky, she felt a sudden surge of pride. How privileged they were to live here, above the rest of the world! It was her success at the Reynolds public-relations agency that had made it possible to buy the house two months ago. Peter's salary as an engineer—even a senior project engineer for Lang-Madson Corporation—couldn't quite swing view property like theirs, nine hundred feet above the ocean. But they both agreed it was a great, smog-free, wide-open spot where the kids could grow and thrive. And with their combined salaries, they could handle it.

One last hairpin turn brought her to Pacific Coast Highway. Traffic was heavy, but moving. Good. It should be an easy drive along the ocean, breathing the fragrant salt air, hearing the percussion of the surf. Then she'd connect with the Santa Monica Freeway into L.A.

She appreciated this time of separation, a space that allowed her to disconnect from home and focus on work. After a week off for the holidays, and especially after Joy's fussiness this morning, she needed the time to reconnect with the business of the day.

What a jewel this new, $200 million resort on the ocean would be! Today she'd meet with the owner and the general manager. It seemed unusual to have the owner involved, and Renato Crivello would be a tough sell. With his small dark eyes and his powerful jawline, he reminded her of a pit bull, bred to fight. Still, she saw a sentimental side to him that she hoped to tap. He was, after all, a man with a dream. Now, after making his bundle in international finance, he could return to his roots, for he'd grown up in the hotel business in Italy. She wondered how long he had dreamed of building this luxury hotel in southern California.

The general manager, Anthony Britton, was a smoothie—magnetic, a charmer. He'd be wonderful in his job and seemed to be on her side, or was that part of his please-everyone game? She'd find out.

She smiled as traffic stopped beside the Seaview Inn, one of her accounts. That success story should help her with Crivello, for none of her competition had her experience with the hospitality industry. The Inn shone with class. Then she looked above it to the church, its wood structure obviously losing its battle with the salt air. Made the neighborhood look a tad tacky. Still, she thought for a fleeting moment about asking God to help her with her presentation.

But when traffic began to move again, her thoughts flowed back to the day ahead. She felt confident her public-relations campaign was strong, her budget realistic, and that her creative approaches would appeal to them. After her dress rehearsal, just before Christmas vacation, her agency's staff had applauded her, and they were probably tougher critics than the client.

❧

Andrea's anticipation rose as the floor numbers illuminated in the ascending elevator. Ten—eleven—the door slid open, and she stepped into the Reynolds Communications reception room. Elegant beveled mirrors and chrome-framed furniture accented the mauve carpeting and upholstery.

"Hey, Ms. Lang!" The blond behind the receptionist's desk greeted her with a wave of a perfectly manicured hand. "You've got a new suit. Christmas present? A size six petite, I bet." Her face registered envy before she nodded her approval. "Right in your color palette too. Matches your French blue eyes."

"French blue eyes! You're been reading too much ad copy!" Andrea grinned as she crossed the reception area. "The execs from Oceanfront should be here at eleven. Give me a call as soon as they arrive."

Starting down the hall, she glanced in the conference room, with everything at the ready since her dress rehearsal the last day before vacation. She moved on past the office of her boss, Jason Reynolds. Once she'd had to walk all the way back to the tiny partitioned cubicles where the copywriters worked. But now, halfway down the hall, she turned toward her office. Slipping into her desk chair, she set a stack of incoming mail to one side and began reviewing the agenda for the meeting.

By two that afternoon, Andrea felt the flush of impending victory. Despite Renato Crivello's stubborn, impassive face, she was sure she had overcome his initial grumbling this morning with her visual blitzkrieg of promotional ideas. She thought Reynolds sensed the positive response too. During her three years with the agency, she'd learned to read the pursing of her boss's lips, his way of holding back a smile.

And her carefully orchestrated lunch in the elegance of Salvatore's, which Crivello obviously relished, had also set the stage for her next move.

"Now about the restaurant," Crivello began, flicking an invisible piece of lint from his handsomely cut Armani suit.

Thank you, Mr. Crivello, she said to herself, for he'd set her up neatly to play her trump card. "Mr. Crivello, I was thinking about your concept of a casual café, and I can see that you want something that reflects the laid-back beach life to guests. But this is a gracious, elegant property, with marble in the floors and a view almost all the way to Hawaii on a clear day. And you have an extensive background in the hotel-restaurant business. Here's your opportunity to create a restaurant that will dazzle the community. It could be a fabulous PR tool, pulling in the VIPs, who would in turn recommend the hotel to out-of-towners." She stood by his chair, leaning toward him. "Think in terms of white cloths, handsome china, a 'name' chef, an innovative contemporary menu with gorgeous presentations. Make a name for yourself with your food!"

She dropped a gold-and-black matchbook from their lunch restaurant on the table in front of him. "You know food and presentation better than Salvatore or anyone else—and did you notice the crowd there?"

She saw Britton nod. "I've been thinking the same thing." He turned to Crivello. "It isn't too late, Renato. We could do a casual terrace eating area—more of a café. And then on the oceanfront—here, I'll show you on the plans." He produced a thick set of renderings, and as he and Crivello bent over them, Andrea looked at Reynolds. No doubt of the upturn of the corners of his mouth.

"We can work with either concept," she assured them. "But I urge you not to ignore this opportunity! Now let me show you—"

She broke off as the phone rang.

Reynolds muttered an expletive. "I told Madge we're not to be interrupted."

He picked up the receiver. "Madge, didn't you understand—" He listened and frowned, looking toward Andrea. "Tell her she'll call back." His mouth drew into a tight line. "All right," he said. He hung up, scribbled a note, and passed it to Andrea.

She felt her face flush, knowing how Reynolds hated interruptions, especially if they were what he termed "domestic crises." And what would Crivello think?

She sensed them all watching as she scanned the note: "Housekeeper on line. 'Emergency.'"

3

ANDREA STARED AT THE NOTE, hesitating. Esther wouldn't interrupt unless . . . she took a deep breath and flashed what she hoped was a confident smile. "Let's take a short break, gentlemen. I'll have coffee brought in."

She made it a point to walk slowly from the conference room to her office. "Coffee in the conference room," she said to her secretary as she closed the door. Hurrying to her desk, she picked up the phone. "Yes, Esther?"

"Miz Lang? We're at the toy store and-and-Joy-ohhh—" Her voice became a thin wail.

Andrea felt the sweat rise on her palms. "What is it, Esther? What's wrong?"

"Joy—she's just—disappeared. We've looked and we've looked. Can't find her anywhere. The manager just put in a call to the sheriff, but I had to call you. Oh, Miz Lang, I was just having the present wrapped for Scott's birthday party, and Joy wanted to look at the dolls, so Tim took her back—" She began to cry.

Andrea could hear her own panic mounting, thudding in her ears. Over it, Tim's voice rose in the background.

"Tim wants to talk with you," Esther whispered.

"Mom?"

Andrea held the phone away from her ear at Tim's strident shout. "Mom, I don't know what happened. Honest, I was only away from Joy for a minute. We can't find her anywhere. We've looked and looked. She's just disappeared!"

Remembering Joy hiding in her closet that morning, she tried to reassure him—and herself. "Honey, are you absolutely sure she isn't just hiding, trying to scare you?"

"Mom," he cried, "we've yelled 'Joy!' all over the store. We've looked out in the parking lot and on the other side of Coast Highway. She's just outta here. Gone!"

Her cheeks burned, while a cold knot of fear formed in her stomach. "Hang in there, Tim. You're at the store on the Coast Highway, right? I'll come as soon as I can. Let me speak to Esther again."

"Yes, Miz Lang?"

"Esther, have you called Mr. Lang?"

"Yes. He's coming right away."

"Good. I'm on my way too," she promised. "You stay there." She slammed the phone down. Every fiber of her being wanted to flee, to be in Malibu immediately. She'd have to walk out on the presentation. Chuck it all, after all that work. She grabbed her purse.

No, wait. She blinked rapidly. *Think a minute. The sheriff's been called. Peter's on the way.* She pushed her sleeve back to look at her watch. Just after three. *Would five minutes make any difference? Couldn't I finish here?* She heard her own rapid breaths. *Can I pull myself together enough to finish?*

Closing her eyes, she forced herself to concentrate on slow, even breathing. Then, stopping only for a sip from the water fountain, she reentered the conference room.

Forcing a smile, she asked, "Shall we continue? I think we can wrap up quickly."

She wasn't sure how she closed, but Mr. Reynolds was smiling and Britton shook her hand. "Very comprehensive job!"

Crivello—well, it was hard to tell when he muttered, "Give us time to go back over this. It's very detailed. We'll be in touch."

She waited for them to leave, hating the small talk, trying to hide her impatience. At last she dashed to her office, grabbed her purse and briefcase, and called, "I'm gone for the day," to her secretary as she rushed for the elevator.

や

Andrea could feel her terror mount as she raced along the Santa Monica Freeway. "Oh, God," she said aloud, "let Joy be OK." Quickly, she assured herself, *I know she's OK. She has to be. By the time I get there, she'll be back, the center of attention. Somebody will probably have bought her an ice cream cone, and they'll all be fussing over her.*

She glanced at her speedometer. Seventy-five. She slowed as the freeway ended, and she swept through a short tunnel. Usually when she emerged to the sudden splendor of the Santa Monica Mountains rising from the sea, she felt an instant balm, even after the hardest day. But this afternoon, her pulse only quickened. She glanced down at her hands, clamped with all their might on the steering wheel. *I'm holding on for dear life,* she realized.

Suddenly, an image of Joy's terror the previous night flashed before her. *Had* someone been outside her bedroom window? Surely not. A few weeks ago, Joy had wakened her to tell about a bear in her room.

Traffic grew more congested at Topanga Boulevard. Would she ever get there? She remembered weeping over newspaper stories about missing children, wondering how parents could handle such a nightmare, hoping never to have to face it herself.

At last she rounded a curve along the coastline, and the toy store swung into view. Even before she turned into the parking lot, she spotted a sheriff's car. If it was still here . . .

Her knees went spongy, and she had difficulty braking as she pulled into a parking space next to Esther's elderly faded blue Buick. It was true. It was happening—the nightmare she couldn't possibly endure.

Mouth dry, heart racing, she tried to summon, from somewhere deep within, a semblance of positive thinking. Even though the sheriff was still there, they could have missed Joy. She could be there, somewhere. Andrea jammed the gearshift into park, grabbed her keys, and rushed toward the red door. *She'd* find Joy.

She collided with Peter in the doorway. "Peter!" she cried. "I have to—" She fought to get past him. He held her and eased her back outside.

"Peter, I have to look for Joy!" she shouted.

"She isn't here," he said softly. "Everyone's looked everywhere."

She shook her head vehemently. "I have to look. I know the kinds of places she'd hide."

She saw his stricken face and felt him release her. "Go ahead," he said.

She flung the door open and swept past the startled clerks,

marching up and down the three empty aisles. But of course, Joy wouldn't be there. The storeroom. That was the place. Joy could easily crawl into a carton, maybe even fall asleep. She rushed toward the door in the back of the store and into the storage area. It wasn't what she expected. She'd envisioned piles of empty cartons, but instead found shelves of games and toys and just a few cartons, all sealed. She poked behind them, calling, "Joy! Joy, are you there?" She pushed open the back door. Nothing but one sport-utility vehicle and a dumpster. Could her daughter . . . ? No, there was no way she could climb up into the dumpster. She hurried to look in the vehicle. Nothing. She'd been so sure. She felt numb, disoriented. Sensing Peter behind her, she let him walk her around to the front of the store. "She's not here," she murmured, still not quite believing it.

"That's right," he said gently. "She just vanished during those few minutes no one was watching. She's gone."

Slowly, the reality of the word "gone" penetrated. She turned toward him and fell into his arms. Then, face against the rough tweed of his jacket, she wept.

He stroked her hair. "The sheriff's department's putting together an all-out search. We'll find her."

Footsteps crunched on the gravel. Turning, she leaned against Peter, holding his arms around her, and saw a beefy man in immaculately pressed green pants and beige shirt bearing the sheriff's department insignia.

Holding out her hand, she said, "I'm Andrea Lang."

"Mrs. Lang, Deputy Maxwell."

"Yes." She looked up at his smooth-shaven face. "What are you doing to find my daughter? Have you—"

The deputy gave her a sympathetic smile and said, "Let me catch you up on what we're doing." He pointed across the highway to the oceanfront. "We have lifeguards combing the beach as well as looking for anything in the water."

In the water! The very thought of the chilly January ocean raised goose bumps on her arms. She knew the water couldn't be much more than fifty-five degrees. "You think she could . . . "

"Probably not. But we have to check it out."

"Could she have started up the hill toward home?" she wondered.

"We're checking that too. I expect a helicopter any minute. And we're patrolling the roads. If necessary, I can call out reserve deputies to search on foot."

"But that wouldn't be like Joy, would it, Peter?" She tilted her head back against his chest. "I mean for her to wander outside the store? She'd be too interested in the toys." Without waiting for an answer she looked toward the deputy. "Did anybody see her with anyone? I mean, we've taught her not to talk to strangers. But could someone have . . . " She couldn't bring herself to use the word "kidnapped" or "abducted."

Maxwell shook his head. "We've interviewed everyone who was in the store. Nobody saw her leave—either alone or with someone. Not the store owner, the clerk, or the three other customers. Not your housekeeper or your son."

Tim! Ever since the phone call, all her thoughts had been on Joy. "Where is he?" she cried. Suddenly, she needed desperately to see him, to know he was all right.

"He's in Esther's car, right beside yours," Peter said.

She ran toward the car and saw a small figure huddled in the far back corner. "Tim!" she exclaimed. He sat, arms wrapped around his legs like a person trying to reduce his exposure to the elements, his face hidden on his knees. When she opened the car door, he started so violently, his arms and legs flew out as though released by springs.

"Sorry I startled you, honey," she said, seeing the tears on his cheeks. Climbing in beside him, heart aching for her son, she put her arm around him and spoke softly. "Honey, you OK?"

"What do you think?" he muttered, burying his head once again in his knees.

"Tim, I love you. Don't be so hard on yourself." She tried hard to inject a tone of certainty. "It's going to be all right."

"Oh, Miz Lang!" She heard Esther's voice just outside the car. Looking out, she saw the housekeeper's mouth quiver, beaver-like teeth overlapping her lower lip. Her tall, thin frame shook with sobs.

"I'll be back," she whispered to Tim and got out of the car. The housekeeper embraced her, and Andrea patted her shoulder in a perfunctory attempt at reassurance. But all she could manage was, "It's hard to understand how this could happen, Esther."

"I know," the woman wailed, pushing a strand of mousy blond hair away from her face. "I feel so bad!"

I don't even want to talk to her, Andrea thought. "Stay here with Tim, will you, while I finish with the sheriff?"

Shivering in the penetrating wintry breeze, Andrea turned, smelling salt and seaweed and dead things from the ocean. There was little comfort in the sun, which seemed as cool and pale as the moon, low in the colorless afternoon sky. She walked slowly toward Peter and the deputy and welcomed her husband's arm around her.

"Do you have any ideas, any thoughts about what happened?" she asked the deputy. "Does it seem most likely that, uh, someone took her?"

"Honey," Peter's voice was steady, quiet. "It's too soon to jump to any—"

"But Peter, did you tell him about last night?"

He frowned and shook his head. "Didn't think of it. Figured it was a kid's nightmare. You know how imaginative Joy is, asleep or awake. Once there was a bear in her room. Another time, it was a crocodile."

"Maybe." She turned toward Maxwell. "This may not be anything. But sometime around 12:30 this morning Joy began screaming. Seemed to think someone was looking in her window."

"We turned on the outdoor floods," Peter added. "Couldn't see anything or anybody."

"Did you go outside, look around the yard?"

Peter exhaled heavily. "No."

Why didn't we? she wondered. *Why did we just dismiss it as a nightmare?*

"We'll check out the yard," Maxwell promised.

"There's a patio outside her window. There wouldn't be any footpr—" She stopped. "Sorry." Her thoughts were jabbing out in every direction, wanting answers *now*. She had to focus, take one thing at a time. Forcing a quiet, reasonable tone, she asked, "Tell me what we can do to help, Deputy."

"Right. I want you to check this description your housekeeper gave us. And we need to know if there's any place she regularly goes to play."

"No, only the play area in our yard. We just moved here the middle of November," she said.

He nodded. "Also, you should check very carefully *everywhere* in your house and yard—closets, under beds, garage, tool shed—to see if she might be there. And I need some pictures of her. We'll get them out to assisting units. And if she doesn't surface within the next hour or so, we'll want to get some photos to the TV stations. That OK with you?"

"Of course."

She examined the sheet on the deputy's clipboard.

"Yes, this is right. Her age, height, weight. The description. Ah, good, her medication." She looked up. "That's important. Now that she takes it every day, she's even more likely to—" she swallowed, "to have a convulsion if the medication's stopped." She thought a moment. "Oh, yes! Dimples. Joy has deep dimples. When she smiles." Her voice caught and she cleared her throat. "Anything else?"

"Yes. We may want to use bloodhounds to help us look. So I'll need a couple of items of your daughter's clothing—something she's worn recently, unwashed."

She nodded.

The deputy hesitated. "Of course, we'll do a check on the housekeeper. She says she's been with you three years."

She nodded. "She's been perfectly trustworthy." She felt her anger rise. "Until now." She bit her lip. "But if you're wondering if she could be part of some plan—oh, that would be hard to believe." She looked away. *Or would it*, she wondered.

Maxwell nodded and made a note. "I think that's it for now, then."

"Why don't we get on home, then?" Peter asked.

Home! Home without Joy there. In three and a half years, there had never been an evening without her sunny presence. *I can't*, she thought. *Oh, God, I can't go home to that empty house.*

4

From Zoë's Prayer Journal

January 2: Dear Lord, thank You for giving me this time, waiting for clients to come in, to return to my prayer journal. Father, I do pray for all my children and grandchildren. But again, I especially have on my heart my Malibu family. It's more than Andrea's immersion in her work, I realize. You know how distressed I am that Peter and Andrea no longer seek You, that they've fallen away—for years now. Oh, Lord, turn their eyes back to You. Bring back my steadfast son, Peter, and my dynamic daughter-in-law, Andrea. May my grandchildren trust you—both my special buddy, Tim, and my little angel, Joy. Draw them to Yourself, heavenly Father, in Jesus' name, amen.

ANDREA STOOD, hugging herself in the chill winter wind. From somewhere, far away, it seemed, she heard Peter's voice. "We really need to get Tim out of here."

She swallowed against the constriction in her throat and nodded. "You're right."

OK, then, Mr. and Mrs. Lang," the deputy said. "We'll be by in about an hour."

"Thanks, Deputy," Peter said. His arm still around Andrea, he walked her toward the car. "You OK to drive, honey?"

"I think so. Why don't you take Tim?" She put her hand on his arm. "Oh, Peter, be sure he knows we don't blame him." She looked toward the housekeeper's car. "I'll tell Esther to leave. In fact, I'll tell her not to come tomorrow." She frowned. "I just don't feel good about her, Peter."

"But surely you don't think she—"

"I don't know *what* to think!" she snapped.

The housekeeper sprang out of the driver's seat as they approached her car. Peter opened the rear door and gently eased Tim out. "C'mon Timmer. Let's head for home." The boy stared desolately at his Reeboks as Peter led him toward his Olds.

"You want me to come back home with you?" Esther asked.

"No!" The word blurted out with such conviction, Andrea instantly regretted it. She saw the woman flinch and forced softness into her voice. "Thanks, no, Esther. No, you get on home." She paused, realizing she didn't want the woman back in her house. "Esther, I won't be going to work tomorrow. I'll call when I need you."

It seemed an enormous effort for the housekeeper to meet Andrea's gaze. "I feel so bad," she murmured.

"I know you do," Andrea said as she stepped into her own car.

Inside, she slumped against the seat. *If only I'd been there. No, that isn't fair. It could have happened even then.* She closed her eyes against the sting of tears. *But oh, Esther, why didn't you keep Joy with you?*

She looked out the window to see the outside lights of the

store snap on and felt the muscles of her stomach tighten. Darkness came so early these winter afternoons. There was so little daylight left for finding Joy. What if she was wandering in the hills, lost? Andrea thought of the coyotes that howled outside their house at night and the great horned owls, half-again the size of a cat, waiting to swoop down for their prey. Where was that helicopter? Were the sheriff's department's cars really covering the roads?

She twisted the key in the ignition and slowly drove along the Coast Highway, foot pressing on the accelerator, lifting, pressing again. She looked on both sides of the road, praying to see a small figure in denim pants and a blue-and-white-striped sweatshirt. Then she turned off and inched along the steep, mile-and-half drive up the hill to their house. Peering off from one side to the other, she hoped against hope for a glimpse of strawberry blond hair.

Nothing.

Reluctantly she pulled into their driveway, not even bothering to pull into the garage. *This isn't real*, she told herself. *I'll wake up and this will be the dream.*

How different their house looked from when she'd left that morning. Then it was their special, privileged spot. She sat, staring at the low, rambling lines of the cedar ranch house. Since first she saw it, she'd loved the entryway, with the floor-to-ceiling glass panels flanking the door and the stone-edged planters that seemed to flow from the outside through the glass to the inside. Now the entry seemed to leave them exposed, vulnerable.

She sat—she didn't know how long—before trudging toward the house. Pushing through the front door, she closed it and leaned against it. Before her, the living room with its planked wood floors and stone fireplace was dark. To her right lay the bedroom wing, and to her left, past the dining room, she heard Tim and Peter in the kitchen.

She moved slowly toward them and found Peter offering Tim graham crackers and milk. This gentle father-to-son nurturing brought tears to her eyes. The sight of her daughter's koala bear by the kitchen table precipitated more tears. Suddenly, *everything* drew tears.

The drone of an approaching helicopter reminded her there was no time for weeping. She had to search the house and maybe, maybe there would be a miracle. Her hope rekindled as she began. Surely Joy would be there, somewhere. Systematically, she searched every corner of the one-story house—all three bedrooms, linen closet, playroom, toy closet. "Joy? Honey? Are you here?" she called, her voice sounding hollow, empty. As she approached her own closet, her pulse quickened. Perhaps, like this morning, Joy would bound out from behind the dresses with a jubilant, "S'prise!"

"Come out, come out, wherever you are!" she sang and stood at the closet door, waiting, hearing only her own breathing. She switched on the closet light, parted the clothes to look behind them. Nothing.

"It's no use," she told Peter as she met him in the hallway.

"Well, Tim and I'll recheck the house and the yard." He clasped her arm. "Just in case."

She nodded and watched them go out the door. She already knew they'd find nothing.

When they returned, Peter shook his head. "Zilch."

She felt rooted to the floor. What else were they to do? Oh, yes, the pictures. She'd get the album. No. The most recent pictures were still in the photo store envelopes in the kitchen desk drawer. She seemed to be walking through glue as she made her way down the hall, slid the drawer open, and pulled out the packets. She spilled the pictures onto the counter. Joy's dimpled smile wavered as tears rose once again. She could feel Peter looking over her shoulder. "I'm not sure I can do this, Peter. You're going to have to help me. You too, Tim."

Peter bent over the counter. "Let's see." She watched as he spread the pictures out, then looked back at her, eyes glistening. "Yeah. I see what you mean." He turned away, then managed a determined breath. "But this is important. Got to pick the very best likeness."

He was always so *logical*, this engineer husband of hers. She forced herself to examine the photos. "No, now here she's squinting. You can't even see her eyes. And here she's mugging. Cute, but not typical. How about this?"

She held out a picture of a pensive Joy, fingering the "wuz," that handful of fuzz plucked from her blanket.

Peter studied it. "Maybe."

"This is good." Tim pointed to a shot that showed Joy at her merriest, blue eyes bright and impish, her grin engraving the dimples deep into her cheeks.

"Oh, yes." Andrea said. "Definitely."

As they finished their selection, Peter turned to her. "Think we ought to call our folks?"

"No!" She heard the intensity of her voice and saw his surprise. "I mean, Joy could be back tonight. Let's don't upset them."

"But Mom could see it on TV in Orange County," Peter pointed out.

"OK," she nodded. "But not my folks. It won't be on TV in Chicago."

Peter picked up the phone, punched the buttons, waited, then shook his head. "Answering machine," he whispered. "Mom? Peter. Call us when you get in, will you?"

"Probably swimming her laps," he said, hanging up just as the doorbell chimed. Andrea caught her breath and grabbed Peter's arm. "Maybe there's news."

Hurrying together to the front door, they opened it to a dumpling of a young woman, all rounded curves, from the auburn ringlets that surrounded her full, open face to the generous hips swelling from a surprisingly small waist. The visitor smiled gently and held out her hand. "I'm Connie Hendrix. I live down the hill, on Sand Dune, but I was in the toy store this afternoon when—" she hesitated. "Well, I was wondering. Is there anything new?"

"I'm afraid not." Andrea could hear the coolness in her own voice. The last thing she needed right now was a nosy neighbor. But she'd better be civil. "I'm Andrea Lang and this is my husband, Peter. Our son, Tim."

Connie shook their hands. "Pleased to meet you." She turned to Andrea. "Well, why I'm here is—my husband, Jeff, and I—we'd like to get a search party going. I mean, your daughter might just be in the hills. If the sheriff's department uses a helicopter, well, y'know, it might scare her. I can get a bunch of people from our church out in the next hour."

Andrea stared at Connie. "You'd do that? You don't even know us!"

"Why, shoot, what difference does that make?" Connie seemed surprised.

Tears welled up again, and Andrea could only shake her head. At last she managed, "That's so kind. But you know, the sheriff's department tells us they'll call in reserve deputies, even cadets."

"That's just terrific. Surely they'll find her." Connie's tone was warm, encouraging. "Tell you what, then. We'll help the helpers with coffee and stuff." She turned away from the doorway. "Talk with you later."

"Thanks." Andrea shut the door slowly.

"Nice neighbor," Peter said.

She nodded, already wondering what to do next. She glanced at her watch. Almost six. "Guess we ought to eat something," she murmured.

Just as she started to heat some soup, Maxwell and two other deputies arrived. "The search parties are out," he assured her. "Now let's see what we can find here."

Flashlights beaming, they looked for footprints outside the house and dusted the window to Joy's room for fingerprints.

"Oh, let there be something!" she said aloud as they worked.

But when they'd finished, Maxwell shook his head. "Nothing. So, we'll just take the pictures then. And you have some of Joy's clothes?"

She handed him a sack with Joy's blanket sleeper and two shirts from the laundry basket. "A little grubby." She pointed at the grape-juice stain on the top shirt.

"Just what we want," he assured her. "We'll keep in touch."

"We want to join the search. If Joy is out there somewhere, she's going to want her mom and dad," Peter declared.

Maxwell shook his head adamantly. "No, you'll do more good here. If someone calls with information, you'll both need to be here."

While Peter showed him out, she went back to the kitchen and stood, arms hanging at her sides. She felt so helpless and empty. Empty arms. She felt empty through and through.

Later, as they sat down to eat, Andrea murmured, "Maybe we ought to pray." She was surprised at her own statement. They always said grace at Peter's mother's, but somehow, at home, it had fallen by the wayside.

"Absolutely!" The heartiness of Peter's response pleased

her, and she looked expectantly toward him. As he reached for her hand and for Tim's, she took Tim's other hand, feeling its tension.

"Dear Lord," Peter's husky voice began, "You know we're in shock. Take care of Joy. Keep her safe, wherever she is. And bring her home to us. Amen. Oh, and bless this food, Father. In Jesus' name, amen."

She gave each hand a little squeeze before letting go. *When,* she wondered, *had they stopped asking a blessing?* Before they were married, she and Peter had "made a decision for Christ." But after she started working—to be honest—she hadn't really prayed for a long time.

As she released Tim's hand, she smiled at him, but he turned away.

"You know," she said, as much to herself as to him, "I kind of feel Joy'll be back with us tonight. There's bound to be some simple explanation for her disappearance."

Tim didn't respond.

Despite the confidence of her words, she found it a tremendous effort to eat.

She glanced at Tim, watching him move the vegetables around with his soupspoon and shred the bread on his plate. He looked relieved when the phone rang.

Peter and Andrea leapt up together. "I'll get it," she exclaimed, waves of fear and hope swelling within her. When she heard the sales pitch for patio covers, she slouched against the counter, emotionally spent. While she managed her firm, "No," Tim carried his dishes to the sink and headed toward his room.

As she and Peter loaded the dishwasher, she thought, *I've got to keep calm with Tim. Maybe if I try to preserve some of our usual evening routine.*

"Come on, Tim," she called. "Let's see what's happening in *The Jungle Book*."

They settled together on the blue sofa by the fire Peter had built in the great stone fireplace. But she soon realized Tim couldn't concentrate on the adventures of Shere Khan and his friends. Finally he murmured, "I'd like to go to bed, Mom." No point in pressing him to stay.

Later, sitting on the edge of his rugged oak bed, she cupped his face in her hands so he couldn't turn away. "Tim, we do not blame you in any way."

His eyes blazed. "Well, I do! I told her this morning I'd take care of her. I messed up big-time."

"Oh, honey!" She leaned over to embrace him, his pain compounding her own. "Please don't. I know you just went a few feet away for a couple of minutes. I could easily have done the same thing. You had no way of knowing. It's not your fault, love."

He turned away from her, face toward the wall. "Night, Mom."

She started to reemphasize her point but knew immediately it wouldn't help. She patted his shoulder. "Good night, darling. I *love* you."

Wishing with all her heart she could make it right for him, she stepped out of the room and saw Peter down the hallway. "Honey." She hurried to him. "Talk to Tim, will you? "You tell him it's OK."

"I did when we were driving home."

"Do it again, Peter. Please."

She turned out the living room lights and stared out into moonless darkness, punctuated by the flashlights of searchers down the hill. The helicopter cast a broad circle of light on the hillside, moving down and up, back down again.

They'll find her, she assured herself. *Or someone from the toy store will drive up with her. She'll be back.*

Just as Peter came out of Tim's bedroom, the phone rang. He ran to their bedroom to catch it. "Hello? Oh, hello, Mom." He listened. "Well, you were right."

He went on to explain the situation, and Andrea, beside him, could hear her exclaim, "Oh, dear Lord, no! Not my little angel!"

Zoë's voice grew softer and Peter interrupted, "Mom, please don't try to drive out tonight. You've had a long day, and there's really nothing you could do." He waited and nodded. "OK, first thing tomorrow's fine. He listened a moment. "Yes, she's right here."

Andrea picked up the phone. "I knew you'd come, Mom. You're always there when we need you."

Andrea could hear the incipient tears in Zoë's voice. "Honey, you can't possibly think this grandmother could stay away. Oh, my darling, this is so hard. I can't begin to think of anything harder. For every one of you! Oh, give my buddy Tim my special love, won't you? I'll be in continuing prayer for all of you. And—oh, please, Lord—maybe Joy'll be back yet tonight."

"Thanks, Mom." Andrea replaced the phone and looked at Peter. "It's true, you know. Maybe she won't need to come."

↭

The hours dragged past. Peter spread out a topographic map of the Malibu area on the kitchen table. Glancing now and then out the windows at the lights of the searchers, he calculated their location and progress on the map. But Andrea could only pace, sit briefly, get up and pace again.

Instead of the nightsongs of poorwills and owls, she heard the relentless thuck-huck of the helicopter, bullhorn blaring, "Joy Lang. Joy, are you there? We've come to help you."

"Hear them, Joy," she pleaded under her breath.

"Don't be afraid. Your mommy and daddy are waiting for you," the voice on the bullhorn continued.

"We are! Oh, we are," she affirmed.

"Wave to us so we can see you. We want to take you home."

"Home," she begged. "Joy, come home!"

As the helicopter moved away from their house, from time to time the voices of the searchers drifted through the still night air. "Jo-oy! Joy Lang? Can you hear us, Joy?"

God, she pleaded silently, *You could bring her home tonight. Please, Lord!*

5

ॐ

From Zoë's Prayer Journal

January 2, 10 p.m.: Dear Lord, You tell us how You love the little children. Watch over our Joy. Keep her from harm and oh, Father, wrap Your arms around her so she's not afraid. Help the helpers. Give them wisdom on where to search, who to question. Show them where she is! Father, I can see that sweet face blowing kisses to me when I left, the last time I visited in Malibu, and I think my heart would utterly shatter if—No, I won't get caught up in the ifs. Your Word tells us not to be anxious about anything. Oh, Father! I just thought—is this Your answer to my prayer to bring that family back to You? That would be one tough answer! Help me to trust You. And please, Lord, may Peter, Andrea, and Tim cry out to You and draw close to You in their distress. God, may they not blame You. Show me how I can best serve them and You, in Jesus' name, amen.

LATER THAT NIGHT, the eerie baying of the bloodhounds echoed through the hills. Andrea, listening by the window, turned toward Peter. "That sound sets my teeth on edge."

"Me too," He clasped her shoulder. "But remember how Joy loves dogs? If she's out there, she'll for sure want to find them and pet 'the nice dogs.'"

He was trying so hard to be positive, she realized. She forced a smile. "That's true. Remember when that big chocolate lab knocked her down? She picked herself up and yelled, 'He likes me! He likes me!'"

Her smile ebbed as she glanced at her watch. A little past ten. Would there be anything on TV yet? As she started toward the television set, she heard a truck in the driveway. As Peter sprinted for the door, she followed swiftly behind him and saw the network mobile television truck through the glass panels of the entry.

"Oh, Peter," she groaned, "I can't deal with this."

The doorbell rang, but she felt paralyzed. Peter grabbed her hand.

"Think a minute, Andry. What's our main object? To find Joy, right? The more people who know she's missing, the better the chances. We need these people. We have to give them a story."

She stared at him. Peter, the engineer, touting the merits of public relations to *her*? The role reversal seemed outrageously funny, but when she began to laugh, she sensed she was perilously close to tears.

The doorbell sounded again. He took her by the shoulders and shook her gently. "Andrea, they're waiting."

Wiping her eyes, she took a deep breath. "OK, I'm ready." She ran nervous fingers through her hair. "I must look like I've run a marathon. I *feel* like I have."

He took her hand. "Think of it as just another press conference, a photo op." He opened the door.

"Mr. and Mrs. Lang?" A tall woman with a profusion of

golden hair, dazzling in a cardinal-red jacket, looked from Peter to Andrea. "I'm Sandy McConnell, News Network. We've been following the searchers in the hills, and now we'd like to talk to you."

"Of course, Ms. McConnell." Peter smiled. "Come in."

Andrea could feel the newswoman warm to her husband. "Whatever it takes," she muttered to herself as she, too, willed herself to smile.

To her surprise, the McConnell woman conducted a sensitive, sympathetic interview, allowing them time to describe Joy's mannerisms and all the little traits that made her unique. She made the plea for Joy's need for medication seem urgent.

As the newswoman left, mobile units from two other channels pulled into the driveway, followed by three other cars. Andrea and Peter moved outside to meet them.

"Mrs. Lang," one reporter asked, "do you think your daughter is still alive?" And another: "How does it feel to think of the possibility of your daughter being kidnapped?"

She wasn't sure how she managed or precisely what she answered.

Just as they wrapped up one interview, Andrea looked up to see Tim wander into the glare of the lights, rubbing his eyes. "Oh, honey!" she exclaimed. She went toward him, turning back to Peter. "Let's get him back—"

"Get a shot of the son," several voices cried.

Peter put an arm around Tim. "Hey, let's get out of the cold, Timmer." And to Andrea he whispered, "I'll take him in and see if I can get him settled down."

During Peter's absence, photographers and reporters from two newspapers and a coastal news radio station arrived.

Bombarded with several questions at once, she held up her hand. "Please!" In the silence, she shivered in a cold blast of wind. Blinking in the light, she continued, "Look, I'll try my best to answer all of you, but please, one at a time." She recognized a writer from the *Times*. "Yes, Mr. Kelly?"

Carefully and with a calm that surprised her, she replied to each question. Then a TV newsman pressed her, "So, Ms. Lang, you believe your daughter was abducted from that store while your son failed to watch her?"

She took an angry breath, but before she could respond, Peter stepped in beside her. "No." His voice was calm but firm. "That isn't accurate at all. We don't know where Joy is. And we don't in any way blame our son for her disappearance."

She squeezed Peter's hand. "Absolutely not!" She shook her head for emphasis. Then, drawing on all her press conference experience, she added smoothly, "We appreciate your trying to help us and showing Joy's picture. And we do want to stress how important it is that she receive medication every single day to—," her voice faltered, "to prevent an epileptic seizure. So, please, we urge anyone who thinks they might have seen our daughter to contact the sheriff." She gave the phone number and repeated it slowly.

"And," added Peter, "we'd really appreciate any of your viewers and listeners who would pray for us."

As the bright lights went out, Andrea turned toward Peter, pressing her face against his chest. A flashbulb went off. And then, as quickly as the media had swept in, everyone was gone.

Slowly, they walked arm in arm back into the house. "You were wonderful, Andry," he said softly. "A real pro. Cool, collected."

"Well, I don't feel cool at all. But I do know one thing. I'm so exhausted, my ears are ringing."

"Let's lie down for a bit," he suggested. "It's way after midnight."

"I couldn't go to bed."

"No." He led her into the living room. "On that fluffy rug by the fire." He reached for some pillows from the couch and the blue mohair afghan.

Together they stretched out on the soft wool rug. How she ached inside and out. With Peter's arms around her, images of Joy flicked through her mind, like pages flipping in a photo album. "Wake me when 'happily ever after' comes," she murmured.

When at last she dropped into a fitful sleep, she dreamed of a dark presence reaching through the window to snatch Joy away and saw herself watching, paralyzed, unable to help or even to scream.

❧

Peter tried to lie still beside her as his anger smoldered. The most logical explanation was that someone had taken his daughter. But who? The thought of child pornographers and child-sellers kindled a physical heat in the pit of his stomach. Joy was a perfect target: pretty, appealing, innocent.

But no matter what, somehow, some way I've got to stay calm, stay in control, he reminded himself. *Got to be the rock, the one Andrea and Tim can lean on. Someone could be watching this entire family. Have to focus my skills to protect the rest of us, keep us safe.* His mind darted from one thought to another. *Make the house secure. A top priority. Start tomorrow by cutting rods for the sliding windows and door. Should have put an alarm system in. Better do it. Purchase a gun? Might be a good idea.*

His arm, beneath Andrea, was going numb. He moved it carefully, pleased that she didn't waken. He could see her profile, her delicate straight little nose, in the flickering firelight—like a duplicate of Joy's—and he felt the muscles around his heart tighten.

Got to focus on good things, he told himself. *God*, he prayed silently, *watch over our little girl. Keep her safe and take away any fear she may be feeling.*

Gradually, the anger dissipated, and he drifted in and out of a restless sleep.

⌇

Andrea's dreams of peril and helplessness flowed, one merging into another, till she jerked awake and checked her watch. Almost three. Stumbling to the window, she peered at the indoor/outdoor thermometer. "Peter!" she cried. "It's thirty-seven degrees."

Peter roused with a "Huh?"

She came back and knelt beside him. "It's thirty-seven degrees. And Joy's wearing such a light little sweatshirt. Could she possibly survive like that?"

"She's sturdier than you think, Andry." His voice sounded convincing, but she wondered if he really believed it.

Peter made coffee and brought it to Andrea just as Tim crept into the living room, dragging his quilt.

"Trouble sleeping, scout?" Peter asked.

Tim blinked at the firelight. "Yeah. It feels like crumbs in my bed. Everything's all mixed up. And it's kinda scary back there."

They settled him between them on the couch and sat, listening to the old clock on the mantel and the voices of the searchers. At last she felt the tension in Tim's body ease, and when at last he slept, Peter carried him back to his bed.

At 5:30, Connie Hendrix arrived at the door, bundled in a

down jacket, her nose red from the cold. She shook her head wearily. "Nothing, the last I heard. But the searchers are fed and coffee-d."

"Come in," urged Peter. "Is that your husband in the car? I'll go get him."

"I'll bet you didn't take time for coffee. Peter has some ready. Come out in the kitchen." Andrea led the way, surprised at how readily she slipped into the old hospitality ritual, even at a time like this. "You must be frozen and exhausted," she said.

"And disappointed," Connie added. "They seemed to be doin' a real thorough job of looking. Why, those dogs were somethin' else." Connie consistently dropped the "g" from her "ing" words. She shook her head. "But evidently there wasn't a sign of your little girl. Some TV crews were there covering it though."

"Yes. They came here too."

"Good. The more people that know, the better." Connie leaned over and laid her hand on Andrea's. "How are you? I know some of what you're feeling."

"Do you?" She heard her own tone of confrontation.

"Yes," Connie spoke softly, "I do. I lost a son. Last year. I mean, he's not coming back."

Andrea stared at her. "What happened?"

"Hit-and-run."

Andrea's eyes filled with tears. "Oh, I'm so sorry," she murmured. "I didn't know."

"Course you didn't. But you see, I *do* understand. And I've been praying for all of you ever since this afternoon in the toy store." Connie looked up as Peter and a wiry, sandy-haired man with a weathered face came into the kitchen. "Andrea, this is my husband, Jeff."

She took his hand. "Thank you for being out there."

Jeff nodded. "Least we could do."

Peter poured the coffee, and Andrea put two chunks of cheese on a plate with some crackers.

"How nice! I really am starving, now that I think of it." Connie cut a huge slice of cheddar and balanced it on a wheat wafer. "Andrea and Peter, I've been thinking. If Joy isn't back by noon, I'll set up a hotline at our church. I'm sure they'll go along with it. That'll give people a place to call—especially if they're kinda skittish about calling the sheriff. And most important, they won't bug you."

Andrea and Peter stared at each other. Turning to Connie, she protested, "But that would take so much time! I couldn't ask you to do that."

"You didn't ask. I want to."

Embarrassed, Andrea glanced at Peter. "That would be terrific," he said huskily.

"Good. Then it's settled." Connie stood, putting her hand on Jeff's shoulder. "Now we'd better get on down the hill. I'll talk with you tomorrow." She hesitated. "No, it already *is* tomorrow, isn't it?" She shrugged. "Anyway, we'll both be praying."

Peter and Andrea lingered at the table after the Hendrixes left. "Can you believe that? Complete strangers reaching out," she murmured.

"Christians, I guess," he added.

She nodded and thought a moment. "But Joy could be back by noon." When Peter didn't reply, she put her hand on his. "Oh, Peter. I know you. You've charted out all the possibilities in that orderly engineer's mind of yours. Well, I have too. No, not charted, really. More tumbling around, like pieces in a kaleidoscope. First one pattern, then another. Most of them, I don't like at all. But rock bottom, I think she'll be back soon."

"Hope you're right." Grabbing her hands across the table, Peter shoved back his chair and as he rose, pulling her to her feet. "Let's see what's on TV. I think the first morning newscast comes on at six." Waiting in front of the TV, she rubbed her palms together while he flicked the remote control. "Looks like all national," Peter protested. "No, wait."

"Local news," an anchorman in a blue suit promised, "including the search for a missing child, just after these messages."

Andrea groaned impatiently.

Two commercials, a third, and a fourth. Finally the program returned to the news set and . . . "Drama in the Malibu hills! Yesterday afternoon, three-and-a-half-year-old Joy Lang disappeared in Malibu." This is Joy." Joy's smiling picture brightened the screen. "Joy Lang was last seen in this toy store on Pacific Coast Highway in Malibu. A picture of the toy store appeared. "Her brother and the housekeeper who was with them said she hadn't been out of their sight for more than a few moments. A search of the beach and highway revealed no trace of the child."

The camera panned along the beach, showing lifeguards with binoculars scanning sand and sea. The scene cut to the darkened hills, with footage of the helicopter and of a line of flashlights moving up the hill. "While a Los Angeles county sheriff's department helicopter covered the Santa Monica Mountains, more than fifty deputies and cadets, aided by bloodhounds, searched the hills foot by foot. But still this morning, there's no word."

Now they saw a closeup of Andrea's weary face. The camera pulled back to show her standing, fists clenched, with Peter beside her. "All night long, the anxious parents—Andrea and Peter Lang—waited, hoping for news. But none came."

Joy's picture flashed back on the screen as the anchor described Joy. An 800 number appeared beneath the photo.

For the next hour and a half, they channel-surfed the newscasts. The McConnell interview came across well, but when they switched to another channel, they saw a closeup of a sleepy-faced Tim. The voice-over identified him as "Joy's brother, Tim Lang, who left his sister alone in the toy store and when he came back to where he'd left her, she was gone."

She spun around, fearful that Tim might have seen and heard. Relieved not to find him, she exploded, "Peter, they're practically accusing him—saying it was his fault!"

Peter's eyes flashed with anger. "I was afraid of that."

"A good story at our son's expense." She grabbed a pillow from the sofa and pounded it. "What a cheap trick! I don't care if it's bad PR, I'm going to march right into their newsroom. I'm going to . . ." She buried her face in the pillow and muffled a scream. When she looked up, Peter was watching her, concern deepening the dark shadows under his eyes.

She sighed. "I know. Be grateful the word's getting out." Clasping her hands she closed her eyes. "Oh, please, Lord, let someone know something."

Peter added a fervent "Amen!" Then he said, "You know that thing about Tim reminds me. We'd better prepare him for some static at school. You know how kids can be."

She winced. "You're right." She leaned against Peter. "I feel so sorry for that kid, Peter. He's sensitive and quiet. He's going to need a lot of help."

"For sure." He waited a moment before he stood and stretched. "Well, I'd better call the office and tell them I won't be in."

She grabbed him around the middle and hugged hard. "Right. I will too."

Later, as Tim joined them for breakfast, the sliding doors began to rattle, and a trash can sailed past the window.

"Santa Ana winds," Peter nodded. "Our Realtor warned me they funnel down from the mountains with a force like nowhere else."

"It's like a giant, humongous fan's been switched on," Tim exclaimed, rallying for the first time from his despondency. He laughed as the weather stripping in the front door began to hum. Then the sink resounded with a bass tone like someone blowing into a huge glass jug. "Hey!" he shouted. "We've got a musical house."

They gasped in unison as pieces of roofing lifted from a house below them and floated down the hill.

"It's like the tornado in *The Wizard of Oz*. Can I go out, Mom? Dad?"

"Good grief, no, Tim. You might blow away too," she said, "and land in Kansas. Hey, and stay away from the windows. I don't like the way they're moving and shaking." And, she thought, *I don't like the idea of Joy out in this wind either.*

Still watching out the window, she flinched as she saw a familiar old blue Buick round the last curve below their house. "Esther!" She slammed her fist on the table. "I thought I made it clear she wasn't to come."

She met Esther at the front door, bracing herself against the blast of the wind. Avoiding Andrea's eyes, the woman handed a small red sweater to her.

Joy's! Andrea held it to her face as tears coursed down her cheeks.

"It was in my car," Esther explained, her voice little more than a whisper.

Andrea nodded, unable to reply, and started to close the door.

"Miz Lang," Esther said. "I left my um-berella in the closet. And a jacket."

Reluctantly, she waved her in. "Go get them."

"Yes'm." Esther stepped into the hallway and quickly retrieved her belongings from the closet.

Andrea waited impatiently, pressing her lips together hard, still crying, wanting only to see her gone. But when she heard Esther weeping, she relented and put her arms around her. "It could have happened even if I'd been there." She felt Esther nod and released her, watching her let herself out the door.

As Andrea slowly returned to the kitchen, the doorbell rang again and she called to Peter, "Oh, no! She's back."

"No," Peter assured her. "She's just leaving. I saw another car, a gray Chevy, coming up the hill."

As they started for the door, the phone rang.

"I'll take that. You get the door," Peter said.

He hurried to the kitchen phone. "Lang," he said.

"Mr. Lang," came a man's voice with a British accent. "I think I can tell you where your daughter is."

6

ʒ

PETER GRIPPED THE PHONE, leaning forward, straining to stay objective above an emotional seesaw of optimism and skepticism. "Excuse me?" he said. "You say you know where my daughter is?"

"Are you interested?" The voice came again, resonant, but with a gravelly edge that spoke of age or too many cigarettes.

"What's your name? What can you tell me?"

"Name's Martin." The caller drew the first syllable out in a long British ah. "Martin Walker. I'd like to meet you and your wife at the toy store where your daughter disappeared."

"Yes?" Peter said, his voice guarded. "And then what?"

"Why, I get out my divining rod and my pendulum, and we see which way she went."

Peter slumped against the counter, hope evaporating. "Ah. Thank you, Mr. Martin."

"Walker," the voice corrected.

"Yes. But I don't think so."

"Ah, now, Mr. Lang, I've found more things than you could possibly—"

"Mr. Walker," Peter broke in. "Thank you. Good-bye."

⤳

Andrea opened the front door, squinting into the wind, and saw a lanky, fair-haired man, wearing beige gabardine pants, an off-white dress shirt, and regimental striped tie. "Mrs. Lang?" he asked. "Detective Jansen, Sheriff's Department." He held out his I.D.

Andrea gasped. A detective. Alone. Fear caught in her throat and she couldn't speak.

He saw her face and quickly added, "No, I don't have any news, but I've been assigned to your case."

She held out her hand to him, and his grip felt firm but careful, as though he recognized how fragile she felt. His tanned face, the color of fresh-cut cedar, surprised her with its sensitivity. Though she saw no softness in its planes and angles, the lines etched around his eyes seemed to speak of compassion—perhaps even sadness.

"Usually I'm not assigned this early in a case, but the sheriff asked me to get on it PDQ," he explained as Andrea motioned him into the house.

"Come in. My husband will be right in, and I'd better get Tim, our son, hadn't I?"

"Please." Jansen nodded.

"I'm here," Tim said, emerging from his room down the hall.

"Hi, Tim." Jansen gave Tim a warm smile as he shook his hand.

They started into the living room as Peter joined them and Andrea introduced him to the detective.

46

"The call?" she asked Peter.

He shook his head. "A kook."

Jansen took the chair by the fireplace, while Tim, Andrea, and Peter sat on the sofa.

"First, let me give you a progress report," Jansen said. "As you can imagine, this wind doesn't help our search."

"I guess not! Does it do this often here?" she asked.

Jansen nodded. "Yes, this time of year. Some people call it the 'devil wind.' Sometimes it rips the buttons off your clothes. We clocked some gusts at fifty-eight miles an hour out here this morning." He glanced from Peter to Andrea. "It's hard to get a helicopter close to the hillsides in these conditions. But we'll keep looking on foot and by car. As you know, we saw no sign of your daughter last night, and the door-to-door search didn't turn up anything either." His eyes, a deep golden amber, were full of regret. "A couple of places with no one at home. Like across the road."

"Oh, yes," Andrea interjected. "There's just Dolores Cooper over there—a widow—and her son, Brant. They went skiing in Mammoth the day after Christmas." She thought a moment. "I think they're due back later today."

"Did your daughter ever play over there?"

"No. We moved in here just before Thanksgiving, and I've only barely met the Coopers. Dolores signed for a UPS package for us just before Christmas, and when she brought it over, she said they'd be away."

"OK," Jansen said, leafing through his legal pad. "Now I'd like to verify what I have." He reviewed the information he'd received from the other deputies.

"That's right," Andrea said. She looked to Tim for confirmation. "Tim?"

"Yeah. I sure didn't see anyone near Joy in the store except us—Esther and me."

Jansen nodded. "Frankly, we don't have a lot to go on. One witness said there was a blue hatchback in the parking lot when she got to the store. After your daughter turned up missing, the car was gone. But we don't even have a make or model. We've checked your housekeeper, and she looks clean. So let's see if we can get at anything you might know that could help."

"Of course," Peter said, leaning toward Jansen.

"Have you noticed anyone, anywhere, watching the kids—Joy in particular? Taking a special interest?"

She frowned, then shrugged. "I really can't think of anything. Can you, Peter?"

He shook his head.

"Oh, wait!" she exclaimed. "There was a work gang cutting weeds just up the hill by the water tank. Somebody said they were from the county jail. Anyway, there were two men with rifles watching them." She glanced at the detective and saw him nod. "It was just after we moved in, and I had the kids out in the driveway playing a little game. There was one man especially, who would kind of lean against the fence and look down at us." She frowned, trying to visualize him. "Dark complexion, mustache, pot belly."

"Do you know what the date would have been?" Jansen asked.

She thought a moment. "Let me get the calendar." Hurrying to the kitchen, she brought back the wall calendar. "Let's see, I'd taken the day off. So it would have been December third. No, I think the fourth."

Jansen made a note. "Anything else you can think of?"

"Tell about Joy yelling and screaming the night before," Tim interrupted.

"Tim exaggerates a bit," Peter said. "But did Deputy

48

Maxwell tell you about Joy thinking there was someone outside her window?"

Jansen nodded. "Couldn't get any prints though," he said. He waited a moment. "Anything else?"

Andrea shrugged, feeling helpless. "I wish!"

"OK, here's what's going on right now," Jansen said. "We've got Joy's picture out nationwide. We're continuing the search in the hills. Oh, and we'll be putting a tap on your phone—just in case."

"What do you mean?" Her voice was anxious.

"In case someone calls with information on Joy."

"You're thinking ransom," she persisted.

"Not necessarily," the detective replied.

She turned to Peter. "Who in the world would kidnap Joy, Peter? We don't have that kind of money."

Jansen stood and came over to her, putting his hand on her shoulder. She was surprised at the warmth, the healing it seemed to impart, just for a moment. "Don't try to second-guess," he said gently. He turned toward Peter. "You haven't had any calls about your daughter so far?"

"Only this fruitcake just now. Said he could tell us where Joy is."

Andrea sprang to her feet. *"What?* And you didn't tell me?"

Peter stood, putting his hand on her arm. "He was a loony. Wanted to meet us at the toy store so he could use his divining rod and his pendulum."

"And you told him no? How dare you?" she shouted.

"Now, Andry." His condescending tone made her furious. Then Peter looked at Jansen. "Tell her, detective."

She whirled to look at the detective and saw him hesitate. "Mrs. Lang, generally these things are not reliable," he said carefully.

"But I've read you can sometimes get information from psychics."

"We don't discount them, but they're not always accurate."

She turned back to Peter. "Oh, Peter! I can't believe you wouldn't—Did you even get his phone number?"

Peter shook his head.

She bobbed her head and groaned, angry and frustrated beyond words.

"It probably wouldn't have been very informative," Jansen offered, and even in her fury, she knew he was trying to soothe this "domestic difference."

"You don't really believe that, do you?" she demanded of Jansen, then sighed. No sense putting him in the middle. "Sorry. Anything else we can tell you?"

"Not at the moment." Jansen started toward the door. "Just know that we're doing all we can to find her."

"We appreciate that," Peter said.

She looked up at Jansen, and his eyes seemed so empathetic, she knew he understood her frustration. "Thanks," she said softly.

As Andrea opened the front door for him, she saw her mother-in-law's silver-gray Lincoln, fifteen years old but still in mint condition, pull into the driveway. Zoë emerged quickly, her jacket flapping wildly in the gale, wavy salt-and-pepper hair blowing forward. She gave Jansen a friendly wave and held out her arms like airplane wings as a gust propelled her toward the front door.

"Look who just blew in!" Andrea exclaimed.

"Right!" Zoë laughed. If I'd known I could just hold out my arms in the wind, I wouldn't have bothered with my car." She leaned against the door to force it shut against the wind, then held out her arms to Andrea.

Andrea moved toward her, welcoming the warmth of Zoë's embrace, murmuring, "I really need one of your hugs. They're healing."

In a moment, Andrea sighed, "I'm just going to stay here for the rest of the day."

Zoë reached out to draw Peter and Tim into a fourfold hug. "My darlings," she whispered. "I love you so!"

When they released one another, Zoë, eyes bright with tears, looked from one face to the next. "This is so hard! I wakened again and again through the night, praying and praying. Then when I swam at six this morning, I prayed through the alphabet like I always do. A different letter for every lap. Oh, and I called your dad and Leslie and Tracy. They're praying, too. Couldn't get the other kids, but left messages on their machines." She hesitated, "I just feel like we four ought to pray before we do one other thing. Would you like to?"

"Yeah, Gram." Tim nodded. "I knew you'd do that."

Zoë rumpled Tim's hair. "That's my special buddy! You know me pretty well." She turned to Peter.

"Sure," he said.

Andrea sighed. "We definitely need it. In fact, your arrival may have prevented a homicide." She made choking motions with her hands, glaring at Peter.

Zoë looked quizzically from Andrea to Peter. When neither elaborated, she muttered a thoughtful, "Okay," and led the way to the breakfast table.

They sat down and joined hands. "I'll start," Zoë offered. "You all join in, as you feel led." She sighed as she bowed her head. "Dear Lord, we feel Your power in the wind this morning, and it reminds us that there is power and strength in You, that You are in charge. And so we turn to You with our plea that You would send Joy safely home and that wherever she is, she is well cared for. And Father, I want to pray for all the hurting hearts at this table. May none of us chastise ourselves over what we should have done or shouldn't have done. May nothing come between our love and support of one another and of You. Help us to press on with hope and trust in You."

As Zoë paused, Peter began, "Lord, we're a little rusty here. Forgive us that we're using prayer as a last resort, instead of a first. Yes, we ask You to protect Joy and keep her and bring her back to us and to comfort us as we wait."

They were quiet a moment. Then, "God," Tim's voice sounded strained, "if You'll just bring Joy back, I promise not to bug her—at least as much as I have." He swallowed and Andrea wondered for a moment if he'd be able to continue. "And I'm sorry I didn't take care of her like I promised."

Andrea put her arm around him and felt him draw a shaky breath. She waited till she could trust her own voice. "Lord, I know there's some logical explanation for Joy's disappearance. Please show us. Today, Lord? You know I always want everything now. But never as much as at this moment. Please, hear our prayers and give us our Joy again, safe, smiling, and as full of fun as always."

"Yes!" Zoë exclaimed, adding, "God, You are gracious and merciful and full of loving-kindness. Thank You that You do hear our prayers. And oh, Lord, I want to add a prayer that if someone did take her, for whatever reason, You'll work powerfully on their conscience and move them to return her quickly. We thank You and praise You that Joy is in Your loving hands. In the name of Your Son, who loved us and died for us, amen."

They sat awhile in silence before Tim said, "I'm going to my room."

Andrea nodded and stood. "I feel so grubby. Think I'll go take a shower."

"Sure. Take your time," Peter said.

She looked at him, wondering if she could trust him to answer the phone, but said nothing and made her way to their bedroom.

Pausing by the sliding glass door, she stared out at the ocean as the offshore wind picked up sheets of water and blew them out to sea. "Reverse surf," Tim had called it.

If Joy drowned, Andrea thought, it would carry her out, rather than in. How long would it take to find her?

7

AS ANDREA LEFT THE KITCHEN, Zoë decided not to ask why Andrea was ready to wring Peter's neck. But as though reading her thoughts, Peter said, "I'm afraid Andrea's pretty miffed at me."

"So I gathered."

He described the phone call from Martin Walker, adding, "Mom, he was a loony. I couldn't see getting mixed up with a divining rod and a pendulum. Doesn't the Bible say not to?"

Zoë nodded. "Makes it pretty clear we shouldn't be around anyone who practices divination or sorcery or witchcraft."

"That's what I thought. But man, Andry was furious that I brushed the guy off."

Zoë put her hand on his. "Honey, I think you were right. But Andrea's a *mom*, and right now she's crazy with worry, ready to grasp at anything. And you know her—always in a hurry. Try to understand. She wants answers. Right now, however, wherever."

He gave her a quick grin. "You're right as usual, you wise old lady."

She bristled and smiled at the same time. "I am not!"

"Not wise?"

"Not an old lady."

"Ri-i-ght!" Peter was silent a moment. "Mom, remember when we were all little and Leslie was in the hospital in ICU?"

Zoë nodded. "We nearly lost your sister. I spent more nights than I can remember at the hospital. It was a miracle when she suddenly got well."

Peter nodded. "But it was Dad I was thinking about. I wasn't very old, but it seemed like he hardly showed any emotion. I wonder now what he felt."

"He was very, very worried. He tried so hard to keep it all together for the rest of you kids."

"Ah, so that—" He stopped as he saw Tim wander down the hall, silent and brooding once again. He and Zoë exchanged concerned glances.

"Let's have a cup of coffee, guy," Peter suggested, winking at Zoë.

"OK." Tim's voice sounded lethargic.

"Good idea," Zoë said. She poured for Peter, and he fixed a cup of milk with just a splash of coffee for Tim. "Now," she added, "I'll just go start a load of wash."

Dear Mom, Peter thought. *Knows Tim and I need to talk.* As they sat down at the kitchen table, he looked across at his son, pale and silent. "Let's talk, Timmer," he said.

"About what?" Tim didn't raise his eyes from his cup.

"About how you're doing."

"How do you think?" Tim looked up, frowning.

"Crummy, I bet. Like the rest of us."

"Yeah."

"Anything else?"

"Like what?" Tim seemed to be stalling.

"Oh, I don't know." Peter shrugged. "If you're thinking about what happened, maybe you're feeling mad and even scared. Seems to me that'd be real normal."

"Yeah," Tim allowed. "I am, I guess." He fell silent and his dad waited. Finally, Tim added, "Somebody might want to come and get me, too, you know?"

There it was, just what he'd thought. But Peter forced a light tone into his voice. "Are you serious? What makes you think anybody'd want *you?*"

For the first time, Tim smiled. "Naah, I guess not."

"But," Peter held up a finger. "Just in case—I mean you *are* a pretty neat kid—I thought you and I might go around and see what we can do to make this house more secure."

"Like what?"

"I'm going to get a security system put in. But meantime, I want to cut some rods to fit into the windows and sliding glass doors, so they're not so easy to open. Want to help me?"

"Sure."

"Great. I'll change my clothes and meet you in the garage in a few minutes," Peter said.

He headed down the hall as Zoë came in with a basket of clothes. She slipped into a chair at the table with Tim and took his hand. "Tim, love, I want to tell you a little story about something that happened a long time ago."

Tim looked at her, and his brown eyes seemed to have lost their luster.

"It was when your dad was very small, about six months old. I had him on what we called a changing table. You know,

56

where I changed his diapers. And one of the other kids—Tracy, probably—started yelling, and just for a moment, I stepped into the doorway to see what was going on. In that second or two, your dad rolled over. He'd never done that before, and he fell off the changing table. He landed, head first, on the hard tile bathroom floor."

"Wow!" Tim breathed. "Did it split his head open?"

"No, but it raised a huge bump, he started throwing up, and I thought he had a terrible head injury. Of course, I rushed him to the emergency room. The good part is that he was OK. But oh, Tim, you can't believe how scared I was—or how guilty I felt."

"I bet." He thought a minute. "But it was an accident. You just turned away. You didn't know he could roll over."

She looked into his eyes. "Right. And Tim, you just turned away for a minute at the toy store. You didn't know there was someone there with an eye on Joy."

He looked down at his hands. "I guess not."

She squeezed his hand. "Tim, you have a choice now. You can wallow around in self-blame, or you can confess what happened."

"You mean to God?"

"Right. Just tell Him what happened, how you feel. You know, God promises not only to forgive us, but to 'remember our sins no more.' They're gone! And if He's not going to keep bringing them up, you don't have to either. Think about it." She stood and clasped his shoulder. "Now, better go help your dad."

"Yeah, OK."

"That's my buddy. You know, I love you yesterday, today, always."

He smiled. "You always say that, Gram."

She nodded and lifted one finger. "Ah, that's because it's true."

❧

Later, while they ate the lunch Zoë had prepared, the phone rang, and both Andrea and Peter sprang up.

Peter picked up the phone. "Lang." He listened. "Oh, hello, Mr. Reynolds. Yeah, it's tough. Right. Well, thank you. Yes, Andrea's here." He held out the phone to her. "Says he has good news."

The office! Andrea hadn't even thought about the Waterfront account since she left the agency yesterday afternoon. And yesterday morning it had been more important to her than almost anything.

She reached for the phone and heard Reynolds's smooth tenor. "Andrea, sorry there's nothing yet on your daughter." He waited a moment. Then, "But I have some news to cheer you. Andrea, you did it! We've got the Waterfront account."

She gasped. "Already? I didn't think we'd hear—"

"Got the call just now."

"Got the Waterfront account," she whispered to Peter. Then, to Reynolds, "That's great. Just great!"

"I agree. Congratulations."

"Well," she hesitated. "Well," she tried again and heard the words rush out as though a tape had been turned on. "We've got our work cut out for us. We'll need to get the creative group together. Set up a time schedule. We can begin with—" She stopped. "The only thing is, I'm not quite sure when I'll be back."

"I don't want to press you," Reynolds said.

"Thanks. I appreciate that. I'll keep you posted."

She replaced the phone, feeling an inner heaviness. How quickly she'd switched back into the corporate mode! How quickly it had become important to her again. Was it that important? Was *anything* more important than Joy? What if she'd been home with Joy, instead of making that presentation?

She could feel Peter and Zoë watching her. "I'm proud of you," he said quietly. He came to her and put his arm around her.

She knew he was trying to help her find satisfaction in her triumph, but it didn't lift the weight she felt inside. "I can think of some greater news," she said slowly.

Time seemed suspended after lunch that day as they waited for news. The dryness from the Santa Ana winds crackled through the house. Andrea's eyes felt scratchy, her sinuses and mouth parched, her skin flaky and itchy. She made out a shopping list with Zoë, who left for the store. Then, as she paced restlessly through the house, she found an airplane model on the floor of the playroom where Tim had left it, an open bottle of paint beside it.

"Timothy!" she called. "You know better than to leave this out. What if Joy . . ." She stopped midsentence.

"How can she get into it?" he shouted defiantly. "Joy isn't here! She's been gone more than a day."

"Hey, hey, Timmer," Peter intervened. "That tone of voice is not acceptable!"

"Well she has," he insisted.

"Nevertheless, please do not speak to your mother that way. And if you're not going to work on the model now, please close the bottle of paint and put it away. Then you and I can get back to our security system."

Mouth set and eyes smoldering, Tim met his father's persistent gaze, then looked down at the model, lifting his foot. For a moment Andrea thought he would stomp it. But at last he mumbled, "*Okay.*"

She watched as though in a dream as Tim picked up his model and fled to his room, tears on his cheeks. She heard only his three words repeating in her mind like an echo-chamber effect in a commercial. "Joy isn't here . . . Joy isn't here . . . Joy isn't here . . ."

Stumbling into Joy's room, she sank to the floor in the corner, hugging her knees and rocking back and forth as the reality of the words seared her mind and pierced her chest. When the tears began, they burned, as though brimming from a steaming abyss.

She wasn't sure how long she sat sobbing till she felt Peter gently lift her and carry her to their bed. Her head throbbed. Even her teeth ached.

"Rest," Peter said softly, spreading a blanket over her. "That's what you need. I'll take Tim out for a while so he won't bug you."

No! she wanted to shout. *Don't leave me alone. I need you to hold me, comfort me.* But she hadn't the strength to form the words. She heard him ease the door shut.

Joy's not here. Now nobody's here, she thought. She curled into a fetal position and wept till the pillow felt cold and clammy beneath her face. Then she lay still, too spent to move.

When the doorbell rang, she jolted upright, a sudden hope rising. Grabbing tissues from the bedside stand, she wiped her face and eyes as she hit the floor and ran to the door. Outside she could see an all-beige woman—from her shoes, skirt, and blouse, to her skin and hair. She held a Bible under her arm.

Andrea opened the door and her visitor said, "Mrs. Lang, I want to give you Romans 8:28."

Andrea blinked. "What?"

"Romans 8:28. That's what you need to cling to." The visitor smiled ruefully. "Oh, I'm so sorry. I'm Betty Nolan. I live in Santa Monica. And the Lord just laid on my heart to bring this verse to you. May I come in?"

"N-no!" She wasn't about to let a stranger into her home, and she definitely didn't want to encourage a lengthy discourse.

"Well, then," said Betty Nolan, tucking her purse under her arm and prodding her forefinger into her Bible where a red ribbon protruded. She held the open Bible out toward Andrea. Pointing to the text, she recited, "And we know that in all things God works for the good of those who love Him, who have been called according to his purpose."

She remembered the verse from a couples' Bible study many years ago. But today . . . "Ms. Nolan," she declared, "I do not need your empty platitudes!"

"But my dear, that's your hope. It's what you need to hang onto. It means God will use your daughter's disappearance. It means even if she's dead, He'll—"

Andrea snapped the Bible shut and shoved it toward the woman. "Don't you dare say another word!"

"Oh, dear." Tears shone in the woman's eyes. "I didn't mean to—" She watched in dismay as Andrea began to close the door. "I'll pray for you. I'll pray for you."

Andrea banged the door shut and leaned against it. "Don't be upset," she repeated. "Oh, *sure!*" She took deep breaths, trying to relieve the pain that gripped her chest. *Why do I feel so angry?* she asked herself. *The woman was trying to help. But she's so different from Connie, with her understanding, her practical help.* Gradually the ache eased. But she jumped at a gentle tap at the door.

She's back, Andrea thought, and swung the door open, ready to do battle.

A tall, slender woman with a dancer's bearing waited on the doorstep, dark hair pulled into a French braid. A black ski sweater with a turquoise and hot pink design emphasized her dramatic coloring and impeccable makeup.

"Dolores," she said, relieved to see her neighbor. "I thought it was—never mind."

"Andrea!" Dolores exclaimed. "I saw it on the news in Mammoth. I can't believe it. Your little Joy. Oh, how terrible!"

Andrea gave a little nod. "Can you come in?"

She hesitated. "You have too much going on. I—" She held out a colorful sack. "I just brought you some scones. From that little boutique bakery."

"Oh, thanks. But do come in. I'm alone and I—please."

"Well, just for a minute." Dolores followed her into the living room and settled into the rocking chair by the fireplace. "Is there anything new?"

Andrea shook her head. "Nothing at all. But people have been so kind. Do you know Connie Hendrix and her husband? They fed all those deputies and volunteers last night. And she's even offered to set up kind of an information center at her church. But then, just now," she smiled ruefully, "one Bible-thumper tried to give me a sermon." She stared at the toe of her shoe and sensed Dolores watching her. Determined to change the subject, she added, "Tell me about the skiing."

"Glorious. Snowed at night and cleared during the day. Fresh snow and sunlight almost every day. Perfect. And Brant—well, he skis rings around me already." She frowned. "I was disappointed, though. Marcy didn't show. My daughter."

"You expected her and she didn't come? Aren't you worried?"

Dolores shrugged. "She's twenty-four and, well, she does this sort of thing lately. I'm not so much worried about her specifically not showing as I am about her general well-being. But," she shrugged again. "She doesn't want my help. S-o-o-o . . . And you don't want to hear about all that. You have enough on your mind. Do you feel satisfied with what's being done to find Joy?"

"It's only been———" Andrea looked at her watch in amazement, "it's hard to believe—a little more than twenty-four hours. It seems a lifetime! But so far, yes. The Sheriff's Department seems efficient. And they've contacted the National Center for Missing and Exploited Children. You've seen their 'Have you seen me?' mailings."

Dolores crossed her fingers. "Let's hope and keep a good thought that there'll be news before the day's over."

Dolores studied Andrea for a moment. "But, Andrea, if it should turn out that this drags on longer than we both hope—

"Yes?"

Dolores leaned forward. "I want to be your friend." She gave a quick smile. "No, that didn't come out right. I want to be your friend, whatever happens. I'm so glad you've moved in, and I get the feeling we could get along well. Please feel free to come to me whenever, whether you're down or up or whatever. I really think I may be able to help you."

Andrea looked into Dolores's dark brown eyes, which seemed to grow almost black with her sincerity. "That's so kind. I really don't know anyone on the hill except Connie, and I just met her last night. We're close—your house and mine, I mean. It would be nice if we could be friends."

Dolores clapped her hands together. "Good!" The front door flew open and Tim burst in, bellowing, "Mom!"

"Yes?" she answered quietly.

"Oh, you're right here."

"Dolores, I'm not sure you've met my son, Tim. This is Mrs. Cooper, Tim." She heard the door close as Peter came in. "And my husband, Peter."

Peter came into the living room to shake hands while Tim continued, "Mom, the wind's stopped, and on our way back, we hiked up in the hills behind the house. Man, we saw deer tracks. And racoons'. And some prints we need to look up. And there are pack-rat nests. It's so cool!"

Andrea shuddered. "Pack-rat nests. Lovely."

"No, they really are. You gotta go see!"

She smiled, happy to see this shift from his depression and anger.

"My son, Brant, spends a lot of time in the hills," Dolores said. "You know him, Tim?"

"Uh-huh," Tim nodded. "I met him out on the road after school one time."

"It seems like you two might have a lot in common," Dolores said. "In fact, he's home right now, playing with a new computer game he got for Christmas. Why don't you come back over with me?"

Andrea felt her entire body tense. Let Tim out of their sight? What if someone was waiting for him too? She stalled, "But do you think, I mean, isn't Brant in junior high? Tim's only eleven, you know."

"Aw, Mom," Tim protested, and she realized how much he wanted to go.

"They'll be fine. What's two years?" Dolores smiled.

"But," Andrea took a deep breath and looked at Peter.

He smiled. "Why don't you go ahead, Tim? You really haven't had a chance to meet many kids here, with Christmas vacation and all."

With tremendous effort, Andrea forced herself to see his viewpoint. *He's right*, she realized. *I can't make Tim paranoid by being overprotective. And after all, Dolores has lived on this hill for fifteen years. She and our Realtor are friends from way back.*

Tim shrugged. "Yeah, I'd like to go."

"Good." Dolores stood, smiling. "I'll get him home by, oh, say 5:30."

Watching out the window as they left, Andrea felt Peter come up behind her and slip an arm around her. "It'll be fine," he assured her.

She nodded. "I know. I can't watch over him every second of the day. But oh, Peter," she choked and the tears began to flow, "if anything should happen to our Tim. . . ."

8

A LITTLE AFTER FIVE that afternoon, the ring of the phone sent both Andrea and Peter running like sprinters responding to the starting gun. *This time, maybe this time*, she thought as she headed for the kitchen phone, almost colliding with Zoë. As Andrea grabbed the receiver, she heard Peter pick up the line in the bedroom.

Detective Jansen's bass lifted her hopes even further. "Wanted to update you," he said, and she felt her balloon of optimism deflate.

"The search of the hills didn't turn up anything," Jansen explained. "But we've sent Joy's photo and description out nationwide. We also have a contact at the Mexican border. And they've posted her photo there."

"Mexico!" she exclaimed. "Is that a possibility?"

"We have no specific reason to think it applies to Joy,"

Jansen said carefully. "But crossing the border is a way to get away from U.S. jurisdiction. It's hard to trace people after they cross over."

"Oh!" she murmured, picturing Joy held captive in a hut with a dirt floor.

"Mrs. Lang," Jansen cautioned, "let me emphasize that we have no specific reason to think Joy is in Mexico."

She swallowed. "I understand."

"Now," the detective continued, "we've run a more thorough check on your housekeeper. She looks clean."

"Good," Peter said. "We didn't really think there was a chance, but we're glad you checked her out."

"So that's about it for the moment. Don't hesitate to call if you have any questions."

After they hung up, Andrea leaned against the counter, watching as Zoë sliced onions and carrots. "Nothing new?" Zoë asked softly.

Andrea shook her head. "Maybe the next call . . . "

She let her voice trail off.

"Yes. Please, Lord." Zoë's voice conveyed optimism, but her eyes were so full of concern, Andrea felt tears spring to her own eyes.

Zoë cleared her throat. "I'm doing chicken and dumplings," she said. "Comfort food."

"You remembered," Peter said, as he joined them in the kitchen. "My old favorite."

He turned to Andrea. "Glad to hear Esther's clean. If you're sure you don't want her back, let's give her severance pay."

"Fine." Andrea looked up at Peter. "So what can we do next?"

He hesitated. "I was thinking we ought to call Dad and your folks."

She winced. "That crossed my mind too."

He glanced at his watch. "Five-fifteen our time. Seven-fifteen in Chicago. Let's do it now, while Tim's not here."

She took a deep breath. "You go first."

"OK." Peter punched in the eleven digits. "Want to get on the other phone?"

"I guess." She started down the hall just as Peter said, "Hi, Dad."

In the bedroom she hesitated, staring at the phone. She picked it up and heard Peter's father exclaim, "Peter! I've wanted to call, but I figured you didn't need the old man butting in."

"Hey, what are dads for?" Peter asked.

"Right. Then tell me what happened," came Benjamin Lang's steady voice. Practical. Like Peter.

Peter sketched in the details.

"How's Andrea taking it?" Peter's dad asked.

"I'm right here," Andrea interjected. "I'm—what is it they say? Doing as well as can be expected."

"I'd expect you're completely worried and scared. And so, frankly, is this granddad," came the voice from Chicago.

"You've got it," Andrea said.

"I've put your names on our church prayer list. And you know I'm praying for you and my granddaughter. I have her picture right here on my desk. Big grin. Dimples. What a sweetie!"

"She's that for sure, Dad." Andrea heard the taut edge in Peter's voice.

"It's only been a day. She'll be back." Benjamin Lang's voice rang with assurance.

"Right," she said, trying for a positive tone.

After they said good-bye, Andrea thought about her father-in-law's expressions of love and concern. They were sweet, touching. But gradually she saw that nothing anyone could say would make her feel better, and nothing she could ever say would convey her anguish to others.

"Your turn," Peter called from the kitchen.

She eyed the phone warily, her sense of dread growing.

Somehow, telling her parents seemed an admission of the horror she wanted so much to deny. It was as though once verbalized to them, it would really be true.

"Andry?" She jumped as Peter sat down beside her. "Your turn," he repeated, placing a gentle hand over hers.

She nodded, picked up the phone, and pressed the familiar sequence of numbers, listening to the tune of the tones.

"Busy!" She slammed the phone down angrily. "Wouldn't you know?" She grabbed a pencil from the nightstand and snapped it in two.

"It's OK," Peter said, with a maddening tone of calm.

"It's not OK!" she shouted. "I just want to get this call over with! Don't you understand?"

They sat in silence. Finally she seized the phone again. "Maybe she's hung up. You can bet it's my mother on the line, not Dad."

She pressed the numbers as hard as she could, as though a really firm attempt would get through.

"Still busy!" She threw the phone on the bed, not bothering to hang up, and paced across the room. "Wait! All we do is wait!" She knew her anger was unreasonable, but she didn't care.

"Want me to get you a soft drink?" Peter asked quietly as he replaced the phone.

She glared at him. "I'm not thirsty." Tears seeped from the corners of her eyes. "I'm sorry. Yes, sure, I'll split a soda with you. I'll try to dial it once more."

This time she heard her mother's terse, "Yes?"

"Mother," she began, "we've got a problem here, and I thought you and Dad ought to know. Is he there?"

"What sort of problem?" her mother demanded.

"Get Dad, will you please, Mother? Then I'll explain."

Her father's gentle, "Is that my Punkin?" took her back thirty years. If only she could climb on his lap and he'd make it all right, like he always had.

Her mother responded to the news just as Andrea expected, with a barrage of questions, her tone strident: "What are they doing to find her? How many people are working on the case? What do they think? What are you and Peter doing to help? Why isn't it in our Chicago papers?"

Patiently, Andrea tried to answer, but she couldn't control the quaver in her voice.

"Of course, if you'd been there," her mother put in. Then came the lecture. "Now, Andrea, you've got to pull yourself together for Peter and Tim's sake. Be strong! Control yourself."

"And whatever I do, don't embarrass you. Right?" she interjected.

Her dad's voice came as a gentle contrast to her mother's. "It's going to be all right, Punkin. You want us to come?"

All I need is Mom criticizing everything I do, she thought. But she said, "Oh, Dad, thanks, but not now."

"Stand tall, Andrea!" her mother interjected.

"OK, Mom, you get the last word, as always. I'll keep you posted."

After they said good-bye, she looked up at Peter. "Quite a difference between your mom and mine."

"They both want to help," he said softly.

"I know. But your mother *does* help and with so much love. Mine is just all heart, isn't she?" she asked, her voice rich with sarcasm.

"Sure is."

"This reminds me of when my mom's mother died. My grandmother was precious to me. At the funeral, I lost it—fell apart, cried and cried. My mother was so embarrassed, kept telling me to pull myself together. She never, ever shed a single tear. I tell you, that woman *has* no heart."

"Maybe," Peter offered, "she has a hard time showing it."

"Sure." She began pacing the room again, slowly gaining momentum as an idea began to form. She stopped and looked down at her husband. "I am *not* going to play the noble little woman role. Repeat: *not*! And I am not just going to sit around and wait. I'm going to *do* something!" She could feel her face flush as the ideas began to flow. "I can use what I know best to—well, publicize Joy, advertise for her. I can get clients to donate media time and space. We need to get a banner up by the toy store right away with her picture." Her mind raced and the words tumbled out. "And I'll get someone to underwrite printing a whole bunch of flyers."

She resumed her pacing, then stopped and pointed at Peter. "Then you know what we need? A reward. Why didn't I think of it before? Think, Peter, think! How can we get some money together—a really worthwhile amount?"

"Maybe they'd start a fund at work," Peter said.

"Yes!" she exclaimed. She hurried down the hall to the kitchen. "Mom! I'm going go start the most important PR campaign of my life. It's called, 'Find Joy!'"

Zoë wiped her hands on a dishtowel and turned to give her a quick hug. "That's my dynamic Andrea! No one could do it better than you."

Andrea nodded. "It's what I know. Now, first thing, we need to get some reward money together. Peter thinks they might do something at work."

"And I'm really good at fund-raising." Zoë paused and laughed, adding, "And modest about it too."

"No, it's true," Andrea agreed. "You are good at it."

"I'll get on it tomorrow," Zoë promised.

~

The next morning, Andrea began planning her "Find Joy" campaign.

But when she asked Peter to join her in a brainstorming session, he shook his head. "Look, I'm an engineer, not a publicist."

His refusal hurt. She stared into her coffee cup. Seeming to sense her disappointment, he added, "I can be a sounding board, though. I'll give you my opinion if you want to run anything by me. You're the best, honey. Go for it."

Later that morning, Andrea drove down the mountain, up the Coast Highway, and headed through Malibu Canyon toward the sheriff's station.

Inside the Lost Hills station, she asked at the counter for Detective Jansen. After a brief wait, he appeared, looking surprised and, she thought, pleased.

"Could I talk with you?" she asked.

"Of course." Leading her into a conference room, he motioned to a seat. She sat on the edge of the chair and leaned toward him, outlining her ideas for a publicity campaign. "What do you think?" she asked.

She saw the excitement in his amber eyes. "I like it."

"Any suggestions?"

He loosened the brown patterned necktie that enhanced the rugged tan of his face. "The important thing is to keep her name in front of the public. The more people hear about her, the more likely you are to find her, OK? Now, you may not need long-range plans. But if it turns out you do, don't forget national TV, those unsolved-mystery, missing-kids type programs." He paused and smiled when she nodded eagerly.

"Yes, yes, of course," she said. "Now, do you have any thoughts on how to keep the momentum with the press going right now, when there's really nothing new?"

He hesitated. "Well, I noticed the media latched on to your boy."

She winced. The last thing she wanted was to give Tim negative attention. "Yes?"

"So how about Tim putting a yellow ribbon around a tree for his sister?"

"Yes! Great press angle. And then, you know, he's having a hard time. This could make him feel good—like he's part of the effort." She thought a moment. "And of course a press release on the reward. Peter's mom's working on that."

"Definitely."

She jumped to her feet and shook his hand. "Detective Jansen, did you ever think of a career in public relations or advertising?"

He stood and smiled. "No, this is my career. But I'm glad to see you feel like getting to work. This is a tough time for you. The not knowing."

She stared at the lines of compassion around his eyes. "You really understand, don't you?" She looked away, embarrassed at the intimacy she suddenly felt with him. She ran her fingers along the chair's edge. "But you deal with this sort of thing all the time. I'd think you'd be hardened to it all."

"I thought I was. Till my own loss. My wife—" He looked down at his hands and pressed his lips together.

"Cancer."

"Oh," she breathed. "I-I'm sorry."

He extended his hand to her. "Good luck on your campaign, Ms. Lang. I'll do anything I can to help."

She clasped his hand, feeling so grateful for his input and empathy that she blurted, "Detective Jansen, we're going to be a terrific team!"

9

From Zoë's Prayer Journal

January 6: Heavenly Father, thanks for turning Andrea's despair into a program of action. Here I fretted to You about all the time she spent at work, and now You're using the skills she learned there to help find Joy. You prepared her for such a time as this! You are an awesome God! Again, I pray for protection for our darling Joy, and oh, Lord, please lift Tim from his guilt and depression. As for Peter, You know he's never expressed his feelings well, but I can see the deep pain in those brown eyes. Help him, help all of them to trust You. Be glorified in this, I pray in Jesus' name, amen.

WHEN ANDREA TOOK A BREAK from work on her Joy campaign Sunday afternoon, she found Tim sprawled on the floor staring at the TV. "Thought you were helping your dad work on the car, honey."

"We finished. He's doing paperwork."

"I see." She glanced at the screen. A chase scene with gunfire. "This the best there is?"

He shrugged.

"How about doing something else?" She glanced across the road. "Want to have Brant over?"

"Nah. I saw him go out with his mom."

"Well, maybe when he gets home. You enjoyed your time with him yesterday, didn't you?"

"Yeah." Tim's face brightened for a moment. "That place is radical, Mom. You ever been over there? Like I told you, Brant has a snake named Simon. And some neat tapes and games."

"Really?"

"Yeah, and his mom is kinda different."

"Oh? In what way?"

He shrugged. "It's—uh—hard to explain."

She started to question him further, but Tim stood and stared past her, out the window.

"Want to go outside?" she suggested. "It's nice out."

"And do what?"

"You could bang a ball against the garage door. Practice for that game you said you play in PE."

"Yeah." He shrugged and slowly moved toward the closet. *He's in the same slow-motion world I inhabited yesterday*, she thought as she watched him reach for a handball and head out the front door.

♪

Outside, Tim gave the ball a couple of lethargic bounces as he started toward the driveway. *Would his mom and dad feel as awful if he'd disappeared?* he wondered. Joy was cute. She made them smile a lot. He bit his lip, remembering the times he'd felt mad because she got so much attention—attention *he'd* had when he was the only kid. He thought of the times he wished Joy wasn't there to bug him. Did thinking things like that make them happen?

He scuffed one foot against the rock he and his dad had unearthed when they planted their living Christmas tree. Fossils of seashells showed clearly in its triangular planes. Did the sea once come all the way up this mountain? Or did the mountain rise out of the sea? As he bent over to look at the intricate pattern, he heard a tiny mew.

Straightening quickly, he scanned the yard. "Kitty, kitty?" he called softly.

Another mew. It seemed to come from the plants with the purple blooms by the house.

"Here, kitty!"

The foliage parted and a multicolored kitten, no bigger than Joy's little stuffed Siamese, appeared.

He laughed out loud. "Hey, that's some suit you've got!" he exclaimed, surveying the patches of white, black, and orange. "Like a clown!"

The kitten carried a crooked tail, bent at forty-five degrees near the tip, at a jaunty tilt. Outsized feet exaggerated the animal's kittenish clumsiness as it started along the sidewalk toward Tim.

"How can such a skinny cat have such big feet, huh?" He stooped, hearing the kitten purring as it approached him. Then, in a flash, the cat leapt onto his bent knees and walked up the front of his shirt.

"Hey, kitty, those are sharp claws!" he protested, supporting the kitten against his chest. The purring grew louder. The kitten reached up one paw and, claws sheathed, gently placed it against Tim's cheek.

"Aw," he exclaimed, stroking it softly. He'd forgotten how good it was to hold a cat. He'd had one till just before Joy was born. All black. Named Spooky. But when it disappeared, his mom had thought they should wait till Joy was older to get another.

The cat's whiskers tickled his chin. Rubbing his face against his shoulder to relieve the itch, Tim cradled the bit of fluff in his arms, feeling its warmth.

"Wonder where you came from," he murmured. "You sure look like you could use a good meal."

A desperate hope rose in his heart. Maybe somebody hadn't wanted the cat and dumped it off in the hills.

Careful not to jostle the kitten, he rose and walked to the front door, touching the latch with his elbow.

"Mom! Dad!" he called as the door swung open. "Look what I found!"

His mom appeared first. "Oh!" she exclaimed. "What a funny kitten—a little girl."

"How can you tell?"

"Calicos are always girls, or so I've read." She rubbed the kitten between the ears. She'd always had a kitten when she was growing up. How soft it felt! She knew already he'd want to keep her.

"What's up?" Peter stepped into the hallway from the bedroom. He smiled as he saw the kitten. "Hey, that is a pretty wild paint job! Were you done by Picasso or Dali?"

"Yeah, Dad, and that's not all." Tim set her gently on the floor. "Look at her front paws."

"Catcher's mitts," Peter said. He picked up the kitten and examined one oversized paw. "She's got an extra toe."

"No fooling. I knew she was special. Oh, Dad, Mom—" Andrea heard the earnestness in their son's voice.

"Can I keep her, huh? Can I? I'll feed her. Train her to a box. She won't be any trouble, I promise. Puleeze?"

"You sure she doesn't belong to someone?" Peter asked.

"I've never seen her before. Somebody probably dumped her off in the hills," Tim said.

"Still, I think we should put an ad in the paper and nail up a 'cat found' sign, just in case," Andrea said.

Tim's smile disappeared. "But we can keep her while we do that, right?" he persisted.

"Well . . ." Peter pursed his lips thoughtfully.

"If nobody turns up to claim her, I'll pay to have her fixed," Tim offered. "I've saved enough, I think."

Peter grinned. "How about if we get the ad in and put the sign up, and if no one responds, give her a one-week trial? You agree, Andry?"

She nodded, hoping the owner wouldn't surface. The cat would be so good for him. "Sure. Give her a try."

"Oh, thanks!" Tim's face glowed with excitement. "But—"

"But what?" she asked.

"I can't just call her 'Kitty.' Let's see." He thought a moment. "She's so loving. Mom, she put her paw against my cheek." He took the kitten from Peter and demonstrated. "Remember that ballet we saw? Romeo and—"

"Juliet?"

"Yeah! That's it. Juliet. C'mon, Juliet. Let's see if we can find you something to eat. Could I try her on some milk, Mom?"

"Sure."

As Tim headed toward the kitchen, an exuberant Juliet bounded behind him.

⌇

Later Sunday night, with no news from the sheriff's department, they agreed that Peter should return to work the next day. "And," he suggested, "school starts again for Tim, so what if I take him to school on my way? He'd be a little bit early."

"You've been worrying too!" she exclaimed. "Oh, Peter, please! I find myself wondering what sort of loony might be out there, waiting to compound what's already happened."

"So I'll take him."

"And I'll pick him up after school," Andrea said. She thought a moment. "I hope the kids don't give him too hard a time. Maybe we ought to talk to him."

He nodded and they went together and found Tim lying on his bed with Juliet purring on his chest.

"Now there is a contented cat," Peter said. "You know, she'll be good company for your mom when I go back to work tomorrow and you go back to school."

Tim flinched and sat up, transferring the cat to his lap. "School," he groaned.

"I know," Peter's voice was sympathetic. "I don't want to go back to work either. But it's time." He sat down beside Tim. "Tim, you could get some flak from the other kids."

Tim looked up at him. "You gonna give me that 'sticks and stones' bit?"

Peter grinned. "I'll spare you. But try not to let anything anyone says undermine the facts. And they are, number one, that you are not responsible for what happened to Joy."

"And number two," Andrea interjected, sitting next to Tim on the bed, "we, your dad and I, are behind you 100 percent. We believe in you and we love you, and you can count on that, no matter what."

"And number three," Peter continued, "the other kids may let you down from time to time, but God never will. He promises to be our refuge and strength."

Andrea put her arm around Tim. "One other thing, honey,

this isn't forever. Kids'll find something else to focus on before you know it. Remember when we were at Gram's for Thanksgiving in Orange County, your cousins, Scott and Michelle, told about getting a lot of static at school after their dad was arrested? After a while, it all died down."

Tim nodded. "Yeah, I suppose."

"OK, then, we're agreed on tomorrow," Andrea said, relieved he hadn't protested more.

But the next morning, Tim balked. "Mom," he pleaded, "please don't make me go. I don't feel good."

She felt his forehead. Not a trace of fever. Putting her hands on his shoulders, she stooped and gave him what she earnestly hoped was a look of understanding. "I have an idea how you must feel, honey. Especially when you're still kind of new at school and don't have any real friends here yet. But waiting won't make it easier. It's hard for all of us to get back to our regular schedules. But the sooner we do, the better. Vacation's over, and you need to go back to school with everybody else. Your dad's going to work, and I'll be working at home." She paused a moment and then added firmly, "Tim, I want you to go."

He sighed. "All ri-i-ight."

After Peter and Tim left, she called her office and explained to Mr. Reynolds that she needed time to launch her "Find Joy" campaign.

"OK," he agreed. "We'll help any way we can. Art department says it'll donate some work."

"Terrific! But Mr. Reynolds, Joy could be back today, tomorrow, anytime."

"Right. And we'll have to get going on the Waterfront account by the end of next week."

"Yes. Right. I understand."

She made a point of working only when Tim was in school.

The days passed in a strange contradiction of time accelerated—with not enough hours to get everything done—and time dragging—as the old clock on the mantel gonged another hour and another and still no word on Joy.

Then, on Friday, Tim's teacher called. "Mrs. Lang," she said, "it's Jenny Whitson. I'm so very sorry about your daughter's disappearance. I can't imagine anything worse." She went on, "I know there are so many things to cope with right now, Mrs. Lang, but I'm calling because I'm concerned about Tim."

"Oh," she murmured, instantly feeling new tensions build in the back of her neck. "What are you seeing?"

"Two things, really. He's not with us much of the time. I call on him, and he hasn't heard. And his fuse can be extremely short. The littlest thing seems to set him off." She hesitated. "He may also be getting some needling from the other kids. I tried to talk with them when Tim was out of the room, but you know how they can be."

Andrea responded, "I appreciate your concern, and I think we'd better see about some counseling. Can you make some recommendations?"

Ms. Whitson sounded relieved. "Of course."

Andrea jotted down the names and numbers and a description of each counselor, slumping in her chair as she said good-bye. "Oh, God," she said aloud. "Do You see all this pain? Do You?"

She thought Peter would balk at the idea of counseling, but when she mentioned it that night, he said, "I agree. The poor kid's come dragging his sleeping bag into our room every night since he went back to school. I think he needs a neutral party to talk to."

She nodded. "Somebody who isn't emotionally involved." She ran the three referrals past him.

"I like the one who's a Christian."

"Dr. Hadley?" She hesitated. "Well, OK."

"Good. That's settled. Now, meantime, back at the ranch house?" he prompted.

"Oh, this ranch house? I've accomplished quite a bit." She detailed her campaign to date. "And a full-page ad in the *Advertiser* and one hundred thousand flyers with Joy's picture."

"Great! I'm proud of you." Peter beamed. "And I have some good news from work. Management's come up with five hundred dollars for reward money. And the employees have taken a collection to pay for ads or however we want to use it."

"That's wonderful!" she exclaimed. "Maybe there's enough to do a banner on Malibu Canyon Road. There's so much more I could do!" She sighed.

She made it a point to spend time over the weekend away from the computer, and even took in a movie with Peter and Tim. But Sunday night, as she lay in bed, ideas for the Joy campaign mingled in a jumble with her strategy for the Waterfront account. She wasn't aware of sleeping at all—till the piercing scream of a frightened child propelled her from the bed. Standing, she shivered in the dark, waiting. She heard the furnace click on and Peter's even breathing. Nothing more. A dream, she slowly realized. Or was it?

Shaking, she grabbed her robe at the foot of the bed and hurried into Joy's room. The night-light still shone, revealing the aching emptiness of the bed, its patchwork quilt neatly in place.

Stifling her sobs, she knelt beside the bed. "Oh, God," she cried, "are You there? Do You care? This is more than I can bear! Is it my fault for not staying home? Are you punishing me for not being a better mother? Is that it?"

Tears spilling on the bedspread, she waited. She wasn't sure for what.

It's true, she admitted to herself. *I could have been a better mother. I was always rushing to get to work and pushing her aside to finish the work I'd brought home. But wait. Because of my job, we could buy this house,* she thought. The house Joy knows as home now, the house she should come back to. *If I stopped work, could we handle it financially?*

She did some calculations. With what she'd saved, they had put a substantial amount down, so monthly payments weren't too horrendous. It would be close, but not impossible.

Still kneeling, she said, "Lord, You know I'll do anything to get her back. Whatever it takes. If it's giving up my job, then I will. You know how much I love it. But it's nothing—*nothing* compared with what I feel for my daughter. Is that what You want? For me to stay home, be a twenty-four-hour-a-day mom? Is that what it takes to have her back again?"

Drawing a long, tremulous breath, she stretched out her arms, palms up. "Then here—take it. My job for my child. I offer it to You. And, oh, God, how I'll praise You when she's home!" A sudden thought made her catch her breath. "Why, You might even bring her home for her birthday!"

She wasn't sure how long she knelt there before she rose unsteadily to her feet. A sense of relief washed over her as she groped her way in the dark to the kitchen, shut the door, and turned on the light. Pulling stationery from the desk drawer, she sat at the kitchen table and began writing a letter of resignation to Mr. Reynolds.

The words flowed with surprising ease, as though they had waited, already composed in the computer of her mind, ready to be called up.

She signed her name. "There, I've done it. Now it's Your turn, Lord."

10

THE NEXT MORNING at breakfast, Andrea propped her letter in front of Peter's plate.

He read it and looked at her, eyebrows raised, brown eyes questioning. "Sure you want to do this, honey? You've worked so hard, come so far. And with this new account—"

"I know." She nodded. "But I talked with God about it. I think it's what He wants."

Peter's expression softened and he smiled. "I'm glad you talked with Him. And if you're sure . . ."

She nodded. "My only concern is the money. This'll be quite a cut in our income. But I think we can make it."

He frowned, stared into the distance, obviously calculating. At last he said, "It'll be tight." He looked across the table at her. "But thanks to you, our house payments are low. And I should get a raise next month."

She reached across the table for his hand. "Oh, honey, I'm so glad I married you. Some husbands would go ballistic, insist they need two incomes." She thought a moment. "Maybe I can do some consulting."

"Maybe this is our chance to believe that God will meet our needs." He paused and gazed intently at her. "I think this is also a time when we need to get back to church. With everything going berserk, seems like we need something in our lives that's dependable, true—an anchor."

"I was thinking about that," she said slowly. "You know, I've been to the Hendrixes' church. It's up the hill from that account of mine, the Seaview Inn. That's where Connie's set up the Joy Information Center. Wouldn't that seem, well, appropriate?"

"Very appropriate."

She looked up as Tim joined them at the table. "How goes it?"

"Pretty good." His voice sounded listless.

"Did you get back to sleep OK last night?" Peter asked.

Tim bit his lip. "After a while."

Andrea studied his averted eyes, hangdog posture. He was becoming as silent as his dad. She'd definitely call the psychologist today.

Peter glanced from Tim to Andrea. "Your mom has some news, Tim."

"Yeah?"

"I'm resigning my job," Andrea explained. "Going to stay home, be a mom, work on my campaign to find Joy."

Tim seemed preoccupied. "OK."

Nothing more? She felt disappointed.

Tim looked from one to the other. "Dad, Mom, we've had Juliet a week now. And nobody's called about the ad or the sign."

"Hmm. Is that right?" Peter put on his serious, thinking-it-over expression, but Andrea saw the twinkle in his eye.

"Yeah. You know, she trained to the box right away. Doesn't scratch the furniture. And she's very comforting."

"You haven't heard anything?" Peter looked at her.

"Not a word."

"Well, then, I guess Tim has himself a cat," Peter said.

"All r-i-i-ght!" Tim exclaimed, giving first his dad, then his mom a high-five.

She smiled. *Juliet's good for him*, she thought. *What could be more comforting than a cat purring on your lap or cuddling up beside you in bed?*

Later, as Tim left for school with Peter, he turned to Andrea. "Take good care of my cat, Mom," he grinned.

She bent to kiss him. "I will, and I'll be there to pick you up."

In the car, Tim groaned to Peter. "I hate it when she picks me up. When am I gonna get to ride the bus like everybody else? I feel like a baby. Nobody's gonna come take *me*."

Good, Peter thought. *He's not worrying about that anymore.* "I sure hope not," he said. "We need you."

"Well, if they tried, I'd fight and yell, and they wouldn't get me."

"I know you would," Peter said as they started down the hill. "But hang in there, Tim. You'll be back on the bus one of these days."

"Yeah. When I'm in high school, probably." Tim slid down in the seat and stared out the window. "If somebody took Joy and they find him, what do you think they'll do to him?"

"Kidnapping is heavy-duty, Tim, a federal offense. I guess the exact sentence would depend on a number of things. Like if a kidnapper crosses state lines, that's a death penalty. It's a very serious crime."

"I guess! Boy, if I found the guy, I'd take care of him."

"How so?" Peter glanced at his son's clenched fist, feeling the charge of his anger.

"Oh, boil him in oil. Do a Rambo." Tim pointed his finger and moved it in an arc, doing machine-gun sound effects. "Hang him by his thumbs." He gave a wicked grin, waiting for his dad's reaction.

Peter heard his son's words echo his own deepest inclination toward vengeance. "Put him on a rack, maybe? In other words, get even?"

"Well, *yeah!*" Tim turned sideways in his seat toward his dad. "Don't you want to?"

"Sometimes," Peter admitted. "I've thought of buying a gun, all sorts of things. But I'm beginning to get to where I can pray that whoever might have her is taking good care of her. That's what's most important, don't you think?"

"I s'pose so." Tim's tone was grudging.

He glanced at his son. He wanted so much to be the steadfast father for Tim, the rock he could depend on. Now, as they traveled the Coast Highway and neared the school, he tried to switch Tim's focus to the day ahead. "What are you looking forward to in school today, Tim? PE?"

"Yeah. We have a cool handball game we play."

"I saw you practicing against the garage door. Looking good." Peter braked to a stop by the school playground. "Go for it!" Leaning over to open the car door, he gave a thumbs-up.

As Peter left the school grounds and began his winding route through Malibu canyon, he shook his head, trying to clear it of thoughts of Joy and to focus on the day ahead. But one truth crashed through his concentration again and again. *She's gone. Joy's really gone.*

Without warning, he felt himself plunging under a huge wave of grief. It was like the time, body-surfing, when he found himself caught in a swell that was far bigger than he'd anticipated. It broke over him, holding him under in a wash of turbulence till his lungs felt ready to explode.

Gasping, he found a spot to pull off the road. The suffocating pressure modulated into a pain in his chest so sharp, he wondered if he might be having a heart attack. He felt his pulse. Rapid, but regular. *If only I could cry*, he thought. But he couldn't. After a few moments, the pain relented enough for him to get out of the car. He stood at the canyon's edge, gulping in the clammy morning air, welcoming it into his tortured lungs. Across from him, in the midst of green foliage, rocks gleamed with moisture. He looked down into the dizzying depth of the canyon, with its massive boulders and outcroppings, realizing that another few steps would end his pain. "God," he cried, "I don't know if I can make it. Help me! Help us all!"

Then, as though his words had tapped a deep well within him, he began to cry.

He had no sense of time as he stood there, hearing the muffled flow of the stream below, interrupted by the steady noise of cars speeding past behind him. He turned at last, hastily wiping his eyes as he heard a car stop and saw the black and white of the highway patrol.

"Got a problem?" the officer called.

What a question. Peter almost laughed out loud. He took another deep breath. "Thanks," he said, "I wasn't feeling too great. But I'll be going on now."

"OK. Watch the traffic from behind when you ease out." The patrolman pulled away.

⟋

Two days later, as Andrea worked at her desk, she answered the phone and heard Reynolds's voice. "Andrea, say it isn't so."

"Oh, Mr. Reynolds. You got my letter?"

"I did. I'm hoping that by now you see this isn't necessary. You can work on your campaign to find Joy and handle your job. We'll help you."

He's making it hard. I knew he would, she thought. "Oh, that's very kind, Mr. Reynolds. But truly, I've made my decision."

"I can't believe you'd bring us this far with the Waterfront account and give it up to someone else. We need you," he said.

She was ready for him. "That's the hardest part for me, Mr. Reynolds. I'd love to work on this campaign. But I've set it up pretty thoroughly." She swallowed hard. "You've been very good to me. Nothing—believe me—nothing but a crisis like this would make me even think of leaving. But I have to."

"I think we could make it worth your while," Reynolds persisted.

"Mr. Reynolds, you are a class-act marketing man, and I admire you enormously. But the answer is still no."

She heard him sigh. "Tell you what. I won't accept a resignation. But I will consider a leave of absence."

She felt her pulse quicken. Maybe, after Joy was back. No, she'd told God . . . Her mind spun, but she heard herself say, "All right, if that's the way you want it. And by all means, call me if you have any questions."

"Definitely." He paused. "Uh, one more thing. I want to send out your computer. We're redoing our office system."

"Oh!" she exclaimed. "The computer I have here is ancient, a Model T. But this is too much."

"Look, what could I get for a used computer? Peanuts."

Tears seeped from her eyes and she could only say, "Thank you."

"OK. Got a meeting now. Good luck with your campaign to find your daughter." And he was gone.

She replaced the phone and gave in to the tears. How she loved her work. How she would miss starting and finishing a project, the satisfaction of seeing effective results.

She blew her nose and coached herself aloud, "No, I can't look back. I've got to look ahead. I have work to do here. Got to use all my skills to find Joy."

She dug into her file drawer for a folder just as the phone rang.

"Good morning, dahling." No mistaking Dolores's deep, theatrical voice.

"Ah, Dolores. Glad you called. I'm about to take a break for a cup of something. Join me?"

"Lovely! Want to come here?"

"No, I'm waiting for a phone call. You come here."

"Ten minutes?" Dolores asked.

"Perfect."

Andrea hurried down the hall to the kitchen. She'd mix vanilla-almond coffee with Colombian decaf. Dolores should like that.

She started the coffee and ran back to the bedroom to change from her grubbies to a turquoise turtleneck with periwinkle sweats. As she dabbed on some lipstick, the doorbell rang.

She could see Dolores through the glass panels flanking the front door. Wearing black tights and tunic, she'd draped a scarf in jewel tones at her neck. How could this woman always look so perfectly turned out?

Andrea opened the door. "Come in. You just saved me from a private pity party."

"Oh, good. I knew there was a reason I called." Dolores followed Andrea into the kitchen and nodded as Andrea indicated a chair in the eating area. "I take it black," Dolores said as she sat down.

Andrea reached to a high shelf and brought down two Audubon bird mugs and poured the coffee, bringing it to the table.

Dolores sniffed appreciatively. "Smells divine, and aren't these mugs splendid?"

As Andrea sat down, Dolores added, "So you're feeling depressed about your daughter. I'd think you were totally uncaring if you weren't."

"Yes, that. But it's more than that. I resigned my job. Just finished talking with my boss when you called."

"Oh, my dear!" Dolores exclaimed. "That must have been terribly difficult."

Andrea nodded, afraid for a moment she might cry again. "Tell me about it," Dolores said, her voice sympathetic.

"I just felt God wanted me here. And I need the time to work on my Joy campaign." Andrea saw Dolores's questioning look. "I've launched the most important PR campaign of my life: Find Joy."

Dolores clapped her hands together. "Perfect! Use all your experience and expertise."

"It's what I have to do." Andrea stopped. "Oh, I'm being a rotten hostess. Would you like a muffin? I can zap one in the micro."

"No, no!" Dolores waved the idea away. "No way will I undo an hour in the gym this morning."

"I admire your discipline," Andrea said. "It shows. You always look fabulous."

They were silent a moment, tasting their coffee. Then Andrea asked, "So you go to the gym. What else? You don't work?"

"No, not anymore. Oh, once in a while I help with some charity production or other. I used to dance, you know. I go to a yoga class, do the gym three days a week. I spend time with a fascinating group of very 'now' women. So connected—give off a lot of energy. I'd love you to meet them. And then I usually have lunch out. I'm a 'foodie,' I'm afraid. I love finding new restaurants, trying new dishes."

Dolores paused to sip her coffee. "And, let's see: I check out the new films and what's happening in the theater. I entertain guests a fair amount, and I'm entertained quite a lot."

What a life, Andrea thought. *She has it all.* "Sounds busy," she said.

"I like it that way. I have a lot of stamina." Dolores's voice seemed to lower a full tone "But lately, I've been spending more time just—well—I call it getting in touch with the divine. I mean, it's all around us, isn't it? We need to get in harmony with it."

"When you say the divine, do you mean God?" Andrea asked.

"Perhaps that's what you call it," Dolores said. "But to me, this is so much more! It's real! It's experiential! It has so many dimensions!"

The phone rang, and Andrea said, "Hold that thought." She crossed the room to the kitchen phone.

"Ms. Lang? Frank at Universal Sign Company. I have some figures for you on those banners."

Andrea grabbed a pen and paper. "Good. Let's have them." She jotted down the information. "Thanks, Frank, I'll get back to you."

She hung up and picked up the coffeepot on the way back to the table. Dolores put her hand over her cup. "I'll need to be on my way in a moment."

"Sorry about that." Andrea waved toward the phone, setting the coffeepot on the table. "Some figures on some banners I want for my campaign."

"It must feel good to be *doing* something," Dolores said, her eyes sympathetic.

"Yes. I'd go bonkers otherwise. You'd think it'd get easier as time goes by." She shook her head. "Not so."

"Tell me what all you've done so far."

Dolores seemed so interested, Andrea detailed her accomplishments and plans.

"But that's simply spectacular!" Dolores exclaimed. "You are truly a pro. I'm sure you'll see results." She stood. "I hate to leave, but I really must press on."

Andrea stood and clasped her arm. "Oh, and I wanted to hear more about your getting in touch with the divine."

Dolores gave her a penetrating look, almost as though trying to evaluate her innermost being. "We'll get into that," she promised.

11

~

From Zoë's Prayer Journal

January 16: Dear Lord, this is so hard!
Everyone's so affected. My buddy, Tim, tells me
he feels like a slimeball. (What a word!) Oh,
Father, I pray You would show him how special
he is to You, how much You love him and con-
firm that it doesn't matter what he did or didn't
do the day of Joy's disappearance. Thank you
that Peter and Andrea have decided to return to
church. Surely that will help Tim. Maybe there
could be a special friend for him in Sunday
school? And oh, bring our Joy home safely —
soon, please? Thank You for Your mercy, Lord,
in Jesus' name, amen.

AFTER DOLORES LEFT, Andrea returned to her desk, glancing at her watch. Ten minutes past eleven. Better check in with Connie at the Joy Information Center. Maybe there was some news.

"Andrea!" her neighbor exclaimed. "Good to hear your voice. "How you doin'?"

"OK. My boss just called. Tried to get me to stay."

"I bet that was hard."

"Yes. But," Andrea brightened, "can you believe this? He's sending my computer out to me."

Connie whistled. "Hey, that'll be handy. What a guy!"

"Right. My computer here is so slow. Now I can do more and much quicker. For my Joy campaign." She could feel her smile fade as her thoughts returned to Joy. "Is there anything at all coming in today?"

"I'm afraid not. But," Connie's voice lightened, "this afternoon—who knows? Maybe just what we've been waiting for." She paused. "I'm praying an awful lot for you."

"I know and I appreciate that," Andrea said softly.

"Your mother-in-law and I pray together too," Connie added. "What a prayer warrior! I just found out her name is the Greek word for 'life.' And she sure is full of life! You know she was here four days straight, working on raising money?"

"Incredible, isn't she? She got almost a thousand dollars in pledges. And now she's dedicating a whole day every week to come to Malibu to work at the center and cook for us. "

"What a gift!"

"Yes, and for sure, she's a pray-er. Did she tell you how she prays when she swims her laps? Calls it her twenty-five-yard prayer closet. And then she journals her prayers too."

"Yep, I do that too." Connie laughed. "Journal, not swim."

Andrea sighed. "You both seem so—connected—I guess the word is. Even when things are tough."

"Maybe," Connie's voice was gentle, "it's because we're in the habit of coming to Him, when things are smooth and when they're tough."

"Maybe if we started going to church again . . ." Andrea's voice trailed off.

"Well, shoot, yes!" Connie said, eagerness in her voice. "We have services at 8:30 and 10:15 Sunday mornings. And then a real informal little family service at 7:30 Sunday nights. Oh, Andrea, why don't you all come? It's a sweet fellowship, not too big. Warm, loving. And there's a terrific Sunday school program for Tim."

"What denomination is it?" she asked.

"Nondenominational. Not a lot of ritual and stuff. But all Bible-based. Real good teaching."

"Sounds good. A little like a church we attended before—" She stopped, embarrassed, adding, "frankly, before we got too busy."

"Hey, it happens." Connie seemed neither surprised nor shocked. "Anyway, the important thing is that you want to come back." The click of call-waiting sounded on Andrea's line. "You go ahead and get that call. See you Sunday, then!"

As Andrea pressed the button to take the other call, she realized with surprise that she looked forward to Sunday.

"Yes?" she said.

"Eric Jansen here."

"Detective Jansen. What's new?" she asked.

"Just had a call from the producer of *Missing Persons*. You know, the network show. I never give out personal phone numbers, OK? But I have the contact if you want to call them."

"Terrific! We could use some national exposure."

He gave her the name and number and added, "I saw the story you did for that "First Person" column in the *Times*. It was really nice, full of feelings, not overdone."

"Thanks."

"Keep up the good work, Mrs. Lang!"

They said good-bye, and she phoned the TV producer who asked if she could meet with Andrea the following week.

She quickly agreed and hung up, elated. At last, some national publicity. Hallelujah!

ↀ

As soon as she brought Tim home from school the next afternoon, he gloated, "We had a substitute, and I finished all my homework. OK if I go to Brant's?"

She nodded and heard him slam the door as she thumbed through the mail she'd just retrieved from their box. An envelope from Crivello Enterprises, Inc., caught her eye.

Leaning against the kitchen counter, she tore it open.

Dear Ms. Lang:

Even a capable, creative woman such as you needs time off from the job at hand. Enclosed is a certificate for you and your husband to use at the Bayside Inn. It includes your Saturday night stay, Saturday dinner, and Sunday brunch. You may call the number on the certificate to make your reservations. Enjoy.

Grazia for your creative work on our behalf, beautiful lady.

We'll miss you, but I admire your priorities.

Regards,

Renato Crivello

P.S. We're going ahead with the serious restaurant, which will be called Pastels. It will—how did you say it?—"knock their socks off."

She reread the letter through blurry eyes and shook her head. "Thought so," she said to herself. "Under the pit-bull exterior of our world-class financier beats the heart of a teddy bear."

It was a lovely gesture, but of course she couldn't. To go away now seemed—what, she wondered. Ah, a betrayal of Joy.

The phone interrupted her thoughts. "News!" Peter's voice sang out. "Good news."

The only good news she could imagine would be . . .

"Joy?" she asked anxiously.

"No-o-o." He sounded apologetic and hesitated a moment. "I got a promotion."

"Oh!" she exclaimed, sorry to have deflated him. "How wonderful! Tell me."

"Chief engineer."

She caught her breath. "Are you serious?"

"Yep."

"Honey! Congratulations! But I had no idea. Did you expect it?" she asked.

"Knew it was a possibility. Hoped. But didn't want to get your hopes up."

"That's spectacular. Does it mean more money?"

"Yes. So we'll be OK staying in the house even without your working. God," he added, "is good."

"He is. I agree. Oh, Peter, I'm so proud of you."

"Thanks. Now, what about your day?" he asked.

"Reynolds called. I got through that. And Peter, he's giving me my computer."

"Darned decent. Sure will be useful."

"You bet. Oh, and listen to this letter Crivello wrote me." She read it to him.

"Hey, hey! Listen, wouldn't it be good for us to get away? Celebrate the promotion? How about Saturday?"

"This weekend?" She shook her head. "Oh, Peter, I couldn't. Leaving Tim. The house, the phone."

"Bet Mom'd come. I'll call her. She'd love time with her buddy. And can't we leave the Inn's number with the sheriff?"

"I suppose."

"Listen, Andry, it'd be good for us to get out of the house, have a change of surroundings. We'd have time to talk about your Joy campaign and all. Please, look at our calendar."

She forced herself to turn to the wall calendar. "The date's open, but—"

"Good. I'll call Mom and get back to you."

A few minutes later, Peter called back. "Mom's excited about coming. Just so she gets back to Orange County for a noon open house Sunday. That should work. Call and see if you can make the reservation."

She hung up, stood staring at the phone, and finally picked it up. As she dialed the hotel, she hoped they'd be sold out. Not so. Reluctantly she booked for their arrival at the *Bayside Inn* Saturday. Just as she hung up, the phone rang.

"Mrs. Lang? One moment please."

It was the TV producer calling back.

Almost immediately, a man's voice came on the line. "Mrs. Lang. Michael Thomas at the *Daily News*. We like your idea of a picture of your son with the yellow ribbon. Can we come out this afternoon and get it?"

"Certainly," she said, feeling the exhilaration of an effort that paid off. "What time?"

"I have a photographer out in Malibu right now. She could be there in ten minutes."

"Make it fifteen," she said.

"Fine," he agreed.

She looked at her watch. It seemed a shame to interrupt Tim, but he'd agreed to pose for the photo. Better get him home from Brant's. Looking up Dolores's phone number, she called. Busy.

I'll just walk on over, she decided.

The gate to Dolores's house was unlatched, and she followed the patio around the pool, with its dramatic black tile.

At the entrance, she rang the bell and waited.

The door swung open to reveal Dolores, chic in a royal blue jogging outfit, holding a portable phone. "Andrea! How nice! I'm on the phone."

"I know. I won't interrupt. But I need Tim. There's a photographer coming from the *Daily News*."

Dolores nodded. "I think they went up in the hills. See that big gong on the patio?" She pointed to an immense brass gong—a remnant of some pagan temple, Andrea wondered.

"Oh, is *that* what I've heard a couple of times since we moved in?"

Dolores nodded. "Give it a good whack. It could wake the dead. But it's Brant's signal to come home."

"Right. You go ahead with your call. I'll wait in back for them." She waved. "Come over when you have time."

Dolores nodded, returning to her phone conversation as she shut the door.

Dolores is full of surprises, she thought, smiling as she approached the gong. With two hands, she grabbed the striker that hung next to the gong and gave it a mighty blow.

The tone reverberated through the hillsides. "Wake the dead is right," she murmured.

Just as she began walking toward the back of Dolores's lot to wait for Tim and Brant, she heard laughter behind her. Turning, she saw Tim and a taller boy who, with his dark hair, strong nose, and slender face, was almost a photocopy of Dolores.

"You rang?" Tim asked, breaking up once again.

She laughed too. "I did. Would you call that overkill or what? Dolores thought you were up in the hills."

"Nah, just around the other side of the house," Tim explained.

She held out her hand to the other boy. "You must be Brant."

"Right," he said, giving her a flaccid handshake.

"I hate to interrupt. But Tim, the *Daily News* called and they'll be here soon to take that picture we talked about." She saw his disappointment. "You can come back afterward—if it's OK with Brant."

"O-kay." Tim drew the last syllable out to register his annoyance.

On the way home, she eyed Tim. The look was just right: jeans and sweatshirt. All she needed was the yellow ribbon.

"Which tree will we use?" he asked.

In her mind, she'd already pictured him by the big Aleppo pine, but after all, it was his show. "You have a preference?"

"Uh-huh. The big pine tree. I like to climb up there and think. And I hear the wind blowing through it when I'm in bed."

"Perfect."

The photographer was late, and Tim paced impatiently. But when the petite Japanese woman arrived with her cameras, Andrea was surprised at how well Tim responded. She'd expected him to be shy and stiff. Instead, he looked easy and natural as he wrapped the wide ribbon around the tree and tied an awkward bow. They were almost finished when Tim spied Juliet. "Hey! Could we get my cat in a picture?" he asked.

"Why not?" the photographer replied.

Tim picked up Juliet and held her so she could reach out to the shiny ribbon as the camera clicked and whirred.

"You did a terrific job," Andrea told her son as the photographer drove away. "Maybe we'll get you a job modeling."

"Yeah, sure." He struck a hands-on-hip stance. "Big Shot

from Malibu wears Big Shot jeans." He broke the pose. "Can I go back to Brant's?"

"OK. Oh, and for your info, Gram's coming to be with you Saturday night. Your dad and I have an invitation to go stay at a hotel on the beach."

"Cool," he said as he hurried back toward Brant's.

12

From Zoë's Prayer Journal

January 19: Dear heavenly Father, thank You for that Italian tycoon's giving Peter and Andrea an overnight at his posh resort! Oh, may it be a time of rest and restoration and renewal. And speaking of renewal, I'm tickled pink they plan to go to church when they get back tomorrow. How I pray that, as they worship with the Body, and feel the support of the fellowship, they'll trust You. And thanks for the opportunity to be with Tim. Oh, Lord, You're doing good things, just as You promised, and I exalt You, in Jesus' name, amen.

THE BAYSIDE RESORT, built on the jetty, looked out on the surging, open ocean on one side, the tranquil channel into the harbor on the other. As Peter and Andrea pulled up to the entrance, her reluctance about coming began to fade. Then they stepped into the sunlit lobby with its teak floors, whitewashed walls, and profusion of blooming bromeliads. It was right to come, she decided. Peter's promotion called for a celebration. And maybe here, just for a little while, she could escape the nightmare of the last seventeen days. Maybe she and Peter could actually talk.

After they settled into a beautifully appointed room over-looking the channel, they watched the boats sail and power in from a day on the water.

"The salt air makes me hungry," Peter said. "How about an early dinner?"

"Suits me."

Andrea took a leisurely shower and spent time on her makeup, realizing how casual she'd become since she'd stopped working. As she changed into the black crepe dress Peter loved, he said, "You look great!"

Downstairs in the hotel restaurant, they found few tables taken at six-thirty.

"Where would you like to be?" the maître d' asked. He looked at them carefully. "May I suggest this?" He pointed to a semicircular booth, set apart from the rest of the tables and tiered up to capture the ocean view.

"Good," she said. "Nice and private."

In the fading light, they watched the surf foaming white on darkening sand. A row of palm trees, silhouetted against the sky, reached up like upended feather dusters. A few surfers caught the last rides of the day.

"You liked to body-surf when we first moved to California," she remarked. She saw Peter wince and wondered what unpleasant memory she'd triggered but decided not to ask.

They were silent as they studied the evening's offerings till Peter lowered his oversized menu. "Anything grab you?"

"All of the above. I'd love the rack of lamb with rosemary and garlic, but it's for two people."

"Well, you're in luck. That's my number-one choice."

She reached for his hand. "We're so compatible!" Keep it light and loving for his sake, she decided.

The sommelier brought the "lovely nonalcoholic wine with a lively sparkle" that he'd recommended and poured it into delicate champagne flutes.

She held up her glass. "To you, Mr. Chief Engineer."

They touched glasses and sipped.

"Tell me, is this going to mean a lot more hours at work for you?" she asked.

He wrinkled his brow. "It's stress time, for sure. In this economy, we've had to let people go. The euphemism is 'rightsizing.' That means we have to put out fires—troubleshoot problems—and try to get new business, all with fewer people. But," he smiled, "it's a challenge. This is a chance to take over, make a difference."

As they waited for their first course to come, she heard snatches of a conversation at the table beside them. She caught the word "windsurfing" and "trying to come about." Then the man's voice rose. "I hate situations where I don't feel in control!" he exclaimed.

She glanced at Peter. He hadn't heard. But she knew he too hated situations where he had no control. *It's good that this job came right now,* she thought, *something where he does have some power. Because having Joy missing without a clue—he has no control there. How hard that must be for him. It would be good if he'd talk about it. Maybe that can happen tonight. Maybe we can both really communicate.*

When their entrées arrived, Peter eyed the baby carrots. "Good thing Tim's not here."

"I know. He loves raw carrots, hates them cooked." She smiled. "Bet he's having fun with your mom."

After the rack of lamb, Andrea moaned, "I'm stuffed." But

when the waiter brought the dessert cart, she gave in, as she knew Peter would.

The coffee service that followed was a separate ceremony, with individual pots brewed at their table, and a silver tray of condiments.

"Cinnamon sticks, shaved dark chocolate, sugar sprinkles, orange peel," she recited.

"And whipped cream," Peter grinned.

She leaned back. "I hate to admit it. You know I didn't want to come. But this weekend is a special gift. Especially to have some time alone with you. It's hard to talk when we're trying to keep Tim's spirits up."

"I know." He dropped a spoonful of whipped cream on his coffee and sprinkled chocolate on top.

She took a deep breath. "I want to tell you what I've been feeling, and I want to hear what you're feeling." Suddenly, the words spilled out in a rush.

"I think I've been through every emotion in the book since Joy disappeared," she began. "The first twenty-four hours weren't real. Joy wasn't truly gone. She'd be back anytime. Then, as days went by, I got so angry! How dare Joy disappear? Why hadn't she paid attention to what we taught her? And then I was mad at Esther. If only she hadn't left Joy. If only she'd been more responsible."

She picked up a paper doily from the coffee condiment tray and began pulling tiny pieces from the edge. "Then I got absolutely furious with myself. Why had I let Esther take care of her in the first place? If I'd only been there instead of Esther. If I'd been a good mother. If I wasn't working. If I hadn't worked so hard. And then that I had to move to Malibu, that I ever thought it would be so good for the kids. What did it bring? Disaster!" She looked across the table at Peter's stoic face, then continued working at the doily in vicious little pulling motions.

She couldn't stop and didn't even try to organize her thoughts, letting them come as they would. "I get so furious sometimes," she continued, "I pound the wall when you're gone. Once I opened the cupboard and looked at all the dishes and started hauling them out so I could smash them against the wall. The only thing that stopped me was that I'd have to clean it all up, and I'd have to go get new dishes." She shook her head. "And I'm sorry, but I have to admit this—I'm mad at Tim too. Why didn't he watch her just for those few minutes? And I'm mad at the kids at school who're giving him a hard time about Joy being gone."

She stacked the torn bits of doily in a little pile. "I'm sorry, but I'm mad at you for being so in control and not even crying. And I hate my mother and her lack of feelings, and it goes way, way back, to all the times she told me to keep a stiff upper lip, not to have an unhappy face, and for goodness' sake, whatever, don't cry! She even told me how to feel. 'Be happy!' It makes me want to gag. What a bunch of _____!" She deliberately used a graphic word she knew her mother wouldn't like.

The doily grew smaller and smaller. "I'm mad at the searchers, the authorities. Why didn't they bring Joy home that very first night? I want them to do more. I want people to care more, to understand how I feel, that I'm shriveling up, dying inside, that my head hurts all the time. But I hate it when they say, 'I know how you feel,' because they don't know at all. I hate people who won't even ask me what's happening, talk all around the subject. I hate the woman who came with her Bible and told me how God works everything together for good. Well, whose good, I'd like to know!"

She dropped the remains of the doily, a one-inch circle, and wiped her eyes on the corner of her napkin. "And I have to tell you, I'm furious with God. He's always been so good to us. Always gave us everything we really, really wanted. Oh, not absolutely everything, but you know, the things that mattered. Each other, our jobs, our house, our kids. What's He doing now? Why has He turned on us? How did we fall out of His favor? I can't figure it out. It makes me crazy. Maddening. All I want is my daughter back and He—won't—do—it. Now I've quit my job and—"

She looked up at him. He hadn't said a word. No reaction whatsoever. His impassive face stopped her short of telling him about her bargain with God. She closed her eyes and felt tears on her cheeks, dimly aware that the waiter had approached the table, then retreated. After a while, she wiped her eyes and took a sip of her coffee, which tasted cold and bitter. She shoved it aside. She felt drained, but at the same time, there was a sense of relief to have said it all. Well, almost all.

She looked across at Peter and saw him bracing himself against the seat, shoulders hunched, as though to ward off a blow. "Sorry I ran on so. I know you're hurting too," she said softly. "Now, your turn. How're you feeling?"

He didn't answer. His head ached from her verbal outpouring, his helplessness to do anything to make her feel better. Now she was asking for something he couldn't do.

She knocked on the table. "Hel-lo? Anyone home? I was asking how you feel, Peter."

"I think the chances of finding Joy are still good." He heard the matter-of-factness in his voice. "And I also think God is about the only sure thing we have right now."

"No, no!" she cried. "I didn't ask you what you think. I asked you how you *feel*. Didn't you hear a word I said?"

Peter could sense his panic mount, the tightness in the chest begin. *I can't go through that again,* he thought desperately. *I can't let myself be held under by that huge, crashing wave of grief like I was the other day driving to work. If I talk about it, it'll all come back again.* He shut his eyes and swallowed hard. Slowly, another realization seeped into his awareness. He was angry too. He knew that. But he hadn't realized till this moment that he was angry with Andrea—angry that she hadn't been there with Joy, that she'd put her blasted career ahead of her child. If only she'd stayed home like his mother had. If a woman truly loved someone, wouldn't she personally care for that someone? So what if she hadn't worked? Then they wouldn't have lived in Malibu, and maybe this wouldn't have happened.

But *I can't say these things to Andrea,* he realized. After all, I've gone along with her goals and dreams. To tell her now would devastate her.

He saw her watching him. "Well?" she said. It was almost a command.

"Andry, I can't."

"Yes, you can," she urged. Her voice gentled. "Don't be afraid to talk about feelings, Peter. It's good for you."

"Good for you," he said. "Not good for me."

"Nonsense! Good for everybody. Come on, Peter, if you love me, please don't shut me out. Share with me. It'll make it easier."

No, no! His mind raised a barrier against the wave. *It won't make it easier. It will destroy me.* He shook his head. "I can't."

He watched her flop back against the chair cushion, her face a study in disappointment. No, more than disappointment. Disgust, repugnance. His heart raced. *Now I'm really losing her,* he thought. He felt impotent to do anything, to make anything better, to change anything.

Out of the corner of his eye he saw the waiter and, welcoming the distraction, signaled for the check. He charged it to the room and, after a protracted silence, asked her, "Ready?"

She sat motionless.

He tried again. "Want to take a walk?"

"If you wish." Her voice was cold and formal as she stood and strode before him, out of the dining room.

They strolled around the perimeter of the hotel without saying a word. He could hear the thunder of the breakers on the beach, strains of a jazz trio, and laughter from the bar. Finally, she said, "I think I'll go take a long soak in the tub. At least I won't have to clean it."

Back in the room, Andrea stripped out of her dress and saw she'd spilled lamb sauce on the front. Who cared? She put on the thick terry robe the hotel had provided and went into the bathroom, slamming the door behind her. Tearing open the packet of bubble bath, she ran the water in the tub as hot as she could bear. It was only when she settled into the cool suds, feeling the heat of the water beneath, that she began to cry. She didn't care if Peter heard her. She didn't care about anything. She cried for Joy, yes. But she also cried for herself. *Alone. I'm totally alone,* she mourned. *Peter isn't here with me at all. He can't be. But I need him. I feel so—what's the right word? Forsaken. That's it. Totally forsaken. Isolated. Forsaken."* She cried until the water began to cool. Then with her foot she turned the spigot on until the water in the tub was hot again. And she cried again in terrible, gulping, suffocating spasms. It occurred to her that there might be less pain if she let herself slip all the way down beneath the bubbles.

At last, exhausted, she rose from the tub, dried, used the lotion by the tub. Slipping on the lacy nightgown she'd brought for what she anticipated as a special time together, she crawled into the king-sized bed. Propped on the other side,

Peter watched TV. Keeping to the far edge of the bed, she put a pillow over her head.

He snapped the light off. "Want me to turn off the TV?"

"No."

"I'd just like to see the end of this," he said.

Drained, she fell into a deep sleep, dimly aware only of the clanging of the bell buoy in the channel beneath their window.

⌘

She awoke before dawn, disoriented by the unfamiliar surroundings. Her eyes burned. Then she remembered the night before. Putting on the robe, she stole across the room to the sliding-glass door and pulled the draperies to one side. In the gray light, the channel water gleamed, mirror-smooth. A lone fishing boat, a weathered red contrast to the silver of the water, hummed its way out the channel, the V of its wake pursuing it. *One boat, all alone, venturing into the turbulence of the ocean*, she thought. *Like me. All alone.* She glanced up at the lights on the hillside in the distance. God, she prayed, are You there? I know You promised in the Bible never to leave me or forsake me. But I don't feel You with me at all. Please, I need You!

Peter turned over in bed as she stepped back into the room, his face creased from folds in the pillowcase, cheeks slightly flushed, like a small boy sleeping.

If only, she thought. *If only . . .*

Counseling! The word popped into her mind, startling in its suddenness. If Peter had such difficulty expressing his emotions, maybe a counselor would help. Dr. Hadley already seemed to have helped Tim in his first appointment yesterday. "Post traumatic stress syndrome," he'd called it. Maybe—she felt a small glimmer of hope. Maybe she'd bring it up at brunch.

☞

Later that morning, Peter and Andrea selected from a sumptuous buffet and returned to their table by the window of the dining room. Andrea looked out and watched a father and daughter launching a kite on the beach. Silver, magenta, and cobalt mylar glimmered in the sun.

As the proud bird rose higher and higher in the brisk breeze, Andrea was surprised to feel her heart lift with her new hope. Perhaps the weekend could still be salvaged.

She gave Peter a quick look and reached over to brush her hand against his. "Peter, sometimes relationships fall apart in a crisis. Let's don't let that happen to us."

He looked up from his plate and set his fork down.

"Honey," she continued, "we're having trouble communicating. And that's understandable, considering all we're going through. But what I'm thinking is, we've agreed counseling's important for Tim. Maybe we need to—"

Watching him carefully, for a moment she thought she saw terror in his eyes. But his face seemed impassive.

She finished the sentence, "—see about maybe talking to someone. Not necessarily a therapist. Maybe a minister."

He shook his head and looked down again at his plate. "Andry, try to understand. I've got just about all I can handle right now. Please don't add anything more."

Tears stung her eyes, and she turned away, looking out the window just in time to see the breeze slacken and the kite plummet to the ground.

13

ZOË LISTENED as the door from the garage to the Malibu house unlatched.

"We're home," came Andrea's voice. A flat-toned statement of fact. No lilt, no joy in her voice.

"Uh-oh," Zoë muttered to herself, as Tim stood from the board game they were playing.

"Hey, Dad! Mom!" he yelled. "You back already?"

Peter appeared at the door of the playroom. "Clearly we were desperately missed."

Tim hurried toward him and Peter hugged him.

"Me and Gram had a great time."

"Gram and I? Good."

Andrea came up behind them. "I need a hug too." As Tim turned to embrace her, Zoë thought she detected new lines of pain in Andrea's face.

Andrea released Tim and moved to the opposite side of the room, away from Peter, looking toward Zoë. "You weather the challenge of your grandson OK, Mom?"

Zoë looked from Peter to Andrea. The alienation was palpable, but she simply said, "Nothing to weather!" She winked at Tim. "We just got into trouble together. That's all."

Tim nodded. "We hiked in the hills." He gave Zoë a sly grin. "And we found these mega footprints. I thought they were Big Foot's—" He began laughing, unable for a moment to continue. Then, between bursts of laughter, he managed, "Till Gram put her foot in the print, and it was the same length!"

Zoë nodded, laughing. "But Tim, be fair, that print was a lot wider."

Tim shook his head. "So I call her Gram Big Foot now. But," he added, "she does make this way-cool white chocolate fudge. We did it together."

"And ate it together, I'll bet," Andrea suggested.

"Don't worry, Mom. We saved you some."

"Glad of that!" Peter said. "Sounds like you two had a good time."

"Yeah. Did you guys?" Tim asked.

Peter nodded. "Great hotel, right on the beach. Terrific food."

When Andrea said nothing, Zoë said, "Good." Grateful that she had something to cheer them, she looked toward Tim. "Show them this morning's paper, Tim."

"Oh, yeah!" Tim exclaimed. He hurried into the living room and returned with a section of the newspaper. Andrea and Peter bent over to look.

"Oh, Tim, your picture!" Andrea exclaimed. "Full color. The yellow ribbon. And even Juliet."

"Hey!" Peter added. "You two look great!"

"Yeah, I'm stoked they used the one with Julie," Tim said.

"I told you, Tim. You're a natural," Andrea gave her son a tender nod. She looked at Zoë, but not at Peter. "This is great coverage, isn't it, Mom? Maybe someone will see it and call with information!"

"That's just what I prayed this morning," Zoë said.

Andrea glanced at her watch. "Mom, don't make yourself late to your open house on that lake property listing."

"I can take a hint!" Zoë feigned a pout. "But you're right. I'd better go. I have all my things together." She turned to give Tim a hug. "Thanks for being my buddy, Tim. I love you yesterday and today and always."

"Love you too, Gram. Thanks for being here. Uh," he hesitated. "You wanna take some fudge?"

Zoë laughed. "Are you kidding? That stuff's terrible for you." She waved. "Enjoy!"

Peter and Andrea walked her to the door, each with an arm around her.

"Any important calls, Mom?" Peter asked.

"Just your dad, Peter, wanting an update."

Peter nodded. "Good. Thanks for coming, Mom."

"Appreciate you, Mom." Andrea looked toward her, and Zoë sensed a silent question, an unexpressed need.

She squeezed Andrea's hand. "Be back on Thursday," she whispered. "We'll talk."

After Zoë left, Peter disappeared into the bedroom and Tim headed outdoors. *Alone again*, Andrea mourned. *Guess I've got to stop expecting empathy and understanding. At least the press coverage is an upper. I needed that. Now, what other story possibilities can I figure?*

The ring of the phone interrupted her thoughts. As she picked it up in the kitchen, she could hear Peter answer in the bedroom. An oily, foreboding voice began, "Mr. Lang. It's no use, you know. Your daughter is dead, sacrificed—" Andrea slammed the phone down and screamed.

A moment later, Peter joined her. "Honey," he began.

She covered her ears. "What is the matter with people?" she shrieked. She looked up at Peter. "I know! Don't think about it! Don't feel it!"

"What's the matter, Mom?" Tim hurried into their room.

"Nothing," she said automatically, then changed her mind. "No, something. Some depraved person telling us Joy's dead."

"Yeah. That's what some guys at school say." Tim's mouth drew into a tight line.

"Oh, Tim!" she exclaimed, bending down to hug him for a long moment. "That is so cruel!"

"Yeah. Dr. Hadley says they just want to get my goat. So I'm gonna try not to react."

"Smart," Peter said.

The phone rang, and Andrea bit her lip. "If it's that sicko again . . . "

Peter picked up the phone. "Yes? Ah, Detective Jansen. Yes, we're back." He gripped the phone tighter as he listened. "A little girl in Seattle?"

Andrea caught her breath and leaned toward the phone, trying to hear. She saw Tim's eyes widen.

"You can patch us through to her? Sure, we want to talk to her. We'll hold." He turned to Andrea. "It's a long shot, he says. The child says her name's Suzie."

Andrea sighed. "I can't imagine Joy would—" Then she remembered. "But you know, Peter, she does have a book she likes about a little girl named Suzie. Maybe she's nervous, scared, confused. Oh, honey!" She clasped Peter's arm. "I think we'll know, don't you? Joy's always been good on the phone.

She'd recognize our voices. But if there's any doubt, we'll go right on up to Seattle. We could even be there tonight. Oh, Peter! Just think!" She turned toward the hall. "I'll go get on the other phone."

Hurrying to the bedroom, she picked up the phone, hearing only Peter's breathing. *He's anxious too*, she thought. She paced back and forth until at last she heard a husky voice. "Mr. and Mrs. Lang? Sergeant Decker, Seattle PD. I'll put the little girl on now."

Silence. Then, "Say 'hello,'" prompted Decker.

"Hew-wo," came a tiny voice.

"Hello!" Andrea exclaimed. "Is your name Joy?"

"Yeth," the child said.

Andrea caught her breath. "How old are you?"

No answer.

Wanting with all her being to hear the right answer, Andrea asked, "Are you three and a half years old?"

"Yeth."

"Or are you five? Peter interjected."

"Yeth."

"Honey, is your name really Suzie?" she asked.

"Yeth."

"And," Peter continued, "are you as big as the policeman with you?"

"Yeth."

Andrea sank to the edge of the bed. They continued questioning the child, but no matter what they asked, her answer repeated like a broken record. "Yeth." Nothing more. At last, Sergeant Decker came on the line once again. "Mr. and Mrs. Lang? What do you think?"

"It doesn't sound at all like our daughter," Peter said, his voice cautious. "But, ah, does she show any signs of trauma?

Drugs? She keeps giving the same answer, even to the most bizarre questions."

"We've tested. No drugs. And no signs of abuse."

Andrea's last hope drifted away, like a helium balloon floating out of view. "It's not Joy, then," she declared. "Oh, I wish with all my heart it was." She sighed. "But our daughter doesn't lisp. And she's quite bright."

"Right." Decker hesitated. "Uh, you got a fax?"

"Why, yes," Andrea said.

"Let me fax you her picture—just to be absolutely certain."

"Good," Peter said. He gave the officer their number, adding, "Thanks so much, Sergeant."

Slowly, Andrea replaced the phone, the tiniest whisper of hope remaining, somewhere deep down.

She went to her desk and waited for the ring, Peter moving beside her. "This is taking forever," she fretted.

"He probably had to go to a different room—maybe even a different floor," Peter said.

"I suppose."

They both jumped when the phone finally rang. The fax machine began to hum and very slowly the edge of the image appeared.

"It's upside down!" she exclaimed, trying to pivot her head to see. At last the entire image appeared, and Andrea shook her head. Even upside down, she knew.

"Wait, now!" Peter cautioned, tearing off the paper and turning the picture. "Oh," he sighed. "I see what you mean."

He turned and put his arm around her. She couldn't cry. Hope and despair, she thought. Hope and despair. Will this seesaw go on forever? She heard Tim come into the room.

"Bummer," he said.

"Bummer," she echoed.

꒛

That afternoon, Peter enlisted Tim's help in the yard, and Andrea tried to work at her desk. Unable to concentrate, she found herself writing letters, filing papers, never really getting into a project. At four Peter came in to shower.

"Good afternoon?" he asked.

"No!" She almost snapped the word, then looked up at him. "Sorry. Just not very productive."

He put a gentle hand on her shoulder. "You OK to go to church?"

"Church?" Tim's voice came from the hallway. "Do I have to?" Tim added.

"Yes," she said firmly. "I think we all need it."

꒛

As they walked toward the church, Andrea heard Connie's voice behind them. "Hi, Langs! I'm mighty glad you're here."

Connie and Jeff caught up with them. "Welcome," Jeff said, shaking their hands. "Hope you like this little service. It's plain-wrap. Mostly praise and just a short message and then time for prayer. More intimate than the morning services. Probably a good introduction for you."

The sanctuary was simple but serene, with pale peach walls interrupted only by clerestory windows. Behind the raised area before them stood a polished oak cross inlaid with copper.

The two families settled into a pew toward the front of the church, and eventually about a hundred people gathered, including many young children. Peter glanced at his program and the title, "With All Your Heart—A Series on Trust." *Sounds like something we could all use*, he thought.

Two young men mounted the steps to the raised area. One held a guitar and strummed a melody Peter didn't recognize. "Words are in your program," the guitar player noted and began singing, "Trust in the Lord with all your heart and lean not upon your own understanding. In all your ways acknowledge Him and He will direct your paths."

Peter recognized the quote from Proverbs and concentrated on learning the melody. When they repeated the song, he joined in tentatively, hearing the strength and conviction in his voice grow. He could hear Tim singing, but not Andrea, seated on Tim's other side.

They sang a half-dozen songs, several focusing on trust, others praising God. During the second verse of "Take My Life and Let It Be," he glanced to one side and saw Connie and Jeff, arms uplifted, faces radiant. *That's what I want*, he said to himself, *that kind of relationship with God.*

The second young man introduced himself as Kent Narver, an associate pastor. "We've been talking these past weeks about trust—what it means and how we get it, how it grows. We found that we can't just have blind trust. We need to know who, or should I say in whom, we trust. Our coins say 'In God We Trust,' but do most Americans do that?" He heard the chorus of no's and smiled. "So in what do we sometimes trust?"

"Money," a woman suggested.

"Definitely," Kent nodded. "And we're pretty surrounded by that ethic here in Malibu. What else?"

"Position, achievements," a man offered.

"Good. Another?" Kent asked.

"Ourselves," two voices called out at the same time.

"Ah, yes!" Kent exclaimed. "We can do it. We're capable, cool, in control. Until—" He paused for effect. "Until we come to the end of ourselves, until things go out of control."

I can relate to that, Peter thought.

Kent spoke about God's trustworthiness, then focused on biblical examples of the trust of David. But when he pointed out Psalm 37, Peter read and reread the passage from verse 5 through 9. It seemed written especially for him. "Commit your way to the Lord, trust in Him and He will do this. He will make your righteousness shine like the dawn, the justice of your cause like the noonday sun. Be still before the Lord and wait patiently for Him; do not fret when men succeed in their ways, when they carry out their wicked schemes. Refrain from anger and turn from wrath; do not fret—it leads only to evil. For evil men will be cut off, but those who hope in the Lord will inherit the land."

Peter closed his eyes. "Lord, right now, I declare that I *will* trust in You. With all my heart," he prayed silently.

He heard Kent finishing his message. The young man paused and looked around at the congregation. "Let's pray now. This is the time to bring your concerns to the Body, so we can pray together."

There was a moment of silence before a woman prayed for her father, terminally ill with cancer, and a man confessed his despair over being out of a job. Another man gave thanks that his son had entered a drug rehab center and another for his new granddaughter. Then Peter heard Connie's voice.

"Lord, I want to lift up our friends, the Langs, to You. It's been more than two weeks since their little daughter, Joy, disappeared. Oh, Lord, comfort her parents and her brother. Give them a solid trust in You. Give them faith and help them see that faith is the substance of things hoped for, the evidence of things not seen."

Jeff picked up the thread of his wife's prayer. "Lord, help the authorities. You know exactly where Joy is. Reveal it to them. Father, we ask You to return her unharmed, in perfect condition, in Your perfect timing."

Then a child's voice began, "Father, wherever Joy is, don't let her be scared. Be her daddy while she's gone. Hold her tight."

"And God," another small voice added, "I see kids at school being mean to her brother. Help them stop it."

Andrea wept quietly as the prayers unfolded and felt Connie, beside her, take her hand. *I'm glad we came*, she thought. *Here, I don't feel so alone, so forsaken. There's so much pain out there, besides ours. And people care. And oh, I could hug that precious child who prayed for Tim.*

She listened quietly as Kent brought the service to a close. "Now, may the God of hope fill you with joy and peace as you trust in Him, so that you may overflow with hope by the power of the Holy Spirit."

Lord, Andrea spoke to Him in her heart, *I'm going to trust you to respond to my giving up my job and to bring Joy back.*

14

✍

From Zoe's Prayer Journal

January 24: Father, as I head for Malibu this morning, I give this day to You and ask You to use me. I thank you so much that Andrea and Peter went to church Sunday and felt Your presence. But something must have gone wrong with their weekend away. Andrea obviously wasn't happy when they came back. So if I can be helpful in that respect, or any other without being intrusive, please show me how. Above all, please, may there be more of You and less of me manifested. In Jesus' name, amen.

PASTA WITH CHICKEN, sun-dried tomatoes and spinach, salad, crusty bread. Zoë mentally reviewed the menu for the dinner she would prepare at Peter and Andrea's as she drove up the hill to their house. As she negotiated the last hairpin turn, she saw Tim start across the road.

"Hi, Gram!" He came to her car window and she lowered it.

"How's my buddy?" She reached out to grasp his hand.

Obviously in a hurry, he flashed a smile. "Fine. I'm on my way to Brant's."

"Oh, OK." She motioned him on. "See you!"

"See ya!"

She watched him, all arms and legs, cross into the neighbor's yard, just as a woman in a bright turquoise pantsuit came out the gate. Her dark hair caught into a smooth chignon, she walked with the fluid movements of a ballerina. Dolores, no doubt.

Zoë's focus switched back to Tim. *I called this the golden age when my kids were growing up,* she remembered. *Old enough that you can let them out of your sight without worrying, but young enough that they're still eager to come back to you.*

She waited as Dolores approached the road, evidently heading for her mailbox. Might as well know the neighbors, Zoë decided. Lowering the right window of the car, Zoë leaned toward her. "You must be Dolores. I'm the grandmother, Peter's mother."

"Ah!" Dolores exclaimed, her dark eyes brightening as she leaned down to look in the car. "Would you like to adopt my family too? Tim tells me you're terrific."

Zoë laughed. "Tim must inherit some of Andrea's PR gifts. I just wanted to thank you for being so cordial to him. This has been a tough time for him."

Dolores nodded. "I'm happy he enjoys coming over."

Zoë moved back behind the wheel. "Come see us."

Dolores waved and Zoë shifted gears, turning into the driveway and parking by the front door. She sat for a moment, watching Dolores head back into her house. *Why am I frowning?* she asked herself. *She was congenial and polite. Why do I have this reaction of—it isn't dislike. Nothing that strong. More like a sense of caution. Reminds me of a feeling I had about a client with ulterior motives.* She shrugged. *Maybe my blood sugar's just low.*

Zoë got out of the car, grabbed the groceries from the back-seat, and marched up the walk. She rang the doorbell, and in a moment Andrea opened the door, a pad of paper in her hand. "Hi. Just making some notes," she explained. "I'm ready for a cup of coffee. How about you?"

"Perfect," Zoë said, hanging her coat in the closet.

While the coffee brewed, Zoë said, "I just met Dolores."

"Isn't she a stunner?"

"Definitely. Quite a contrast to Connie—plain-wrap, heart of gold. With Connie, what you see is what you get. But the joy of the Lord really shines in her face! I look forward to seeing her, praying with her when I come to the Joy Center. And," Zoë raised a triumphant finger, "while I was there today, I got another five hundred toward the reward from the think tank down the road."

"Mom!" Andrea gave her a quick hug. "You're sensational."

When the coffee was ready, they took it into the living room.

"I didn't get to hear much about your weekend," Zoë said as they settled on the sofa.

Andrea raised one eyebrow ever so slightly.

"Didn't live up to your expectations?" Zoë asked carefully.

"Oh, the hotel was charming. Gorgeous room with a channel view. Fantastic food. But it was hard not to think about Joy." She twisted her wedding ring on her finger. "I thought Peter and I'd have a chance to talk. I mean, really talk about how we're feeling about this nightmare. I didn't hold back, I talked and talked. I realize he's maybe trying to protect me, and that he's not as verbal as I am. But, Mom, Peter just closed up—silent as a mime, but minus the facial expressions."

Zoë could picture her son's stolid face. "Peter's never been very good at talking about feelings." She smiled. "But oppo-

EVIDENCE OF THINGS UNSEEN

sites do attract. We tend to fall in love with opposite strengths. Later, we see opposite weaknesses. Being different isn't necessarily wrong."

Andrea sighed. "Guess I'm majoring on the weaknesses." She thought a moment. "But Peter talked about feelings when we first met."

Zoë nodded. "Haven't you read how the goal-oriented male pours on the personality to win the female? No doubt that's what Peter did with you. Then with that objective achieved, he moves on to a new goal, and the woman wonders what's happened."

"Yes, but we *have* a new goal. Finding Joy. Why can't he tell me how he feels about what's going on?"

Zoë pursed her lips. "I'm afraid that's not Peter's nature. My experience is that when things are tough, he clams up. I remember when his dad left us—"

Andrea leaned forward. "That must have been so hard." She hesitated. "Did the kids know it was about another woman?"

Zoë nodded. "Yes. And you know, the other kids vented their anger or cried or something. Peter just went to his room. He never talked about it. If I asked questions, I got the briefest imaginable 'I think' sort of responses."

"Sounds familiar." Andrea sighed. "You're saying this is how he is. I guess I'm saying I need more right now."

"I understand what you want from him, dear heart," Zoë said softly. "And I would too. But Peter's lack of response doesn't mean he doesn't care. I'm encouraged that he—all of you—are going to church again. Maybe by getting in touch with God, he'll get in touch with himself. I've been praying all along that somehow, through this experience, he'll learn to express his heart better."

Andrea shook her head. "Lovely idea. But I know I can be honest with you, Mom. I can't imagine him ever reaching that point." She sighed. "I guess I need to stop expecting anything of him, and just get on with the business of finding Joy."

"Expectations," Zoë mused. "I used to have such big expectations of my husband. Then I found out Benjamin couldn't, in fact, no human being could meet my every need. Only God can."

"I think," Andrea said, "you're right about Peter. And instead of focusing on him and what he does or doesn't do, I need to really concentrate on my Joy campaign."

Zoë sighed inwardly. Hadn't Andrea heard what she said about placing her expectations in God?

"Yes," Andrea said, more to herself than Zoë. "That's what I need to do."

༦

In the weeks that followed, Andrea pursued her Joy campaign with a fervor that transcended even the high energy she'd previously poured into her job. Through the remainder of January and all of February, her obsession seemed to escalate rather than diminish. Peter watched with growing concern.

On a bright March morning, with sunlight flooding in the kitchen window, he looked across the breakfast table at her. The sun accentuated the dark shadows under her eyes, the prominence of her cheekbones.

She's going to burn out, he thought for the hundredth time.

At first, he'd been pleased that her mind was occupied, that she found satisfaction taking an active part in the effort to find Joy. *But now, it's consuming her*, he thought.

"What time did you come to bed last night?" he asked. "I didn't hear you."

She stifled a yawn. "I didn't notice."

"Quite a bit after midnight, wasn't it?"

"I guess," she said, a so-what tone in her voice. "And the night before.

And the night before that." When he saw her mouth tighten, he reached across the table for her hand. "I'm worried about you, honey."

"Peter," she said, as though speaking to a small child, "I'm trying to get our daughter back."

"I know," he said quietly. "And you're doing a fantastic job. I just wish you'd ease up a little."

She shook her head vigorously. "I can't. Don't you see, Peter? Time's so important. The longer it takes, the harder it'll be to trace Joy." She stared at him as though he were stupid. "Can't you understand? This is the most pressing deadline I've ever tried to meet. I'm running a race. A race against death!"

The word seemed to hang in the air. It was the first time she'd verbalized that horrendous possibility. Of course he'd wondered if, after almost three months, Joy was still alive. But to hear his wife say it . . . He felt his gut tense, and he studied his toast. When he glanced up for a moment, he saw the almost feverish brightness of Andrea's eyes, and he sighed inwardly. It was unbearable to think of losing his daughter forever. But if Andrea kept driving herself, he could lose her too.

"Hey," he said, "look at all you've accomplished. You've put out thousands of flyers with Joy's picture, bumper stickers, ads, bus-stop signs, banners. You've even managed to plant a news story every couple of weeks."

She said nothing.

He knew she was trying hard, in the midst of her campaign, to be the "good wife and mother," to confine her efforts to the time he and Tim were away or sleeping. But even when they were together, he sensed her distraction, her mental focus light-years away.

He tried again. "Your work's brought in a number of leads."

She shrugged. "Sure. Leads that got our hopes up, then fizzled."

She was right, and it seemed to him that every episode took a greater toll on her, with higher, almost unreasonable highs and ever-deepening lows.

"That's why I can't give up," she said, clasping her hands together. "That would be deserting Joy."

"But honey, you talk about this 'race against death' as though you're the only one who can win it. There are others working—"

"Sure," she interrupted. "And I don't see a lot happening." She banged her coffee mug on the table. "The sheriff doesn't come up with anything tangible. And by the way," she pointed at him. "What are you doing? I thought you were going to find out wonderful things with the computer at work. I sure haven't heard anything wonderful."

"Yess," he drew out the consonant. "I am working with the computer whenever I can—at lunch, after work." He measured out his words for emphasis. "But I can't do it full time, because I need to earn enough to keep on living in your dream house."

Eyes smoldering, she blurted, "Oh, I'm the one who wanted it, huh? May I remind you that you were pretty hot on buying this house too? I didn't exactly cram it down your throat." She paused. "Now, would you mind answering my question? Is it too much for you to tell me what's happening with the computer programs?" Her voice was condescending, as though she was addressing someone of limited intelligence.

It was hard not to react to her tone, but he mentally took a breath and lowered his voice. "What's happening?" He stalled a moment for control. "Well, Hank Willis—remember, I told you, he's our computer wizard—he couldn't be more determined to find Joy if she were his own kid. 'Modern technology is the key, Peter,' he keeps telling me. And he's spent a lot of time finding databases, working out programs, checking on-line sources."

"And?"

"Nothing substantial, really." He couldn't lay more false hope on her. She was already running on overload. He'd wait till he had something substantial.

"Maybe—" She stopped as Tim came into the kitchen.

"Wow! I could hear you guys all the way down the hall to my bedroom," he exclaimed. "What are you so mad about?"

They glanced at each other, united for the first time that morning in their concern for their son. "Guess we're both edgy about Joy and all."

"Yes," Andrea added, "and sometimes you take it out on people you love."

Tim nodded wisely. "That's what Dr. Hadley said."

"And," Peter added, "frankly I'm bothered that your mom's wearing herself out with the Joy campaign."

"I'm fine," Andrea insisted. "I don't work every second, you know. I'm out running every day, like you suggested."

"Yeah, Mom, twenty-two times around the driveway makes a mile." Tim drew circles with his finger.

She gave a quick smile. "You guys were great to measure it for me, so I can run right here and keep my portable phone handy."

Right, Peter thought. *Mustn't miss a single call.*

"And hey!" Her face came alive. "I have a new idea I was working on last night. I know it'll fly!"

It's no use, Peter thought. *She can't let go.*

❦

Later that morning, after Peter dropped Tim off at school and turned onto Malibu Canyon Road, Andrea's words, "a race against death," replayed in his mind. He thought back to his father-in-law's exclamation when Joy was born. "A girl, Peter! Just you wait. A father's love for his son is a given, but for a daughter—well, it's a very special, particular thing!"

And he was right. There was something about "Daddy's little girl." He lifted one hand from the steering wheel to wipe a tear. *I want her back so much,* he thought. *I love her so much, I'd give my life for her. But it's so hard to talk about. How can I tell Andrea about the constant battle I have against the thoughts that keep surfacing, hard as I try to hold them under? It's like trying to sink a plastic bottle in the water. It keeps popping up again.*

He could feel them coming again, those thoughts of all the unspeakable things that could have happened to Joy. Just the other day, Willis's computer search had revealed a newsletter for pedophiles and a list of organizations, one with a Malibu mailing address. Even now, the idea of his daughter help-less, subjected to the perversion of some degenerate—or degenerates—roused such a primal rage that, in the privacy of his car, he cried out loud. As he entered a short dark tunnel, he shouted, "No!" slamming his fist on the dashboard, trying to force the idea down again.

When he emerged into the bright light, he willed himself not to dwell on dark thoughts. Work, that was the only answer. He had to zero in on the day's work. One project was definitely in trouble, with the customer's reporting intermittent failures in the testing of one of the valves. He'd managed to avoid out-of-town trips since Joy's disappearance, but he might have to go to Texas if they couldn't iron out the problems in a day or so. He half-hoped he'd need to go, just to get away for a while.

He thought back to Andrea getting ready for her day,

another day of preoccupation with Joy, Joy, and more Joy. At least at the plant, he could become completely absorbed in something that didn't relate to Joy in any way. He'd always loved the challenge of creating new designs, the satisfaction of seeing the finished hardware go out the door. At work he could see something happening, something productive.

Guiding the car around the last curve before the road straightened and headed toward the freeway, he wondered how much more time the sheriff's department would give to the case. They'd been so thorough, spent thousands and thousands of man-hours looking for Joy, following up on hundreds of leads. And they were cooperative about feeding data to him. But when would they decide they'd done enough, that there were other people, other cases to spend their time on? Would he and Andrea eventually give up hope too? And if so, when? Next month? A year from now? Ever? No, he thought, there would always be some glimmer of hope. But still, practically speaking, at some point in time they'd have to get on with life. Would Andrea ever be able to let go and go on? Would she ever come back to him and Tim?

15

SITTING AT HER DESK in the bedroom, Andrea smiled with satisfaction over the layout of her newest project, the Joy Lang Keep-Safe Packet. A moment later she phoned the director of promotion and advertising at California Consolidated Savings. "Gwen. Andrea Lang. I have an idea for you. You have a moment?"

Quickly, she described the packet detailing the insert space for a child's picture, fingerprints, and concise medical information, including blood type. Blanks to fill in with physical description and noting right- or left-handedness and distinguishing marks, such as moles, freckles, or birthmarks.

"Gwen, the big thrust is prevention, being prepared for an emergency. You could invite people to come in to have their kids' pictures taken in your branch offices."

Her enthusiasm escalated as she heard Gwen's positive reaction, and Andrea promised to bring in the layout and copy that afternoon.

She started to make another call, but remembered she'd promised Connie she'd come into the Joy Center that morning. Half an hour later, as she swung her minivan out of the driveway, she saw Dolores heading out from the house across the road carrying a stack of letters. Andrea pulled up beside Dolores's mailbox at the edge of the paving and opened the car window. Her neighbor looked impeccable, her hair held back with a silver headband, her electric-blue jumpsuit without a wrinkle. How can a woman look so put-together at home, mid-morning? Andrea wondered.

"Want me to mail those, Dolores?" she asked. "I'm going right by the post office."

"Would you? I'd love to get these out right away."

"Of course." Andrea reached for the letters. The words "blessed be," printed in blue, danced across each envelope flap. She stared at them. Dolores's spirituality remained an enigma to her. "Unusual stationery," she murmured.

"Oh, yes. These are to members of my women's group." Dolores smiled and bent down to look in the window at Andrea. "How is it with you?"

"Oh, pretty good. Nothing new."

Dolores shook her head. "I'm so sorry. It's about time we get together. Come over soon. I want us to get better acquainted."

"Thanks, I'd like that. You and Brant have already been wonderful friends to Tim. I appreciate that."

Dolores dismissed her thanks with a toss of her head. "He's a delightful boy." She straightened. "Thanks for taking my mail."

Andrea smiled and slipped the car in gear, easing down the winding road. Already, the hills, nourished by the winter rains, had turned a brilliant green. Spring. It had been winter when Joy disappeared. Such a long time . . .

She stopped by the mail drop on the Coast Highway, then hurried on to the church. Maybe someone with a solid clue would call today.

Turning into the church parking lot, she reflected on the support she'd received here since they began attending the Sunday services. People had been so generous with their prayers and expressions of concern.

A secretary waved as she entered a side door and made her way through the office to the Joy Center, a cubicle so tiny, there was room only for two people. A poster with Joy's picture smiled down from the wall.

As Connie saw her in the doorway, her round face broke into a broad grin. "Hey-hey!" she exclaimed. "I'm glad to see you!" She rose from a battered wooden desk to give Andrea a quick hug.

Feeling Connie's plump warmth, she remembered Peter's assessment of their neighbor: "a hugger and a grabber."

Connie gestured to a chair. "Sit. I've just been playing back the messages from the answering machine. Nothing but some kids acting loony. Sometimes I think these Malibu kids have too much time on their hands." She shrugged. "But what do I know? I grew up in a little Midwest town. I mean, it was so small, we gave our telephone numbers in four digits. All had the same prefix. Jeff and I could never afford to live in Malibu if his folks hadn't paid off the house and left it to us."

Andrea nodded. "I know what you mean. There are some spoiled kids and grownups here." She leaned on the desk. "There isn't much coming in anymore, is there?"

"To be honest, not this week, at least. But," Connie added quickly, "I'm sure all your hard work's gonna pay off. And

Peter's mom getting the reward up to ten thousand dollars will attract more interest too. It only takes one call, you know." She took a close look at Andrea. "You OK? You look—"

"Burned out? That's what Peter said. But Connie, I can't stop. I have to do everything—*everything* I can possibly think of. To stop would be so disloyal to Joy." She looked at Connie carefully, inviting her reaction. "I'm even thinking about hiring a private detective, but I don't have the funding."

"Aren't you OK with what the sheriff's department's doing?"

She nodded quickly. "Oh, yes. But you wonder if they could have missed something." The rugged planes of Eric Jansen's face played across her mind. "As far as moral support, Eric—"

"Eric?"

"Detective Jansen," she explained. "He's been fabulous. Always on the case. And he's certainly more understanding of how this is for me than—" she hesitated, "some of my family."

Connie studied her face a moment. "You talking about Peter?" She nodded before Andrea could reply. "It's a guy thing," Connie continued. "Most of them need to be macho. They have an awful time letting it all hang out. God put them here, they figure, to protect the family, to be the rock. They mainly want to get the job done. Most guys just aren't heart-to-heart sharers, like women." She smiled. "Sometimes I think that's why God gave us women friends. We can kinda spill our guts to each other, and we understand. But shoot, I learned all this the hard way after Greg died. Jeff seemed to be able to sort of pack his grief into a jar and put a lid on it and tuck it all away somewhere. He'd get into bed and be asleep before I had the covers pulled up. And I'd lay there with my eyes glued to the ceiling. I thought he wasn't feeling anything. He was, but he couldn't talk about it."

"That's what Peter's mother says. That he's never been good at talking about things that are tough." She sighed. "But sometimes I think Peter just looks at me and my pain like it's another personnel problem."

Connie reached across the desk and squeezed her hand. "I know."

She thought back to Connie's statement the first night they met: "I know what it is to lose a child. Only mine's not coming back. Greg died in a hit-and-run a year ago."

"Connie," she began, "tell me something. How did you survive after Greg died, especially if you didn't feel Jeff was with you? I mean, the shock, the pain! To kiss your son good-bye in the morning, and then to find the highway patrol at your door that afternoon."

The brightness faded from Connie's hazel eyes and she swallowed. "It was almost unbearable. I felt like there was a rhino on my chest, like I'd swallowed a shag rug. I'd find myself doing dumb stuff like looking for the detergent in the refrigerator." She smiled briefly, then frowned. "We never found the yellow-livered scum who did it, you know, and I had a terrible time letting go of that." She thought a moment. "I kept planning meals for three, thinking that Greg would be there with us. It seemed to take forever before I realized, really knew he just plain wasn't going to be with us again." Her eyes teared. "And then, it was just so *final*. To know he'd never come home, never hug me, never ask what's for dinner. Every time I read a newspaper story about a hit-and-run, it was like Greg's being killed all over again. When I'd look at his picture, it was like an electric shock went clear through me."

Connie paused and rubbed the back of her neck. "To survive someone you love so much, someone you thought would be around long after you're gone, it's not the right order—it's not the way things oughta be. Know what I mean? How do you bury your child? You never expect it. I thought for a while I'd go nuts. And it seemed for the first six months, the more time that passed, the worse the pain got."

"I know. I don't find that it gets better either."

"I bet you're finding like I did that people can be so weird. They'd talk about my 'getting over it.' Bull!" Connie tossed her head. "You don't get over it. What you do is you get through it." She looked across at Andrea and her tone lightened. "But hey, you still have hope. I didn't."

"True. But not knowing is the most hellish limbo. Joy's never out of my mind—she's the last thing I think about as I go to sleep, and the first thing that pops into my mind in the morning."

Connie looked thoughtful. "I guess, in a strange way, I was blessed. At least it was a done deal. Over. For you it can't be over till—"

"Not till we find her." Andrea could not, would not consider any other outcome to this nightmare. Joy had to be alive, somewhere.

They sat in silence for a moment. Then Connie continued, "It took me awhile to understand that we don't own our kids. They're lent to us. Some of us just get to keep them longer than others." Her brown-lashed eyes shimmered, but her voice was firm. "And God really does comfort those who mourn. I don't know what I would've done without Him."

"Sometimes I envy you and your great faith."

Connie smiled warmly, shaking her head. "No, not great faith. A great God. The only way I can survive is knowing God's in control, knowing His character."

"But," Andrea hesitated, "didn't you ever ask why?"

Connie frowned. "Seems to me the question's not why, but

how you're gonna relate to God in the midst of it all." She gave Andrea a gentle smile. "It seems to me you never needed Him more to be your comfort and hope." She thought a moment. "Would you be interested in learning some more about Him? It's in knowing Him that faith comes."

Connie's face, splattered with freckles, wasn't really pretty, but there was a glow that somehow made her seem almost beautiful. "The joy of the Lord," Zoë called it.

"I might," Andrea replied tentatively.

"Come to our women's Bible study here. It's all about just who God is. A chance to really understand His character. We meet on Wednesday mornings. Ten to twelve."

Andrea dismissed the idea immediately. Take more than two hours away from her campaign? Impossible! "Thanks, Connie. But I couldn't concentrate. There's still so much I need to do."

"I understand. But that's a standing invitation."

Connie hesitated. "In the meantime," she said gently, "you could think about getting into the Word by yourself." She smiled. "It couldn't hurt! For me, when I do it first thing in the morning, it gives me something to focus on, hang on to for the rest of the day."

"I'll think about that," Andrea promised. "I certainly appreciate what I'm learning here at church on Sundays. Remember two weeks ago, the sermon on praying and believing you'll receive what you prayed for?"

"Of course. In Matthew 12."

"Well, I decided to really, truly try that when I pray for Joy's return." She looked down at her hands. "It probably sounds silly—I haven't even told Peter. I don't think he'd understand. But I've set a sort of target date, I guess you'd call it."

Connie frowned ever so slightly. "God's timetable isn't always the same as ours. Sometimes He says, 'Not yet.'"

"Sometimes, when He doesn't seem to answer, He may want us to learn something."

"I suppose," Andrea murmured, slightly rankled at Connie's response. "But maybe He thinks I've waited long enough. Isn't that possible? What I said to Him was just, 'Lord, if You're there—if You really do hear prayers, then I pray right now, believing that You will bring Joy back to us by her birthday.'" Andrea smiled, "There's time. It's next month—April 17."

There. She'd said it. And verbalizing it for the first time to someone else sent a rush of exhilaration and expectation through Andrea. She felt her face flush. Reaching across the desk, she grabbed Connie's hand. "Oh, Connie! Wouldn't it be just like God to bring Joy back on the same day He first gave her to me?"

16

From Zoë's Prayer Journal

March 20: Father, I wish I could look over Your shoulder just one minute, and see all this as You see it, the whole scroll unrolled. Ah. You're saying, "Not yet." The point is not knowing but trusting. I confess I waken sometimes with such fears for Joy. Please, help me with those "vain imaginations." I want to "think on the things that are true and noble and pure and lovely and good." I will trust You! And dear Lord, please use this crisis to make Peter and Andrea stronger in their marriage and stronger in You. I love You, Lord. In Jesus' name, amen.

TOWARD THE END OF MARCH, Andrea wakened with her hopes building, her expectations focused. *God keeps His promises,* she assured herself. *Today I'll shop for Joy's birthday. Oh, what a festive day it will be.*

Midmorning her enthusiasm spiraled as she entered a Santa Monica mall party shop, with its festive, colorful wares. Prowling the aisles, she grabbed a rainbow of balloons, streamers, party poppers, birthday plates, and napkins.

Now, a dress. She hadn't dared look in a children's clothing store these past three months. But today she hurried down the mall to her favorite shop. Inside, she fingered the fabrics of dresses with intricate smocking, wide sashes, and eyelet collars. She changed her mind a dozen times before settling on a dainty print, blue the very color of Joy's eyes. The perfect birthday dress!

Only as she turned to leave the shop did she wonder, *Am I getting carried away? Is something a little out of balance here?* She shoved the store's door open, pushing the idea away at the same time.

Reentering the mall, she pondered what present Joy would love best. The very idea of a toy store—even a different one, far from that fateful shop in Malibu—filled her with trepidation. Then she remembered the drugstore with the menagerie of stuffed animals. She half-ran toward it, filled with an energy she hadn't felt in months. Racing down the aisle to the back of the store, she congratulated herself on this inspiration. What wonderful toys! Paddington Bear in his red rubber boots. A sad-faced walrus with wide, spreading whiskers and soft tusks. Then she spied the tiger-striped cat with the quizzical golden eyes and luxuriant fur. "Oh! He's wonderful!" she exclaimed to no one in particular.

"Yes," said a clerk arranging merchandise in the corner, "but you must hug him."

"What?"

"Hug him," she repeated.

Andrea embraced the animal, which immediately rumbled with deep purrs. "I *have* to have this, whatever it costs," she exclaimed, turning over the price tag. It was so expensive! Never mind. How often did they celebrate a fourth birthday—*and* the return of a lost child?

She didn't tell Peter that night about her purchases. He'd think she'd gone off the deep end. He wouldn't understand how important it was to be ready.

⁊

A week later, still two weeks before Joy's birthday, she considered the birthday cake. Better make it and have it waiting in the freezer. Last year Joy had wanted chocolate. But during this year she'd discovered angel food. Why not a daffodil cake, a marbled version of both yellow and white angel food? So pretty, so springlike. She baked it one morning after Peter and Tim left. All through the afternoon, she labored, frosting it and adorning it with yellow butter-cream rosebuds, as she'd learned when she handled the Pacific Foods account.

Just as Andrea put the finishing touches on the cake, the phone rang.

"It's Mom," came Zoë's cheery voice. "You in the middle of some marvelous new creative thought?"

Andrea laughed. "Well, more accurately, I'm in the middle of a marvelous creation. It's Joy's birthday cake."

"Oh?" Zoë said, her tone guarded.

"Mom, I just know God's going to bring her back for her birthday!" Andrea exclaimed. "It's part of the agreement we made—He and I."

"Oh, sweetheart," Zoë said slowly, "I know how much you long for Joy's return. We all do. But you know, God doesn't generally give us a road map or a timetable. What He wants is for us to trust Him, day by day, no matter what."

"Well, I'm trusting Him," Andrea insisted.

"Dear heart," Zoë said, her voice soft, "you're telling Him what you want, then trusting Him to do it."

"So?" Andrea heard the edge of impatience in her own voice. She wanted to hang up, get on with the cake.

"It's just that it may not be His will to bring Joy back just yet."

"But Mom, I have this strong feeling . . . "

Zoë gave a soft sigh. "I understand. But I've found my feelings maybe 50 percent reliable. They depend on the weather, what I had for lunch, who smiled or frowned at me, time of the month, so many things." She paused. "But God and His word are reliable."

Andrea looked at the ceiling and said nothing.

Zoë's voice brightened. "But I hope with all my heart you're right." She hesitated. "Well, I'll let you get back to the cake. See you Thursday."

"Great. Love you, Mom. Bye."

As Andrea replaced the phone, she stood thinking about what Zoë had said. Then she shrugged. "She doesn't have enough faith," she said aloud.

She turned back to the cake. OK, so it wasn't the perfection required for a color cover shot. Still, it was darned pretty. Carefully, she slipped it in a plastic container and slid it to the back of the freezer.

⁓

That week, remembering Connie's suggestion about time in the Word, Andrea began getting up thirty minutes earlier. If God was going to bless her with Joy's return, surely this was the least she could do. The caned rocker by the fireplace, she decided, would be her "prayer chair." Early in their marriage, before the kids, she'd enjoyed these quiet moments, then had given them up as life grew busier. In fact, she hadn't opened her old Bible outside of church in years. Now she began reading a different psalm each day. Afterward, she tried to meditate on the words. At first, it was hard to keep her mind from wandering to the upcoming day and to thoughts of Joy. But gradually she began to look forward to these quiet times.

On Friday, she looked up to see Peter, sleepy-eyed, in the doorway.

He blinked at his wife, rocking in her fuzzy turquoise robe, her leather-bound Bible open on her lap. With the wall lamp backlighting her hair in a golden glow, she looked beautiful once again. He felt an immediate surge of hope and gratitude. Maybe she was going to be OK. Maybe they'd be together in their faith again, as they'd been in the beginning, when they committed their lives together, at the premarital conference in Wisconsin. But even as he rejoiced, he wondered if this would last. Still, he told himself, surely this was a tangible, positive sign.

"Sorry, honey," he apologized. I heard you get up and wondered if you were—"

"OK?" She finished the sentence, nodding. "Yes."

"I," he hesitated, not wanting to say the wrong thing, neither too much, nor too little. "I like your choice of reading material." He started toward her, longing to embrace her, but she looked back down at the Bible. He watched for a moment, then moved quietly back to the bedroom. If she could believe that God was in control, perhaps she wouldn't have to run so hard and so fast in her "race against death."

But in the days that followed, she didn't let up a bit. Each day he could sense her pressing herself harder.

One evening she announced, "Now I've got to alert the press to Joy's birthday. It's only a week away."

He'd thought about the upcoming date and dreaded it.

Reluctantly, he agreed. "Yeah, I guess that's a good peg for a story."

"Well," she said for the hundredth time, "we have to keep her name out before people. Whatever it takes."

But she didn't tell him that deep in her heart, she believed that instead of a little paragraph tucked in the paper's second section, a front-page story would break.

She could see the radiant pictures and the headline, "Joy Lang Safely Home."

Privately, she began her own countdown, her faith flagging only on the eve of the birthday. Still, there could be a phone call during the night, couldn't there?

~

It was the silence that wakened her the next morning. Night after night in her dreams she'd heard Joy's frightened wail and rushed to her daughter's room to find nothing. Now, she listened. An owl hooted somewhere behind the house. Peter exhaled gently. She lifted her head and in the pale dawn watched the fog wrapping around the house. *Like a shroud*, she thought. Quietly she eased out of bed, her sense of dread building as the silence seemed to intensify. Though she didn't want to look, she knew she needed to. Clad only in her nightgown, she walked to the door of Joy's bedroom, took a deep breath, and willed herself to look into the room.

Joy wasn't there. The now-familiar emptiness engulfed Andrea. The neatness. Not a toy out of place. The yellow-and-blue patchwork bedspread with the stuffed koala bear reposing on top, wavered through gathering tears. The burning tension in her chest spread to her throat.

She felt rather than heard Peter behind her. He draped a

robe over her shoulders and, as he pulled her gently back against him, whispered, "Honey, don't."

Whirling to face him, fists clenched against her chest, she mocked him. "'Don't'? Peter, it's Joy's birthday. I was so sure she'd be back today. She's been gone almost four months. What am I supposed to do?" She paused but didn't wait for an answer. "Pretend Joy never existed? Like you?" Letting her hands drop to her side, she saw the hurt in his unshaven face and felt a stab of remorse.

"I'm sorry," she whispered, reaching out for him, grateful for the comforting warmth of his embrace, hoping to draw strength from his solid body. She stroked the prickly roughness of his dark-stubbled chin, then pulled away and turned to reach down for the koala.

Twisting its fur, she remembered Joy's ecstatic exclamation, "Mr. Bear!" when she found him Christmas morning. She stared out the window at the fog. "I was just so sure we'd have her back. That we could have a party, a birthday party today. I wonder *how* can God let me suffer so."

Peter's voice was husky. "I know. It's hard. So hard." He patted her arm, a question in his eye. "You need me to stay? Will you be OK?"

For a minute she considered crying out, *No! I won't be OK. Don't abandon me!* Instead, she nodded. "I know. You need to get going." In her heart, she knew even if he stayed home, his silent presence wouldn't help.

She moved slowly toward their bedroom, forcing herself to put on jeans and a bright blue sweatshirt.

In the kitchen she stared a moment at the "Missing!" poster, attached with four golden butterflies on magnets to the refrigerator. She touched each picture of her daughter in a gentle caress before she opened the refrigerator, stared dully inside and reached for the eggs.

"No eggs, Mom," came Tim's voice behind her. "Just toast," he insisted.

She'd thought his appetite had improved recently. Maybe he was thinking of Joy's birthday too. "Honey," she protested, "if you only eat toast, pretty soon they'll start collecting for a CARE package for you."

"Honest. That's enough." He pushed his brown hair back, and it immediately fell back again over his forehead.

A determined meow from the hallway made him laugh. "Juliet's talking. She's giving orders. 'Now,'" she says. He went to the cupboard, measured out the dry cat food into a dish, and held it at waist level. Juliet rose on her hind feet. "Is she one smart cat or what?"

He set the dish in the laundry room as Peter came to the table and broke two biscuits of shredded wheat into a bowl. They ate so silently, she could hear the faint click of Peter's jaw as he chewed.

Afterward, she walked outside as her men climbed into Peter's car. Ah, the fog was beginning to burn off. That helped a little. Now their house and Dolores's basked in a private spot in the sun, while everything below lay eclipsed by fog, thick and white as snowbanks.

"Bye, guys," she called as Peter backed the Oldsmobile out of the driveway. She forced a smile. "Take it easy in the fog."

Standing a few minutes longer in the driveway, she watched the silvery-blue car round the curve. It was hard for Tim always to be driven. But he was all she had now.

The sound of the phone brought her running inside, heart pounding. Each time it rang, hope rose again.

"Yes?"

"Andrea, it's Connie," came the soft voice. "I won't keep you. I'm on my way to the Joy Center to see if there's anything new. I know this is a hard day. I'm praying for you."

"Thanks, Connie. I appreciate that. I may come around later."

"Don't feel you have to."

"I know. Thanks."

As she replaced the phone, she glanced at the kitchen clock: 7:30. Would Eric Jansen be in yet at the sheriff's office? On a Wednesday, yes. She grasped at a wild hope. Perhaps something had happened overnight. Maybe he was checking it out. Maybe Joy could still be back today!

Hastily she dialed the familiar number, heard a laconic voice answer, "Sheriff's station. Watson."

"Detective Jansen, please."

In a moment, "Jansen."

His deep voice never failed to soothe her. She hesitated. "Eric—" She'd thought of him on a first-name basis for some time now, but when it slipped out, she felt embarrassed. "Detective Jansen, it's Andrea Lang."

"I liked it better the first way," he said. "Hello, Andrea." The way he said her name, drawing out the first syllable, sounded so intimate, it caught her off guard.

"What can I do for you?" he asked.

"I just wondered," she felt as flustered as a schoolgirl and suddenly foolish to bother him. "Wondered if there was anything new about my daughter."

"We're still checking out those leads I told you about Monday. It'll take a few more days before we know if we're on to anything."

She blinked back the tears, not trusting herself to speak.

"Andrea?" he asked. "You still there?"

"Yes," she managed. "Sorry. It's just that it's Joy's birthday."

"Oh." She could hear his concern. "A tough day for you. I'm going to spend most of today on this, okay?"

"Thanks, Eric, I appreciate that."

So there it was, she thought as she said good-bye. *Joy wouldn't be back today. Would she ever come home, ever sit down to meals with them, ever want to play "owl" again?*

She stood in the quiet kitchen, feeling a strange counterpoint of emotion. First there was the heaviness of sorrow. But beneath it, an anxiety simmered. Ah, she realized, it was the question of how to fill the interminably long day ahead of her.

The media wouldn't be around till later. With so much work completed on the Joy campaign, there wasn't a lot more to do without additional funding. And going into the center, sure, there might be another lead—and another dead end. But staying home opened time for thinking. Even as she stood there, the now-familiar progression of ideas began, like the pop-up pictures in one of Joy's books, springing into being with the turn of each page. The image she'd held close all these weeks, of Joy in her birthday dress, puffing out those round little cheeks to blow out the candles on her birthday cake, collapsed. In its place, she saw Joy being sold to a couple who wanted a child of their own desperately enough to do anything. She could even envision the man and woman in their late thirties, smug and self-satisfied.

But before she could fully rage against these images, a new picture burst into her mind: Joy in captivity, Joy held down by a greasy-haired, leering sadist. She squeezed her eyes shut to break the terrible picture. But quickly her mind slipped in the impression of Joy, her hair dyed black and cut spiky—no longer her bright, golden child. Then she saw Joy before a camera, naked, exploited in child pornography.

She blinked the image away, but quickly her mind took a new path. Maybe Joy wasn't even alive. She felt bile rising in her throat. Which was worse—imagining Joy in torment or thinking of her dead? Her daughter could have been battered, then thrown somewhere, her little body decomposing.

She could feel the break in the rhythm of her own heart-beat. Premature ventricular contractions, the dispassionate doctor had called them. Stress, he'd explained, to which she sarcastically replied, "No fooling!"

She shook her head. *Stop focusing on those pictures*, she told herself firmly. *Do something*.

But what? Something that wouldn't take heavy concentration. Maybe bake some cookies. Oatmeal cookies. She opened a cupboard and, reaching for the oatmeal, frowned at the carton's telltale lightness. Well, then, chocolate chip cookies. No, she'd eaten the last of the chips in frustration one afternoon last week. She banged the cupboard door shut and thought suddenly of the birthday cake in the freezer. Maybe she should deep-six it in the toilet. But no, she'd wait, just in case.

Now what? She sighed. The master bathroom could use a cleaning. She gathered the cleaning supplies, moved slowly to the bathroom and began scrubbing the tub. She leaned on the sponge, putting her whole body into the effort. But, with only one end of the tub done, she slammed the sponge down and stood, backhanding the tears away. "Forget it!" she cried out loud. "Who cares?"

She moved out of the bathroom into the bedroom and stood looking at the peach-and-yellow room with its puffy quilted bedcovering, the matching valance over the sliding door. Did she have so much that God decided to take something away? Wouldn't keep His part of the bargain? But she'd given up her job. "I've prayed, I've believed," she said aloud. "Why haven't You brought her back?"

17

MIDMORNING, after she'd abandoned her cleaning and tried unsuccessfully to focus on a new story angle, Andrea wandered, frustrated, into the kitchen. Maybe a cup of coffee would help. She glanced across the road at the white stucco house with its contemporary interplay of curves and planes. *Dolores*, she thought. *Maybe that's what I need. Someone whose lifestyle is exciting—and who's not involved in this whole thing.* She checked her directory and punched the numbers on the phone.

"Goood morning," came Dolores's throaty Tallullah Bankhead voice.

"Dolores, it's Andrea. Feel like a cup of coffee?"

"Not only do I, darling, I've just made a fresh pot. Why don't you come over?"

Andrea hesitated. "You sure? I didn't mean to invite myself."

"Nonsense! I'd love company."

"Well, fine. All right. Thanks. Be there in a minute."

Replacing the phone, she reached for her keys, started out, then headed back to the bedroom to pull a comb through her hair. She stared in the mirror. "Looking a mite peaked, girl," she said to her reflection. Indeed, her skin, once described by a makeup artist as "peaches and cream," looked pale and blotchy. Her whole face seemed less rounded, more angular, and her hair had lost its golden highlights. No wonder Peter was concerned. Her clothes were looser too. She poked at the puffiness that diminished the impact of her blue eyes and realized that even they seemed faded. She sighed and brushed a little peach blush on each cheek, then looked again, doubting it was an improvement.

Sliding open the door from the kitchen eating area, she stepped out on the ocean side of the house. Fog still obscured the view, isolating her house and Dolores's from the world below. For a moment, she wished she could simply walk away on the puffy whiteness.

She picked her way down the wood stairs set into her iceplant-covered bank and started across the road. "Hi!" she called as she saw Dolores standing tall at the gate to her house. Put-together as always, Dolores's embroidered Mexican blouse accented her dark, dramatic beauty.

"Come in," Dolores invited. "I'm so glad you called. I hesitate to bother you, knowing how busy you are." She motioned Andrea through the gate, smiling down at her. "It's been much too long."

She followed Dolores across the patio into the family room and heard dreamy melodies of bells and flutes. As Dolores snapped off her stereo, Andrea puzzled what to make of her. Dolores's brooding darkness could be a bit unnerving. Yet there was an engaging, outspoken liveliness that appealed to Andrea.

"Aren't you glad the Santa Ana winds are over?" Dolores chattered. "It was so dry for a while, I'd wake up in the morning and my eyelids would go 'click.'"

Andrea laughed. "I know what you mean."

Dolores gestured toward a glass-topped table surrounded by rattan chairs, cushioned in brilliant crimson, purple, and blue. "Sit down, and I'll get the coffee. It's unleaded, with cinnamon. You'll love it."

"This is so attractive." Andrea looked around the room.

"My late husband was good to me." Dolores poured the coffee into cobalt-blue mugs and joined her at the table. "Now tell me. What's happening? Anything new?"

"Not really. Days go by, and there's nothing. Then there's a rash of calls from people who say they may have seen her. I think there've been more than six hundred leads the sheriff's followed through on. Some have looked so promising, but—" She shook her head.

"You poor love. That has to be excruciating!"

Andrea leaned toward the table and gazed into her coffee mug. At last she took a sip. "This is good."

"My secret blend. When I—" Dolores broke off as the phone rang. She reached over her shoulder to the counter behind her and picked up the phone. "Good morning! Oh, yes I can, Kit." She put her hand over the phone. "Andrea, this will just take a minute. Why don't you take a look at the rest of the house?"

Carrying her coffee cup, Andrea strolled into the living room. Over the fireplace hung a painting of a moonlit scene in a flower-laden glen. Dreamy figures dressed in white evoked a sense of—of what? she pondered. Ancient pagan worship, perhaps. To her left, the huge glass cube of a cocktail table caught her eye. Staring, fascinated, she moved closer to examine the rocks and branch inside the glass. Just as she leaned down, she saw something move. Stifling a cry, she watched as very slowly, a pale green snake slithered along the branch.

"Yuck!" she muttered and retreated quickly for the family room, just as she heard Dolores say good-bye.

"Dolores, that snake, . . ." she began.

"Oh!" Dolores smiled her reassurance. "You saw Simon. That's one of Brant's collection, and I thought it would be an evocative conversation piece. I guess junior high is a big time for boys and snakes. Hasn't your Tim told you? He's quite fascinated whenever he's over here."

"Uh-oh! Does that mean I'm going to become a mother of snakes too?" She grimaced.

"Oh, they're really rather nice when you get used to them. Remember, they're infused with the Life Force. You can live in harmony with them." She smiled. "Besides, they're quiet and don't ruin the furniture. And they only eat disgusting things you don't want around anyway. This one came from the pet store, but the kids find them in the hills, too, you know."

"Just so Tim doesn't press me into duty as a snake-hunter, now that I'm not working."

Dolores nodded. "You'd just quit the last time we talked at any length. Has it been a hard adjustment?"

Andrea ran her fingers up and down her cup. "I loved the excitement, the creativity, the bright people, the thrill of making a name, a product, a service known. But I know the Joy campaign is what I'm supposed to be doing."

Dolores nodded. "And look at all you've accomplished. I've seen the posters, the banners on Coast Highway. And you've had a lot of news coverage."

"That's the idea. Whatever it takes! Keep her name and her face out there."

"How marvelous." Dolores gave an encouraging smile. "I hope your husband appreciates all that you're doing."

"Yes, well . . ." She stopped, but Dolores looked so sympathetic, so genuinely interested, she plunged ahead. "Actually, he's handling all this a lot differently than I am." Remembering Connie's comment, she added, "But I guess maybe it's a male/female difference. Still," she added, "sometimes I think he doesn't really care."

Dolores peered at her over her coffee cup then set it down. "Are you saying you don't feel his concern and his support?" She seemed to read the answer in Andrea's face. "Why, that's terrible for you! I can't imagine having to go through this all alone!"

Andrea bit her lip.

"Do you have anyone else you can talk to? Your mother?" Dolores asked.

Andrea laughed bitterly. "My mother? Not exactly. The abominable ice woman. 'Be brave. Don't let anyone see you cry.' That sort of thing. But Peter's mother is a love."

"Hmmm. Zoë, right? I met her. Imagine her coming out from Orange County every week! That's lovely." Dolores got up to pour some fresh coffee. "What about friends?" she asked.

"Connie Hendrix, down the hill, has been the most help. You know her?"

Dolores gave a deep, rich, throaty laugh. "Little Miss Holiness? The one who comes to a neighborhood party where people are bringing carpaccio and blackened ahi, and she shows up with a tuna casserole made with canned soup, for God's sake?" She laughed again, adding with disdain, "With potato chips on top."

Andrea felt herself bristle. "Come on now, Dolores. Connie set up the Joy Information Center. She spends hours there every day. She may be homespun, but she's given me practical help, and she cares a lot."

"Forgive me." Dolores looked genuinely contrite. "You'll have to get used to me, I'm afraid. I call it as I see it, and maybe sometimes I go a bit far." Her voice turned to velvet. "I'm truly grateful Connie's being helpful." She paused. "But honestly, I wish that husband of yours would get a heart." She winked. "Sometimes I think marriage is the root of all evil."

"I hope not!" Andrea gave a quick laugh. "I guess I shouldn't be too surprised. He tends to be quiet. Always has, according to his mother. But it gets to me. In fact, one night, several years ago," she smiled at the memory, "a night when he was totally incommunicado, I went out the back door, around to the front, and rang the doorbell. And when he came to the door, I said, 'Hi. Just checking to see if anyone's home.'"

Dolores clapped her hands. "Bully for you!" Hands still together, she nodded at Andrea. "The more I know you, the more I like you." She pursed her lips. "So you have a quiet husband, a simpatico mother-in-law, and a homespun friend. You must miss the more sophisticated people you've been working with. But surely they'll want you back, as soon as your daughter's found."

She shrugged, unable to think beyond today's wounds, and glanced at Dolores's alert, interested countenance. Something about this woman's own ability to tell it like it is made Andrea feel comfortable opening up to her. And, remembering Connie's reaction to Andrea's "deal" with God, she wondered how Dolores would respond. "Actually, my quitting was part of a bargain. Or maybe you'd call it an agreement."

"Oh?" Dolores raised her eyebrows, listening attentively.

"With your husband?"

"No." She looked at her coffee cup. "With God."

Dolores leaned forward, the darkness of her eyes deepening. "I see," she encouraged.

"You know I was at work when Joy disappeared. I thought I'd arranged excellent care for her. Obviously, it wasn't good enough. I've wondered a thousand times if I'd been there . . ." She shrugged helplessly. "I told God that I'd quit my job and take care of the kids if He'd bring Joy back." Her voice caught and she stopped a moment. "I thought He was telling me He'd bring her home by her birthday."

"Ahhh." It was more an exhaled breath than a word.

Inexplicably, Andrea felt compelled to tell more, to elucidate. "I went back to work when we first moved to California from Chicago because houses are more than twice as expensive here. I wanted to give the kids a good home. Then I fell in love with Malibu. We found this house, with that view all the way up to Point Dume one way, and around to Palos Verdes the other, the whole coastline all spread out, and the unspoiled mountain behind. And I thought I'd already died and gone to heaven." She took a sip of her coffee. "It was my job that helped us get this house. My campaigns won a couple of awards. I could see results, and I loved it. It was hard to just toss it all away, but I was willing to give it to God. Now, I wonder why He's punishing me? Why didn't He keep His part of our deal? Does He even *know* what's going on? Does He care?"

"Of course you wonder, Andrea. Who wouldn't?"

"I'm wondering a whole lot today. Because this is Joy's birthday, the day I prayed—*really believed*—God would bring her back." She exhaled in a soft moan. "In fact, I wonder if this whole belief system we call Christianity is bull." The words began to tumble out of her mouth as they had that night in the hotel restaurant with Peter. "What if we've just dreamed it up to make us feel more comfortable about ourselves and about dying? What if it's all just a fairy tale and we're a bunch of poor deluded fools, feeling smug and secure, when we've got it all wrong?"

Andrea stood and paced to the doorway, jaws clenched, hands clasped tightly behind her. "What if God isn't really good? Or what if God doesn't even exist?" She could feel Dolores watching her. "I prayed believing that God would bring her back for her birthday. So here we are on Joy's birthday. *So where is she?*"

For several seconds she stood with her back to the room. Then, turning, she strode back toward the table. "In faith I resigned that job." She could hear her voice rising to a shout, but she didn't care. "In faith that He would restore Joy to me. It was my sacrifice. And what has He done in response? *Nothing!* Not one thing!"

Agitation accelerating, she grabbed the edge of the table and leaned down on it, looking Dolores full in the face. "Do you know what I feel like?" she almost whispered. "I feel like doing what Job's wife told him to do—to curse God and die."

A faint smile played across Dolores's face. "You won't die," she said quietly.

Curse God—yes, that's what Andrea wanted. Curse Him, curse this teasing, cruel God who didn't keep His end of their bargain. Free herself from a God who did nothing.

"Yes?" Dolores murmured.

That single hushed word kindled something deep inside. Andrea stepped back, jabbed her fist high above her head, and closed her eyes. Then all of her fear, frustration, and anger funneled into a searing cry. "Are You there at all, God? Can You hear me? If You are—then—*the hell with You!*"

18

EYES STILL CLOSED and fist clenched, Andrea slowly lowered her arm to her side. She stood silent, listening, waiting. Waiting for what? She wasn't sure. To be struck down? To die, right there? That was what Mrs. Job expected, wasn't it, that if you cursed God, you'd die?

At last she sank into a chair, heart thudding painfully, gasping for breath. Was this how a heart attack began? Would she indeed die, right here in Dolores's family room? Gradually, the frightening beat subsided, but she felt cold and clammy. Her whole body seemed drained, depleted.

She felt her face go slack.

She wasn't sure how long she sat before she began to wonder at her outpouring before this woman she barely knew. It was as though she'd been caught in a rush of heavy freeway traffic, with no off-ramp for twenty miles. Once she began, there was no turning away. Embarrassed, she glanced across the table at Dolores. "I'm afraid I shocked you," the words rasped in her throat and she coughed. You must think I've really lost it."

Dolores studied her thoughtfully. "Not at all. I believe I understand what you're feeling. Think what you've been through! Of course you feel like your God is playing games, mocking you." She was quiet a moment. "But I do think . . ." She pursed her lips, hesitating.

"What?"

"No, I don't believe this is the time." Dolores's voice seemed to come from far away.

It was such an effort for Andrea to reply. "Really," she managed. "For what?"

"Just this. What kind of God would let you down like this? How do you know He's real? How do you hear from Him?"

Andrea groaned. "If you want to launch a deep theological discussion, Dolores, your timing is not the greatest."

"Forgive me," Dolores answered quickly.

She lifted one weary hand in protest. "No, maybe it's a valid question." She closed her eyes. Too much effort keeping them open. At last, she heard herself answer, "I've believed I hear from God—if that's what you'd call it, through prayer and the Bible. But," she sighed, "I'm not a scholar. I haven't even read it all the way through."

Dolores steepled her fingers, her long nails meeting in five apexes of scarlet. "Maybe there is more. Maybe you are limiting yourself. Is that possible?" Her eyes narrowed as she watched Andrea carefully.

She blinked as a mixture of caution and curiosity seeped through her. "Like what?"

"Oh, experiences." Dolores's eyes widened, as though challenging her.

Experiences? Meaning? she wondered. "Uh, I suppose that's possible," she mumbled. It was such an effort to talk, or even to think. She rested one hand wearily on the table. "I'm sorry, Dolores. My mind's turned to mush."

With a sweep of her hand, Dolores dismissed the subject. "Of course. Why don't you see if you can get some rest? I'm sure you're not sleeping well."

"No, I'm not. The nightmares never seem to stop." She stood, her legs trembling, and Dolores reached for her. "I'm all right," Andrea said quickly, mustering what she hoped was a look of assurance.

"Would you like me to walk you home?"

"No. Thanks. Thanks for not being shocked. For being here."

Dolores put her arm around Andrea's shoulders. "I am here. Whenever you need me."

"I appreciate that," she murmured as she willed her unsteady legs to carry her out the door.

꒰

At home, Andrea fingered the gaily wrapped birthday packages she'd stashed in the back of her closet. It was possible that Joy still might . . . possible, yes. Likely, no. She heard her own sigh tremble in the silent house.

She tried to think about what she'd just done at Dolores's house. Had she actually cursed God? Was she now completely separated from Him? At least He hadn't struck her dead on the spot. And Dolores seemed to understand the pressures that had precipitated her outpouring.

It seems odd, she thought, *that I don't feel anything. Maybe I'm in shock, like the time we had three aborted landings on an airplane.* When they'd begun the fourth descent, she remembered, she was too exhausted to care any longer.

Exhausted. That was all she felt right now. Pausing only to remove her shoes, she sprawled on the queen-sized bed. *I should take the spread off,* she thought. *Too much effort.*

A moment later she felt a gentle thud on the foot of the bed. Juliet. The kitten's purrs came in passionate throbs as she kneaded the bedcovering with her outsized paws. Then, with dainty, careful steps, she walked along Andrea's legs, up to her waist, turned around twice and settled on Andrea's chest.

She rubbed the side of the kitten's face and the volume of the purrs rose. "You've grown so fast since January," Andrea murmured. She felt tears sting her eyes. How much Joy must have grown and changed since January! Sighing, she settled Juliet into a more comfortable position, welcoming the warmth, feeling her own muscles begin to relax. Juliet eyed her briefly, then slowly closed her eyes. Sleep. Yes, that was the answer.

She dreamed of Joy. Joy wearing the blue-and-white dress purchased for her birthday. Joy admiring the frosting flowers on her cake. Joy, face aglow, blowing out the four candles and clapping her hands with delight. Joy smiling through a frosting mustache. Joy unwrapping the stuffed tiger cat and laughing when she hugged it and felt it purr.

She watched Joy leave the table and go out to her swing. As Andrea pushed her, Joy swung higher and higher. The chains on the swing grew longer and longer, till she almost touched a sky that glowed with peach and blue and gold. How beautiful it was! But then darkness covered the sun, enveloping Joy. Demons with glowing eyes and fearsome claws snarled and swirled out of the blackness. They called Andrea's name, reaching out for her, closing in around her till there was no escape. Crying out, trying to push them away, she wakened to find herself sitting upright, with a wide-eyed Juliet clinging to her shirt. She lay back to release the cat's claws, hooked painfully into her shoulder. Drenched with perspiration, as though a terrible fever had just broken, she struggled back to reality and glanced at the clock. Two already.

At last Andrea found the strength to strip off her clothes and stand in the shower, sighing with relief as the warm, welcome water coursed over her skin. She shampooed her hair and lavished liquid soap over her entire body. Opening her mouth, she let the needles of water pelt her tongue. Somehow, she needed cleansing everywhere. Finishing with water as hot as she could stand it, she toweled dry and styled her short blond hair with a few quick flips of her brush. She was almost dressed when the doorbell chimed. Zipping her cords as she hurried down the hall to the front entry, she saw Connie outside. As she unlatched the door, Andrea's cheeks flamed, knowing how distressed her friend would be if she knew of this morning's episode at Dolores's.

"Connie! Come in."

"I walked up," her neighbor explained breathlessly, her rounded face pink from climbing the hill, ringlets of auburn hair damp on her forehead. She thrust a basket into Andrea's hands.

Lifting the brown checkered napkin, Andrea said, "Muffins. How thoughtful!" She shook her head in wonderment. This tireless woman had already done so much.

"Well, you know, when in doubt, cook! They're apple-spice."

"Thanks so much." She realized she had to invite Connie in. "Come sit down a minute." Andrea led the way to the living room. Turning to face Connie as they sat together she murmured, "You get so much done every day and today I just—I might as well confess. I had coffee with Dolores in the morning, came home, and slept almost three hours."

"I did that too." She put her hand over Andrea's. "And I also know how hard birthdays can be. But Andrea, I just want to tell you, I believe wherever Joy is, God has angels all around her, protecting her. I honestly do."

Andrea felt the tears gather. "Do you? I hope so!"

"Yes, I do." Connie's eyes were earnest. Then she smiled. "Meantime, my diagnosis, Miz Lang, is that right now you're totally exhausted. You've been running like somebody was after you, gaining on you."

"Or getting away from me."

"Really. Think about it. You've put together a giant campaign singlehanded."

Andrea sighed. "If the right person would just see her picture and know where she is."

Connie squeezed Andrea's hand. "It only takes one. Each time I answer the phone at the center, I pray it's the right call."

"Anything today?" Andrea asked.

"Nada. But some donations came in. I was thinking we might do some more flyers and I could go to LAX and hand them out to people who're flying to other parts of the country."

"Connie!" Andrea chided. "That's a fantastic idea, but don't you think you've done enough? There wouldn't be a Center if it weren't for you. I can never even begin to repay you."

"That's true." Connie winked. "My services are priceless." Her voice softened. "But someday you'll pass it on; you'll help someone else."

"Me?" Andrea asked dubiously. "It's hard to see how." It was difficult to think of ever being able to do anything but wait for Joy's return. She glanced at Connie. "About being tired, you're probably right. I seem to have run out of steam. I can't think of anything else that's practical to do in the way of PR, but I don't like the idea of not having any reason to get up in the morning."

She waited for Connie to tell her how important it was to carry on for Peter, for Tim, but instead her friend's hazel eyes searched her face. "Andrea, now that you have the campaign going, maybe it's time to look outside of yourself. Remember I mentioned the Bible study—about knowing God? Getting into God's Word, especially with support from other women, you'd see how much He has that can help you. Couldn't you find time now?"

I can't, she wanted to scream. *I've cut myself off from God.* Instead she stalled. "I've been reading the Bible in the morning." She hoped that would satisfy Connie. "Great. But how about an in-depth study? I've told you about our Wednesday group. Great women. It'll help you understand God's character, find out who He really is."

Andrea felt her pulse quicken. *A God who's mocked me, failed me. Forget Him,* she thought. She glanced at Connie. *It really is bizarre,* she decided. *I've basically renounced God, yet I'm hearing about Him from two totally different women. Dolores, the sophisticate. Connie, the earth mother.*

"Funny," she murmured, looking back at Connie. "Dolores started to talk to me about God today too."

"Dolores?" Connie's brown eyebrows arched higher. "Well, that surprises me, I admit." She paused thoughtfully. "How well do you know her, Andrea?"

"Not well. But she's been kind, and Tim likes to play with Brant."

Connie took a breath, then seemed to think better of what she'd started to say.

"Is there a problem?" Andrea asked.

"Let's put it this way," Connie said cautiously. "I have a problem with some of her—philosophy. She's into stuff that to me is on the fringe, New Age, not reliable. She and some other women—" She cut her sentence short and picked up her purse. "Think about the Bible study."

Connie's persistence grated on her, like a pebble stuck in her shoe. But no, the problem wasn't really Connie; she obviously wanted only to help. But after what Andrea had done and said that morning, to turn around now and seek God in a Bible study seemed ludicrous, the epitome of hypocrisy.

"What is it, Andrea?" Connie's bright eyes seemed to look into her very soul. "What's holding you back? I love you. Don't you know that? And I see such torment in your eyes today. You think God's let you down?" She took Andrea's hand. "Oh, Andrea, He knows how you hurt. He hasn't forgotten you. He sees the big picture. He has a purpose in all this, and it's for good, not evil."

Andrea thought she'd dismissed God from her life, and good riddance. But some small crevice of her mind told her she was still connected in some inexplicable way. She wanted to shake free. Why couldn't this woman let her go? She looked into Connie's face, and the certainty of her faith, the genuineness of her love filled Andrea's own heart to overflowing. "God wouldn't want me there," she blurted, as tears flooded down her cheeks.

She felt herself gathered against Connie's full bosom. How good it was to be able to cry freely, as she never could with her own stiff-upper-lip mother—or even with Peter. She could feel Connie's own tears mingle with hers and felt the depth of her understanding. She wept till there were simply no more tears.

When she drew back, Connie fumbled in her purse and found one clean tissue. With a flourish, she tore it in two and handed one half to Andrea, who laughed in spite of herself before she mopped and blew. "This is ridiculous," Andrea sniffed.

"No, it isn't. It's good," Connie insisted. "It's good to cry, to be honest with your feelings."

"Yes," she admitted. "It's good."

"Tell me," Connie asked, "why in the world wouldn't God want you at the Bible study? Surely you don't feel you have to be 'worthy' to come."

"Well . . ."

"Of course you're not worthy!" Connie said. "Me neither! I mean, none of us is. That's what makes God's love for us such a miracle." She gazed at Andrea, thinking a moment. "I know you don't believe it, but God is holding you right now. Why are you resisting Him so?"

Andrea swallowed hard. If only Connie knew . . .

"Think about the study."

"Sure. I will," she said.

"Good!" Connie stood as a door slammed in the back of the house. "Sounds like Tim."

"Yes. Kevin Jackson's mother started picking up the boys on Wednesdays so I don't have to go every day."

"And I'm on my way." Connie hugged Andrea briefly, then smiled. "I've just got to give you a new commandment I heard: 'Hangeth thou in there!'"

"Mom? Got any cookies?" Tim called from the kitchen.

"I'll just let myself out," Connie whispered.

"Thanks, Connie. For everything!" She turned toward the kitchen, hoping her son wouldn't see the aftermath of her tears. "Hi," she said. "How're you doing, honey?"

Tim nodded but turned away from her, climbing on a chair to reach an upper cabinet.

"Sorry, no cookies. But how about an apple-spice muffin?" She held out Connie's basket. "You can zap it in the micro, if you like."

He grabbed a muffin, opened the microwave door, and looked back toward her, frowning. "Mom?"

"Mm hmm?"

"You might get a call. I socked a guy at school."

She kept her voice calm. "Oh? How come?"

"I know Dr. Hadley says to flow with the mean stuff. But this kid said if Joy was cut up into little pieces and thrown in the ocean, we'll never find her."

"Oh, Tim." She hurried to put her arms around him. "That is gross and unspeakably cruel!" His body, taut and tense, resisted hers and pulled away.

"I think there was a better way to handle it than socking him though. You know that, but frankly I don't blame you." She searched his face, seeing the pain. "I know you took a lot of flak right after Joy disappeared, but it's still going on?"

He shrugged. "Jay Carter keeps saying if it was me that got taken, nobody would care like they do about Joy."

Andrea exhaled sharply. "Ter-rific." She coated the word with sarcasm. The cruelty of kids constantly amazed her. "And how does that make you feel?" she asked.

"Well, I've wondered if—if you'd have felt as bad if it'd been me instead of Joy."

There. He'd said it. She'd known it must be on his mind, though he'd never verbalized it, and she'd tried in every way she could to show him how much she cared for him. "Oh, Tim! Don't you know I'd feel just as terrible if you were gone?"

"Yeah, but see, she's special. She's a gir-rull." He accented both syllables heavily. "And she's cute and she even looks like you, Mom."

She stooped so she could look her son in the eye. "Timothy! You are special! You're my firstborn. No one could ever, ever take your place. No one is more special!"

A tear slid from each of his eyes, and he fell into her arms, sobbing. She could feel the ribs, the backbone of his spare body.

She was amazed that somehow, from deep within her, her

own tears rose again. Stroking his hair, she whispered, "I love you so, Tim. I don't know what I'd do without you."

When his tears subsided, she pushed him gently away from her. "Boy, look at us. I've got a wet shirt front, and you have wet hair!"

"Yeah!" he wiped his nose with his forefinger.

She grabbed tissues from the counter, handed one to him, and dabbed at her own eyes and nose. "Now you heat the muffin and I'll get some milk."

He set the microwave timer. "Can I go over to Brant's?"

"After you do your homework."

She went to the refrigerator and took out the milk. Too bad they didn't put missing kids' pictures on milk cartons anymore. She poured for him, setting the glass on the table and sat down, waiting for him to join her with his muffin. To distract him from the day's events, she asked, "What do you do at Brant's these days?"

"Oh, just hang out."

"I saw Simon the snake today," she offered, grimacing.

"Oh, yeah! Isn't he cool?"

"I think I prefer Juliet as a pet. She took a nap with me today. She's warm and cuddly. But a snake!"

Tim sat down and took a bite of muffin. "Simon's really very friendly. And he doesn't bark and bother people, and he only has to be fed once a week."

She held up a hand. "Spare me the details of his diet."

"Aw, don't you wanna know?"

She shook her head. "But I would like to hear what else you and Brant do."

"Oh, we play some games, like I told you. Listen to some music."

She nodded. "What kind of music does Brant like?"

BEVERLY BUSH

"He's into rock, mostly."

"Oh? Like Pete and Mike?"

"Aw, Mom!" Tim wrinkled his nose. "They're so nerdy. He likes heavier stuff."

"Such as?"

"Oh, Devil's Triangle. Or The Adominations."

She groaned to herself. She'd heard their music, read all the articles about their influence on adolescents. "Heavy is right! More like punk or heavy metal, isn't it?"

He nodded enthusiastically.

She had to take a stand. "Tim, I don't think that's appropriate for you."

"Aw, Mom!" He gave her a what-do-you-know look.

"Listen, Tim." She tried to keep her voice quiet, reasonable. "I've worked with some of these groups." She thought back to some of the song titles—"Raising Hell" and "Love and Hope and Sex and Dreams"—and remembered their emphasis on violence, death, the wild, the weird, the illegal.

"Yeah?" Tim's dark eyes shone with defiance.

"They are destructive. Sometimes they have Satanic undertones."

"Satanic?"

"Yes, dealing with Satan, the devil. Even worshiping him."

"So?" His tone grew more belligerent.

"Tim, Satan's evil and dangerous. He's called 'the enemy' for good reason. It's God who's good."

Her words hung in the quiet room, and she dug her fingernails into her palms. *How glibly I said that*, she thought. *What a hypocrite!*

Tim's chair scraped on the floor as he stood, glaring down at her. "Well! I'd like to know what's so good about God. I don't exactly see Him bringing Joy back!"

172

Every muscle in Andrea's body seemed to tense. Her face burned. She stared up at her son. "He will," she said and heard the hollowness of her statement. How could she urge him to have faith after the scene she'd played this morning? She sagged in her chair, realizing how impotent she was to help her son. Hours seemed to pass, as though the two of them were caught in a single frame of a film.

At last she cleared her throat, but her voice sounded strained. "Honey, I want what's *best* for you. And that does not include listening to that trash."

"No!" he shouted, the color in his face deepening. "What you want is to spoil things with the only friend I've got!"

He rushed out of the kitchen, and in a moment she heard his bedroom door slam with wall-rattling force.

19

From Zoë's Prayer Journal

April 22: Heavenly Father, once again I bring my Malibu family before you. I see Peter trying so hard to be the rock, but I know that pain in his jaw is tension. Show him it's OK not to always act like Clint Eastwood! And Lord, you know Andrea feels You've let down her down. She doesn't yet understand who You are—and bless her, she's always, always in a hurry. Help her to trust You and not to be bitter. Then, my buddy, Tim. Is this relationship across the road good for him? Please, bring him a godly friend who's more his age. And, oh, loving Father, our Joy! It's been so long! My heart aches so! Wrap Your arms around her, keep her from all evil and bring her safely home—in Your time, in Jesus name I pray, amen.

THE SUN ROSE from behind the mountain, brilliant in a powder-blue sky, and Tim came to breakfast grinning. "Look at this perfect day. Not even a cloud. Just right to help Brant build his new snake cage."

"Oh?" she asked. "He needs a new one?"

"Well, yeah! His best rat snake escaped the other day."

She thought a moment. She'd taken a stand against Brant's music, not the boy himself. And being outdoors learning to build something sounded healthy. She recalled a year or so ago how Peter and Tim spent time together building a picnic table. But since Joy's disappearance, since Peter's new job, he'd had so little time for Tim. Face it, so little time for her.

She glanced at Tim's eager face. "Sounds like you better help him."

Tim nodded enthusiastically as Peter came in and slipped into his chair at the breakfast table.

"Grape Nuts?" she offered.

Peter touched his jaw. "Hard to chew."

"Is that a problem?" She looked at him with concern.

"No." He flashed a quick smile. "I just don't need that much exercise this early in the morning."

"Let 'em soak awhile," Tim suggested.

"Sure, make me late for work. And me with a project in trouble." Peter reached for the other cereal box. "I'll go for the flakes."

She studied his face as he poured the cereal into his bowl. How intense he looked these days. She wondered if it was the new responsibilities at work, or Joy, or both.

Beneath that calm exterior, Mr. Cool has to be hurting, she thought. *Truth is, I've been so busy with my own agenda, I haven't done much to try to lighten his load. In fact, I've been so preoccupied with the Joy campaign, I haven't even planned our meals the way I did when I worked. When Mom Lang's not here to cook, I mostly open a package and stick it in the microwave. Maybe what the poor guy needs is a real homemade meal.*

She smiled across the table at him. "I thought I'd take some time off today from the campaign and fix something special for dinner. Maybe even—" she paused for emphasis, "apple pie."

"Really?" His smile clinched it. She'd work in the kitchen today.

After Peter left to drop Tim off at school, she opened the freezer door and grasped the leg of lamb with both hands. She smiled in spite of herself, remembering the day she'd broken a window pane with a frozen lamb roast. A bride of six months, she'd lost her grip on the slippery, icy mass and grabbed in vain as it slid past the freezer onto the glass on Peter's workbench.

"You did what?" Peter had laughed, shaking his head incredulously when she showed him the damage.

Tonight when she served the lamb, he'd remember and chuckle again. A bit of laughter—how nice that would be. How little merriment there had been in the house lately! As she set the lamb carefully on the counter, she planned the rest of the menu: mint sauce, potatoes browned with the meat, salad, and homemade apple pie. She'd use candles on the table. Already she could visualize Peter's earnest grin, the warmth in his brown eyes.

But late that afternoon, just as the aroma of the lamb spread through the house, Peter called. "I'm sorry, hon. Got a problem, a sick valve. I'm going to have to sit up with it for a while. Don't hold dinner. I'll grab something from the machine here."

She bit her lip and tried to suppress the anger that began to bubble deep inside her. "I'm disappointed," she said. She heard the silence at the other end of the line and waited. When he didn't respond, she continued, "I spent most of the day preparing a very special dinner—especially for you."

"Oh," he murmured, "the pie. I forgot." His voice took on a tone of reasonableness that annoyed her. "Honest, I didn't plan this."

"Of course not," she said. Then she couldn't resist adding, "Or last Wednesday. Or the week before, or . . ."

"I know." He was quiet for a moment. "Look," his voice held a lilt of promise, "why don't we plan to do something this weekend, the three of us? Maybe go to Sea World, or the wild animal preserve."

A voice in the background called Peter's name. "Got to get back now," he said. "See you as soon as I can. Love you."

Leaning against the counter, she blinked back hot tears. Stop it, she chided herself. *It's only a leg of lamb. No, it isn't only a leg of lamb. It's another dinner without Peter. What? The fourth or fifth time this month. Seems I have a missing daughter and a missing husband. Doesn't his company understand? Doesn't he understand?*

She walked across the kitchen and stared at the apple pie she'd labored over, peeling all those tart Granny Smith apples, mixing the pastry from scratch. She wasn't sure if she should take it outside and smash it against a tree or sit down and dig into it with both hands and stuff it into her face. Better yet, plant her face in the pie like a contestant in a pie-eating competition.

She sighed. She wasn't even hungry.

As she brooded, a darker thought intruded: Did he really have to stay late again? Would the Alaska pipeline shut down tomorrow because of this faulty valve? Did a jillion-dollar contract stand in jeopardy? She sponged off the counter. He'd never had so many late nights before. Maybe it wasn't just the new job. Maybe he was deliberately burying himself in work trying to forget.

Forget! The very idea infuriated her. How *could* he? Reluctantly, she tried to give him the benefit of the doubt, to consider that deep down he must care and suffer as much as she. But sometimes he seemed more like a robot than a husband.

Maybe he's given up, she thought as she scrubbed at a stain on the tile. *That could explain how disconnected he seems. He just stands back and watches my emotional seesaws. Total detachment. It's as though I'm just another management situation he has to deal with, part of the job description.*

Maybe Peter didn't want to come home. Could he be—no, she didn't really think there could be another woman. But, she recalled, that was exactly what her secretary thought, till her husband stunned her by filing for divorce.

Squeezing her eyes shut, she tried to force the idea away. "What if?" she said aloud. She'd become an expert at playing that game. "They'll take me off to the mental hospital and shut me away with the crazies if I don't stop," she muttered. Still, she'd worked hard on that meal. What a shame to . . .

Eric! The name flashed into her mind with such suddenness, she gasped and felt her cheeks flush. She looked at her watch. He was probably just getting off-duty. He couldn't have been more helpful, and he really looked like he could use a good meal.

She turned toward the phone. And wouldn't it be good for Tim to talk with another man?

Who was she kidding? It might be good for *her* to have a male adult, a really empathetic male adult, to talk to. She stared at the phone. *Could I? Yes, I could! Will I?*

She picked up the phone and dialed the sheriff's station. When a man's voice answered, she panicked and replaced the phone. Annoyed at her lack of daring, she chastised herself, *What a goody two shoes! Why can't I loosen up? What did Dolores call me? Narrow. I bet she wouldn't be so inhibited.*

She looked across the road to Dolores's house, where Tim had gone as soon as he finished his homework. She still wasn't happy with that relationship, but Tim so desperately needed companionship with another boy. She'd grown weary of suggesting that he invite someone home from his class.

Grabbing the newspaper, she sat down in the living room to try to read, but it was all so depressing. Bombings in Paris. Death on the freeway. Disease spreading in the Southland. A headline caught her eye: "Photo Leads to Discovery of Missing Girl." She spread the paper out to read the full-column story. An eight-year-old girl, abducted by her father four years earlier, had been found when someone recognized her picture on a flyer in a gas station.

Four years! She sighed. She was sure she couldn't survive waiting that long. Wondering how the mother had kept her sanity, Andrea stared at the picture of the radiant woman embracing her smiling daughter.

Will I ever, ever be in a picture like that? she wondered. *Imagine what it must be like for them after all that time. Think how much the girl must have changed. She looks as though she was well cared for, but after all, she was with her father, who presumably loved her. What about Joy? Who's she with? It could be someone who wanted her, cherished her.*

She pictured someone else tucking Joy in at bedtime and had to shake the painful scene out of her head. A memory took its place, as she saw herself one night, a year or so ago, looking down at Joy in her bed. How startling it had been when, in Joy's blue eyes, she saw her own image. *How amazing,* she'd thought. *She is a reflection of me, and I will go on and on and live forever in her and her children and her children's children.*

But now, she wasn't so sure.

She folded the paper and wandered slowly to the corner

windows, looking out at the view up the coast to Point Dume. The sun had already set behind a cloud bank, graying the ocean, turning the canyons from green to charcoal, a scene as colorless as she felt. Restless, she turned toward the TV, then thought better of it.

Starting toward the kitchen, she made a quick decision. Forget the roast lamb. She'd take Tim out for an early burger and a chocolate shake. She knew just the place. She turned the oven off, took the roast out, and hurried to the phone to call Dolores. Busy. Well, then, she'd just go over and get him.

With a nubby sweater tossed over her blue-and-white striped turtleneck, she headed out across the road. Opening the gate to Dolores's yard, she crossed the patio and knocked at the door. In a moment, Dolores appeared, a flaming exclamation point in a scarlet jumpsuit, her blue-black hair hanging smooth and loose about her face.

"Andrea!" she exclaimed warmly. "How nice! Come in!"

She stood outside the doorway. "Sorry to bother you, Dolores, but your phone was busy, and I thought I might take Tim out for an early burger."

"Oh," Dolores dismissed the idea with a broad wave of the hand, "give him a little more time. They're enjoying each other."

"I knew they planned to work on the snake cage."

"N-no. They're in Brant's room at the moment."

She frowned, wondering if Tim had made up the snake-cage project so she'd let him come over.

But her neighbor's gaze distracted her. Dolores's dark eyes explored her face with such intensity, Andrea wondered if they could penetrate her innermost being. "Is your husband not coming home for dinner?"

Andrea exaggerated a pout.

"Then come in and sit!" Dolores grabbed her arm and

pulled her inside, pushing the door shut with her foot. Indicating the cut-crystal glass in her hand, she offered, "I'll get you something to drink."

She started to shake her head, then gave in. Why not? "Soda would be nice."

"I can give you something stronger."

"Soda's fine." Andrea trailed behind her into the kitchen.

Dolores brought out a matching glass and went toward the refrigerator. Andrea heard the clank of ice cubes.

"Perrier or Diet Coke?"

"Perrier."

Dolores nodded approval. "With lime," she decided, reaching into the refrigerator.

Watching her, Andrea felt ashamed of her petulance over Peter not coming home for dinner. After all, Dolores no longer had a husband to come home to her. "Dolores?"

"Mm?"

"Is it hard without your husband? I mean, how long has it been?"

"Since Nate died? Let's see. Three years? No, almost four." Dolores stopped and faced Andrea. "Hard without him? Want an honest answer?"

Andrea nodded.

"No." Dolores cocked her head to one side. "Nate was ridiculously straight. Let's be candid: He was a cold fish." She assumed a rigid posture and a grim, serious expression. "He signed his letters to his mother, 'Sincerely, Nathan.'" She laughed and spread her arms wide. "I'm having a fine time. For instance, I've completely redone the house, to 'de-Nate' it and make it more me. As you know, I'm plenty busy. I'm doing just fine, thank you." Dolores started toward the living room. "Let's get comfortable."

She led the way, pausing to point out a window. "Isn't it

beautiful? That pearly quality of the ocean. And look, it shines like mercury along the shore, especially in the canyons."

Smiling ruefully, Andrea remembered how bleak the same scene had looked to her earlier. Her neighbor really did have an eye, a flair for enjoying.

Following Dolores, she remembered the snake that had startled her on her last visit. With relief, she saw he wasn't there.

"Where's Simon, Dolores?"

"Oh, I think the boys took him out." Dolores kicked off high-heeled black pumps and tucked her feet beneath her on the plump-cushioned sofa. She watched as Andrea settled into a chair of leather slung over chrome. "Now tell me about Andrea."

"I'm fine." She flashed a smile and felt it fade under Dolores' scrutiny. "Who am I kidding? It just doesn't get any easier— the waiting."

"Of course it doesn't! But you know what I think? That you need to lighten up, have some diversion, some fun." Dolores smiled conspiratorially. "I'm available. Why don't we do lunch Wednesday and see what mischief we can get into?"

"Oh, thanks, Dolores, I'd love to. But Connie invited me to a Bible study, and I thought I might go."

Dolores tilted her head back and broke into a deep, throaty laugh. "Forgive me. But I seem to remember your being rather—shall we say, upset?—with God the last time you were here." She pointed a scarlet-nailed forefinger toward Andrea. "What's the matter? Feeling guilty?"

"No. Well, I . . ." She felt her face color.

"You see!" Dolores spread her hands for emphasis. "That's the problem with so much religious teaching. You must do this and you must do that, or God's gonna get you. I thought Jesus came to set people free. I don't see a whale of a lot of freedom. And where's all this *joy* Christians are supposed to have?"

Dolores seemed to speak in italics, and to punctuate her last sentence, she leaned toward Andrea fixing her with her wide eyes. "Don't let Christianity put you in a box, Andrea! You could suffocate."

She felt a tight pressure on her chest as she forced herself to meet Dolores's gaze. "So what do *you* believe?"

"I believe," Dolores paused, "there are many different ways to get to St. Louis." She smiled, one carefully penciled eyebrow rising to challenge Andrea.

"Meaning?"

"Meaning there's more than one way to be in harmony with the universe. You would probably tell me that you try to achieve it through the Bible. Yes?"

Andrea nodded. "Yes, His Word. Which seems one good reason to do a Bible study, wouldn't you say?"

"But that's so limiting, Andrea! You know, I really get annoyed with the exclusivity of some Christians. It's like, 'This is it, and there's no other way.' So intolerant! They have this smug, 'I have something you don't have!' attitude. What I would say is, first, that we have more than one lifetime to get our acts together, and second, that there are other ways to experience the divine."

"Such as?"

"Through *experience*. I pity those narrow people who are missing it all. Why, it's straitjacket living! I mean, let's think about the Bible. How can we be sure that plain ordinary men remembered things accurately? And we all know that the Bible's been changed through the centuries, that it isn't the same as when it was first written. So does it make sense to trust its every word? I believe we can learn so many things if we get in harmony with the universe and open ourselves to all that's there, waiting for us to access it. I believe you can even learn—" She stopped, staring past Andrea, then very slowly almost chanted the words, "where—Joy—is!"

A chill traveled along Andrea's backbone. She shook her head. "I've heard that from a man from Oregon who had 'vibrations' that Joy was in Anchorage, Alaska. And a woman who said she'd been put in a box and shipped to China. So what I'd like to know is, if God can show us where Joy is, why hasn't He?"

Dolores's mouth curved in a tight smile. "Maybe He doesn't know."

Andrea recoiled. God not know? It was unthinkable.

"Or maybe," Dolores continued, "it's a matter of *how*, not why. I know you're dubious, and I won't press you now. But there are ways to delve into the unknown. You're intelligent. Don't you want to try anything that might help? Don't you want to *know*?" Dolores looked at Andrea carefully, as though trying to diagnose her.

"Yes, of course," Andrea murmured, feeling unease in the pit of her stomach. *Am I being chicken, or is my body warning me in some way?* she wondered.

But before she could comment, Dolores stood, and her voice took on such a briskness, Andrea looked up to be sure another person hadn't entered the room. "Now, about that hamburger, Andrea. Is your heart really set on it? I have some lovely poached salmon left from a party last night. Why don't you and Tim join us?"

"Oh, no, Dolores, we couldn't im-"

"Impose? Nonsense." Dolores led the way to the kitchen. "You talk to me while I fix up some plates."

She watched in fascination as Dolores went to work, an

artist painting with food. She spooned a golden sauce onto the stark white plates, fanned Chinese peas along one edge, accenting the pink of the salmon with red dollops of tomato, green sprigs of cilantro. "That is gorgeous, Dolores! I'll trade it for a burger and a chocolate shake any day."

Dolores smiled. "I have some pasta salad we can have with it. Want to call the boys? End of the hallway to the left."

Andrea searched without success for a light switch, shrugged, and made her way carefully in the fading light. At least she didn't hear the beat of heavy rock pounding from the room. Come to think of it, why was it so quiet? She'd expected to hear conversation or exclamations or the sound effects boys make when they're playing. The door was closed. She hesitated, listened a moment, then knocked, startled at the loudness of her hand on the wood. Whispers. A rustling noise. Then a voice that leapt from baritone to soprano in a single word. "Ye-es?"

"Brant, it's Mrs. Lang. Tim's Mom. Tim, we're going to have dinner here because Dad's not coming home. And it's all ready, so come on, boys."

More whispers. The click of the door being unlocked—or was it locked? The scrape of a drawer. "Coming," Brant called. And in a moment both boys swept past her, shutting the door behind them.

She followed them, uneasy with their secrecy.

As they began their dinner, Tim seemed to avoid eye contact with her. But at least he was eating, and she was grateful for that.

She looked across the glass-topped table at Brant. "I thought you guys were going to work on a snake cage this afternoon."

Brant glanced at Tim. "Yeah, we were, but I don't have all the materials."

She nodded. "So what were you two up to?"

"Oh, magic." Brant's dark eyes challenged her.

"Magic as in rabbits out of hats? Or snakes?" The very thought distracted her. "By the way, where *is* Simon?"

"Don't worry." Brant's soothing tone sounded remarkably like his mother's. "He's in a cage in my room."

"Promise I don't have to worry about him slithering up my leg?"

"Promise!" Brant flashed a brilliant orthodontics-in-progress grin.

"Mom," Tim interjected, "can I have a snake? It wouldn't be any trouble at all. And you only have to feed it—"

Andrea finished the sentence for her son, "once a week. I know. I think for the moment Juliet is enough, Tim." She smiled at him. "Oh, and that reminds me. I found her walking along the wrought-iron railing in the hallway today. No problem at all. Very surefooted!"

Tim nodded. "'Cause she's big-footed." He looked at her, persistence in his eyes. "But how about a little later? Could you think about a snake then?"

"Maybe if you petted Simon; he's not slippery or slimy. I could go get him," Brant offered.

Dolores came to Andrea's rescue. "Brant, please do not spoil Mrs. Lang's dinner."

Dinner concluded with what Tim termed "humongous" long-stemmed strawberries, which they dipped in yogurt and brown sugar.

Later she and Tim stepped out into a crisp, clear night with the Milky Way arching so white, it seemed to help light their way.

"I like not having streetlights," Tim said.

"Me too. Listen." They stopped. "You can hear the surf breaking. Amazing. That's nine hundred feet below us."

"Yeah. Kinda mysterious sounding."

"Speaking of mysterious—what was going on in Brant's room when I called you for dinner?"

"We were playing with a ouija board."

Magic indeed, she thought. She remembered Zoë cautioning, "Ouija boards and tarot cards and palm reading are unreliable and rooted in the occult. They open the door to the enemy."

Not a good idea, she decided, *and I definitely need to find other people for Tim to play with.*

"Well, that is mysterious," she said carefully.

"Yeah. Brant would ask questions and the thing would just move. It wasn't like we were doing it."

She stumbled on a rock. "Questions such as?"

"Oh, just dumb stuff." Tim seemed to be hedging. They were silent as they started up the stairs. "I had an idea of a question I want to ask next time though."

"What's that, Tim?"

"Where Joy is."

Her breath caught in her throat and she coughed. Rapidly, she considered how she should respond. At the top of the steps she stopped, turned toward him, and put her hand on each of his thin shoulders. "Tim, don't."

"Why not?"

She wasn't sure why she felt so defensive, so on guard. "It's . . ." she paused. "It's not dependable. It's hocus-pocus or maybe worse."

"But it works, Mom!" he insisted. "It gave Brant answers."

"Tim!" she snapped. "I don't like it. Period."

"I was just trying to help." She could hear the nearness of tears in his voice.

"I know, honey." She hated to find fault with everything he wanted to do. "But I don't think that's a good way. In fact, I really believe it's a bad way."

But as they stepped into the house, Dolores's cryptic, "There's more than one way to St. Louis!" echoed in her mind.

Are we both getting into things that are best left alone? But no, she thought, *of course not. That's silly. Dolores just wants to help.*

20

THE EDGE OF SARCASM in Andrea's voice rang in Peter's ear as he told her good-bye. Sure, he'd missed several dinners at home. But this had been a cruddy, one-step-forward, three-steps-back day, and he needed time alone with the office empty. Apple pie couldn't solve his problems. *Admit it*, he told himself. *You don't want to hear Andrea's and Tim's problems after the day you've had.*

He looked up as Hank Willis laid the pieces of a valve on Peter's desk. "Look here. No wonder the crazy thing won't go together. Here's our problem." Willis pointed with a pencil to the valve stem. "It's ten-thou oversize. No way we can make it work on a hospital oxygen-supply system." He looked up at his senior engineer. "You sure?"

Willis nodded, handing Peter a micrometer. "Look for yourself."

Peter took a measurement and checked it against the plans on his desk. "I don't believe it!" he muttered. "Might as well be off a mile. And it's due in Texas tomorrow." The piece of equipment wavered before him as sudden anger rose in an almost blinding heat. Grabbing the drawing and the part, he stood, knocking his chair over, and strode out of the room, down the hallway, out of the building, and across the court-yard toward the machine shop. *So help me*, he told himself, *I'm gonna punch out whoever did this. I told Keller how critical this measurement is. And not just once. We went over it and over it and over it.*

From the corner of his eye he saw heads turn as he stalked toward the foreman's desk. It was all he could do to wait for Keller to finish a phone conversation.

A pudgy man whose perpetual frown had etched a deep V above his nose, Keller looked up at Peter with questioning milky blue eyes.

Peter willed his fists to release at his sides and took a deep breath. "Now, Keller," he began, hearing his own tone of exaggerated patience, "let's take a look at the drawing and at this valve stem." He spread out the plans, pointed to the stem dimensions and asked the foreman to measure the stem.

Keller measured, shook his head in disbelief, measured again. "Good grief. It's way off, isn't it?" He shook his head, then added quickly, "But listen, Mr. Lang, I told the machinist twice!"

Peter shook his head. "The point is, this valve's due in Texas tomorrow. They're waiting. What can you do?"

Keller glanced at the clock. "We'll stay. Stay till she's fixed."

"How long would you estimate?"

"Two, three hours at the most. I'll get Dawson on it right now."

"You do that." Peter turned and knocked over a stool as he marched out of the shop, clenching and unclenching his fists. "Stupid Neanderthals! Careless! Just plain careless!" he muttered. He started out of the building, hesitated, and detoured into the auxiliary men's room. The wooden door to the nearest stall was closed. He stared at it a moment, fury and frustration mounting. Then, raising his fist, he swung hard, shattering the first layer of plywood and punching through the second. He heard an exclamation of profanity from the other side of the door. The toilet flushed and the latch scraped. The door opened a slit. As the pain began to register, Peter blinked and managed, "Sorry. That wasn't directed at you." A curly headed young man wearing the gray uniform of the maintenance crew let the door swing back and cautiously moved past Peter.

"Hey, man, lighten up," he protested. Glancing at Peter's bloody hand, he repeated his earlier expletive. "You're dripping on the floor I just mopped," he added, pushing out through the door.

Peter held his hand under the faucet, watching the red blood swirl around the bowl and down the drain. He wiggled his fingers tentatively. Good. Nothing broken. Darned fool thing to do. But better the door than Keller. Looking up at the mirror he gave his reflection a little nod of affirmation. He felt better.

He applied pressure with towels until the bleeding stopped and wrapped a clean handkerchief around his knuckles. Using his left hand and his teeth, he was tugging a knot tight when Hank Willis came in. "Been looking for you." Willis saw Peter's hand. "Hey!"

"Looks like I'm going to have a repair bill here." He pointed toward the damaged door.

"Whew!" breathed Willis. "Good thing it wasn't Keller,

though I sure wouldn't blame you." He stood a moment before clasping Peter's shoulder. "Hey, we both know it isn't just Keller or the test results. It's been a lousy four months. I don't know how you hang together."

"People tell me how cool I am. But," he measured out the words for emphasis, "I-do-get-angry! I never thought I could kill a person, but I know now I could, if I only knew who." He sighed. "I can't let all that hit the fan at home. It's not fair to Andrea or Tim."

"So how do you handle it?" asked the older man.

"I try to work it off at the gym after work. That helps some. But obviously it's not 100 percent." He touched his left jaw gently. "I've got this pain in my jaw—TMJ, they call it. The joint. Dentist says it's tension. And today," he shook his head sheepishly, "guess I just had to blow off some steam." He looked at his watch. "Two or three hours to wait for the redo. At least I can get out the 'Joy' file and see if I can come up with anything."

"Sure. I'll stay and work on it too," Willis offered as Peter headed out the door.

In his office Peter found someone had righted the chair he'd overturned. Willis, no doubt. Mr. Neat. Once he'd watched Willis fold his lunch sack in precise thirds, tucking in the end with great care before throwing it away.

From his file Peter pulled out the folder and thumbed through the papers. The graph of reported sightings of Joy wouldn't yield any sort of pattern, no matter how you cut it. The pedophile angle hadn't paid off either. The sheriff's department had traced down the Malibu lead, but couldn't tie it to Joy. They were all at a convention the day Joy disappeared. He shook his head in disgust. A convention of pedophiles!

Tracing down what witnesses described as "a blue hatch-back" from the parking lot of the toy store seemed impossible. He'd have to let the authorities work on that one. But there were a couple of possible suspects who couldn't be found. Working with the databases he'd bought, he could try to run down their license plates, employers, or credit records. Maybe they would yield some new lead.

"Pete?" Willis stood at his doorway. "I don't know if I should show you the latest or not. You might punch my computer out."

"Nah, you're safe now."

Willis waved a computer printout. "I cannot tell a lie. A hacker—a young kid in our neighborhood—showed me how to check out that list of suspects connected with the adoption rings. Real unsavory characters." Laying the papers on the desk, he pointed to a name. "Seems like there's drug traffick-ing involved. I'm gonna check further."

He looked up at Willis. The idea of *selling* a child, like a piece of horseflesh or a car, made his blood boil. How could they? Yet if he could look at it dispassionately, he realized Joy would be highly marketable. Blond, blue-eyed. Who wouldn't want her? She'd probably bring a handsome price. "Scum!" he said aloud. "I—" He stopped as the phone rang. "Lang."

"Peter," came a voice with a folksy twang. "Jeff Hendrix. Tell me if you've got a minute or not."

"Jeff! Sure."

"Why I'm calling is a group of guys are going to start meet-ing at church early Tuesday mornings, fifteen or twenty minutes max, to pray. Wondered if you'd want to join us."

"What time were you thinking?"

"Early. Six-thirty or seven. Could you make that?"

Peter thought a moment. If he could get someone else to

take Tim to school. "Sure. Count me in and thanks for think-ing of me."

"Great. We'll start week after next. And Peter? We've all been praying for you and your family all along."

"Thanks, Jeff, we need it."

Peter replaced the receiver and looked up at Willis. "A men's prayer group. Couldn't hurt."

"You a Christian?" Willis seemed surprised.

"Why? Do I come across like some kind of pagan?"

"No, it's not that. But how can you believe in a God that would do this?" Hank pointed at the printouts.

He pursed his lips. "How? Well, I don't hold it against God personally." He thought a moment. "The bottom line is, Hank, I know God can use all this for good. I don't know how yet. But He does."

⌇

It was after eight before the remachined part was finished and the valve assembled, boxed and ready for hand-delivery to Texas. Peter breathed a sigh of relief as he climbed into his car and headed for the Coast Highway.

He wondered how he'd find Andrea when he got home. No telling if she'd be on a high with a new "Find Joy" scheme or in the pits. He hated emotional scenes. Andrea's tears, the fear he often saw in her face made him feel so helpless, so useless. He wanted to fix it like he'd fixed the valve.

But he couldn't.

When he arrived home, he found her staring at a magazine, her Bible beside her on the couch. She reached up to hug him, moving the Bible so he could sit beside her.

"Sorry I was so miffed when you called," she said. "You heal the sick valve?" Her voice was barely more than a whisper.

"Yep. Alive and well and ready to go to Texas."

"Good. Feel hungry?" She gave him a quick smile. "I definitely have leftovers. Tim and I wound up having dinner with
Dolores and Brant. Roast lamb sandwich? Apple pie?"

He smiled. "Pie." He stopped her from rising. "In a
minute." He tapped the Bible. "Glad to see you've been in the
Word."

She looked away. "Not exactly. Something Dolores said
made me pick it up, but I just couldn't get into it. I felt—
blocked."

"That happens sometimes."

"No, this is different. Somehow I feel separated from God."

"Oh, honey!" He tried to make eye contact with her. "Don't
you remember back when we studied the Book of Romans?
There's no separation from God." He recalled the verse,
'Neither death or life, or angels or demons, or things present or
things to come.'"

"Oh, sure!" she said. "Well, maybe the Bible's wrong. Ever
think of that? Frankly, I don't see one shred of evidence that
He sees or knows or cares about Joy or us."

Alarmed, he took her hand. If she didn't trust the Lord, she
didn't have anything to draw from. How could she go on?
"Andry, that just isn't true. He knows everything and He does
care. He sees the big picture, and we only see a tiny corner."
He put his arm around her and tried to draw her closer, feeling
her resistance. "Honey, don't give up the comfort you could
have from Him. You're not cut off. He's patient. He waits for us.
He waited twenty-two years for you to come to Him in the first
place. He's waiting for you again."

She didn't answer.

He kept his voice calm, gentle. "Want to pray together?"

She shook her head and sat motionless, head lowered, face
hidden from him.

He waited, heartsick, hoping she'd soften. But it seemed the subject was closed. He glanced helplessly about the room, sighed, and finally murmured in resignation, "So. About that pie." Pie, he thought. Who gives a . . .

She rose slowly. "I'll get it. Cheese with it?"

"Sure."

She led the way into the kitchen, cut into the untouched pie, and lifted a generous slice onto a plate. He could smell the cinnamon as he brought out the cheddar and poured a glass of milk. "Want some?" He held up the milk carton.

She gasped, staring at his right hand. "Peter! What happened? A machine? You're so careful."

He grinned sheepishly. "Punched out a door."

"You *what?*"

He nodded.

"You? Coolhand Pete? Oh, honey, is anything broken? Are there splinters in it? Do you need some ice?"

"It's fine. Sit down."

She joined him at the kitchen table. "I don't believe it," she said. "I've never seen you that angry. It must have really been a bad day." She looked at him carefully. "But I guess there've been a lot of bad days since last January." Tears glinted in her eyes and she reached over to gently stroke his hand. "You know it's kind of a relief to know you're human!"

"Oh, come on!"

"I mean it. You've seemed to compartmentalize everything so neatly. I thought I was the only one in this marriage who was struggling."

"I'm struggling," he assured her.

She watched as he tasted the pie. "This is fantastic," he said. "Definitely not from the supermarket freezer."

She shook her head.

"I appreciate all your work," he said softly. "Sure you don't want some?"

"No. I had plenty to eat at Dolores's."

He measured off another bite with his fork. "Tell me about that."

"She's a fabulous cook and very stylish. In some ways she's a little off-the-wall, but intriguing, vibrant, and challenging. She enjoys life."

He couldn't explain the uneasiness he felt as she described Dolores. And what had their neighbor said about the Bible? Cautiously, he asked, "So, she's someone you'd like to spend more time with?"

"Yes. In fact, she's invited me out to lunch with her next Wednesday. She likes to check out the new restaurants, and there's one up the coast she's heard good things about."

He frowned. "Wednesday. Thought you were going to that Bible study with Connie Hendrix." Before she could answer he remembered, "Oh! That reminds me, Jeff Hendrix called today and asked me to meet with a group of men for prayer early Tuesday mornings. Can we figure a way for Tim to get to school those days?"

She shrugged. "Sure. I can take him if you really want to go."

"I do." It would be a twelve-mile round trip for her, and he was grateful. "So what about you and Connie's Bible study?" he asked.

She straightened in her chair. "I didn't say for sure I'd go. Frankly, I'm really tempted by Dolores's offer. Maybe get away from the house, enjoy a pretty setting, and eat good things. Sounds like *fun* to me."

He caught the glint of defiance in her eyes, the set of her jaw that signaled she'd already made up her mind. "And fun," she added, "is something I haven't had much of lately!"

21

From Zoë's Prayer Journal

April 24: Dear Lord, sweet Father, I sense our Andrea losing touch with You. She told me the other day that ever since she was a preteen, she feared that life would just happen to her. That's what she thinks is going on now. Everything is just happening, and it seems out of control to her. You and I know that's not true, that it's all by design, and You are in control. Oh, help her see the big picture and reach out to You. Use that sweet Connie to get through to her. And bless all Connie's selfless work at the Joy Center. May it bring our Joy back. Be glorified in all this, dear Lord, in Jesus' name, amen.

ALMOST OVERNIGHT, the mountain lilacs bloomed, frosting the hillside with the palest blue. The faint perfume of the wild-flowers hung in the still morning air as Andrea walked around to the ocean side of her house to marvel at still another spectacle of blues. Sapphire tones of the Pacific stood out against the watered-down blue of the sky, sharply defining the broad arc of the horizon. Though no swells rose on the water's surface, small wind ripples sparkled in the sunlight, with a calm, paler streak here and there.

Andrea held out her arms to embrace the panorama. What a glorious spring day! How foolish it would be to waste it inside. She congratulated herself for telling Dolores yes to lunch. She needed to get out.

The ring of the phone sent her hurrying into the house. It would be Connie, she knew.

"Just checking in with you about this morning's Bible study," Connie said. "Let me pick you up around 9:30."

"Oh, Connie, thanks. But I can't, after all. Something's come up." She listened to the silence. "Tim told me last night he had to have some things for school tomorrow. Don't you love it when they wait till the last minute?" She felt her face flush at the lie and hurried to add, "I appreciate your thoughtfulness though."

"Oh, shoot! I'd counted on seeing you. We usually kinda adjourn to John's at the Beach for lunch afterward. Thought it might do you good to take off and relax for a spell." Connie paused before suggesting, "Maybe next week." Her cheerful voice turned warm and urgent. "Andrea, *people* are fragile. They'll let you down, but God never will. It could be such a help right now for Him to be your rock. Trust me, I know."

Some rock, Andrea thought. "Connie," she protested, "He *has* let me down."

"It might seem like that to you. But I believe with all my heart you'd see it different if you could begin to grab ahold of *His* way of looking at things. See, that's why I want you in this study."

Connie was becoming tiresome with all her God-talk. *But*, Andrea thought, *she's so earnest. And she's been so kind. Maybe if I go once she'll get off my case.* She heard herself say, "I'll try for next week."

"That's what I was wanting to hear!" Connie said.

She hung up, half-amused, half-annoyed with Connie's tenacity. She hated lying, but at least she was free for today. What a pleasure it would be to spend time out in the real world. With a sigh, she realized how she missed it.

Andrea dressed carefully. Reaching past her business suits, she selected a soft silk print dress in shades of peach, yellow, and pale green. "Perfect with your spring coloring," the shopkeeper had told her.

Evidently she'd chosen well. "You look smashing!" Dolores called as she turned her sapphire Porsche 944 into Andrea's driveway and reached over to open the door.

As Andrea slid into the car, she saw that Dolores had pulled her hair back in a French braid. Shocking-pink flowered earrings echoed the color in her scarf and her spike-heeled pumps. Her dress, a sheath of white linen, rode high above her knees as she eased out the clutch and headed down the hill.

"Love your car," Andrea said, settling back into the ivory leather upholstery.

Dolores laughed. "I had so much fun buying this! Nate always drove a Cad-i-lac." She stretched out each syllable like taffy. "I was so sick of that stuffy big car. This is a delight." She shifted gears expertly as they curved around the hairpin turns. "Mustard's coming into bloom," she noted, waving at an expanse of brilliant yellow. "It's a killer to clear out and keep us firesafe, but it's so glorious. Sometimes I cut it and bring it inside. Doesn't last but a day or so, but I like its sculptural, Japanese-y look." She glanced at Andrea. "You hungry? I do hope so."

She nodded. "I skipped breakfast so I could eat lots." She smiled. "Seems like such a long time since I've done anything like this. I feel sort of wicked."

"Why?" Dolores asked, surprised. "You deserve it." She checked traffic and turned right onto Coast Highway.

"I'm playing hooky from a Bible study," Andrea admitted.

"With Connie? Her church is big on Bible study, isn't it? And on 'being saved.'" Dolores waved her hand impatiently. "I know all about that." She shot her a probing glance. "So, feeling guilty again? Well, don't! I'm sure your God wants you to take care of yourself. It'll be good for your whole family for you to have some R and R."

Dolores's tone was so emphatic, so reassuring, Andrea felt her tension ease. *She's right*, she told herself. *Relax and enjoy. That's what this day is all about.* She turned toward Dolores. "Tell me about this restaurant. Have you been there?"

"No, but I knew the owner, Antonio, when he had a bizarre little place in Beverly Hills. A little larger than a postage stamp and almost impossible to get into. Now he has this fabulous location, and he's hired a chef who won awards at the Four Seasons. It's got to be a knockout."

She smiled at Dolores's superlatives, the sense of adventure she invoked. "Were you by any chance a cheerleader when you were in high school?"

"Why, yes." Dolores seemed startled. "How did you know?"

"Just a wild guess."

Several miles past Malibu Canyon Road, Dolores swung off the highway. She turned toward the ocean, up a winding road shaded with live oak trees, then down a ramp flanked by cascades of geraniums. A circular concrete structure came into view. Only about twenty feet in diameter and domed with glass, it rose in the center of a ring of paving that was swirled with shades of peach and green.

"Is that all there is?" Andrea asked.

"You'll see," Dolores promised, as she pulled up to the entrance. A valet helped them out and opened a thick glass door with a huge pewter disc for a handle, revealing a spiral staircase plunging downward. They wound their way to a circular dining room, cantilevered over the ocean.

Andrea caught her breath.

"Told you!" Dolores said.

A tall, dark-mustached man in a European-cut suit bowed and kissed Dolores's hand. "Ah, signora, what a privilege to have you in our new restaurant!"

"Thank you, Antonio." Dolores turned to Andrea. "This is my friend, Andrea Lang, and I've told her how wonderful you are. Don't disappoint us."

Antonio bent to kiss her hand. "A privilege, signora," he murmured, his voice deep and warm. His dark eyes twinkled. "And certainly I could never disappoint two such bee-yoo-tee-ful young ladies! Here! Come! I have ready for you a table by the window. Or would you prefer to be outside?" He gestured toward the patio tables, where umbrellas in Maypole colors fluttered in the breeze. Without waiting for a reply, he declared, "Outside! Yes. That will be better. Give me just a moment to set up."

Andrea studied the dining room, the white-clothed tables with peach overlays, chairs upholstered in seafoam green. "This is wonderful! The colors are so gentle and it's so light and pleasant. And look how the mirrored ceiling reflects the surf."

Dolores nodded. "Very architectural. Uncluttered. Someone knew just when to stop."

"Anything more would have been too much," she agreed.

She watched Antonio approach from the patio. "Everything is now ready for you. Come!" He led them through the plushly carpeted dining room to a glass-topped table outside. Pulling back a softly upholstered pale-green chair, he declared, "I have something very special for you today. You would like first to order some wine?"

"Of course," Dolores nodded.

"I'll bring the wine list."

As Antonio glided away, Andrea took a deep breath and turned toward the ocean. "Will you look at that view? There's Catalina! It wasn't even 'there' earlier this morning. Now it looks close enough to swim to."

A moment later, Antonio handed a heavy book to Dolores. "The wine list, signora." While she leafed through it, Andrea studied the guests at other tables. Casually dressed, under-stated, like the restaurant, but elite, sophisticated. Natural fibers everywhere. And white seemed very in. Sophisticated women with pricey haircuts. Plenty of diamonds and emeralds. Elegant men with silver-edged hair. She recognized one movie star, then another.

Dolores looked up from the wine list, and Antonio materialized from inside the restaurant. He must have been watching through a peephole, Andrea decided.

"Let's have the Grgich Hills Chardonnay," Dolores said.

"An excellent choice, signora."

"And I'll have iced tea, please, Antonio," Andrea said.

Dolores pouted. "Perhaps you'll have some wine once we order. After all, this is a celebration." She leaned toward Andrea. "Surely you don't have a hang-up about wine." Her voice was soft and almost seductive. "Wasn't Jesus' first miracle turning water into wine?"

"Wine is good for the stomach," Antonio said, motioning to a waiter dressed in a soft gray blazer. "This is Carmelo, and he'll take good care of you." He lowered his voice. "But let me tell you that the lobster tail is . . ." He kissed his fingertips and hummed an ecstatic, "Mmmmmm!"

"Ladies." Carmelo presented the pale green menu with abstract brush strokes of watercolors. "In addition to our regular menu, may I suggest the lobster tail that Antonio mentioned. It's poached and chilled and served on a confetti of spring vegetables. Very colorful and very delicious." He continued listing the day's specialties, then smiled. "I'll give you time and come back to see if you have any questions."

Andrea read through the menu. The prices were definitely downtown. Oh, well, how often did she do this sort of thing anymore? She was here and she would enjoy it. She looked up at her companion. "This is not easy! Everything sounds fabulous."

"This chef is particularly good with seafood," Dolores suggested.

They pondered in silence until at last Dolores announced. "All right. I'll do the vegetable terrine with sun-dried tomatoes and the *pot-au-feu* of seafood."

"Sounds wonderful," Andrea murmured, closing the menu, "but I can't resist the lobster."

Carmelo arrived with the wine, presenting it for Dolores's inspection. Uncorking the bottle with a flourish, he handed her the cork. She nodded and waited as he poured a sample. Swirling it in the glass, she lifted it and inhaled deeply before tasting it. "Lovely." She smiled across the table. "You're going to love it." He poured more wine for her and moved around the table to serve Andrea.

Dolores is right, Andrea told herself. This is a celebration. She watched as the pale amber liquid flowed into her slender-stemmed glass.

Dolores offered a toast. "Here's to you and your reentry!"

She touched her glass to Dolores's. "I'll drink to that!"

Taking a sip, she swallowed slowly, set her glass down and smiled, feeling an instant sense of exhilaration. "You know, I feel as though I've emerged from hibernation." When the food arrived, it was all her neighbor had promised. Andrea's dish was as colorful and prettily arranged as a painting, and Dolores's entreé arrived in a copper pot, the seafood fragrant with saffron.

Andrea took her first bite. "This is incredible." They dined slowly, savoring the lunch, the wine, the vista, chatting easily as they learned about each other, discussing the theater, music, books.

She's a dynamic woman, Andrea decided. *Such a capacity for enjoying life. But also bright, perceptive, and well-read.*

"My father was a great reader and passed it along to me," Dolores was explaining. "I've really tried to instill a love for books in my children. My daughter was such a voracious reader, she grabbed everything that came into the house, including my husband's professional journals."

"So your own family—there's Brant and your daughter?"

"That's it. Nate had a daughter by a previous marriage, but she never lived with us, and she died awhile back. Brant and I are quite close and alike in a number of ways, I think. My daughter, Marcy, has always been a bit of an enigma to me. She seems to have totally withdrawn. In fact, right now, I don't even know where she is."

"How awful! What happened?" Andrea leaned forward, feeling Dolores's pain, wanting to understand.

Dolores looked out at the ocean. "She had a stillborn child a few years ago and then couldn't get pregnant again, and the depression has been consuming. I haven't heard a word from her since she was supposed to come up to Mammoth with us over the holidays. Her phone's been disconnected. She and her husband separated several months ago and," she raised both eyebrows, biting her lip. "I've tried to help, even got her into therapy, and I've agonized. And now, it seems she won't let me do any more."

"But you're not giving up!" Andrea protested.

Dolores shrugged. "What else can I do? I can't fix her. If she doesn't want my help—" She shrugged again, blinking rapidly.

"I guess there's more than one way to lose a daughter, isn't there?" Andrea reached across the table and touched Dolores's hand, sensing a new bond.

Dolores nodded and glanced down at the beach.

Andrea waited a moment before speaking. "Forgive me, but you said there are ways to know certain things, to find answers. Haven't you been able to learn anything about Marcy?"

Dolores shook her head. "I think her karma is really messed up." She held up her water glass, and a waiter hurried to pour for her. Andrea sensed the subject was closed.

After she'd sipped her water, Dolores looked over at Andrea's clean plate. "Do you want a doggy bag?"

Andrea laughed. "I am completely, delightfully, decadently stuffed!"

"Ah, but we haven't finished yet." Dolores pointed as Carmelo rolled the dessert cart up to the table

"Oh, no, I couldn't! I'll just have some coffee." She looked up at the cart filled with temptations. "What is that affair with raspberries?" she asked.

"A cold white and dark chocolate soufflé with fresh raspberry sauce."

"Better have it," her companion urged.

She groaned. She didn't need it. She wanted it. "I'll have it," she said.

Dolores applauded. "And I'll have," she hesitated and gestured toward a tart with lemon slices arranged in the center to form a flower, "that!"

Later, as they sipped their coffee, Andrea heard a woman's voice from a nearby table. "Dolores!" She turned to see a woman with snow-white hair, styled in an impeccable pageboy, rise and come toward them.

"Sybil!" The two women embraced, and Dolores gestured across the table. "Let me introduce my neighbor, Andrea Lang. Andrea, this is Sybil Vance."

The woman turned to reveal a youthful face and eyes of such a startling jade green that Andrea stared into them, transfixed.

"So happy to meet you," Sybil murmured, her eyes still fastened on Andrea's as she turned back to Dolores. At last she looked down at Dolores. "Lovely spot, isn't it? By the way, I'm having a gathering this Saturday. Why don't you join us?" She moved aside as the desserts arrived. "Call me." She blew a kiss as she returned to her table.

"Interesting woman," Dolores remarked. "I'll tell you about her sometime."

"More coffee?" The waiter had appeared from nowhere.

"Please." Dolores watched as he filled her cup and Andrea's. Then she leaned back and gave Andrea a warm, almost tender smile. "You know, I think one reason I'm so attracted to you is that you remind me of myself at your age."

"How so?"

"I wasn't really being me. Partly because of Nate. But also because I limited myself." She stirred her coffee. "Do you mind my asking, did you—do you—have restrictive parents?"

Andrea smiled. "Have you been tapping my phone line? My dad, no. A teddy bear. Mom, yes. I sometimes think Hollywood could type-cast her perfectly as the matron of a woman's prison." She shook her head. "Oh, she's not really that bad."

"Oh, my. No wonder," Dolores commented. "And I feel that in a way, Peter is restrictive."

Andrea sat up very straight. "Wait a minute, Dolores! He's never stopped me from doing anything I wanted to do."

"Forgive me. I just have the feeling he might subtly limit what you want to do. Not deliberately, mind you. He probably doesn't even realize it." She placed her hand on the table, close to Andrea's, her voice warm and earnest. "I see so much of your true essence waiting to be released. A capacity for play-fulness, lightness, and at the same time a lot of depth that you haven't fully tapped."

Andrea leaned toward her, listening.

Dolores's eyes sparkled mischievously. "I can imagine you, if you'd really let go, trying bungee jumping, exploring some new areas of your spirituality, maybe even having an affair."

Andrea held up a hand in protest, but Dolores continued. "I'm exaggerating, of course. What I'm saying is what Einstein said a long time ago, that we're all prisoners of our own ideas. We limit the possibilities. Why, scientists see this all the time, when a breakthrough comes from a direction they'd left unex-plored."

Andrea felt a surge of defensiveness. "I understand what you're saying, but I've always thought of myself as a pretty open and creative person."

"You are. You are!" Dolores nodded. She cocked her head. "I'm just suggesting that there's more out there, and you are such a beautiful, capable, really remarkable young woman. You deserve it." She gave her a smile that could melt an ice sculpture.

Andrea couldn't help but smile back. She lifted her coffee cup. "Here's to growth then."

"To growth," Dolores echoed.

A little later, as they left the restaurant, Dolores's eyes brightened. "I have an idea. There's a new boutique right on our way home. Gorgeous things, handmade in South America."

"I don't know if I trust myself," Andrea confessed. "I feel positively giddy, and it's not just that little bit of wine. This has been like a mini-vacation."

A few minutes later, they turned off the highway to the beachside boutique.

The clothes were gorgeous. Dolores held an appliqued blouse up to Andrea. "Nice, very nice. The blue's just the color of your eyes."

She sneaked a look at the price tag. Not as bad as she'd expected.

"Slip it on," the proprietor coaxed.

A moment later, when she emerged from the dressing room, both Dolores and the owner chorused, "Yes!"

She looked at herself in the mirror. It was becoming.

"You deserve it!" Dolores said. "Now just let me try on this caftan."

Half an hour later they left the boutique, elated and laughing as they stashed their purchases in the trunk.

"I'm not sure you're good for me, Dolores," Andrea said as she settled into the car.

"Nonsense! Of course I am. Bet you haven't laughed this much in a long time."

"You're right. And something else." She glanced at her watch. "We've been gone more than three hours, and I've only thought about Joy once."

Dolores pulled the car onto the highway. "And you get a gold star for that!"

As they drove in compatible silence, she thought, *It's*

interesting, the way we become different people when we're with different people. With Dolores, I feel full of life, ready for fun and free.

She reviewed the day. The boutique with all its pretty things, the restaurant, the food, the conversation, Antonio. And Sybil, with her white hair and jade green eyes. "You promised to tell me about Sybil."

"Oh, a fascinating woman."

"What does she do? What sort of gatherings does she have?"

Dolores glanced at Andrea. "She's a channeler." Andrea turned sideways in her seat and laughed. "Are you serious? One of those people who 'become' a person who lived a long time ago? Like Napoleon. Or Rembrandt?"

"Some channelers do go way, way back. But Sybil is more contemporary. And quite good at it, judging from the one time I went. One man was able to communicate with his son who had committed suicide."

Andrea felt her pulse skip a beat and then another. "So then, people come to her home and she summons the spirits of the dead and talks to them?"

"No, that would be more like a medium. Sybil actually becomes a channel for that dead person. I mean, her voice changes, and she talks like that person, and the communication is really direct. I mean, that man believed he was talking *with* his son!"

"That's creepy!"

Dolores braked for a stop signal and turned toward Andrea. "Sometimes it can be very informative." Her tone was light, but her deep eyes challenged Andrea.

Was Dolores suggesting Sybil could be a channel for Joy? But if Sybil could, that would mean Joy was . . . She didn't dare finish the thought. "No!" she cried. "No, I won't even think of it."

22

COULD A CHANNELER possibly be a link to Joy's "spirit"? The question nagged at Andrea all the rest of the week. Her instincts told her to stay away, that the channeler would give more dramatic performance than truth. Yet her mind wouldn't let it go.

*Some part of me keeps saying that if Sybil could become a channel for Joy, surely I'd know if I were really hearing Joy's voice. Maybe I could learn something. But what I'd learn is that she's—*she had to force herself even to think the word—*dead.*

She shuddered. *Am I ready for that?* she wondered. *If I knew, it would be all over. Not knowing, I have hope. But the waiting gets harder each day. Knowing would end the pain of hanging suspended.*

Then a new thought surfaced. *But what if Sybil was wrong, and I stopped working to find Joy and lost my chance of finding her?*

The internal dialogue was so persistent, she felt grateful when Saturday came, the day Peter had promised to take them to the wild animal preserve. Tim, she saw, shared her anticipation, ready long before she finished packing their picnic lunch.

A light mist fell as Peter backed the car out and they headed down the hill. What the radio termed "early morning coastal clouds" enveloped the Coast Highway too. But as they entered the southbound freeway, the sun broke through. "You are my sunshine," she began singing, and first Tim, then Peter, with his well-trained baritone, joined in. She felt her spirits lift, the same feeling she'd had as a kid when she and her family set off for the circus, zoo, aquarium, or natural history museum. How good it was to be doing something as a family.

Family. From the corner of her eye she caught a glimpse of the empty portion of the backseat. No, she would not think about that. She segued to "Row, row, row your boat," and Peter quickly turned it into a round.

Grateful when Peter took a turn at song-leading, she relaxed and remembered his solo work in college, and then the night he'd serenaded her in her sorority house. She smiled as they traveled south and inland, where the sun had already parched the spring green of the hills to a monochrome of tan.

As Peter turned off the freeway, she saw the sign announcing the wild animal preserve: "No trespassing. Violators will be eaten."

"No way!" Tim exclaimed. "I don't wanna be lunch for a lion! We're safe inside our car, right? I hope those big cats come real close."

Peter reached for his wallet as they pulled up to the preserve entrance. "They might do just that. So remember to keep your window up."

Peter paid for their tickets and raised his window as they began their tour.

"An ostrich and another and a whole bunch," Tim laughed. "Hey, their knees bend the wrong way."

As they drove slowly over the barren plains, Tim exclaimed over the zebras, and Andrea used the park brochure to identify antelope, wildebeests, and water buck.

"Radical!" Tim declared. "Better than a zoo. Here, *we're* in a cage." He glanced around the inside of the car. "And the animals come to us."

As they drove through a gate into the forest area, they immediately sighted the lions. Andrea wasn't sure who was having the better time, Tim or Peter.

"Look at them!" Peter pointed. "Over there, Andrea. Get a picture."

"They're everywhere," Tim exulted.

She focused on two lions waging a tug of war over a stick. Nearby, a young male washed himself.

"Same technique as a little kitty we all know," Peter pointed out.

"Juliet!" Tim agreed.

All during the ninety-minute drive through the wildlife preserve, Andrea tried to concentrate on the animals and on Tim's and Peter's enjoyment. But she continually fought the reflex reaction to point out the high spots to Joy. *Will I ever stop missing her so much?* she wondered.

"That was g-r-r-eat!" Tim growled like Tony the Tiger as they emerged from their safari and parked by the display and entertainment area.

"Let's stick together in this crowd," Peter said. Andrea walked toward the schedule of animal shows. "Look! We're just in time to see the domestic animals." She led the way into the arena, where they found places on the wooden bleachers just as the dogs began to perform. All sizes and breeds rode bicycles, and did tumbling, balancing acts, and clown routines.

Peter leaned toward her. "See how smart dogs are?" he needled.

She smiled. Peter loved to hassle her about the relative intelligence of dogs and cats. When a trainer played ball with two Siamese cats, he persisted, "You see, cats' brains are smaller than dogs'."

"Juliet can retrieve," defended Tim. He stopped as a cat with the coloring and markings of orange marmalade began walking two parallel tightropes.

"Uh-huh," scoffed Peter. "It takes two tightropes. One for the two right feet and one for the two left."

"Yeah, but he's *doin'* it," Tim said softly. "Bet Juliet could too."

"She's got the big feet for it, all right," Peter said.

Tim's eyes brightened. "She walks that iron railing. I bet I could train her."

The performance ended with a cat-in-the-hat trick and the Langs left laughing. "Not bad for a bunch of cats," Peter allowed.

After lunch in the picnic area, Tim urged, "Let's go to the reptile house. OK?"

The park was growing more crowded, and they had to elbow their way.

Inside, Tim stopped by a colorful striped king snake. "I saw one of those in the hills. I sure would like to catch him. And a gopher snake too."

"Fine, but I want you to take a real close look at the Western rattler," Peter said. "You could mix him up with the gopher. See, the rattler has that flat, spade-shaped head. So if you ever go to catch a snake, make sure you see the head before you grab."

Tim looked carefully. He sure didn't want to tangle with a rattler. And Brant said they were all over the Malibu hills. He left the reptile house reluctantly. Snakes were so cool! He'd like to have a dozen. But there were still monkeys to see and another domestic animal show in a few minutes. Maybe if he watched the trainers carefully, he could get Juliet to do tricks too.

Now his parents wanted to go into the desert garden. He groaned. "Just for a minute," his mother promised. He knew how long "a minute" could last. He dragged his feet through the gravel, lagging behind.

"Those!" his mother pointed at a plant with tinges of red on the leaves. "That was what I was thinking of putting in the planter outside Joy's room."

There it was again, he thought. Joy, this. Joy, that. His Mom still talked like she'd be back any minute. Heck, she'd been gone since just after Christmas. Sometimes it was hard to remember what it was like when she was with them. Sometimes he was glad not to have her bugging him. He sighed. But sometimes, yes, he missed her, dreamed about her, and woke up crying.

Now his mom and dad had stopped and it seemed they were never going to get out of there. He looked at his watch. After one-thirty. The show had already started. "Mom?" he began. She was pointing at another plant and didn't seem to hear. "Mom!" he repeated.

"In a minute, Tim."

He tried to be patient. After what seemed at least an hour, he tried again. "Dad?"

"Yes, Tim," Peter said without turning to him.

"Dad, could I just go and watch the cat show again? I could meet you afterward by the Safari Store."

"Yes." Peter nodded, still looking toward Andrea.

Was his dad talking to him? Tim hesitated. His mom wasn't looking at his dad. So his dad must have meant his "yes" for him.

He hurried out to the arena and squeezed into a seat near the stage.

⨝

Andrea pointed to one of the plants. "This one looks like a man-eater, doesn't it, Tim?" She turned to where he'd been just a minute ago. He wasn't there. Her throat tightened and for a moment she couldn't breathe. But surely he was just behind that palm tree. No. He wasn't. She grabbed Peter's hand. "Where's Tim?" she cried.

He glanced around the garden, and she saw the color drain from his face. "Tim!" he bellowed. "Timothy Lang!"

Heads turned toward them. Curious faces stared.

"He was—just here—a minute ago." She inhaled sharply between words. "He can't—have gone far."

"I told him. I told him!" He shook his head.

She tried to think, to stay calm. "Maybe he's gone on to the monkeys."

"Or maybe back to the snakes," Peter suggested. "I'll go look. You stay here, in case he comes back."

She couldn't stand still. Pacing the length of the garden, back and forth, she watched, waited, emotions seesawing from expectation to despair.

At last Peter returned, shaking his head, muttering, "That kid! I told him!"

"Did you look in the children's area?" Her voice sounded harsh, demanding. "Let's go look there."

"I still think one of us should stay here."

"All right. You go," she snapped, resuming her pacing, fiercely planting each foot in the gravel. Each time she reached the end of the garden, she prayed she'd turn and see Tim's blue plaid shirt, his unruly brown hair. Each time she failed to find him, inwardly she cried out, "Oh, please! Please!"

She saw Peter reenter the garden, alone. "Not a trace?" Fear closed in around her, black and blinding, and she began to shake uncontrollably. He was gone forever. Snatched away from her! First Joy, now Tim.

Peter enclosed her in his arms. "He's just wandered off." His tone was steady, reassuring.

Words poured out in a shrill voice that couldn't be hers. "You don't understand, Peter. You don't understand! He's been taken! Taken just like Joy. Whoever took Joy has been watching and waiting and planning. Followed us here. Waited for their chance. Now we've lost our son too."

Pain, beginning in her chest, radiated through her body with such intensity that she broke away from his arms. "Both children. Gone! Both children."

She felt herself falling.

She came to, lying on a slatted wooden surface. Someone held a cool cloth to her forehead. She looked up and gradually two forms came into focus: Peter and a man in a beige brimmed hat and shirt emblazoned with the wild animal preserve logo.

"Mrs. Lang," the man said, "we're putting out an announcement on the PA for your son. I'm sure we'll find him directly. Can I get you anything?"

She struggled to sit up, suddenly aware of a ring of curious faces around her.

"It's all right," Peter's voice was gentle. "Just rest a minute."

Leaning against him, she tried to explain. "It's like a repeat performance."

"It's all right," he repeated.

"But do you know what I mean? It's like that terrible, endless drive out the Coast Highway that afternoon I heard Joy was missing. But it's worse. I know now it can go on and on, without any answers. And to have both—" She began at last to cry.

"Your attention, please!" The voice over the loudspeaker boomed and crackled. "Would Timothy Lang please come to the preserve office by the flagpole? Tim Lang, please come to the preserve office by the flagpole."

By the flagpole. She had to be there. "Peter—"

"OK. Can you make it?"

"Have to."

As he walked her slowly across the grounds, she saw the crowd brush and bump against her but felt nothing.

Peter pointed to a bench by the flagpole. "Let's sit here in the shade."

She watched and watched, willing her son to materialize in the crowd. Now and then she saw a plaid shirt and sprang to her feet, only to sit again in despair. There was strangely little comfort in Peter's presence. Her son was all that mattered.

A crowd oozed out from the arena. "Show must be over," Peter said.

She climbed up on the bench, watching, hoping. Peter stood up beside her, steadying her. The stream of people exiting the arena thinned. She leaned against Peter.

"There he is!" Peter cried. "Here, Tim!" As the boy headed toward them, Peter stepped down and turned away, face flushed with anger, jaws clenched.

She rushed toward her son, gathering him into her arms, weeping. She felt him stiffen, embarrassed at her display.

"Aw, Mom! Didn't you hear me say I was goin' to see the cats again?"

"Honey, no, I didn't. I was so worried."

"I asked Dad. Honest. I thought he heard me."

"No," Peter growled, coming toward them, "I did not hear you."

Tim's voice grew defensive. "So is that my fault?" His gaze wavered under Peter's glare.

"When you ask a question," Peter said, emphasizing each word, "it is your responsibility to be sure you have the other person's attention." He turned and began walking. "All right, the party's over. Let's go to the car now."

"Aw, Dad! Can't we even go to the gift shop?"

Peter grabbed his son's hand, pulling him toward the exit. "You, young man, have blown it."

In the car, Andrea licked her parched lips, too emotionally drained to reach for the lipsaver in her purse. She looked back at Tim, slumped in his seat, staring out the window and reached back to pat his knee. Despite her own torment, she felt sorry for him. He'd committed a mistake in judgment, not an act of defiance. She glanced at Peter, grim-faced as he concentrated on driving the busy freeway. Once before, years earlier, when Tim had been an hour late getting home from school, she'd seen Peter's fear and concern channeled into anger. Men react by getting mad, she realized, and women cry, then welcome back the prodigal son. Leaning back against the headrest she closed her eyes. So much for her fantasy of family togetherness. How long had it been from the time they missed Tim till he reappeared? Not more than twenty minutes. Yet for her it stretched into an eternity. The uncertainty, the not knowing. That was the terrible part, a distillation of all these weeks and months she had not known about Joy.

She felt her camera on the seat beside her and remembered the time she'd shot thirty-six pictures, painstakingly setting the exposures, focusing, composing each one. Then, when she tried to rewind the film, nothing happened. She'd forgotten to load the film in the camera. What if all her efforts to find Joy were as futile as taking pictures without film? What if her daughter was dead?

She remembered Connie's telling about *her* son's death and saying, "At least it's over, and I know where he is."

Her eyes snapped open. It would be better to know. She saw that now. Far better than the wondering, far better than all the what-ifs that continually ran through her mind like some macabre musical round that never ended.

She thought back to Sybil and her astonishing eyes. It was more than the color, she realized. There was a depth, a discerning in her gaze. Maybe . . .

Why not? she murmured to herself. *Why not?*

23

From Zoë's Prayer Journal

April 30: Dear Lord, I feel sometimes as though Andrea is beating her fists against Your chest. How I pray that somehow You'll take her to Connie's Bible study, and that she may see and experience how, when people truly love You, love spreads out to one another with such depth and sweetness! Oh, Father, as I pray, I see my critical spirit regarding Andrea. I ask You to forgive me, and help me focus on the basic and awesome truth: You are God and Your ways are best. Oh, my Abba, I thank You for this time in Your presence and praise You in Jesus' name, amen.

"CHECKMATE!" Tim proclaimed.

Andrea stared at the chessboard, shaking her head. "You're getting too smart for your dear old—" She stopped as they heard Peter's car in the garage.

"Dad's home early!" Tim exclaimed, running to meet Peter as he came through the door.

Peter bent to hug him. "Hi. Want to toss a ball?"

BEVERLY BUSH

"Sure!"

"Let me change my clothes." Peter started down the hall, loosening his tie.

Andrea came out of the family room to kiss him. "Hi! You have a good day?" she asked, following him back into the bedroom.

"Yeah, one of those days where everything clicked." He smiled at her. "Probably because I met with the prayer group at church first."

"Oh, *right!*" She heard her own skepticism.

He turned to stare at her as he pulled his striped necktie from beneath his collar. "I wasn't being flippant. That's a good group of men. I felt focused—that's the word—when I left. And strengthened. It wasn't just that they prayed for us, though that was great. But there are a lot of other people with problems. It was good to have a chance to pray for them."

"You'll keep going then?"

"You bet." He clasped her arm. "I wish you'd find a group of women to support you. Whatever happened to that Bible study of Connie's?"

She glanced away. "I didn't make it last week."

Well, how about this week? Tomorrow, isn't it?"

"I guess."

She couldn't avoid his earnest gaze as he urged, "Try it, hon, please."

Resenting the pressure, she stiffened. "I'll see how I feel tomorrow," she hedged, pulling away from him. "I'd better check on what's in the oven." She shook her head as she started for the kitchen. *What is this?* she thought. *Some kind of conspiracy? Connie. Now Peter. But I did say I'd go this week, didn't I?"*

In the kitchen, she peered into the oven at the chicken and turned up the heat. "Maybe if I go once, it'll shut them up," she grumbled. She picked up the phone and called Connie. "About tomorrow's Bible study. I'll come."

"Hey! Super!" came the cheery response. "Pick you up at nine-thirty."

※

The next morning, as she stepped outside to wait for Connie, Andrea glanced across the road to see Dolores, a slash of violet in her long robe as she watered her geraniums. Andrea waved, thinking once again of her neighbor's channeler friend, Sybil. *Why am I wasting my time when I could be calling Sybil? When I get back*, she decided, *I'll do it.*

A crackle of brush near the road diverted her attention, and she watched a red-tailed hawk rise into a cloudless sky. Quickly gaining altitude, it soared in a broad loop, then stopped in midair. Wings outspread but motionless, the bird hung as though suspended from an invisible wire. Andrea caught her breath, marveling at the updraft that held the hawk so secure, so still. Suddenly, the bird plummeted like a fighter jet, landed in the sagebrush, and swiftly rose again, carrying a small rodent in its mouth. She shivered. The living and the dead. How quick the transition is.

Watching the hawk wing away, she scarcely heard Connie's car enter the driveway. She turned, surprised to see the white Ford Tempo with the red and blue racing stripes. "You've got new wheels!"

"Yeah," Connie grinned. "I had the stripes put on so it wouldn't look so much like a Girl Scout oxford."

Andrea laughed, slipping into the car.

"I'm so glad you're coming," Connie beamed, waiting for her to pull the door shut.

Casual in a blue denim skirt and turquoise-and-white checked camp shirt, Connie glanced approvingly at Andrea's white slacks and pink cotton sweater. "Pretty. Wish I looked as good in pants as you do."

As they drove down the hill Andrea looked down at the Bible on her lap. It looked so pristine, compared with Connie's oversized, well-worn brown volume, reinforced at the binding with duct tape. "That looks well-used," she remarked.

"It is. It's a parallel Bible with four different versions, side by side. I love it. Sometimes one little word, translated different, gives you a whole new slant on a passage. I've made notes in this Bible and underlined so much, I can't stand to replace it." Connie swung the car onto the Coast Highway. "Look," she said quietly, "I don't want to poke my nose in where it doesn't belong, but one reason I'm so glad you're coming is that last time we were together, I know you weren't feeling real good about the Lord. Seems to me you said you'd felt secure with Him before—?"

"Before Joy disappeared?" Andrea finished the sentence and thought a moment. "It's hard to remember. I just sort of drifted away. I think I told you, Peter and I both accepted the Lord on a retreat just before we were married." She thought back to the evening service, outdoors on the shores of a Wisconsin lake, where the sky turned navy blue and stars blinked on just before darkness fell. When the young pastor had issued the invitation to "accept Jesus Christ as your Lord and Savior," without a word to each other, she and Peter had risen together, compelled by a single sense of rightness. "It was a trains-whistles-and-bells experience," she explained. "United in our love for Christ. United in our love for each other." She turned to Connie. "Sometimes I wonder if it was real."

"What happened after that?"

"After we married, we got active in our local church. Went to a couple's Bible study. When Tim was born, we stood before the church and dedicated him to the Lord. Then Peter had a job offer in California, and houses were so much more expensive. I started working. We did go to church, but we never got really involved. Joy was born, and I was even busier. My career took off, and sometimes I'd have work to do on Sundays. Gradually, we lost touch." She thought a moment. "But to be honest, it seemed like I was doing OK."

"You didn't seem to need God," Connie suggested.

"Could be. Never had a situation I couldn't fix."

"Until—" Connie interjected.

"Right. Until Joy." She turned defensively toward Connie. "But I *did* turn to God when Joy vanished. I believed He'd answer me." She sighed. "Now I don't think He's listening or even cares. This probably sounds stupid and simplistic to you, but frankly, when He gives Joy back to me, then I'll know He's good and just and caring." She stared out the window. "I might as well be honest. The reason I haven't come with you before is that I'm not sure I want to have anything to do with God."

"Oh, but Andrea, He does care." A rich tone of assurance filled Connie's voice. "I know He does. Seems to me the problem is that it's hard for us to feel close to anyone we don't know real well. I couldn't depend on a person 'til I know what they're like, down deep. That's why I've bugged you about this study. It's all about knowing God by looking at His different Old Testament names. When we started three weeks ago, we learned that in Old Testament times a person's name described his character. So when we learn about the names of God, we're learning about God's character, what He's really like."

A little later, Connie turned her car into the church parking lot. "Here we are. You'll like the women. All ages, sizes, and flavors. And you'll love our leader. Mary Lou's from Atlanta. She used to call it, 'Etlenna,' but she wants us to help her speak California-talk. She used to be a model, but now she basically gives her life to teaching."

Inside, several women had already settled on sofas and floor cushions. Others gathered around a table set with a coffee maker and Styrofoam cups.

"Uh-oh!" Connie exclaimed, pointing toward slabs of dark brown cake. "Millie made her famous gingerbread. It's real moist and molasses-y. Try some?"

Andrea reached for a cup. "Coffee's fine."

"And *that*, love, is why you wear slacks so well and I don't." Connie placed a slab of gingerbread on a paper napkin and nodded toward a couch. "Let's sit there."

As they crossed the room, Connie introduced her to several of the other women who welcomed her cordially. "We've been praying for you," declared a woman with close-cropped curly hair and a radiant complexion.

"Indeed we have!" echoed a matron whose Dioressence fragrance wafted toward them.

Nice, she thought. *But a lot of good it's done.* The door swung open and Connie intoned, "Heeeere's Mary Lou, y'all," as a willowy woman hurried in. Her short, sculpted auburn hair set off flawless skin and high cheekbones, and she wore a pale pumpkin-colored pantsuit, fashioned from soft, sheer wool and belted at the waist. Andrea could easily picture her as a high-fashion model.

"Hi, everybody!" she exclaimed. "I'd have been here sooner, but my cat caught a bird and I just hated that. Had to give that sweet li'l hummer a decent burial." She settled into an upholstered chair as latecomers found their places. "My, but you look good," she nodded, glancing around the group till she saw Andrea. "Ah, welcome! I'm Mary Lou."

Andrea introduced herself.

"Of course." Mary Lou waved. "Glad you're here!" Her direct gaze and picture-perfect smile radiated such warmth. They seemed to say, "You're the very person I was hoping would come."

After her opening prayer, Mary Lou looked up. "Now," she said, "we've studied two names of God in the past weeks. And they are?"

"Elohim, the Creator," a woman in a striped boat-neck shirt answered.

"And El Elyon, the most high, sovereign God," a tiny Hispanic woman said.

"Good," Mary Lou smiled. She looked at her outline. "Our new name today is El Roi, meaning—?"

"The God who sees," several women chorused.

"And how did this strike you? What was your reaction to this name?" she asked.

The woman with the short curly hair raised her hand. "I just loved that He's not just powerful and sovereign, like we learned the past two weeks, but that He's watching and caring and understanding. I really saw that in our lesson when He showed himself to Hagar."

Mary Lou opened her Bible. "Uh-huh. In Genesis 16. So what were Hagar's circumstances?"

"Basically tossed out on her ear," said a slender young woman with a ponytail.

"By?" Mary Lou prompted.

"Sarai," someone answered.

"Exactly. So Hagar found herself running. But what were God's instructions to her, and what did she learn?"

"Well," a soft voice hesitated, "he told her to go back and submit to Sarai. And Hagar learned that God knew about everything in her past, present, and her future. So pardon me, but I've got to ask, doesn't that mean that God, if He's sovereign, permitted what happened to Hagar?"

"I believe we can say it didn't take Him by surprise." Mary Lou's green eyes twinkled.

Wait a minute! Andrea fumed silently. *Then does this mean God wasn't surprised when Joy was taken? That He permitted it? What kind of a God is that?*

She heard Mary Lou continuing. "So if we saw God last week as omnipotent, what are we seeing this week? That He is omni—?"

"—present," Connie said. "Oh. And omniscient."

"Good," Mary Lou nodded. "He is omnipresent—everywhere—not limited by time or space. He can be with us right here and with Connie's brother in Indianapolis and my mother in At-lan-ta." She grinned. "See, I'm learnin' California-talk real well." The women laughed and Mary Lou continued, "But not only that, He *knows* everything that's going on. Hard for our finite minds to grasp. Did you see that in Proverbs 15:3? Let's look at that."

Andrea fumbled with her Bible and finally located the passage. "The eyes of the Lord are everywhere, keeping watch on the wicked and the good," she read. She frowned. *If that's true, God knows the wicked person who took Joy. Why, why, why is it taking so long for us to know?*

Mary Lou asked the group to look up some additional scriptures, but Andrea sat wrestling with the concept that God saw perfectly well what she and Peter and Tim and Joy were going through—that He even knew where Joy was—and wasn't doing anything. "That's not fair," she muttered to herself.

But as the discussion continued, she couldn't help but sense the assurance in most of the women, and especially in Mary Lou. She liked her honesty, her easy, nonjudgmental manner. Gentle, yet confident. And her face glowed as her enthusiasm mounted.

Now Mary Lou was concluding the lesson. "So tell me, in what circumstances is it helpful for us to know God as El Roi?"

"When we see evil prospering," a soft voice suggested.

"When Satan seems to be in control," Connie added.

"When we're separated from someone we love. Maybe don't even know where they are. We know God is watching over them," another woman said, giving Andrea a quick glance.

"Good, good." Mary Lou smiled. "So now the question is, has God revealed Himself to you as El Roi, the God who sees, who knows, who cares? Will you accept the peace that He gives when you're in a tough spot? Knowing He's watching and that it's His responsibility, in His timing not ours, to vindicate?"

Peace? What peace? Andrea thought, as Mary Lou began her closing prayer.

"Lord," the leader prayed, "for those who are having trouble getting to know You, not just in their heads, but also in their hearts, I pray You'll make Yourself real and true and tangible in a very personal way. And Father, when we're tempted to ask that unanswerable question, 'Why?' help us to look at Your character, to find refuge and hope in all that You are. We pray all this in Jesus' name, amen." She stood, flashing her perfect smile. "See ya'll next week. Wish I could do lunch, but I have a meeting with our senior pastor."

"We're going to a new place just down the highway called Monica's," Connie explained to Andrea as they rose from the couch. "I'll just get a head count." She crossed the room, calling to the woman with the ponytail. "Ellie, you coming?"

Andrea felt a hand on her arm. "This is such a painful time for you. I'm glad you came," Mary Lou said. "If you have any questions, or if you just want to talk, please give me a call. I'm here on Mondays, Wednesdays, and Fridays."

"Thanks," Andrea murmured, unwilling to meet Mary Lou's gaze. She was afraid the woman might ask her reaction to the lesson. And if Andrea was honest, she'd say, "Humbug!"

Connie returned. "All set. Just six of us going today. Monica's has done catering a long time but just opened for lunch." She picked up several Styrofoam coffee cups and stuffed them in the wastebasket on the way out the door.

A few moments later as they turned into the restaurant parking lot, Andrea saw that it was on the "wrong" side of Coast Highway: no ocean view. But inside, she noted the black-and-white tile floors, chrome trim, and neon signs. Sleek, clean, fun, she decided.

The other four women were already seated, looking over the menu. "I'm having the chocolate pavé and the curried chicken," Ellie announced, "in that order."

"Ellie!" one of the women chided.

"Why shouldn't I have what I like best first, when I'm hungriest?" Ellie demanded.

Andrea liked her logic. "Life is short; eat dessert first," she quoted.

"I knew we'd get along well," Ellie laughed.

Andrea studied the menu. Not exactly tuna casserole with potato-chip topping. Maybe Dolores had exaggerated about Connie's plebeian taste. Every dish here sounded fresh and appealing.

After they'd ordered, Ellie turned to Andrea. "Is there anything new about your daughter?"

Andrea shook her head. "Not really. Not for several weeks."

Ellie nodded, her eyes soft. "We'll pray for you."

Andrea began to relax as the conversation flowed. She'd feared they'd talk about nothing but the Bible. But they had the same problems with stubborn children and rebellious septic tanks as she did. They were also informed and aware. And they laughed a lot.

She felt conspicuous, however, as they held hands and prayed when lunch was served. But how could she object when Ellie petitioned so eloquently for Joy's safety and her family's peace?

The salads were excellent, and as the waitress gathered their dishes, Connie whispered, "Would you consider splitting that apple affair with the caramelized topping?"

Andrea leaned toward her. "With or without ice cream?"

Throwing up her hands, Connie surrendered. "With!"

As they savored the last of the dessert, the woman with the short curly hair said, "That was a great study today, wasn't it? It's so exciting to see that God doesn't miss a thing and that He cares."

Should she let it pass? No, Andrea decided. She took a deep breath. "Well, I'm sorry, ladies, but I don't see it. I look at my situation, and I think, is this the way He shows He's watching and caring? God has taken away a whole part of myself. I've fallen to my knees. I've wept, I've bargained, I've made promises. And," she swept her hand above the top of the table, "I don't see one shred of evidence that He cares at all."

She waited for shock waves or protests, but as she looked around the table, she saw only empathy in the women's faces. At last Ellie spoke softly. "I had three stillborn babies, and I thought I could bargain with God. I'm just starting to understand that, as Mary Lou said, He's God. He's in control. And when I think about it, how presumptuous of me to think I could ever do anything to manipulate a sovereign God."

Three stillborns! The pain of Ellie's situation gripped Andrea. To go through three full-term pregnancies and return home each time with empty arms to an empty nursery. "How did you cope?" she asked softly.

"Not very well, for a long time. God never did give us a birth-child. We finally adopted darling twins, a boy and a girl." She beamed, and the other women nodded. "We are so blessed!" she continued. "God knew they'd need us as much as we needed them. But before that, the scripture that really helped me was Jeremiah 29:11. '"For I know the plans I have for you,' says the Lord. 'They are plans for good and not for evil, to give you a future and a hope.'"

Seeing the confidence in Ellie's face, Andrea sighed. "You and Connie. I envy the trust you have."

"What you see," Connie said, "has grown a little bit at a time as we began to see the big picture and the balance of who God is."

Ellie smiled. "I did not get whammied and trust God in a split second. And there are times even now when some small corner of my mind whispers, 'What if it's all a crock?' But not often. And never for very long."

Connie smiled softly at Andrea. "It's OK to have doubts. Honest!"

A woman at the end of the table stood. "I hate to interrupt this, but I've got an appointment."

Connie glanced at her watch. "We need to get going too."

Ellie reached over to squeeze Andrea's hand. "Hang in there!"

She looked up at Ellie, feeling the kinship of loss. "Thanks," she murmured. "Thanks for being so open."

Later, as they drove down the Coast Highway, Andrea said, "Nice group."

"Yep. There's somethin' special that happens with women who love God. They really love each other. And almost everyone at that table has had a lot of tough stuff. Sarah, the one with the short, curly hair, didn't say much. But she was an alcoholic for twenty-two years and bulimic for eighteen."

"The one with the sweet face? Next to Ellie? No!"

Connie nodded. "She knows what the word 'deliverance' means."

Deliverance. That was what Andrea hungered for. An end to the pain. Looking out the window, she thought again of Sybil, the channeler. She blinked back tears. "Connie, I have to tell you, I'm just so tired of waiting."

"'Course you are."

"I mean, I'm at the point where I just have to know something. I've half-decided to go with Dolores to see a channeler."

Connie glanced at her. "Tell me I heard you wrong."

She closed her eyes, sorry she'd brought it up. "I shouldn't have mentioned it."

"Look, love," Connie said. "This isn't just some notion of my own. The Bible's pretty clear about messin' with the occult. Couldn't you just wait a—"

"Don't you see?" Andrea interrupted. "If I knew Joy was dead, I could get on with my life, like you did after Greg died."

Connie turned off the Coast Highway and started up the hill. "But how do you know you *will* know if you go see this person? How do you know she can give you truth?"

Tears seeped from Andrea's eyes. "Connie, I can't think what else to do. Besides, how do you know she doesn't have access to information? How do you know she couldn't even be a channel for God?"

Connie shook her head. "If she has access to any power, it definitely isn't God."

"So who then? A man in a red suit with a pitchfork? Oh, come on, Connie!"

"I mean the being who was cast out of heaven and is alive and well on planet earth. The liar, the deceiver, Satan."

"Oh, be serious!"

"I am." Connie slowed the car and looked at Andrea, her eyes pleading. "Please don't do this." She paused. "What does Peter say to this?"

Shrugging, Andrea turned away.

They sat in awkward stillness as Connie negotiated the last hairpin turn. When she pulled into Andrea's driveway, Andrea opened the car door. "Thanks for taking me."

Connie nodded. "We can do it again." She put her hand over Andrea's. "Please talk this over with Peter. Please try to hang on just a little longer. You can do it! I'll be prayin' the Lord'll help you to."

Andrea slipped out and closed the door, feeling a tight knot in her stomach? Was it fear? Apprehension? No, it was more like something she felt as a child. That sensation that rose whenever she plotted to do something forbidden by her mother, her take-control, run-the-show mother. She could see her mother with her mouth set in a firm, straight line, proclaiming, "No, no, no! We don't do that, Andrea!"

She started toward the house. Connie is not my mother, she told herself firmly.

24

From Zoë's Prayer Journal

May 1: Father, as I wait for our staff meeting, I thank You for this time to be with You. I know You see the distance between Andrea and Peter. I also know Your desire is that there be oneness in a marriage. I pray that You will renew their closeness, help them be honest and listen to one another. And Lord, I thank You for Peter's excitement about his men's prayer group. Now he says You've taken Andrea to Connie's Bible study this morning, and I pray she truly heard Your truth. Thank You for the work You're doing in their lives, in Jesus' name, amen.

AS CONNIE EASED her Ford Tempo out of the driveway, Andrea stood at her doorway and glanced across the road toward Dolores's house. Her two neighbors were as different as chamber music and country-western, she realized. So was one right, the other wrong? Maybe the truth wasn't black or white, but some shade of gray. She fit her key in the door lock. Surely Connie was too narrow. Intolerant, really. Well-meaning, of course, and kind. But so rigid. Especially about the channeling.

As she pushed the door open, she pictured Sybil with her white hair and jade green eyes. There was a certain presence about her that was hard to dismiss.

In her bedroom, she changed to blue chambray pants and a bright yellow blouse. She'd need to pick up Tim in half an hour, but there was time to call Dolores. She started to reach for the bedside phone, then hesitated, recalling Connie's question, "What does Peter say about this?" She knew he'd say, "Nonsense!" But he didn't understand the terrible need to know that gnawed at her like an internal parasite.

She grabbed the phone. A moment later she heard Dolores's throaty "Hello?"

"It's Andrea."

"Greetings, neighbor! How are you?"

"Hanging in here." She hesitated. "Dolores, I've been thinking about Sybil. I think I'd like to go to one of her—" She searched for the word.

"Gatherings? Good for you! There's one tomorrow. I'll pick you up at seven-thirty."

Tomorrow! Sooner than she'd expected. Andrea felt her palms grow damp. "Oh, uh, P.M., right?" What would she tell Peter? She hated not being honest, but she knew how he'd react. "I'll have to see what I can work out."

"If Peter won't be home and leaving Tim's a problem, I have a suggestion. A very nice high school girl tutors Brant in math on Thursdays, and the two of them could come over to your house when we need to leave. She's intelligent and very reliable."

Andrea hesitated. Might as well admit it. "I guess I'm, uh, a little scared of what might happen at Sybil's."

The voice came, warm as a well-played cello. "Of course you are! But consider this. You could just be an observer for starters, if that's more comfortable."

That's true, she thought. "I suppose."

"Then I'll let Sybil know we're coming?"

Warnings began to ricochet through her mind, but she pushed them away. "OK."

"Fine. See you at seven-thirty," Dolores said.

"Thanks," she murmured, slowly replacing the phone.

~

That night at dinner, Tim carried the conversation with a scene-by-scene description of a film they'd seen at school. Andrea tried to listen, but her thoughts drifted. How could she get away from home the following night?

It wasn't till they sipped coffee while Tim watched television, that Peter told Andrea, "I have to make a quick trip to Oakland tomorrow. I'll be back late tomorrow night."

"Quick is right."

"Flight gets in at ten-thirty."

Well, now, she thought, smiling to herself. *I'll be back from Sybil's before he's home from the airport. Brant and his tutor can stay with Tim, and Peter won't even have to know.*

Immediately, needles of guilt pricked her. She'd never gone sneaking around behind Peter's back. But she knew his unshakable engineer's logic. She'd heard him pooh-pooh Hollywood stars who wrote about past lives and channeling. And he might even remind her of that fortuneteller in the New York tearoom who made such outrageous predictions some years ago. He'd ask how Sybil could be any more reliable, and he'd tell her to wait on the Lord, be patient, that any moment there'd be a breakthrough.

Sure there would! The progress so far had been downright dazzling. Four months and they didn't know one tangible thing more than the day Joy disappeared, but she was supposed to be patient!

She glanced at Tim, wondering how he'd react—especially after her dissertation on the ouija board. But that was before the wild-animal park, when she'd thought Tim was gone forever. Before she'd become consumed by the desire to know whether Joy was alive—or dead.

꒳

Getting away the next evening was as simple as telling Tim that she was going to a meeting with Dolores. Brant came with his tutor and her six different earrings studding each ear. Tim asked no questions.

Andrea made another trip to the bathroom, her third since dinner. Nerves, she acknowledged. Grabbing her purse, she headed out to meet Dolores.

Fifteen minutes later, Dolores turned her Porsche off the Coast Highway toward the ocean.

"Oh," Andrea said, surprised. "I thought it would be way back in a dark canyon, or maybe carved into the mountainside."

"No, it's on the beach." Dolores slowed the car and nodded toward a stark white wall with a wooden gate. "And I think you'll be even more surprised when you see it." She pulled off to the side. "We'll park out on the road."

As Dolores set the parking brake, Andrea laid her hand lightly on Dolores's arm. "Before we go in, tell me a little about how Sybil conducts these, will you?"

She could sense Dolores's smile, even without looking at her. "Still feeling a shade nervous? I did, too, at first." She unfastened her seat belt and turned toward Andrea. "Channelers, as you know, communicate with the unseen in the spirit realm. Sometimes it is spirits that died long ago, like Nero or Caesar. Or maybe even extraterrestrial beings." Her eyes widened. "Sybil, however, specializes in the more recently departed. She channels her master, a beautiful old man who taught her so much. He died just a couple of years ago. It's wonderful!" Dolores lifted her hands and punctuated her words with wide gestures, the way Andrea had seen Europeans conversing. "He continues to teach through her. Now, some people channel just one particular spirit, but Sybil also channels people's relatives and loved ones. It's really quite incredible and takes a lot of courage to open herself to them. But then, she's very advanced, the way she taps into another state of consciousness." She lowered her voice to a confidential tone. "She told me once that it's not unusual for her to spend two or three hours a day out of her body. I suspect that's why she's sometimes able to channel several different spirits in a single night."

"Out of her body?" Andrea asked, visualizing a nebulous, white-haired form floating over Sybil's physical being.

"Yes! Apart from herself, able to see everything, including herself. Able to even travel to other places and see things there."

What in the world was she getting herself into? Andrea wondered. Maybe Peter was right. Suddenly it all seemed spooky, sinister. She should have asked more questions. Her mouth felt parched, and suddenly she wasn't at all ready for what she might learn. "Maybe I'll just wait out here."

Dolores's voice turned to velvet. "Oh, please come. You're here. Just relax and don't force anything; let it flow." She opened her car door.

Andrea hesitated. Then she took a deep breath and unlatched her door and stepped out.

Dolores turned the handle on the gate, pushed it in, and held it open for Andrea to see. An English garden bloomed on either side of a flagstone path. Against the wall, hollyhocks nodded in the breeze.

"Oh, yes!" she exclaimed. "Not at *all* what I expected. Hollyhocks! I made the blossoms into dolls when I was a little girl."

"I thought you'd be surprised," Dolores said.

She looked beyond the garden to the house and laughed. "Why, it's like a David Winter sculpture of a cottage. Even looks like a thatched roof." She stared at the steep-pitched roof, the multipaned, deep-set windows, the dark wood insets laid horizontally in the stucco—or was it masonry? "Storybook stuff," she said.

Dolores nodded. "Isn't it charming? And so unexpected, in Mal-i-bu." She accented each syllable.

Andrea followed Dolores up the path, past the privet hedge, roses in every imaginable shade, the fragrant herb garden. Dolores jingled the hand bell. The sturdy wooden door with its heavy metal bolt opened to reveal Sybil. With her white hair backlit by the house lights, she seemed surrounded by a shining nimbus.

She was dressed in darkness. Soft folds of deep gray crepe draped from shoulder to hemline, caught at the waist with a cord of matching braided silk. Jet earrings swung as she turned her head. She greeted Dolores, then turned to Andrea, her green eyes wide, penetrating.

"Yess," Sybil allowed the consonant to hiss, "I remember you." The channeler took her hand and, rather than shaking it, explored it with her fingertips before she finally released it. "I feel your stress. It's good you have come."

As they stepped through the door into the entry, Andrea saw a woman with an asymmetric short haircut holding a blue pottery bowl, half-full of bills and checks. Dolores pulled Andrea off to one side. "Forgot to tell you. There's a love gift."

"Oh? What's appropriate?"

"At least fifty."

Andrea gasped. "Fifty dollars? I don't have that much. And a check, well, Peter wouldn't understand."

"Don't worry," Dolores soothed. "You can catch up with me." She scribbled a check and added it to the pile.

"There's wine." Dolores pointed to the bar, a step down from the entryway. "Or whatever."

Andrea shook her head, still dazed by the amount of the "love gift." She thought back to Mary Lou and the Bible study. There'd been no collection, nothing said about an offering. Still, if Sybil could help . . .

She glanced around the house. Much too soft and snug for a channeler, she decided. She'd expected ultramodern. Directly ahead, at the far end of the room, a massive glass panel, divided into tiny cottagelike panes and flanked by two doors of similar glass, looked out on the ocean. A roughhewn wood staircase ascended from the hallway. To the right, a stone fireplace rose through the high ceiling. She stepped into the living room, observing its planked wood floors. Bulky overstuffed chairs and couches, covered with beige, rose, and pale-green chintz, rested on Oriental rugs in muted tones.

Turning to look for Dolores, she noted all the people flowing through the front door. A man in tennis shorts, with the sleeves of a cashmere sweater tied loosely over his shoulders, came in with a woman wearing a silky microfiber jogging suit. Others paraded in Rodeo Drive's latest. Designer jeans with blazers seemed to be de rigueur. She recognized a Lakers basketball player, her least favorite TV news anchor, and a rock star. She counted twenty-one people in all.

"Oh, there you are, darling." Dolores took her arm. "Let's find a place to sit."

They found two chairs near the fireplace, and Andrea glanced nervously at her watch. Eight o'clock. As though pre-programmed, a hush settled over the room and she saw Sybil standing before the fireplace.

"Shall we begin?" she asked, as guests hurried to claim seats in the living room, with the overflow perching on the stairway.

Sybil seated herself in a straight-backed wood chair just in front of the fireplace, pressing the palms of her hands together. For the first time, Andrea noticed the extraordinary length of the fingers that had explored her hands earlier. The only sound in the room came from outside—the rhythmic thunder of the surf, which was muted when someone closed the door. The channeler glanced around the room, the faintest smile curving her lips. "Light, love, and peace to you. Tonight, the master, Mehani, has told me he wants to speak to you. And then, Norman," she nodded to her left toward a pudgy-faced man, his dark hair slicked straight back, "has asked that I try to hear from his mother. And—and—" her eyes darted from face to face, "someone else wants to make contact tonight."

Andrea stopped breathing for a moment. *Does she mean me,* she wondered. *No. Not yet. I'm not ready.*

As Sybil closed her eyes, the lights in the room dimmed and she began, "Lord of the universe, we call upon your divine light. I give myself to you, your servant, your vessel, to be placed in the light of the holy spirit, to travel wherever you will take me." Head upturned, she opened her eyes, blinking, and intoned, "Ooooooommmmmmmmm."

Other voices joined Sybil's, and Andrea looked around to see several people holding out their arms, palms up. A nervous inclination to laugh struck her and she coughed to suppress it.

Now Sybil's chant modulated to "Ma-ha-roosh . . . al-ma-keesh . . . a-ma-may-oh." Abruptly she stopped, rising to her feet in superb slow-motion control.

The room seemed to grow colder.

"Little children!"

Andrea's skin prickled. Sybil's voice had dropped at least an octave.

"I come to tell you that you and you alone have the power to create your own reality," Sybil, or was it the master, intoned. "Indeed, nothing you need is outside of yourselves. Look within. The door opens inward." Slowly Sybil moved among the group. "You will be my disciple," she addressed a petite blond who nodded and smiled. "And you," she turned to a balding man with long strands of hair combed over the top of his head, "must learn to love yourself."

She continued in the lower voice, circulating throughout the room, addressing a dozen of the group, one at a time. Then, arm raised as in benediction, she concluded "So—be—it!"

Sybil sank to the floor by the fireplace, assuming the cross-legged lotus position, hands clasped. Long minutes of silence passed, broken only by the muffled surf sounds.

"That which is called Amanda Bennington," she chanted slowly. Again she began her hum. It seemed to Andrea to go on and on. She flicked lint off her pants and glanced at the rapt faces around her. *These people are really into this*, she thought. Sybil's voice diminished to the merest whisper. Rocking her body rhythmically, she shook her head like an animal ridding itself of a fly. Her head dropped forward. Silence. A soft growl and Sybil extended her chin, rose, and stretched. "Norman!" a new voice shrilled.

The man to Sybil's left cried out and scrambled to his feet, like an obedient child.

"Norman," she continued, "it's beautiful here! It's all bathed in a golden light and everyone's so happy. So happy. Oh, Norman!" Tears filled the voice and Sybil rushed to the man, embracing him, rocking him gently, though he towered a good six inches over her. "I know I wasn't a good mother," the voice continued through the tears. "I made so many mistakes, demanded so much of you. And then I wasn't there when you needed me. Norman, I know now that love is all that matters. And I love you."

Norman wept in terrible gulping sobs, allowing himself to rock in Sybil's embrace. "Oh, Mother," he managed at last. "You never told me. You went so fast. And I never told you. I love you too."

"Love your wife, Norman. Love your children. Open yourself to the divine light of love," the voice urged.

"Yes, yes," he promised.

Sybil released her embrace and freed herself from Norman, as he rocked forward and backward, eyes closed, tears cascading down his cheeks. "Yes, yes," he continued, his face radiant.

To her surprise, Andrea felt tears on her own cheeks. The release Norman had experienced seemed so genuine. Oh, if only, if only she could . . .

Sybil returned to the fireplace, where she collapsed to the floor, gasping, her arms twitching. Alarmed, Andrea glanced at Dolores, who gave a quick nod of assurance.

They waited. Was she finished? At last Sybil's voice came, so softly, Andrea had to lean forward to hear her. "There's someone else here."

The temperature of the room seemed to drop several more degrees. Andrea felt the hair rise on her arms. She couldn't bear it. "Is it a child?" she cried, half-rising from her chair. "Is it a little girl?"

Gently, Dolores pulled Andrea back into her chair. "She can't hear you. Just wait."

Sybil's face contorted with effort. "Be with me," she chanted. "Don't be afraid. Come to me. Come." She drew the last consonant out in a long hum. Time seemed to stop.

Hope, fear, expectation, and foreboding mingled in the tears that rolled down Andrea's face. Was it Joy's spirit? Oh, God, the tension was unbearable. *Please, please, break through,* she cried silently, staring at Sybil, waiting, waiting.

Sybil's eyes snapped open. She rose into a crouch and shook herself, like a dog coming out of the ocean. She blinked, as though wakening from a long dream, then smiled, her teeth gleaming in the low light. Norman helped her to her chair.

Whispers mingled. "Wonderful." "Amazing." "Like a current running through my entire body."

Then a male voice advised, "Sign her up, Sammy. She'll win you an Emmy."

Frustration of a magnitude light-years beyond any she'd ever known clenched at Andrea's stomach, her jaws. The buildup, the anticipation had been so intense. She'd felt on the brink of discovery, as though a dark veil was about to be lifted. And now—nothing. "I've got to talk to Sybil, find out what she saw," she muttered.

But the channeler was gone. Where? In desperation, she looked around the room, up the stairway.

Dolores shook her head. "That's it. When it's over, it's over."

No, she cried to herself. *She can't be finished, because I'm not.* She grabbed Dolores by her shoulders. "That's the trouble! Don't you see?" Her voice rose above the murmur in a wrenching wail of despair. "It isn't over."

25

PULL YOURSELF TOGETHER!" Dolores hissed, grasping Andrea's arm. Forcing her to her feet, she added, "We'll leave now," and propelled Andrea toward the door.

Sensing the eyes of the group upon her, Andrea heard the low buzz of conversation. *I've embarrassed Dolores*, she realized. Self-consciousness seeped through her frustration, and she felt her face flush.

Outside, the cool dampness of the evening air helped pull her back to reality, and she heard their heels click along the flagstone walk.

Andrea didn't know what to say as they slid into the Porsche and Dolores started the engine. Did she owe this woman an apology for becoming so involved, getting so upset?

But she hadn't expected to be so drawn in, to sense herself just on the edge of receiving something she desperately wanted.

It was like that hot day, years ago, when she entrusted her last quarter to her brother to buy an ice cream cone. She could almost taste the rich, cold, satiny chocolate as he walked toward her, waving the cone in the air, tantalizing her. Then, as she reached for it, he jerked his hand just out of her grasp, and the glistening scoop of ice cream catapulted onto the dusty ground. Tears of frustration stung her eyes then as they did now.

"Let's go get you a cup of herbal tea." Dolores's voice was softer now, almost gentle.

Afraid she'd cry, Andrea didn't trust herself to speak. They drove in silence until Dolores parked in front of a small cedar structure.

Andrea didn't want the tea, and she didn't want to talk, but there seemed to be no choice. She followed Dolores inside, where racks of vitamins and health foods flanked a few wooden tables and chairs and a profusion of vining plants.

Dolores stood at the counter. "Give me two cups of Celestial Dreams, please," she told the young man with shoulder-length hair. She turned to Andrea. "Anything else? Tofu cheesecake? Beet muffin?"

Andrea shook her head and waited while the clerk poured steaming water into ceramic teapots. She reached into her purse, but Dolores waved away the money. Too weary to protest, she zipped her bag shut and moved to a table in the corner, away from the only other customers, two young women who held hands across the table and spoke in a low murmur.

"Maybe this will help calm you." Dolores set down her mug and teapot. "You look like you need it."

"That is the understatement of the year!" Andrea gripped the handle of her teapot, trying not to raise her voice again. "Do you have any idea how frustrating that was for me? I couldn't help but feel Sybil was close to Joy."

"I know. But you see, Sybil can't control how far she goes. She just has to let it happen." Dolores tilted her head to the side. "But look here, at least you're letting yourself feel! You're opening yourself up to possibilities. That's excellent."

"Not when there aren't any answers."

"But let's think this through." Dolores's tone was all reason. "Maybe it was another spirit. Sybil might not have reached Joy for the simple reason that she is alive." She spread her perfectly manicured hand over Andrea's. "Don't be discouraged. This was your very first experience. And," she added, "you did say you just wanted to observe."

Alive! Yes, maybe that was the answer. But . . .

"To satisfy yourself," Dolores continued, "you may need to come again, or possibly to arrange for a private session, so Sybil can be more specific and you can learn about Joy."

Oh, sure, she thought. *More money.* "And how much does that cost?" she asked. "I thought fifty bucks was pretty steep for starters. Fifty times—how many? Twenty-one people? That's—" She felt too drained to calculate. "Whatever. Not too shabby for an hour's work."

Dolores leaned back, the corners of her mouth curving slightly. Was her smile patronizing? Or patient? Andrea sipped her tea, waiting.

At last the dark-haired woman said, "You might want to try something else. There are other avenues—when you're ready."

A part of Andrea said, *Don't close yourself off on the basis of one experience.* Another told her bluntly, *This is nuts. You're nuts. Forget it.* "I think," she murmured, "that I need a little time to process all this."

"Of course." Dolores's voice was understanding. "Take your time. What harm can there be in taking your time?"

What harm? What harm, indeed! Warning beeps of urgency

sounded once again, somewhere in her mind. Time mattered a lot if Joy was still alive. Her daughter's very life might depend upon finding her as soon as possible.

❦

Peter glanced at the clock in the car as he pulled out of the Los Angeles airport parking lot: five minutes till eight. The meeting in the Bay Area had come off with far less static than he'd expected, and he'd hurried to the Oakland airport just in time to catch an earlier flight home. Street traffic was light now and he'd be in Malibu by eight-thirty.

He found himself looking forward to a little time alone with Andrea. She'd been so tense, so preoccupied when he left. In fact, he realized, she'd been wound up tight as a spring-valve since the trip to the wild animal preserve, when Tim went off on his own.

When he walked into the house, he was surprised to find Brant and Tim trying to coax Juliet to walk across two ropes they'd stretched between chairs. A teenage girl watched. "Where's your mom?" he asked.

"At a meeting." Tim shook a plastic bowl of cat kibble at one end of the ropes to entice the calico.

"With my mom," Brant volunteered.

"Oh?" Andrea hadn't mentioned a meeting.

"This dumb cat!" Brant exclaimed as Juliet jumped down from the chair, ignoring the rope. "She doesn't get it! You're wasting your time, man."

"No, no," Tim insisted. "She can learn. She's smart. I know she can."

"Yeah, yeah," Brant scoffed. Grabbing Juliet impatiently, he tried to plant her in the middle of the ropes, suspending her by her flea collar, smiling as she struggled and hissed.

"Hey!" Tim snatched the cat from Brant and caught an open-clawed swat.

Peter turned to Tim. "Gotcha, huh? Break the skin?"

Brant laughed. "She's hopeless."

Watching Brant, Peter felt a surge of antagonism. *I don't like this kid,* he realized, surprised at the strength of his reaction. Brant's handling of the cat seemed more than boyish carelessness or even teasing—as though he was getting his kicks from hurting her. His smile, the hardness of his dark eyes . . .

Peter looked at the scratch on Tim's arm. "Better give it a good washing with antiseptic soap." He pushed his sleeve back to look at his watch. "Besides, it's time to get ready for bed."

"Yeah, I'd better be going," Brant allowed.

"Me too," the girl said.

"Need a ride? And what do I owe you?" Peter asked.

"I've got wheels," she said, "and Mrs. Cooper paid me already."

"Thanks for keeping Tim company," he said. "Need a flashlight to get home, Brant?"

"Naw. I can see in the dark." He gave a quick grin.

Peter let them out, locked the door, and headed down the hall to check on Tim. He stood in the doorway of the bathroom, watching his son wash his arm and brush his teeth. Tim grinned a toothpaste smile and burbled something unintelligible, then laughed, splattering toothpaste on the mirror.

"Beg your pardon?" Peter chuckled.

Tim rinsed his mouth. "What I said was, Juliet can too learn to walk the ropes."

"With a lot of training, a lot of patience, maybe she could. But not the way Brant handles her."

"He didn't mean to hurt her, Dad."

"I'm not so sure."

"No, really," Tim insisted. "He's cool. We're buds."

250

As Tim struggled out of his clothes and into his pajamas, Peter smiled at his son's lankiness. Every rib, every vertebra stood out, just as his own had at the same age. He could remember admiring and tagging along after a friend who was older, more physically developed and clearly smarter. Tim must look up to Brant in a similar way. Still, he didn't much care for Tim's choice of role models.

"Guess you get to tuck me in." Tim headed toward his bedroom.

"Lucky for me." Peter waited for his son to slip under the covers, then sat on the edge of the bed, realizing how long it had been since he'd gone to Tim's room at night. He couldn't remember why he stopped, why Tim began coming to him in the living room to tell him good-night instead, why Andrea began tucking Tim in. But now he remembered how good it used to be, and somehow he felt privileged to spend these closing moments of the day with his son.

A light impact at the foot of the bed announced the arrival of Juliet, who delicately stepped the length of Tim's body as he laughed. "She tickles." The cat touched his cheek with one oversized paw. "That's better, Juliet," he smiled, stroking her back. "No claws. Good girl."

Peter smiled. "How about a little prayer, pardner?"

"Sure." Tim closed his eyes. "God, thanks for all You do for us, and I just want to ask You again to take care of Joy and bring her back. Bless Mom and Dad and, maybe, do You think You could help Juliet learn to walk the ropes? That'd be way cool. Thanks, Lord, in Jesus' name, amen." He looked up at Peter. "Think it's OK to ask Him about Juliet?"

"Why not? He cares about all creatures, great and small." Peter leaned over and kissed the boy's forehead. "Love ya a bunch, Tim."

"Me too. Love you, I mean."

Tim reached up for a hug, and all the love Peter felt for him came in a throat-tightening rush. How blessed he was to have this son.

"Night, Dad."

He closed the door and headed down the hall. As he passed the front door, he heard footsteps outside and turned to open the door. Andrea stood there, key pointed toward him, staring at him.

"Peter!" she managed, pressing her hand against her chest. "You scared me! I thought you—"

"We finished quicker than I thought, and I caught an early plane."

"Oh." She brushed past him. "That's nice." She seemed unnerved by his presence.

"Tim's tucked away."

"Oh." She looked down the hall. "Well," she hesitated, "I want to hear about your day. I'll just put my purse in the bedroom."

In a moment she was back. "Want anything to eat?"

"No, thanks."

"Oh. Well, I need a glass of water."

He followed her into the kitchen and watched her pour water from a container in the refrigerator.

"So how was Oakland?" she asked.

"Damp, cool. But the natives were friendly. We got a lot done in a short time. Had to run to get the earlier plane, but it worked out." He looked down at her. "So tell me about your meeting. I didn't miss anything at school I was supposed to attend, did I?"

"No," she said. "It wasn't anything about school." She sat down at the table, running her fingers through her wavy blond hair. "I might as well tell you. I went with Dolores to a session with a channeler."

He sank into the chair opposite her, staring in disbelief. He tapped his ear. "For a minute, I thought I heard you say you went to a channeler."

"You heard correctly." Her voice sounded harsh, defensive, and he saw the firm set of her jaw.

He felt not so much shocked as sad. *She's much more upset, more vulnerable than I realized,* he thought. *I feel her drifting farther and farther away—away from me, away from God. And it seems there's nothing I can do. Oh, Lord,* he prayed silently, *help me to help her. Help me proceed with caution.*

"Want to tell me about it?" he asked.

"Well, you probably would have laughed. I mean, she chanted and writhed on the floor." Andrea flung out her arms, eyes closed, then changed to a falsetto tone. "And she spoke in different voices."

He nodded, waiting.

"I wanted to laugh at first too. But then—" She frowned and her eyes focused far beyond him. "I found myself terribly involved. And I just felt that she might be—" she swallowed and her voice caught, "in touch with Joy's spirit. But it didn't come through." She buried her face in her hands. "I was so frustrated!" She paused. "But then, Dolores pointed out that maybe Sybil couldn't reach Joy because she's alive. So I don't really know whether to feel glad or mad."

In his dismay, he didn't know how to respond. "I see."

She looked up abruptly, her eyes accusing. "Please don't say that. You don't really see at all! You don't have the sensitivity. You don't feel things. You won't allow yourself to. Everything has to be *logical* to you. You think it's all silly." When he didn't reply, she persisted, "Don't you?"

"Not silly," he said slowly. "More frightening." He reached across the table for her hand and felt it, unyielding beneath his. "That's a *feeling* response, by the way. Because I'm really disturbed about your being drawn into the occult. I think it's dangerous, and I don't believe there's truth there."

"Where is the truth?" She shook her head slowly, as though it weighed too much to move easily. "I don't know anymore."

"Andry," he pleaded. "I don't blame you for being weary and impatient. But look what easy prey it makes you for someone like this channeler. Don't you see how she's leading you on? Why, she's teasing you just like a girl who gives a man the big sexual come-on and then cops out. She'd love to have you dependent on her and paying her, again and again."

Andrea gave a slight nod. "Well, she isn't bashful about her charges."

"I thought not. How much?"

"Tonight? Fifty."

He whistled. "And how many people?"

"Twenty-one."

He calculated. "That's 1,050 buckaroos!"

"I know, I know!" She closed her blue eyes a moment. "Look, Peter, I'm really bummed, OK? The last thing I need to have rubbed in is that I'm a sucker."

"I'm not saying that. What I'm saying is, please, please, stick with the Bible. Go back to the Bible study at the church. Forget this fringe stuff." He knew immediately he'd said too much.

"Ease off, will you?" Her eyes shone with anger. "Isn't it enough that you insist on church on Sunday?"

He tried to level with her. "Honey, it's just that I feel I'm losing you."

"Losing me? No," she said, "more like driving me away."

The inner dialogue began the next Tuesday as Peter drove toward the church for his weekly meeting with his men's prayer group.

This is a family matter, private, he told himself. *Something you should be able to work out yourself. You can handle it. You know you can.*

No, his other voice disputed, You can't. It's beyond you. You can't get through to Andrea. There's a wall there. It's as though something else is taking control.

You tell them that and they'll think you're crazy, overreacting to the stress. Come on, now, man, this is private stuff. It's one thing to talk about Joy, ask prayer for her, because everyone knows about her disappearance. But you bring this up, and they'll think you're not a leader in your home. I mean, are you the spiritual head or not?

But I need to stop thinking of myself and be real, be honest. Have these guys ever been judgmental before?

No, he admitted. *Anything but. They've been sensitive and empathetic.*

He sighed. He needed their help and especially their prayers.

As the men gathered in the small classroom, several complicated prayer requests unfolded, and Peter had almost decided to let his own go. Then Connie's husband, Jeff, looked around the table of six, one eyebrow raised. "Is there something else?"

Peter took a breath. "Yes." He could feel his underarms tingle. "I want to ask for prayer for—" He looked around at each man at the table, steeling himself for any negative reaction. "For my wife." He looked down at his hands. "I feel her slipping away from me, away from God. I know this sounds ridiculous, but I feel there's something that's not of God gaining a hold on her."

"Ahhh," he heard Jeff exhale sharply. "That's exactly what my wife feels. Connie's real worried about Andrea."

He stared at Jeff, surprised. "She sees it, too, then?" he asked, with a mixture of relief over Connie's validation and alarm over the implications. "Well, I wish this week you guys would pray for her."

"No, no," insisted Walt, a retired Hollywood set designer. "We need to pray now."

The others murmured agreement.

Heads bowed, the men wrapped Peter in a circle of prayer. Voices came from his right, his left, across the table. "Lord, we know that You are in charge," one man began, "that You are far stronger than Satan. We ask You to protect Andrea from any powers of darkness, to free her from any hold they may have on her."

"Father, protect her from the enemy and his demons. Help her to see their lies and to know that You alone are the way, the truth, and the life. Enfold her in Your mercy, grace, and love. Turn her from darkness to light."

"God, please strengthen Andrea so she can withstand the temptation of what seems like a quick fix. Give her patience. And give Peter love and wisdom in supporting and protecting her. Help them both to learn to wait upon You, to trust You, to know that You see their pain and that in Your timing, You will bring answers. And Father, let this whole intense trial bring glory to You. We praise You for the good You will bring from it, just as You've promised. We thank You, Lord Jesus, for it's in Your name we pray, amen."

As he looked up, Peter saw the compassion in each face. He'd felt so vulnerable coming to them, yet they'd understood.

"Thanks, guys," he whispered. And in his heart, he added, "Oh, God, may these prayers not be too late!"

26

☙

From Zoë's Prayer Journal

May 6: Oh, Lord, I just read Isaiah 30, where You say, "In repentance and rest is your salvation, in quietness and trust is your strength, but you would have none of it. Is that our Andrea? I praise You that You go on to say, a couple of verses later, that You long to be gracious. And You also say, "Blessed are those who wait." Oh, Father, may she repent and rest in You. In a way I'm glad she went to the channeler. I pray that she sees now that there's no real truth there for her, and that she'll truly turn to You and wait for You. Please, woo her back to the Bible study. Draw her with Your cords of love and the love of the other women. Oh, Lord, You are good, and I praise You, in Jesus name, amen.

TIM KICKED AT THE DIRT by the side of the road and looked back at Brant's house, biting his lip. *This is the third time I've busted my buns to get my homework done and gone over,* he thought. *And every day I get the same story from Brant's mom.*

"Sorry, Brant's gone to a friend's house." Probably an older *guy.*

He felt a twinge of jealousy and something more: left out, disappointed. Like not getting chosen when the team captains picked players for a ball game.

What's happened, anyway? he wondered. *I thought he really liked me. I sure like being with him. He's funner than anybody in my class.*

Tim thought back to the magic tricks Brant had shown him, how he'd taught him how to catch lizards and snakes and even how to catch mice to feed the snakes. Brant had games they played where "forces" and "powers" fought against each other. And that rad music.

Tim walked slowly back to his house. His mom heard him and came into the hall. "Brant not home?"

"Yeah." Tim bit his lip. "Again."

"Honey," his mother placed her hand on his shoulder.

Here it comes again, he thought.

"Why don't you invite someone your age over? I'll be glad to go pick them up."

Why couldn't she understand he'd rather be with Brant?

Was she still paranoid about Brant's heavy metal music and ouija board? No, she hadn't even mentioned them lately. But he didn't want to worry her, what with Joy and all, so he didn't tell her *everything* he and Brant did anymore.

"Surely there's someone you'd enjoy," his mother persisted.

"Not really." He stared out the window at Brant's house. All the guys in his class seemed like major losers compared to Brant. Except for Paul, but he'd never come over. He lived right at the beach, with the movie stars and people who were rich, snobby, or both.

"Not really," he repeated.

"Honey," his mother stooped to look closely at him. "I know you like and admire Brant. But two years is a big age difference. Don't be surprised that he wants to be with older guys."

She said some other things, but he'd stopped listening.

"Guess I'll go up in the hills for a little bit," he said. "I know: Be careful."

"You've got it."

Just as Tim started out his driveway, he saw Brant coming up the road. What luck! The older boy was alone.

"Hey, Brant. How about we go snake hunting up in the hills? I saw a king snake there last weekend."

Brant shook his head. "Naw. I just came home to get something and I'm going back to my friends."

"Can I go too?" Tim blurted. He knew he was butting in, but he wanted so much to be friends—best friends—and he knew he was losing Brant.

Brant gave him the kind of smile adults use when kids say something dumb. "I don't think so," he said slowly. "See, it's a sort of club." He looked at his watch. "Gotta go."

Tim followed behind Brant. "How do you, I mean, what do you have to do to join the club?" He tried to sound calm and casual.

Brant stopped, turned, and stared at him. A glint of sunlight made his dark eyes flash. "That," he said with finality, "is a secret."

"Oh." Tim couldn't think of anything else to say.

It all sounded *so bad*, so cool!

Brant continued to gaze at him. "But I'll tell you this much." He paused, heightening the impact of what he was about to say. "It takes an act of special courage and boldness."

"So," he knew his voice sounded nervous and high, and he

struggled to lower it. "So does that mean anyone can join if they ... I mean, if I did an act of special courage and boldness?"

He watched Brant's mouth widen slowly into a smile, but it wasn't an expression of pleasure or happiness. It was like—Tim searched the corners of his memory—like the evil-looking guy he'd seen on a TV commercial for a movie his mom said he couldn't see.

Brant seemed to be thinking. "May-be." He accented the two syllables equally. "I could bring it up for a vote."

"Yeah!" Tim exclaimed as Brant turned and started down the road. "See ya!" he called, exhilarated by the possibility of belonging to a secret club with cool people like Brant. But as he headed across the road, fingers of fear grabbed at his excitement. What would he have to do? How brave would he have to be?

⁂

Wednesday morning again, Andrea thought as she poured the orange juice. *It's Bible study day, and I can almost feel the old squeeze play coming.*

Indeed, when Peter came to breakfast, his first words were, "This is Bible study day, isn't it?" He waited for her nod. "I wonder if I could ask you a favor. Yesterday I left my Cross pen on the table where we meet to pray. It's that room at the end of the hall opposite the sanctuary. Could you—"

She almost laughed aloud at his transparency. "*If* I go, I'll look for it," she answered in a tone that she hoped would close the subject. Soon, she knew, Connie would call, all eager-beaver, adding to the pressure. She stared across the road. Maybe she'd call Dolores instead.

But soon after Peter left, Dolores phoned. "Andrea, will you be home midafternoon? I'm expecting a delivery that needs to be signed for, and I'm leaving in an hour. I won't be back till four or so."

"Sure," she agreed. "Leave a note to bring it here." She hung up, empathizing with Tim's disappointment when Brant wasn't available. She shrugged and glanced out the window. The bed of iceplant needed weeding. And inside, a brimming laundry basket caught her eye. In comparison, the Bible study didn't sound so bad. In fact, she might as well have a little fun with it, beat Connie to the draw. She punched in the numbers and heard Connie's spontaneous, "I will bless the Lord at all times! Good morning!"

Oh, brother! That's almost enough to make me hang up, Andrea thought, but she plunged ahead. "Connie? Andrea."

"Oh," Connie laughed. "I was expecting someone else."

"I called to see if I can pick you up for Bible study."

"Can you!" Connie exclaimed. "I'd be tickled pink."

"Fine. I'll be by at nine-thirty."

As she replaced the phone, Andrea realized she hadn't prepared her lesson. Better give it a quick run-through before she dressed and left the house. She sat down in the rocker by the fireplace and looked out at the ocean. The sun shown through windblown clouds, its light moving like a spotlight on the rippled water. Oh, if only a spotlight would somehow shine on Joy!

She sighed and opened her book. El Shaddai. That was the name of God for this week. It meant, she learned, the all-sufficient one. *All*-sufficient? She shook her head. How, with her beloved daughter still missing, could she possibly call Him all-sufficient? She fingered her hair as she thumbed through the rest of the lesson. No way she could finish it. Her hair felt oily; better wash it.

She had to hurry to pick up Connie on time. With her well-used Bible in hand, Connie wore a yellow blouse that set off her freckled, sunny face. "Isn't this a gorgeous day?" she exulted. "Clouds are blowing away, and the ocean looks like someone spilled blue ink all over it. I looked out the window and said, 'Wow, Lord. You're the Creator, and You did a great job!' I don't even care that some of His creations—the deer—ate my geraniums last night."

Andrea couldn't help but smile at her neighbor's upbeat outlook. "So what have you been up to?" she asked Connie, as they continued down the hill.

Connie hesitated. "Yesterday was my son's birthday. He would've been ten."

"Oh," Andrea breathed, remembering the intensity of her own pain on Joy's birthday.

"I thought about digging a hole and crawling in. But I decided to thank the Lord for the years he gave us with Greg, and I spent the day at the Joy Center."

"Oh, Connie!" she exclaimed, marveling at this woman's ability to transform grief into positive action, feeling a stab of guilt at her own negative thoughts about her. "I appreciate that. I appreciate you so much!"

"Had a call from a woman in Iowa who thought she'd seen Joy. Would you believe there's a poster of Joy in Keokuk, Iowa? I passed the info along to the sheriff."

Andrea sighed. "You know something? I don't even get excited about these reports anymore."

Connie nodded. "I understand. But they'll check it out." She glanced at Andrea. "You never know. This could be for real." They were silent a moment before she continued. "So what about you?"

Might as well be honest, she decided. "True confession time? I did go to Sybil's. The channeler."

Connie didn't seem surprised. "And?"

"And it was frustrating. She seemed so close to, to something, but really told me nothing."

Connie nodded. "Uh-huh. I was talking with Carol Spencer yesterday. If she's at the study today, you might want to ask her about her . . . experience with Sybil."

A few moments later, at the church, Connie introduced Andrea to Carol as well as to a young Chinese woman who'd been out of town the previous week. All of the women she'd met before were there, and they all seemed to just love this new name of God.

The door flew open and Mary Lou glided in, her full print skirt flaring around her legs with each graceful step. Her eyes—surely they were blue last week—now reflected the turquoise of her jacket. Her ebullience permeated the room. "Was this a dynamite lesson?" she asked, as she arranged her Bible and lesson book on the table before her. "We're going to have a great time today." She glanced around the room. "Who'd like to open with prayer? Martha?"

The petite blond nodded, and they bowed their heads. "Oh, Father, thank you for this study, this revelation of Yourself. How wonderful to meet You as the all-sufficient one, the one who enables us to handle whatever circumstances we're in." She hesitated. "Oh, El Shaddai, I sense there's someone here who's hurting so much, who needs so badly to see that You are sufficient for her. I pray that You'll become very real to her today. And I ask Your blessing on Mary Lou, that all she says and teaches may be from You and glorify You. We pray all this in Jesus' name, amen."

"Thanks, Martha." Mary Lou turned and wrote on the board the words, EL SHADDAI. "So here is our new name for this week. Where in the Bible do we first find El Shaddai? To whom does He appear?"

"Genesis 17. To Abram," Connie answered.

"Right. And what was Abram's situation?"

Carol raised her hand. "He was ninety-nine years old. God had promised him offspring, but he was still waiting!"

"Right. Ninety-nine and no kids. Things were not lookin' good. And the Lord appeared and said, 'I am El Shaddai; walk before me and be blameless. And I will establish my covenant between Me and you, and I will multiply you exceedingly.'"

Andrea found her mind wandering as the group discussed how it was only when Abram completely surrendered himself to the Lord that he received the total outpouring of God's blessing. She found herself planning the week's menus and reminding herself to make a dental appointment for Tim.

Then, like a television commercial interjected at higher volume, she heard Mary Lou's voice, "God truly poured Himself out for us in the person of Jesus, who shed His lifeblood for us to give us everlasting life. Think of that, and think of what surrender to Him means the next time you take communion."

Andrea blinked and stared at the leader. She remembered John 3:16—that God so loved the world, He gave His only begotten Son. Could a God who loved the whole world stop loving her? Stop loving Joy? Was God, after all, still there, still watching, still caring? Her head ached. She didn't know. She just didn't know.

The class was ending now and most of the women hurried off to a Christian-life seminar. Only Carol was available for lunch.

"Three's good," Connie declared. "Let's get some deli sandwiches and take them to the beach."

Fifteen minutes later they found a spot on the sand, and Carol spread out a blanket she always kept in her car for "emergency picnics."

They ate in comfortable silence, with the warmth of the sun mitigating the cool of the breeze. Andrea watched the shorebirds run away from the breaking waves, then turn and chase the receding water. A pelican folded its wings and plunged from the sky into the water, ungainly but efficient. They could see the bulge of the fish in the bird's mouth when it surfaced.

Sipping her diet drink with a straw, Carol turned to Andrea. "I hear we have something in common."

"What's that?"

"Sybil."

"Oh, yes." Andrea's curiosity mingled with fear, a fear that Carol might try to take away her hope of gaining information about Joy from Sybil. "Connie mentioned you'd had an experience with her." Andrea squinted at the slender woman, as her glossy black hair tossed in the wind.

"Sure did. It's kind of involved, but my parents died in an auto crash when I was not quite two. I was put up for adoption, and so was my four-year-old sister. We went to different families. It was really a botched-up deal, but I didn't even know I had a sister for a long, long time. When I found out, I couldn't find any records about what had happened to her. I was obsessed with finding her, and one investigator came up with some information that indicated she was dead."

Carol took a long sip of her drink. "Well, I was really into that all-roads-lead-to-God stuff then, and I started to hear about how Sybil could channel people who'd died more recently. I was so desperate to have some family, I wanted to know my sister, alive or dead. So I went to Sybil."

"And," Andrea leaned toward her, "was she not quite able to reach your sister?"

"Oh, no. My sister spoke to me, told me she loved me, that she'd been adopted by a good family and lived happily in Eugene, Oregon, till her life, at least that life, ended in a boating accident."

So Sybil had actually given her information. *Maybe*, thought Andrea, *I should see her again*.

"But," continued Carol, "she'd be coming back, have another life to live, so I shouldn't grieve. Stuff like that. I was ecstatic. Sybil could have had me coming back for all eternity, hearing from my dear departed sister."

"And you were convinced it was your sister?"

"Absolutely. Just one trouble."

"What?"

"Not long after I saw Sybil, I got a call from a woman with a French accent who was adopted in 1960 and raised in Paris. She'd had better luck tracing her roots than I had."

"Your sister?"

"Bingo!"

Andrea shook her head. "Incredible." Well, if Sybil was a fraud, there had to be some other way, some other person who could help.

Carol brushed her hair back as it blew across her face. "I understand your desperation." She looked carefully at Andrea. "You didn't ask my advice, but—"

Andrea smiled. "Shoot."

"Go with God. He's solid. He won't let you down."

"That sounds lovely," Andrea said wistfully. "Just one problem: He already has."

27

⁊

From Zoë's Prayer Journal

*May 12: It's Sunday, Lord. Help Andrea
and Peter and Tim focus on You. Help me focus
on You. For right now I confess my fears for
Joy, and I lay them at Your feet. Oh, Father,
sometimes I can almost see You nodding know-
ingly over all You understand, while we fret and
flounder and sometimes even try to manipulate.
What audacity to even try! Eyes have not seen
what You will reveal. That's a promise, a certainty, and I thank You, in Jesus' Name, amen.*

ANDREA GROANED to herself as she entered the church with
Peter and saw the communion table. Baskets lined with white
linen lay stacked at one end, and at the other stood gleaming
brass trays of tiny cups, tiered one upon another, like multi-
storied circular buildings.

As they found seats on the aisle, she wondered, *What
should I do about communion? Sure can't say my life's in communion with God.*

The service began, and she could hear Peter's mellow baritone—certainly good enough to be in the choir—beside her.

"Amazing grace, how sweet the sound." How enthusiastic, how much a part of the service he sounded. *He's a participator, I'm a spectator.* She felt a touch of envy.

Later in the service Pastor Hastings began communion, quoting Luke, "'And He took the bread, and when He had given thanks He broke it and gave it to them, saying, 'This is My body, given for you. Do this in remembrance of me.'"

A group of men and women began circulating the baskets, row by row. Andrea noted Mary Lou in the aisle, chic as always in a beige suit, her scarf the shades of autumn leaves. As Mary Lou started the bread across the row in front of them, Andrea saw another basket coming toward her from the opposite direction. *I'll let it go by*, she thought.

Mary Lou moved back beside her, and for a moment Andrea felt her hand on her shoulder. A simple touch of greeting, of recognition? Or was it encouragement? She wasn't sure.

Beside her, Peter took a piece of matzah and turned toward her as he offered her the unleavened bread. She hesitated and saw him nod. *It's as though he's reading my mind*, she realized. *Well, if it means that much to him.* Raising her eyebrows in resignation, she selected a tiny bit of the matzah. As she sat holding it, waiting till everyone was served, she felt her throat tighten. *Stop being so emotional*, she chided herself.

"Take and eat in remembrance of Him," came the pastor's voice. She placed the crackerlike bread in her mouth, swallowed, and choked as a sharp edge caught in her throat.

"You all right?" Peter whispered, patting her back.

Coughing, she nodded. *Serves me right*, she thought.

A few moments later, the pastor quoted, "'In the same way, after the supper He took the cup, saying, "This is the cup of the new covenant in My blood, which is poured out for You."'"

Now the trays with the tiny glasses of grape juice moved

across row after row in the church. This time, Mary Lou presented the tray to Andrea. *I've come this far*, she reasoned. Hand shaking, she selected a glass and passed the tray to Peter.

She stared down at the cup, almost mesmerized by the shimmer of light reflecting from the ceiling fixture into the purple liquid. And then she saw the paler bubbles along the rim of the glass, like beads of blood.

She remembered Mary Lou's words at the Bible study. "God truly poured Himself out in the person of Jesus, who shed His blood to give us everlasting life."

Beads of blood, Christ's blood, Andrea thought, *poured out for me?* She shook her head, surprised and moved by the thought. It had been a long time since she'd considered the magnitude of Christ's sacrifice and applied it personally to herself.

Maybe God is all-sufficient for us, she thought. She felt one tear, then another slip from her eyes.

❧

Peter glanced at Andrea, surprised. He hadn't seen her weep in weeks. Maybe this was an answer to his prayers. Maybe she was opening herself to receive all God had for her. "Oh, please, Lord," he prayed silently.

Afterward, they met Tim outside his Sunday school, and as they drove home, Tim chattered about "this guy, Jonathan, in my group." But Andrea didn't say a word. *What was she thinking?* Peter wondered. He thought he saw a new peace in her face.

When they turned into the driveway, Juliet leaped from the planter beside the garage.

"Hey, girl! We'll have a little practice session on the ropes," Tim called out the car window.

"After you change your clothes." Andrea finally broke her silence.

"I know." Tim's tone was long-suffering.

As Peter turned the key in the door from the garage to the kitchen he heard the phone ringing. Tim brushed past as Peter hurried to the phone. "Yes?"

A husky male voice: "Is Mrs. Lang there?"

He held out the phone to Andrea, shrugging. "I don't recognize the voice. A man."

She took the phone. "Hello?" She listened, then gripped the edge of the counter, color seeping from her cheeks. With a trembling hand she pressed the com-line button that alerted the sheriff's station to monitor the call. "I'm sorry," she said to the caller, "I didn't quite—" She sagged against the counter and tilted the phone away from her ear. "Gone."

Peter put his hand on her arm. "Crank call?"

She tried to hang up the phone, missed the connection, tried again. "Worse. 'Mrs. Lang, I know where your daughter is, but you'll never find her, because you'll never recognize her, the way she looks now.'"

"A nut," he tried to reassure her.

Looking down, she twisted her engagement ring around her finger. He put his hand under her chin and lifted it so he could look into her face. All the peace he'd seen earlier had fled. Even her eyes seemed less blue. "Honey, don't let this rob us of the peace we found at church. Don't let it ruin a good day."

"Silly me!" she exclaimed. "How could I let a little thing like child abduction ruin a perfectly nice day?"

"Sorry," he said. "People can really be slime." He stood for a moment, not knowing what to do, then tried for a lighter tone. "How about I fix my famous gourmet pancakes for brunch?"

"You mean the secret recipe where you add water to the mix?" Tim asked from the doorway.

"Watch it!" Peter held up a threatening fist, winking. Then, pulling out the griddle, he set to work.

۳

As they finished brunch, Peter said to Tim, "Thought I'd attack the brush down below the house this afternoon. It'll be a fire hazard when it dries. Sure could use some help, buddy."

"Sure, I'll—" The doorbell chimes cut Tim short. "I'll get it."

"No, Tim!" Andrea's voice sounded harsh.

She's right, Peter thought. *It might have something to do with the phone call.* "Let me go." But when he walked past the glass panel by the entry, he saw Brant.

Opening the door, he said, "Hi, neighbor."

"Hi, Mr. Lang," Brant smiled. The kid, Peter noted, could be charming when he wanted to. "Tim here?"

"Sure. Come on in."

Brant followed him to the kitchen, where Tim's face lit up. "Brant! Yeah!"

"Wondered if you wanna go snake hunting. Warm sunny day oughta bring 'em out."

"Hey! Sure!" Tim exclaimed.

Peter cleared his throat and gave Tim his best haven't-you-forgotten-something stare.

"Oh, Dad," Tim turned pleading eyes toward him.

"Well, we could cut the brush starting at three," he offered. "That'll give you almost three hours."

"All right! Let's go." Tim knocked over his empty milk glass, set it upright, and glanced at his mother. "I know, be careful.

Never grab a snake until you know what kind it is. I promise. Oh! I'll need a pillowcase, or a laundry bag or something to put them in."

"Second shelf, linen closet," Andrea said softly.

As the boys headed down the hall, Peter smiled. "Can't say Tim's not an optimist."

"Gets it from his father, no doubt," she said. She looked out at the ocean. "Although sometimes I'm not sure if you're all that optimistic, or if it's just that you're able to shut out things that hurt."

"A little of both, I guess," he admitted, watching her carefully. If only he could give her an injection of optimism, or at least something to look forward to, something to count on. A thought that had hovered in the back of his mind all week began to surface. *Do I dare bring it up today?* he wondered. *She's so darned touchy. But it makes sense. Maybe I should give it a try.*

"More coffee?" he asked.

"Sure. Thanks."

He poured from the carafe and watched her take a sip.

"You'd think I'd be used to it," she said at last, "but that phone call got to me."

"I know." He watched her a moment. Painfully, slowly, in recent days he'd been forced to stand back and face the truth: After more than four months, the chances of finding Joy were slim. All the authorities told him so. His own logic told him so. No, he wasn't giving up. He would continue his computer search, but he had to look honestly at the odds. And they weren't good. What Andrea needed most now was to get her focus on something long term, something that was sure, firm. What was the point to life unless there was a goal?

He took a quick breath and began, "I've been thinking, honey, that it would be great if you had a long-term goal."

"I do." She nodded.

No, he thought. *A goal is the reasonable expectation of a tangible yield.*

He tried to choose his words carefully. "I mean something tangible to look forward to."

"Such as?" Her words came as a challenge.

He reached across the table for her hand. "Andry," he said gently, "I've hated seeing you so unhappy all these months." He traced a vein on the back of her hand with his index finger. "I see all your life and brightness fading away, a little more each day. I can't help but think of the times in our marriage that you've been happiest."

She shook her head. "I give up. When?"

He was amazed that she could forget. "Why, when you were pregnant! Don't you remember how great you felt?" He stopped, astonished at her transformation.

Her face drew into a hardened mask, and she snatched back her hand as though she'd been stung. "Another baby? Is that it? I can't believe it!" Her chair scraped against the floor as she pushed it back and stood, staring down at him, eyes wide with anger. "You scum! How could you even think that anything, anyone, could replace Joy! You're so cold, it makes me shiver. Do you have any heart at all?"

"Honey," he protested, "I'm not suggesting that Joy can be replaced. Of course not. There's only one Joy, and I love her as much as you do."

She started to speak, but he held up his hand. "Hear me out," he said gently. "When I was praying the other day, I thought about how we've always agreed we wanted three kids. With my new job, I figure we can afford it. I just thought if you had something to look forward to, to think about, something sure—"

273

"Oh!" she exclaimed. "Is that it? God told you this was the answer for poor little Andrea? A new product? Well, He was wrong!" She shoved her chair against the table with a thud. "Wrong again!" She gripped the edge of the chair till her fingernails turned pink, then white. "You just don't understand, do you? You don't understand at all."

He stared at her, feeling the ache in his jaw. He hadn't meant to upset her. Maybe his timing wasn't so hot, maybe this came too soon. But wasn't it time for life to go on? His idea seemed so practical. It would give continuity to the family. "Andrea," he began, "I think—"

"You think!" she shouted. "You *think*. That's the trouble, Peter. You think, but you don't feel. Won't feel." She was silent, then added, "Maybe you can't feel." She sighed. "It's hard to believe that two people can be in a crisis together and be light-years apart!"

It's true, he thought, as she left the room. The distance between them was huge. But wouldn't the anticipation of a baby, having a common goal, draw them close once again? He gazed at the doorway long after she disappeared.

෴

Andrea shook her head as she started down the hall. Walking toward the bedroom, she wondered, *What's happening to our marriage? Peter used to be my rock, my steadfast one. Always before our personality differences complemented one another. I'd have a creative idea, and he'd see how to implement it.*

She remembered his logical, straight thinking that helped her reenter the job market, his creative financial planning for saving, investing in their house. Now the very things she'd admired about him were turning hateful. It reminded her of how much she'd loved peanut butter all her life. Then, when she was pregnant, even the smell made her sick. Pregnant. There it was again. How could Peter even *think* of another baby? To become pregnant would seem a betrayal of Joy.

She sat down at her desk and turned on the computer. Had she really changed so much? She had to admit Peter was right about how happy she'd been during her pregnancies, so filled with promise. There was a giddiness, a euphoria, a blossoming. Was it really almost five years since she'd become pregnant with Joy? What a bright time that was, with Tim joining in their anticipation, listening to the fetal heartbeat, putting his hand on her tummy to feel the baby move. How clearly she remembered her first glimpse of Joy, so perfect, so beautiful, even as a newborn. Peter was right. She was happy then.

But, she told herself firmly, she had no right to that sort of happiness today. Not until they found Joy.

She took a deep breath as she stared at the computer screen. She needed to finish a news release, but she was too distraught to concentrate. She opened a file folder. A slip of paper fell out. "Hope is a better companion than fear!" it read. And it was signed, "Eric."

Dear Eric! How compassionate he was. Not at all what you'd expect from a man who'd seen so much human pain. You'd think he'd grow hardened or apathetic, or simply lose interest as new cases came in. But no, he continued to care. In fact, he was the only male she knew who seemed to understand her anguish, to feel with her. For a moment she allowed herself to wonder what it would be like to be married to this tough-gentle man who was so in touch with feelings, always knew the right thing to say.

This is ridiculous, she told herself and turned back to her computer. But she found herself staring out the window at a

California quail strutting across the yard, then filing her fingernails, then rearranging objects on her desk. Maybe, when Tim came back and went out to work with Peter, she'd drive down for a run on the beach.

She looked at the clock. Perhaps it wasn't a good idea to let Tim go out with Brant. Yes, she understood how boys love snakes. It wasn't the snakes so much that worried her, she realized. There was something about Brant.

⌇

As the boys left the house together, Tim couldn't believe his luck. Brant must still want to be friends. Maybe he'd even tell Tim what he had to do to join his club.

Brant led the way up a deer trail behind the house, winding through the holly bushes and lilacs. "Something smells kinda like turkey dressing," he said. "Sage, I think it is. If we head up this way we'll come to a flat, cleared spot. Snakes might come out to sun themselves there, but keep your eyes open as we go."

Tim heard rustling and crackling noises on all sides. He saw lizards, birds, and rabbits, but no snakes. They reached the clearing.

"Bummer! Nothin'," Brant said impatiently. "Let's move on." They'd just started on up the hill when Brant held up his hand and stopped. "Over beside that rock." He pointed to the right. "See the head? Looks like a gopher snake."

"Yeah, but there's nothing to grab hold of. He's mostly under the rock. I'll toss something and see if that'll bring him out." Tim picked up a small stone and lobbed it toward the rock. As it hit, the snake disappeared.

"You fool! You messed up!" Brant shouted angrily. "What kind of a snake hunter are you, anyway?"

Tim's heart sank. "Maybe there are others around," he murmured.

"Yeah. *Sure.*" Brant's tone was sarcastic.

With sticks they prodded the brush beside the deer trail. Just as they were about to give up, Tim saw the motion in the grass just to his left. "Brant," he whispered. For a moment, the snake came into view, another gopher, but even bigger. Tim grabbed, clamping both hands around the smooth leathery skin. The snake hissed, and he almost let go. But he tightened his grip and shouted, "Brant, the bag! Right behind me."

"Hey, that's a big guy," Brant exclaimed, bringing the bag and opening it. "What d'ya think? Three feet?"

"Easy." Tim admired the wriggling, cream-colored reptile, with its dark-brown and black blotches, before stuffing it into the bag and pulling the drawstring tight. He slung it proudly over his shoulder. "I've got the feeling this is gonna be a good snake-hunting day."

A little later a buzzing sound came from dead ahead. "Rattler!" Brant warned.

Tim could feel the hair rise on his arms. He wanted to run the other direction. But that would be chicken.

"Just watch where you step," Brant cautioned. "They're more scared of us than we are of them."

The sound moved away, and Tim took a deep breath and followed a little farther behind Brant. He grabbed a long stick and used it to part the brush ahead of him, stepping with care.

Suddenly Brant lunged and grabbed, turning triumphantly to display a gaudily striped snake. "Red, black, white, black, red. Yup, it's a California king," he announced. "Ain't it a beaut?"

"Yeah," Tim said, running his hands over the handsome snake. "Man, you are lucky!"

By the time they headed down the hill, they had added a garter snake and a smaller gopher to their catch. They paused in the clearing to sit for a moment.

"What a great day!" Tim exclaimed. "You're really a good catcher."

"Yeah, but you got the first one. No, the second. You scared the first one away," Brant needled him.

Tim felt his face grow warm. "Yeah, well." He plucked a reed of grass and put it in his mouth. "Hey, Brant, I never did hear about joining your club. What about it?"

"Oh!" Brant snapped his fingers. "I forgot." He stared at Tim, chewing on his lower lip. He squinted against the sun and ran his fingers through his curly dark hair. "I tell you what," he said slowly, "Yep, I think this'll do it. Your deed of courage will be . . ."

Tim waited, feeling his heart thud in his chest. "Yeah?"

"To catch a rattler." Brant's braces sparkled in the sun as his mouth spread into a smile.

"Alive, you mean?"

Brant nodded.

Despite the heat of the sun, a chill gripped Tim's entire body. A rattler? How could he do it without getting bitten? What if he did get bitten? He could *die!*

"You brave enough to do that?" Brant asked.

"Uh. Guess I have to think about it," he hedged.

"Chick-en?"

"No. It's just that—" He cleared his throat. "I'm not sure how to do it. You don't go and grab a rattler."

"Nah, but it's not that hard. What you do is get yourself a real heavy kind of bag. Like, for instance, the kind salt for the water softener comes in, or sometimes fertilizer. Then you find yourself a nice rattler, and you just kinda use a stick to ease it into the bag. Now, some people use a noose on the end of a stick and try to get them just behind the head." He shrugged. "Whatever works for you." Brant stood. "Let's go."

Tim rose on legs like overcooked spaghetti. Catch a rattler! One mistake and he'd be dead!

28

ANDREA LET OUT A LONG SIGH of relief when Tim returned
from the hills and went out to help Peter cut brush. He was safe
and now she could get away. At this hour, she'd be able to find
a parking place near Malibu pier.

"Hey, guys, I'm going to run on the beach," she called a
moment later as she drove past them down the hillside.

Toward the bottom of the hill, a white Honda Civic headed
toward her, the sunlight reflecting back from its windshield.
She heard the honk and slowed as the car pulled beside hers.
Now she could make out Eric at the wheel. She'd never seen
him out of his "uniform" of dress shirt and necktie before or
in this car. In his short-sleeved turquoise golf shirt he somehow looked more—accessible—that was the word. With the
window rolled down, his muscular arm rested on the door,
blond hair glinting in the sun. Suddenly, she felt embarrassed,

like a schoolgirl in a surprise encounter with her latest heart-throb.

"Hey, lady. What's up?" He smiled easily, revealing perfectly even teeth and one gold filling.

"Restless, I guess. Thought I'd go to the beach for a run. Unless," She suddenly realized he might be heading for their house. "Unless you have something for us."

He shook his head. "Not really. Just got off duty and thought I'd drop off the latest 'Have you seen this child?' mailer with Joy's picture." He handed the postcard to her.

She looked at her daughter's smiling face, then back at Eric. "I hadn't seen this one. Thanks."

He hesitated. "I was headed for the gym, but running sounds better. Would you rather be alone?"

"No. I've had plenty of that lately."

"Good. If you follow me, I know a good place to park."

He backed his car into a driveway and turned down the hill, leading the way onto the Coast Highway and, after awhile, into the Malibu Colony area west of the pier.

I shouldn't be doing this, she told herself. But she followed obediently, pulling into the parking space he pointed out for her. A few moments later they were slipping between two houses, their feet sinking into the sand as they walked toward the ocean.

"My private route," he explained, and she heard herself laugh.

The sun danced off the ripples on the water. "Not much of a surf day," he noted, watching the foot-high waves break on the sand and foam toward them.

"You can't wear shoes on the beach," she said. "Got to feel the sand under your feet." Leaning to untie her sneakers, she slipped them off, standing on one foot, then the other.

She watched him tug off his Nikes and socks. He pulled off his tan pants to reveal white gym shorts and a pair of strong, lean legs that testified to frequent workouts.

"Ready!" he challenged.

She headed for the wet sand, setting a brisk walking pace for several minutes, then breaking into a jog. He ran easily beside her, at the water's edge, splashing her now and then as a wave washed up beneath them. Gradually, she ran faster, stretching her legs to lengthen her pace, her toes gripping the wet sand. How much better this was than running around her driveway! The deep breaths of salt air intoxicated her, made her feel strangely light. The faster she ran, the more exhilarated she felt. She wasn't sure how long or how far they ran, saying nothing, till they came to a chain-link fence barring their way.

They reversed direction, regaining momentum. "You run well," he said.

"I hope I'm not holding you back too much." She was tiring now but hated to slow down.

"I'm fine."

As they rounded a small point of land, her right foot slipped out from under her in a tangle of kelp, and she lurched against him. He broke her fall, but they both splashed into the surf, wet to their hips. As she leaned against him, they both began to laugh, gasping every now and then for breath, until he led her, still chuckling, back to the dry sand.

"Whew!" she sighed. "That was wonderful. I feel much, much better."

"Gets your endorphins going. Helps with depression." He looked down at her, concern in his deep amber eyes.

"How'd you guess?" She returned his gaze.

"Figures." He clasped her upper arm and the warmth of his

hand, a stark contrast to the cool breeze on her skin, seemed to penetrate to the very bone. "I was thinking last week when I had a root canal that you've been living a root canal for all these months."

She cringed. "Good analogy." Looking up at him, seeing the compassion in his expression, she felt something hard and cold and angry inside soften. How different Eric's countenance was from Peter's impassive mask. She searched his face, finally focusing on the curving fullness of his lips, a startling contrast to the angularity of his face. Compassionate and sensuous. He bent toward her and with a great effort of will she stopped him with the palm of her hand against his chin, feeling the invisible roughness.

He nodded, saying nothing, and they began walking back to their cars.

It was just as he helped her into her minivan that she saw Dolores drive past in her Porsche, waving, grinning, and signaling a thumbs-up.

⁓

That night Andrea waited to slip into bed, hoping Peter would be asleep, but he rolled over toward her, gathering her into his arms, his body warm, too warm, against hers. Usually she'd welcome this overture, respond almost instantly, wait for him to say, "Let's lock the door." Tonight she wanted none of it. He took a breath to speak, and she broke in, "Thanks for all your hard work clearing the brush." She forced a yawn. "Sleep well."

He released her without comment and kissed her lightly. "You too."

She turned away, knowing she'd disappointed him, but feeling distanced and, she realized, still angry.

Her thoughts quickly shifted to Eric. She lay quietly, replaying their encounter, relishing every sentence, each nuance of his voice, the warmth of his touch, the tenderness of his eyes. A melting longing swept over her, and she could almost feel the kiss that might have been. What would it be like, living with him?

She wondered if he'd contact her tomorrow. If not, it would be easy to find a reason to call him. She found herself fantasizing little scripts. She heard Eric tell her how courageous she was, as she smiled back bravely. She felt Eric cup her face in his hands as he asked softly, "You getting enough sleep, Andrea?" She drifted off to sleep imagining another run with him, sprinting away, soaring with no effort across billows of soft sand, far, far away from problems and crises and people who could think only of products and goals.

It seemed just a moment later that she heard the rustling of Tim's sleeping bag beside the bed. It had been weeks since a nightmare had driven him into their room.

"What's wrong, Tim?" she murmured. "Bad dream?"

"Gross. Can I just stay here a little while?"

"Sure. As long as you want." She reached down and patted his arm.

In a moment Tim heard his mother's even breathing and knew she'd gone right back to sleep. He wasn't at all sure he'd be able to sleep again, not after his dream of a rattlesnake as thick as his Dad's thigh, looming up over the edge of his bed with a deafening buzz of its rattles.

He wiped the sweat from his upper lip. How was he going to catch a rattlesnake? What if it went up his pants leg? What if he missed and it struck at him? What if he got bitten? He knew lots of people survived rattlesnake bites, but could he? He sure hoped he'd find a snake close to home. That way, he could get help fast if he needed it.

He pictured himself coming in with his hand swelling and his mom flipping out. Better go to Brant's mom instead.

No, now wait. He didn't have to get bitten. He could wear plenty of stuff. Like an armor. And he'd have to plan carefully. Maybe he'd find a snake in a nice open spot. Then he'd put that heavy, empty fertilizer bag in front of it. It would be stiff enough to stay open. Smooth the bottom down flat to the ground so the snake wouldn't crawl underneath. Then all he'd have to do would be to give the snake a nudge with a stick and it'd slide right into the bag. Piece of cake. He just had to be smarter than the snake, that's all.

But first he had to find the snake. It could be days. Where would he look? His dad said he'd seen one where he'd cleared brush near the house yesterday. Maybe it'd come back. He'd look there tomorrow.

It seemed like hours before he slept.

～

The next day was overcast by the time Tim got home from school. Not a good snake day, he knew, but he took a short hike, just in case. Nope. Not a snake to be seen.

As Tim started back home, he saw his grandmother's car heading up the hill. He ran behind it waving at her, until another car drew abreast of it. Zoë rolled down her window, and as Tim caught up with them, he heard the woman in the other car ask the way to Dolores's.

Zoë pointed to their neighbor's house.

"Do you think it's all right to park out on the road?" the other woman asked. "There will be others coming."

"Oh, I think so," Zoë said. "Have a nice time."

"Oh, we will!" the woman exclaimed. Then, in that gabby

285

way some women have, she added, "We're having a croning ceremony. Kind of a coming-to-maturity celebration for one of our group."

"Really!" Zoë said. She looked out and saw Tim. "Hey, Tim, my buddy!" She kissed her finger and reached out to plant it on his cheek. "Want a ride to your house?"

Tim glanced at the hundred yards to their driveway. "I think I can make it."

A moment later, as they met in the driveway, Zoë reached out to hug him. "Ah, my buddy! I love you yesterday and today and always!" She held out a sack. "Brought you some mint chocolate chip frozen yogurt."

"Hey, Gram! My favorite. I'll share."

"You better!" She swatted his rear as they headed toward the door. "Your mom here?"

"She went to the post office."

Zoë gave a conspiratorial chuckle. "Good. We won't have to share with her."

As they walked inside together, Tim asked, "Gram, what'd that lady mean? What's a croning ceremony?"

"She said it was a kind of celebration of someone becoming a mature woman."

"Yeah, but I heard the word crone used about a witch on a TV program."

Zoë nodded. "I know."

"Weird!" Tim said.

Zoë frowned. "I agree."

A minute later, as they sat down with their dishes of frozen yogurt, Zoë looked across the table at Tim. "Tell me what's new."

He hesitated. It was always safe talking to Gram. She never got grossed out, no matter what he said or asked. But how much did he dare say about his problem? Maybe she'd had something like this happen when she was a kid. "Gram," he began tentatively, "you've always said when you were my age you were kind of adventurous."

She smiled. "They called me a tom boy. I climbed trees, did crazy stuff on my bike. In those days, believe it or not, girls didn't wear jeans. But I had a friend with a brother, and her mother let me wear his jeans!" She laughed, and her blue eyes twinkled. "I was in heaven."

"Well, did you ever, uh, have anyone ask you to do something real scary?"

"Another kid, you mean."

"Uh-huh."

"Like a dare?"

"Well, yeah, kinda like that."

Zoë laughed. "Sure. Somebody dared me to fly off the roof of the house like Peter Pan."

"And did you?"

"Yep. Broke my ankle."

Tim winced. "Oh."

"Another time, I was older then, maybe twelve, a boy dared me to jump across this big ravine. Oh, it was wide. I practiced a lot on level ground, and then I took a big run and—"

"You made it?"

"Yes. But I don't think now it was a real smart thing to do. I was lucky. If I'd missed, I could have been badly hurt." Zoë looked carefully at Tim. "Somebody giving you the business about doing something scary?"

He looked away silently.

"That's OK. You don't have to tell me. You have good sense. But please, Tim, you are my special buddy. I want you around for many, many years. Just don't do anything foolish."

Anything foolish. Oh, wow, he thought, smoothing out the frozen yogurt with his spoon. *Maybe Gram's right. What do I care about that old club anyway?*

But later that day he saw Brant driving away from his house with his mom. There were a couple of other big guys in the car, laughing and punching each other. When Brant looked out and saw Tim, he grinned and made motions with his hand, like a snake's mouth opening and closing. Tim felt himself flush as all his earlier resolve melted away.

And he knew that deep down he cared. A lot.

29

๛

From Zoë's Prayer Journal

May 22: Heavenly Father, I have such a list of concerns today. I'm so glad You tell us to ask! First, that son of mine! Well intentioned, bless his heart. But Andrea just isn't ready for another baby. Oh, Father, bring them back together! And then, Lord, I want to pray for my buddy, Tim. My guess is this dare is from Brant. Please, give my grandson wisdom and caution. And keep him in the palm of Your hand. You know that none of us really feels comfortable about Brant. Would you bring Tim a friend who's fun and who also loves and honors You? Thank You for hearing my prayers, and for being my most high, sovereign God. In Jesus name I pray, amen.

I STILL DON'T HAVE A SNAKE *and Brant's going to think I'm not good enough, not brave enough,* Tim thought miserably. *I've gotten myself all dressed and gone out and there's been zero. Zip. Nothing. So what am I gonna do now? Sit inside and suck my thumb or try again?*

As soon as he finished his homework, his mother called, "Tim? I need to run to the supermarket. Want to come?"

"Nope. You go ahead." He tried to hide his elation.

She looked at him carefully. "You sure?"

He grinned. "You don't want me putting junk food in your basket, do you?"

"Not especially." She smiled back. "You stay right here, and I'll be back in forty minutes or so."

As soon as her car was out of sight, he dressed carefully, first wrapping his legs with some ace bandages he found in the medicine cabinet. Extra protection, he thought, as he pulled on two pairs of jeans and leather hiking boots. He tied them securely and headed for the garage to grab an empty fertilizer bag. Ah, yes, and his mom's leather gardening gloves.

Grabbing the stick he'd used on his last snake-hunting expedition, he started down the hill toward the area he and his dad had cleared the Sunday before. That gopher hole might be a good place. As he worked his way through mustard plants taller than he, a lizard with an iridescent blue marking skittered across his path. A monarch butterfly flitted overhead, its wings brilliant as stained glass against the sun. He stepped carefully, watching, listening. He waited and waited. Would he ever find that snake?

Looking out to the ocean he saw a freighter, far out, like a toy boat against the horizon. Flies buzzed as twenty minutes blipped past on his digital watch. He went through several dry runs, placing the bag by the hole, maneuvering with his stick. Nothing. He sat down with effort. It wasn't easy to bend, wearing two pairs of jeans. *Nothing's gonna happen*, he thought in despair. *And I can't go back to Brant's without a snake.*

Maybe he needed bait of some sort. A mouse in a cage, maybe. Could he get his mom to take him to the pet store tomorrow?

He put his head down on his knees and closed his eyes. Then, a rustling in the tall grass. His skin prickled as he slowly raised his head. With all the quiet and care he could muster, he rose to his feet. Good. He hadn't made a sound. What was it and where?

He scanned the grass and saw it move, over to his right. Probably a rabbit. But he picked up the sack and stick, taking cautious, precise steps to the edge of the clearing.

"All right!" he exulted silently as he saw the rattler's triangular head. He could hear his heart pounding in his ears. *Gotta do it*, he told himself. *Please, God.*

If he could just reach the stick into the brush and give the snake a little prod from behind. He poked in the brush and in a flash, the snake lashed out at his leg. He cried out. *I'm dead*, he thought. Then he realized the snake had penetrated only his jeans. Without thinking, swiftly, he reached and grabbed just behind the head, holding his arm up, so the snake dangled.

Oh, Lord, it was a big, fat daddy. Now what did he do? Where was the bag? He took a quick look over his shoulder, saw it and moved it with his foot. It fell shut. "Help!" he muttered as he stooped, holding the snake high, and picked up the bag. "Now, please, God, help me get him in the bag," he prayed. He held his breath, bit his lip, and dropped the snake in the bag with a resounding plop. Exhaling with a rush of relief, he folded the top of the sack down again and again.

He was dripping wet. Gripping the bag tight, he held it at arm's length and hurried as fast as his "armor" would allow. At Brant's house, he pressed the doorbell and waited. Oh no, no one was home.

At last he heard footsteps. The door swung open and Brant eyed him cooly.

"Got the rattler," Tim panted, thrusting the bag at Brant.

The boy took one step back. "No fooling? Let's take it out to the cage. Mom might not want it inside."

They walked around the house together, and Brant slid the top of the cage open. "OK," he said.

Tim hesitated. This could be tricky. He shook the bag to be sure the snake was in the bottom, then carefully unrolled the top and tilted the corner of the bag over the opening. The snake tumbled neatly into the cage, and Brant slid the top in place.

Brant's exclamation of surprise almost made all the danger worthwhile. "Hey, he's a beaut. Not all that long, but fat and juicy!"

"Yeah. Had to grab him with my hands."

Brant's dark eyes glittered in the sun as he looked at Tim. "No fooling. OK, I'll take it to the guys today."

"Will ya?" Tim grinned. "Thanks, Brant. Thanks." He headed for home, shivering as the cool breeze hit his sweat-drenched body, lightheaded with accomplishment. He'd done his deed of daring. Now they'd let him into the club.

~

As Andrea started up the hill on her way home from shopping, she pictured Eric in his car when they'd met on this very road. *Wonder what he's thinking about our run.* She smiled all the remaining way to her house.

Inside, she found Tim lying on the floor in the playroom, a contented Juliet sprawled on his chest. She wasn't sure who looked more blissful. "You look relaxed," she said.

A smile spread slowly across his face. "We are. In a minute, we're gonna do a little work on the tightrope. We'll start pretty soon, so we don't get *too* relaxed."

She watched them a moment. Whatever had bugged Tim these past nights certainly had fled in the sunlight. If only her own dreams would fade away that quickly. Especially the recurring one, where she heard Joy screaming and couldn't get to her.

Sighing, she put the groceries away and called to Tim, "I'm going to do a little weeding."

She grabbed a weed digger and bucket and had just begun on the bank overlooking the road when she heard Dolores cry, "News! Wonderful news!" Her neighbor teetered across the rutted road on sapphire linen pumps, a perfect match to her dress. In one hand she held a hastily opened envelope.

"Tell me."

"It's from my Marcy, my daughter."

Andrea reached out for her hand. "Oh, Dolores. I'm so glad. After how long?"

"Since Christmastime, when she didn't show at Mammoth. That's almost five months."

Andrea sat on one of the steps and pointed to another below her. "Sit, if you dare in those duds. She's OK then? What does she say?"

Dolores shook her head. "Actually, not a lot. But what a relief to know she's alive. I mean, you imagine all sorts of things." She caught herself and grimaced. "As if you didn't know."

"Where is she?"

"It's postmarked Raleigh, North Carolina. Would you believe? I have no idea why North Carolina. No roots there at all. Maybe that's why. But you don't know how relieved I am." She brushed off a step with her hand and sat down.

Andrea clasped her shoulder. "I'm so glad. Does it sound like she might really be getting her life together?"

A shrug. "Who knows. I just hope she'll keep in touch. I'd go see her. But there's no phone number or address. Obviously, she doesn't want to be contacted." Dolores gestured toward the weed digger. "Don't let me stop you."

Andrea reached over and uprooted a weed in the iceplant. "But this is a beginning. I bet you'll hear again." She glanced at Dolores. "You're looking awfully spiffy."

"Well, I did lunch. New place on Melrose. Terribly noisy, that seems to be the in thing. A 'live' room, they call it. But really innovative food—chilled avocado and lime soup, chicken breast with sun-dried tomato compote and polenta. And a dessert you don't want to hear about." Dolores puffed out her cheeks. "I do *not* need dinner."

Andrea pouted. "Here I am starving. You are not a nice person, Dolores."

"Well," Dolores raised both carefully penciled eyebrows. "You could come next time. But it was a wonder I could concentrate the rest of the afternoon."

"You needed to concentrate?"

"Definitely. Lunch was a break from a day-long seminar on visualization, controlled daydreaming, and dreams."

Andrea stabbed a weed. "I hate dreams. I'd give anything to get rid of that one I have again and again."

Dolores's eyes widened as she grabbed Andrea's arm. "Oh, but you can! You need to learn to think in nonlinear time. And you can guide your own dreams. Is this a recurrent nightmare?"

She nodded. "Yes, and it's always the same. I hear Joy screaming, and I can't get to her. There are variations on why I'm not able to get to her."

"But the feelings are always the same?"

"Absolutely. Fear. Frustration." She sighed. "It's the pits.

But I don't understand. Aren't dreams supposed to be the thoughts of your heart? How can you guide them?"

"It's because they do spring out of your innermost being that you can take charge of them. It's very exciting. And something else." She stopped and pointed as Andrea resumed digging. "Oh, I'd leave that."

Andrea looked up, puzzled. "This weed? Why?"

"It's a lupine, a wildflower with a lovely purple blossom. I mean, I don't know what your philosophy is, but sometimes I find it's better to dig up the flowers and leave the beautiful weeds."

She paused and considered. "Makes sense. So tell me more."

"Well, you can definitely determine the kinds of dreams you'll have. There are ways to stimulate the subconscious before you sleep: music, stories, guided meditations. And then, your dreams can give you affirmations! Oh, you'll have to come over and I'll show you some of the material I picked up, and you can listen to some of the tapes. Really, it opens the most fascinating new world. It's just amazing what our bodies and minds and spirits are capable of if we'll just open ourselves."

Like opening to Sybil? Andrea wondered.

Dolores seemed to sense her skepticism. "Not only that," she persisted, "but the divine can speak to you through your dreams."

Andrea frowned. She knew God had spoken to men of the Old Testament through their dreams. "You mean God?"

Pointing a crimson-nailed finger at her, Dolores smiled and cocked her head as she declared, "That's the trouble with you, Andrea. All that God stuff!" When Andrea started to protest, she continued, "Now hear me out. I'm your older, wiser neighbor, remember! I hate to see you so shackled by dogma. I'm sorry, but I get so impatient with all the Christian emphasis on sin and getting saved. To me, the only sin is being unbalanced and out of harmony with yourself and with the earth and its divine energy."

Dolores caught Andrea's raised eyebrow and persevered. "Surely you know the divine is in you and all around you. You just have to get in touch."

"Maybe," Andrea murmured.

"Don't put yourself in a box. You're much too smart for that." Dolores stood up. "Come over and we'll talk some more about dreams." Her eyes narrowed and she smiled wickedly. "You'll find that you could even program yourself to dream of a certain sheriff's detective."

She felt herself blush, and Dolores didn't miss it.

"Aha!" she cried. "You do have something going! Good." She thought a moment. "I got to know him pretty well when he was investigating a major robbery at a friend's where I was staying during my remodeling." She grinned. "I know! I'll invite him to that party I've asked you and Peter to on Friday, remember?"

30

THAT NIGHT, not even one nightmare about Joy troubled Andrea's sleep. In fact, the following morning she couldn't remember dreaming about anyone. Still, she knew that in some undefined way almost the entire night had focused on Eric. Somehow, his presence had pervaded her sleep, like music filling an empty room. And Eric's presence was so agreeable, she was reluctant to let it go.

Later, while pulling socks from the washer, she was startled to find herself fantasizing how it would be if Peter died a tragic death, and Eric was there for her, understanding perfectly because of the loss of his wife.

She wondered if Dolores was serious about inviting Eric to her party. Judging from the conspiratorial gleam in her eye, yes. But would Eric come? Perhaps he wouldn't feel comfortable with all Dolores's "beautiful people." And if he came, would he bring a date? She hoped not. *She* wanted to spend time with him.

Friday, the day of Dolores's party, Andrea pulled six different outfits from the closet, trying to decide what to wear. Dolores had said, "Casual," but casual in Malibu could mean anything from leather pants to a Valentino. She paired a lemon-yellow cotton sweater with turquoise linen-weave pants. No, too informal and not at all feminine. The sleeveless blue cotton-print dress? No, too cool for evening. She brought out a silken flame-red blouse she'd worn only once. She hadn't felt comfortable in the low vee of the neckline, and when she'd tried to pin it higher, the front didn't align properly. She slipped it on. The color was good, and men did love red. The cut wasn't all that low. She held it up to a pair of beige pants, cut full to drape prettily and emphasize her small waist. Rummaging through a drawer, she discovered a silk sash striped with red, beige, and turquoise. Perfect. That pulled it all together.

Ah, this would be a fine night. She was not going to even think about Joy, much less talk about her. She washed her hair, pleased with the golden highlights as she blew it dry. After she did her nails, she fixed dinner for Tim. With the video she'd rented, he'd be fine for the evening by himself, since she and Peter would be just across the road.

"Come sevenish," Dolores had said, and Andrea began to fret when Peter hadn't appeared at six-forty-five. Twenty minutes later she heard the garage door open. Waiting till he came into the house, she heard him call out a weary, "Hi."

"Hi!" she answered. "How you doing?"

"Bushed," he groaned, coming around the corner into the bedroom. "Accident on the freeway bottled traffic up but good. I'm ready to kick back and—" He caught sight of her. "Hey, you look great. Where have you been?"

"Peter! Didn't you remember? Tonight's Dolores's party."

He exhaled in an impatient puff. "I confess. I forgot." He sighed. "Just what I'd like most not to do."

She tried to contain her exasperation. "Well, then," she said evenly, "I can go for a while by myself." The minute she said it, she realized that by herself, without Peter, she could have time alone with Eric.

But he shook his head. "No. I'll go."

"You don't have to."

"No, I will." The martyr.

"Well, then, we're due now," she said.

"Yeah, yeah," he said irritably. He headed for the closet. "Casual, you said?"

"Right." Sitting on the edge of the bed, she rubbed cream into her cuticles with angry vigor.

She glanced up as he emerged from the closet, buttoning his shirt. Oh no, not that shirt, the polyester she'd tried to give away. It looked so corny. She started to protest, and he challenged her with raised eyebrows.

OK. Don't press it, she told herself. *I don't want us to be one of those couples who arrive at a party with sparks of contention flashing between them.*

After giving Tim last-minute instructions on bedtime and not answering the door, Andrea and Peter started across the road. Even before they reached the gate, she knew Dolores had gone all out. The sound of music filtered from the patio, and Japanese lanterns glowed all around the perimeter. Lighted candles floated in the pool, and flames flickered in the firepit. Pink-clothed tables with centerpieces of ginger blossoms rimmed an open area. *For dancing?* she wondered.

Dolores met them at the door wearing a pure white kimono embroidered with deep pink hibiscuses. Her black hair, sculpted smoothly into a chignon, contrasted dramatically with the single fresh hibiscus blossom tucked behind her ear. "Welcome, neighbors!" she exclaimed. "Come in." She gestured toward the bar. "Help yourself to a drink. Then I'll introduce you around."

While Peter went to the bar, Andrea rubbed her fingertips against her palms, glancing around the room. At least twenty people mingled, from a distinguished white-bearded gentleman in white jacket and tie to a well-endowed blond in a shimmering bodysuit. But no Eric.

When Peter brought her Perrier, they followed Dolores around the room, shaking hands with "beach people" and greeting down-the-hill neighbors, who, she noted, did not include Connie and her husband.

They met the author of seventeen spy thrillers and a retired astrophysicist. An eclectic group, just what she'd expected of their cosmopolitan hostess. Dolores led them to a corner where Sybil held court. The channeler gave Andrea a cool nod. Then, introduced to Peter, Sybil held his hand a long time.

"What was that about?" he whispered as they moved on.

"That's Sybil, the channeler."

He shuddered. "Gives me the creeps."

"Find yourselves a place to sit," Dolores urged. "Oh, and by the way, Andrea, those books and tapes I mentioned to you." She pointed toward a table. "Be sure to take them when you leave."

Andrea stopped to glance at the books, as Peter watched. Their titles included, *Dream Work, Spiritual Travels,* and *Earth Power Handbook.*"

"I'll get those later," she said. "Let's go out on the patio. It's a pretty evening."

They joined Patty and Bill Howard, whom Andrea knew

from PTA, at a table outside, and Andrea made sure she faced the entrance gate. A short time later, she saw Eric come through. He stood a moment by the firepit, the flickering light burnishing the angular planes of his face. Looking handsome and at ease in an off-white cotton shirt with a tab collar and vertical tucks down the front, he didn't see her as he made his way through the patio to the house.

A few couples began dancing, and Peter fell into a discussion of oil explorations with Bill Howard. She watched for Eric and, out of the corner of her eye, saw him approach. *Directed by Dolores?* she wondered.

"Ah, the Langs!" he exclaimed.

Peter looked up and introduced the detective to the Howards.

"There's an extra seat you could bring from that table over there if you like," Andrea suggested, feeling as tremulous as a lovesick teen. Chair legs scraped on the pavement as they moved to make room for him between Peter and Patty Howard.

"Isn't this great?" Eric asked, gesturing at the spectacle Dolores had created. "Class act, huh? Dolores even picked a gorgeous night." He looked overhead. "Clear. We should have a nice moon." He leaned back and watched the dancers for a moment. "Dancing, what a great idea." He looked across at Andrea and she smiled.

"Ah, Detective." Eric looked up and stood as Dolores approached the table. "Be a darling, will you, and move that gas heater?" She pointed across the patio. "It's in the way for dancing."

He followed her and picked up the pole-mounted heater, easily moving it in the direction Dolores pointed. Andrea could see the musculature beneath his shirt, and she realized Patty Howard was watching too.

"*Gracias*, darling." Dolores blew him a kiss and moved to acknowledge the guests just arriving.

Eric returned to the table and looked across at Andrea. She raised her voice over the music. "Is it true, Detective Jansen, that you're entering the LA marathon?"

The corners of his mouth twitched as he caught her reference to their run together. "Yes. And the Iron Man triathalon, if I can figure out how to get to Hawaii."

"Oooh," bubbled Patty Howard. She shook her head, with its Medusa-like tangle of hair. "No wonder you're in such fine shape, Detective."

"Wonder when we're going to eat," Peter grumbled, then turned to Bill Howard as the conversation segued to the Middle East. The music modulated to soft and dreamy.

Eric glanced at Andrea, eyes twinkling, and turned to Peter. "Peter, excuse me for interrupting, but may I have this dance with your wife?"

Peter looked up abruptly. "Sure," he said, turning back to the challenge of Howard, a pacifist.

"I hope I can still do this. It's been awhile," Eric said as he took her hand and led her to the dance floor. They turned toward each other and he smiled, his amber eyes crinkling at the corners. "You look great! Red. I like red."

She smiled back, pleased with her success, realizing it was for him, not Peter, she'd dressed.

He moved with ease, fluidity, communicating his intent so perfectly, she immediately felt a oneness with him. Relaxing, moving with him, she knew a contentment she hadn't experienced for a long time. At last she said, "You can."

"Can what?"

"Still do it. Very nicely indeed."

He drew her closer. "That's only because I have a good partner. *Muy simpatico*."

She nodded her head against his chin, wanting the music never to end. When it did, he held her, waiting. They danced another number and another. The flames from the firepit cast a flickering light on the dance floor, and she felt its heat against her legs each time they danced past.

"Do you know," he said, "that this is the first time I've danced since my wife died, a year and a half ago?"

"Oh," she breathed, giving his hand a compassionate squeeze.

"It feels very, very good."

"I'm so glad," she said.

～

Deep in his discussion with Bill Howard, Peter felt a hand on his shoulder and looked up to see Dolores. "We'll serve dinner in a minute. But would you be an angel and help me move that ice sculpture onto the table? The caterer's French and very temperamental."

"Sure," he said, following her across the patio, where the sculpture sat on the ground beside the table. "I think this will take two," he said.

"We two can do it. I work out," Dolores smiled. And together they positioned the sculpture on the table.

"A little further back. *Ah, bien. Merci!*" Dolores said.

Peter started back to the table, pausing to watch Andrea with the detective. Alone on the dance floor, they seemed oblivious to their solo performance. As they glided and spun and dipped, he caught a glimpse of her smiling face. *Great. She's enjoying herself*, he thought.

As he sat down at the table, he looked over to see Dolores scatter something on the firepit. A musty, spicy aroma began wafting toward him. *Incense?* he wondered. Dolores stood staring at the fire, and he realized with a start that the flames, reflecting back in her eyes, had turned them bright as an animal's at night. There was something almost predatory about her posture, the unwavering focus. He became so absorbed in her, he didn't realize at first that Andrea and Eric had returned to the table.

"You're back," he said. "You guys are good dancers."

Andrea blushed then blurted, "Are you hungry? The buffet's ready."

"At last!" he said.

He had to admit the food was worth waiting for. The ice sculpture, which he could now see depicted a woman resting against a crescent moon, glistened on the table, which was laden with salads, entrées, and an iced container overflowing with jumbo shrimp and crab legs.

Andrea picked up a tidbit in her fingers and tasted. "Mm, duck."

He could hear her continuing comments as he began spooning samplings of salad on his own plate. "What am I having here?" he asked the uniformed woman behind the table.

She smiled and pointed. "This is pasta and shredded vegetables with herbs. That's chicken and macadamia nuts with nasturtium blossoms. And this green salad has Greek olives and feta cheese."

"Thanks," he said, adding some shrimp and crab.

Later they returned to the buffet table to select from veal loin with shiitake mushroom sauce, baked salmon with sorrel sauce, and lobster ravioli.

Then there were the desserts: crème brûlée with fresh raspberries, flourless chocolate cake, and caramel-apple tart. He had to admit it was a sumptuous spread. And it gave him pleasure to watch Andrea as she sat enjoying it next to the detective.

New color brightened her cheeks, the old sparkle shone in her eyes. He was just leaning back, mellow with the good food, when Dolores came by.

"Get your coffee, or an after-dinner drink, everyone, and we'll gather in the center of the patio. Now that the moon's high, we'll turn out the lights and we'll just connect with the energy and center ourselves and stay alert for the messages."

"What does *that* mean?" he asked, instantly on the alert. But she was gone, moving among her guests.

"Oh," said Patty Howard. "She's really good at this. It opens you to the heaven within." She glanced at Peter and added, "Don't worry. It's harmless."

"I don't think so," he said to himself. Peter had felt uneasy just watching Dolores's obsession with the fire. Now he didn't at all like what he was hearing. Maybe she'd use that creepy Sybil. There was no way he'd have Andrea exposed to that, maybe get her all riled up again about finding out about Joy. He glanced at his wife, busy talking with Eric, and wondered if she'd heard.

The Howards stood and moved toward the center of the patio. Andrea looked up, her eyes questioning. "What's happening?"

"Some sort of seance with the moon, I gather," Peter said, rising and moving around to pull out her chair. He leaned over and whispered, "I'm not interested in this. Let's slip out before they get started."

She stared up at him. Surprise and anger robbed her face of all the joy he'd seen earlier. "No!"

Eric rose quickly. "I'll, uh, let you two talk and move along with the group."

"Please, honey. It's late. There's another couple going out the gate just now. Trust me. Let's leave."

She gave him a long stare, full of hostility, and just when he was sure she'd refuse, she stood and rushed past the pool and through the gate. He caught up with her as she stumbled across the road and took her arm. Shaking free, she turned on him. "You are the biggest killjoy I know. I was having fun for a change. But no, you just couldn't handle that! You didn't want to go in the first place, and all evening long I could practically see you trying to figure out how to get away as soon as you could. Fill up your belly and run. I hope you're proud of yourself!"

No sense trying to explain his desire to protect her till she cooled down. He went on ahead silently, unlocked the door, and let her in.

She hurried down the hall to Tim's room and, evidently satisfied that he was asleep, walked slowly into their bedroom and began to undress. "Maybe I'll watch TV for a while to unwind," she said.

"OK." He stood in front of the closet. "Look, Andry, I'm sorry I spoiled your fun. But I was worried that what was coming next would not be fun. Dolores gives me the willies. I think she's into some really ungodly stuff."

He stopped as she glared at him. "Well, then, I'm sorry I didn't stay! All I know is that," she glanced at her watch, "for more than three hours I didn't think about Joy. I laughed, I danced, and I had a good time. Then you drag me away so abruptly I couldn't even thank our hostess. Because poor little Andrea is such a bimbo that you have to censor out the ba-a-a-d things. Is that it? Or is it that you have to play *God* for me?"

31

From Zoë's Prayer Journal

May 18: Lord, how I thank You for Your presence in my life! Time spent with You is so sweet. How could I get through a single day without You? Father, I so long for Andrea to experience Your presence, too, to know the fullness of Your love and grace. For I love her as much as any child born to me. But yes, I know it's not for me to do, but for your Holy Spirit. Please Lord! In Jesus' name, amen.

THE MORNING AFTER Dolores's party, Peter found Andrea in the kitchen, preparing the batter for their Saturday waffles. She looked tired and depressed. He wished he could help her understand the sense of urgency he'd felt about leaving Dolores's last night.

"I need to run to the plant for a couple of hours this morning to check on a project," he said as she spooned the batter into the waffle iron. "Did you have anything in particular planned for today or tonight?"

She shook her head. "Not really. I thought you'd look forward to an evening at home."

He knew it was a little jab at his reluctance to go to Dolores's the previous night. "Would you rather go out for a bite?"

She shook her head. "That's all right."

"Look," he said, "I know I seemed like a killjoy last night. But that Dolores worries me. Did you see the titles of those books she wanted you to read? It's on the fringe. New Age stuff. And basically anti-Christ."

"Oh, Peter. Spare me the sermon!" she said wearily.

He knew he needed to tread carefully. Waiting till he had eye contact with her, he said, "Andry, one of the things I've always loved about you is that you're so interested in other people, so nonjudgmental. You are one of the most charitable people I've ever known."

"But?" she interjected.

He smiled, "Yes, 'but.' Please, keep your eyes and ears open around Dolores." He thought a moment. "Maybe it'd be a good idea to get her to define her terms. When she talks about the divine, does she mean the God of the Bible? Is it God a person, or God a force? And what does she say about Jesus? Is He her Lord and Savior, or just a prophet, or maybe a god but not *the* God?"

She didn't answer.

Better let it drop. The most important thing, he decided, was to show her he loved her.

All the way to work he considered how he might do that, how he could cheer her. By the time he'd finished at the plant and started back home, he'd decided, and he stopped by a Santa Monica mall.

༄

That afternoon, Tim interrupted Andrea three times as she worked at her computer.

"Honey, you're restless," she said at last. "Want to take a walk?"

"Not really."

"Oh, come on. We'll go down to Cliff Drive, and I'll race you back up the hill."

"I'll beat you," Tim warned.

"Pretty sure of yourself, aren't you?" She stood and headed for the closet. "Just let me get my running shoes."

A few minutes later, as they started down the hill, Tim pointed to two beer cans by the road. "Litterers!"

"You can dump them in the Coopers' trash can," Andrea said, pointing at the containers by Dolores's mailbox. "She must have a lot of stuff from the party."

Tim lifted the lid and started to drop in the cans but stopped and gasped. The head of a rattlesnake. He pushed open the plastic bag that lay just beneath it, quickly slammed the lid down and cried, "No, no, no! My snake! My big daddy rattler!"

Andrea hurried over to him. "Your what? What are you saying, Tim?" She grasped the handle of the lid.

Tears trickled down Tim's face, but he pulled her hand away. "Don't look, Mom. It's all hacked up." Suddenly, he was sick beside the trash containers.

Alarmed and baffled, Andrea put her arm around him and fished a tissue from her pocket. "Let's go back home."

She walked him up their driveway and into the house, feeling his thin body trembling. "Why don't you lie down?" He stretched out on his bed, and she brought him a cool, damp cloth for his head.

Andrea sat on the edge of the bed waiting. Tim's rattlesnake? Mercy!

At last, Tim lifted the cloth, looked briefly at her, and put it back over his eyes. "Guess I'd better explain."

"I'd really appreciate it."

Tim told her all about the club, the challenge. "And so I caught a rattler," he concluded.

"Tim!" she exclaimed, fear prickling her entire body. "You could have died!"

"Nah, see, I was major careful. Wore two pairs of jeans, hiking boots, garden gloves. Used a stick and a fertilizer bag." Better not tell her about picking the snake up, he decided.

"Oh, Tim. Honey, that was not smart. I—" She felt a physical pain in her heart. The idea of something happening to Tim was unthinkable, unbearable. "Oh, Tim, I couldn't stand it if something happened to you."

"It didn't though. But a whole lotta good it did for me to catch that big daddy. Now Brant's wasted it."

Watching him, she saw it all with a clarity that startled her. "Oh, Tim!" she cried. "You must feel so betrayed. And you wanted so to be friends with Brant because he made you forget about the rest of your life."

Tim looked up at her, brown eyes deep with thought. "Yeah. When I was with Brant I didn't think about Joy or wish I'd—" he waved one hand, "you know." He was silent a moment. "But now, I sure don't want him for my friend anymore, and I sure don't wanna join his club."

"Good."

They were quiet a moment till she asked, "Want something fizzy to drink?"

"Nah. But I'll just stay here awhile." He lifted his head. "Here, Juliet! Joo-lie!"

A meow from across the hall.

"Here, Julie!"

Another meow and Juliet leapt onto the bed. Tim reached for her and she settled on his stomach. "We'll just cool it here awhile," he said.

She studied him a moment. "OK. Call if you need me."

Guilt assaulted her as she headed toward the kitchen. She wasn't spending enough time with Tim. She was still too busy with news releases and media contacts. Too absorbed in finding Joy. She needed some answers so she could be a real mom to Tim.

In the kitchen, she stopped, hand on the refrigerator door. *It's not just that. Be honest*, she said to herself. *I'm absorbed in something—someone else: Eric.*

She stood motionless before the refrigerator, recreating the oneness she had felt with him during that heavenly interlude of dancing. She recalled Dolores's pointed comment as they returned to the table. "Isn't it lovely that touch-dancing is back?" Her neighbor's smile had been positively wicked.

Peter hadn't appeared suspicious. Or had he? He didn't even seem to notice at first when she and Eric came back to the table. And after that, he'd been intent on getting away from Dolores. Or maybe, it suddenly occurred to her, getting her away from Eric. *Face it: That's what I'm most angry about—having to leave Eric*, she realized.

She sighed and reached into the refrigerator.

Later, as she started to serve dinner, Peter said, "Where's Tim?"

"Says he isn't hungry, and I'm not surprised." She told Peter the story of the snake.

"Whew!" he whistled. "You know, there's something just not right in that house. I'll talk with Tim."

"I'd appreciate it."

He looked at her for a moment, then smiled. "It's just thee and me for dinner then?" Reaching into the cabinet he pulled down two goblets as she watched him, puzzled. Flipping a towel over his arm, he strode to the refrigerator and reached in the back to bring out a bottle of sparkling grape juice. "Allow me, Madam?" he said, as he came back to the table, released the cap, and poured for her.

He filled his own glass and held it out toward her. They touched glasses. "Salud!" he said.

She took a sip and played along. "A very good year."

"But of course."

All during dinner, she wondered why the attempt at celebration? His silence didn't give her a clue. So she asked how the project was going at work.

"Moving along well, thank God. Oh, and something new in the computer search. I wasn't entirely satisfied with the rundown the authorities did on that work gang from the county jail. Remember, you came up with how they were working just up the hill shortly after we moved in? So I ran some more checks, and it seems one of them got out of jail just before Joy disappeared. I'm working on that one." He crossed his fingers.

She felt a little lift of hope. "Good. Good, Peter."

He smiled across at her. "That was a terrific dinner."

"Just fried chicken."

"But excellent. Especially with the mashed potatoes. Shall I get the coffee?" He stood without waiting for an answer, brought the container, and poured.

She watched him, sensing something still to come. Finally as they sipped their coffee, he pulled a tiny blue velvet jeweler's box from his pocket. "I think this is for you."

The thought of a gift had never occurred to her. "But it's not my birthday or Christmas or Groundhog Day."

"That's true." He nodded wisely as he handed it to her. "Open!"

She flipped up the lid and saw, nestled among blue velvet, a dainty pendant: a heart shaped from gleaming gold, with a brilliant diamond nestled in its lowermost point. "Oh, Peter!" she exclaimed. "It's lovely! But why?"

"It's just to say that I love you, which I don't seem to tell you often enough or well enough." He came around the table and leaned down to kiss her and she felt his lips still warm from the coffee.

She was astonished and touched, and as he held her for a moment, ashamed of her impatience with him. Peter really did care. He was steady and true.

Guilt assailed her for the second time that day. Had Peter noticed her attraction to Eric? He had never been the sort to bring home flowers or candy, and she'd learned to warn him as her birthday approached, so he wouldn't forget. Well, whatever precipitated the gift, it showed there really was a core of sweetness and tenderness behind all his talk about thinking things through and setting goals. She had to be more understanding of how worried and preoccupied he was, and how hard it was for him to express his feelings.

She wore the heart to bed that night and dreamed once more of Eric.

"This has got to stop," she told herself firmly the next morning as she dressed for church.

32

AS ANDREA AND PETER settled into their seats at church, he reached for her hand, and again she felt a prick of shame. *Wonder how many other guilty consciences are here today*, she thought.

They stood for the first song, and she heard Peter's voice ring out, "We bring the sacrifice of praise into the house of the Lord." She had to admit he really got into the singing, as his head moved from side to side in time with the music. She glanced across the aisle and saw Connie singing, eyes closed, a smile dimpling her cheeks. *Will I always be a spectator?* she wondered.

She forced herself to concentrate on the words. "Sacrifice of praise," she thought. Yes, praise is a sacrifice when your only daughter is gone. Maybe if I sing it, I could feel it. She could barely hear her own soprano voice beside Peter's rich baritone.

But she went through all the songs, from "We Exalt Thee" to "All Hail King Jesus." It didn't seem to help. Nor did the sermon, "The Lord Is My Shepherd."

The familiar words of the twenty-third Psalm held no comfort for her. The only line she could truly identify with was, "Yea, though I walk through the valley of the shadow of death."

I'm in that valley, she thought. *Joy could be in that valley. I want to believe He's with her. But I'm not at all sure He's with me.*

⌁

As Andrea and Peter stood to leave the church, she saw Connie hurry toward them.

"Hi, Langs!" she exclaimed. One look at Andrea's face, and Connie gathered her into her arms.

Connie always knows when I need a hug, Andrea thought, soothed by her friend's plump warmth, her tenderness. She hugged back appreciatively. "Thanks, I needed that."

"Come outside and have a cup of coffee with Jeff and me," Connie urged. "Maybe a little Danish." She grinned, leading the way into the May sunshine of the church atrium.

There Andrea and Peter found themselves greeted again and again by women from the Bible study she'd attended, men from Peter's prayer group, strangers who called them by name, said they were praying for them. *A warm family*, she thought. *A lot of caring.*

Connie, who'd been drawn into a conversation apart from them, came back to her side, hazel eyes searching her face. "Is there anything at all I can do?"

Andrea squeezed Connie's hand. "When you say that, I know you mean it. Not like the perfunctory offers I've heard so often. Thanks, Connie. But I can't think what."

Later, as they headed home, Andrea turned to Tim. "How was Sunday school?"

"Good. We learned about Daniel. Man, when the Babylonians took him captive, they tried to butter him up to make him be more like them. But he was cool."

"Never wavered in what he knew was right, did he?" Peter asked, glancing at Tim through the rearview mirror. "Knew exactly who he was serving."

"Right." Tim nodded thoughtfully. "God. That's who."

Andrea listened as Peter expanded on the idea, pointing out other steadfast men of faith in the Bible. "It was because they really knew God, had a relationship with Him," Peter added.

Andrea couldn't help but admire how much he knew, particularly about the Old Testament. "How can you remember all that?" she asked.

He shrugged. "Guess Mom did a good job. Always pointing me to the great men of the Bible."

She saw him smile thoughtfully. "What are you thinking?" she asked.

"Oh, just that during my rebellious years in late high school and early college, I knew there was one thing I couldn't change and still can't: Mom never stops praying for me."

"Us too," Tim said.

"I know." Andrea sighed, envying Zoë's unwavering faith. How real, how trustworthy God was to her.

Her reflections ended abruptly when they turned into their driveway. A gray sheriff's department Chevy stood by the front door. Eric, waiting beside it, waved. She caught her breath. "Oh, Peter!" Wariness over the reason for Eric's presence mingled with exhilaration over seeing him. Bolting from the car before it completely stopped, she ran toward him and almost tripped. He grabbed her arm to steady her, and she felt the strength of his hand.

"Don't look so worried," he said. "It's not bad news. Could even be good."

Peter and Tim joined them, and Eric tousled the boy's hair. "Hi, pardner!"

He extended his hand to Peter.

"What's up?" Peter asked.

"Just got a report of a little girl in Phoenix."

"Phoenix," Peter repeated thoughtfully.

"Phoenix!" Andrea exclaimed. "That's not far."

"This picture's kinda grainy. But see what you think."

Eric held out a faxed photo, and Peter, Andrea, and Tim gathered close around it.

She bent over it eagerly, wondering at Peter's control, when her own heart leapt within her.

Tim was the first to speak. "Might be."

"I wouldn't say no," Peter said cautiously.

Andrea studied the image hungrily. She wanted so much for it to be Joy! The little girl's hair was fair. She couldn't tell in the black-and-white picture just what shade. But the heart-shaped face was a lot like Joy's. "How about the coloring?" she asked.

"Described as reddish blond. Blue eyes."

"Peter," she turned toward him. "We have to go." She looked back at Eric. "Where did they find her?"

"Police found her on the street. In OK condition. But she couldn't tell them her name."

Abandoned! Memory gone—probably traumatized from shock or abuse. A jumble of thoughts tumbled through Andrea's mind. *Peter'll want to wait for more information,* she worried. *But I've got to go.* "Peter?" she pleaded.

He nodded. "We'll catch the earliest flight we can."

She hugged him in a flood of relief and hope. Oh, Lord, let it be Joy, she prayed silently.

"I'll work on plane reservations." Peter headed for the house.

"Good," said Eric. "I'll get back to the station. Let me know what flight, and I'll have someone meet you at the Phoenix airport." He clasped her shoulder. "Good luck."

She looked up into his steady amber eyes. "Oh, if only—"

As Tim and Andrea came inside, she heard Peter say, "We'll take it. Yes, two. Thanks." He hung up the kitchen phone. "Two P.M. flight from LAX. Can you be ready?"

She nodded. "But Peter, what about Tim? There's no time to take him to Orange County, or to get your mom out here."

"Can I go with you guys?" he asked eagerly.

"Tim, try to understand," Peter said, putting an arm around him. "We're paying top dollar to go on such short notice. Money's kind of tight right now."

Tim groaned but didn't argue.

"I know!" Andrea exclaimed. "Connie. Just this morning she asked if there was anything at all she could do." She turned to Tim. "How would you feel about going to Mr. and Mrs. Hendrixes'?"

"Well, if you're really not gonna let me come with you. Yeah, that'd be OK."

"Thanks, love."

She called Connie. "It's perfect," Connie said. "Jeff just decided to go surf fishing, and I know he'd love Tim's company. You go, and we'll be fine. God be with you and watch over you, and oh, Lord, may this be Joy!"

She thanked Connie and, adrenaline flowing, ran into the bedroom and packed a carry-on bag for overnight, just in case.

Half an hour later, they dropped Tim off at Connie and Jeff's. Tim didn't look back as Jeff led him toward his fishing gear.

$$\mathcal{S}$$

The plane taxied out to the end of the runway and paused. A baby cried, the engines roared, and the plane surged, thrusting Andrea back in the seat. Then at last they were airborne, and her spirits rose with the plane.

After it banked back toward the east, she closed her eyes as thoughts pirouetted through her mind. She visualized the reunion—Joy rushing into her outstretched arms, the feel of her daughter's sweet warm body close to hers. How would she have changed in five months? Bigger, of course. Thinner? Well cared for? Neglected? Dirty? Her mind raced ahead to bringing Joy back home. How Joy loved to fly! She could hear her daughter's little voice rising, "Heeeere we go!" And oh, yes, they'd have to stop on the way home for extra milk and "oh-ohs," her favorite cereal.

Her thoughts rushed on to tucking Joy into bed with Mr. Bear. But would she remember her dream, if it really was a dream, of someone outside her window that last night at home before she disappeared? Maybe she should stay in their room.

"What would you like?" An attendant with a drink cart interrupted her thoughts.

"Oh, uh, a diet—anything. No, just make it club soda."

Andrea let her tray down.

"Certainly." The handsome young Latina, her hair pulled straight back, reached across Peter and placed a napkin on the tray. "Sir?"

Peter looked up from the inflight magazine. "Apple juice, please."

The young woman served their drinks, and Andrea glanced at Peter. He looked so calm. "What are you thinking?" she asked.

"About Phoenix?" He put down the magazine. "Afraid to get my hopes up, I guess," he admitted. "But of course, I do hope."

"Oh, yes! Me too. Hope against hope. I have this elaborate scenario of Joy's homecoming. I see our world finally coming back together. But then my hopes run smack into my doubts and fears." She was silent a moment. "Are you praying?"

He gave her an incredulous look. "Of course."

"But I thought maybe that engineer's mind of yours would be saying, well, what difference will praying make? I mean, either it is Joy or it isn't."

"What does being an engineer have to do with it? I'm her father. I love her. So of course I pray. We can both pray for grace to handle whatever we find."

"I suppose," she said, not even wanting to dwell on "handling" it not being Joy. She grabbed his hand and closed her eyes. "Oh, God, let it be Joy! Let it be Joy!" she prayed.

33

※

From Zoë's Prayer Journal

*May 19: Oh, Lord, is this it? Could this little
girl in Phoenix be Joy? Oh, Father, You know
how desperately we all want this to be the day
we've been waiting for. How I long to hug my
little angel and for the family to be whole again!
But Father, if it isn't Joy, please, use this trip of
Andrea and Peter's for Your good—and help us
all to accept the outcome. Thank You that You
are good and that You loved us enough to send
Your Son, our Lord and Savior. It's in His
name I pray, amen.*

AS SOON AS THE PLANE parked at the Phoenix terminal,
Andrea scrambled to her feet.

"It'll be a minute," Peter said.

"I know. But I want to get there!" She couldn't contain her
impatience and didn't intend to try.

Peter stood and reached into the overhead bin for her bag.
She ducked out from her seat and pressed forward as soon as
the other passengers began to move toward the exit.

The moment they emerged from the narrow walkway, she spotted the two uniformed policemen, one holding a sign lettered, "Lang."

"Here! Here we are," she shouted, hurrying toward them.

"Mrs. Lang?" asked the tall officer with the short blond crewcut. "I'm Sergeant Morrison. Ah," he said as Peter joined her, "Mr. Lang? Sergeant Morrison."

They shook hands, and the sergeant turned to the burly man beside him. "This is Lieutenant Red Hawk."

Andrea held her hand out to a Native American with a linebacker's build, broad hooked nose, and straight black hair. He took it lightly, then gave Peter a hearty handshake and gestured down the concourse.

As they approached the security checkpoint, she saw a cluster of people with cameras and videorecorders. The group pressed toward them. "Mr. Lang? Mrs. Lang?" a man asked. "Do you think this girl is your daughter?"

"We don't know," Peter replied patiently. "We'll see."

"But Mrs. Lang," a woman interjected. "What do you think? Do you have a gut feeling?"

Andrea shook her head. "I just hope," she said.

The lieutenant took Andrea's arm and pushed through the group, which followed as they took the escalator down. Sergeant Morrison led the way outside, where a police car waited at the curb.

Andrea gasped as the hot desert air hit her like a blast from a fiery furnace.

"Only 112 out today," Red Hawk murmured.

The car, shaded by the terminal structure, felt degrees cooler, and as they pulled away from the curb, she leaned into the breeze from the car's air conditioning.

EVIDENCE OF THINGS UNSEEN

"We're taking you to Child Protection Services," Red Hawk, seated beside her, explained. "They'll bring the little girl there from the shelter."

"Is—is she okay?"

"She's fine physically, except her fingertips are kind of raw. Not sure why. Nothing major, but we couldn't get good prints. The biggest problem is she's disoriented, confused. Gives us no information at all."

"Sounds as though she's very traumatized."

He didn't reply. A Rolodex of thoughts flipped through her head. Joy, what had she been through? No, it might not be Joy; she had to remember that. But in almost five months, what fears, what horrors might have been part of her daily life? And then, had she simply been abandoned? Or had she run away, maybe even clawed her way out, hurt her fingers? Andrea swallowed hard, suppressed her fear, and glanced at her watch. How much longer till they'd see her? It was taking forever. "Is it very far?" she asked.

"A ways. All surface streets."

She tried to lean back and relax. It seemed an eternity before Red Hawk announced, "It won't be long now." She saw Peter look back from the front seat and rolled her eyes, telegraphing her will-we-ever-get-there impatience.

At last the car turned into a parking area beside a three-story stucco building. "Here we are," Red Hawk announced.

The heat seared Andrea's lungs and parched her eyes as she stepped from the coolness of the car. She felt Peter take her arm. "Now we understand about Meshack, Shadrack, and Abednego," he whispered.

Sergeant Morrison opened one of the double doors to the building, and they entered a square waiting area, backed by

323

elevator doors and furnished with several metal-framed chairs with Naugahyde cushions. On a formica-topped table, a pothos plant struggled to survive.

Lieutenant Red Hawk joined them and indicated the chairs. "Why don't you sit down? I'll get the social worker." He disappeared down the hall.

"Social worker?" she muttered. "Red tape, I bet. Oh, Peter," she grabbed his hand, "when will we get to see this child?"

She paced the waiting area until at last Red Hawk returned with a woman with short, bleached blond hair. She regarded them somberly from behind small, wire-rimmed glasses with the weary eyes of a woman who'd undoubtedly seen years of desperate family situations. Her peach, short-sleeve polyester pantsuit spoke, too, of years of service.

"Mr. and Mrs. Lang," the chief said, "this is Sylvia Storm, a social worker with our Child Protection Services."

The woman shook hands, first with Peter, then with Andrea. "Pleased to meet you," she said, her voice as deep as a man's. "Come with me." As she turned, she looked out the window and stopped. "Jack!" She turned to Red Hawk. "I see a couple of carloads of newshounds. Get rid of them."

"Come on, Syl," Red Hawk protested with the ease of one who's known another a long time. "They've got a right to their story."

"If there's a story. And then, when there's a story. I don't want this kid made part of a circus."

Red Hawk put up his hand. "OK, OK. I'll call them off till we're ready to make an announcement."

Ms. Storm sighed and led the way down the hall and into a small cubicle. She moved to a chair behind a gray metal desk and motioned toward two orange molded plastic chairs that faced it. "Sit down."

Storm leaned back in her chair, elbows on the arms, touching her fingertips together. "So you think this might be your child?" She didn't wait for an answer. "Please understand, the question for us is, are you her parents?"

"Of course," Andrea said, hearing the nervous quaver in her voice.

Storm picked up a paper from her desk. "According to this sheriff's report, your daughter would be a little over four years old."

Andrea and Peter nodded.

"And she disappeared from a store."

"Yes," she answered.

Storm pursed her lips. She continued reading, "Hair color, reddish blond. Eyes, blue." She glanced up. "Any scars, identifying marks? I don't see anything here."

"No," Peter replied.

"Oh, yes, remember, Peter," Andrea broke in. "I told the sheriff's department. Remember the time she fell against the metal edge of—" Her voice broke as she remembered holding and comforting her sobbing daughter. "The coffee table." Seeing Ms. Storm's stern look, she felt compelled to add, "She lost her balance. Well, actually, her brother was playing a little rough." She saw Storm's cool eyes. *Oh, great*, she thought. *Now the woman sees me as a negligent mother*. "It, uh, left a little scar under the chin."

Storm looked down at the paperwork again. "Anything else you can think of?"

Andrea gave Peter a questioning glance.

"Her build is sturdy," he said. "Not really pudgy, but not thin. Face has almost a heart shape."

"And," Andrea joined in, "she's outgoing, cheerful, and bright."

Looking at her watch, Ms. Storm said, "They'll be here in about five minutes. I want to caution you not to overwhelm her. Give her a chance to get her bearings."

"We understand," Peter said.

Andrea squirmed in her chair and stood up. "It's so hard to wait."

Peter stood and rubbed the back of her neck. "Won't be long," he whispered.

She closed her eyes and tried to relax at his touch, but dizziness threatened. "Maybe some water . . ."

Without looking up from the papers on her desk, Storm said, "Around the corner to your left. You can wait in the reception area if you like."

They found the cooler just past the soft-drink machine and poured water into conical paper cups.

Little clown hats, Joy had called them once, she remembered. But that was a lifetime ago.

"I think," Peter said in a low voice, "that the storm trooper last smiled back in 1937."

She shook her head. "No, she was old enough to know better by then."

They began laughing then and for a moment, she was afraid she couldn't stop. And then what would Ms. Storm think?

They sipped the water. Peter refilled the tiny cups, and they carried them to the reception area of the Child Protection Services office. Through the window they saw a car pull into the parking lot.

"Peter, that must be them!" She clutched his arm.

The lieutenant and sergeant kept the media at bay while a slender young brunette opened the door on the driver's side. She stepped out of the car, slammed the door, and hurried around to the passenger door and pulled it open. The door shielded Andrea's and Peter's views. But she could see blue sneakers hit the pavement. And in a moment, the woman swung the door shut to reveal a child with blond hair that shone with red highlights in the desert sun.

Holding hands, the woman and child started toward the door, and Andrea knew instantly. The child walked with an awkward, knock-kneed, feet-far-apart gait. "It's not Joy," she choked.

"What's that?" came Ms. Storm's voice behind them.

"It's not Joy."

"You can't know from this distance," Storm said.

She spun toward the woman. "Don't tell me what I can and can't know!" she shouted, her eyes filling with tears. "That is not my daughter. A child does not turn knock-kneed in four months."

Peter cleared his throat, but his voice was husky when he spoke. "I agree. It's not our daughter."

She rushed into Peter's arms and buried her face against his shirt. "Oh, Peter. I can't bear it!"

"I know. I know," he murmured, holding her.

As the door opened, they turned to watch as the brunette urged the child inside. "Come on. It's nice and cool in here, darling. Look. Here are the man and lady I told you about."

The child stared at them. The silence was palpable. At last, "Do you know them?" the brunette asked. "Have you seen them before?"

Shaking her head, the child lifted the bottom of her T-shirt and began sucking on it, eyes downcast.

The young woman raised questioning eyebrows, looking from Andrea to Peter.

"They say it's not a go," Storm said.

Andrea shook her head, feeling the tears roll down her cheeks. Oh, why, why, why can't it be Joy? she mourned.

"Be sure," Storm urged.

Andrea forced herself to step closer to the child, to look carefully. "No," she whispered, "Joy's fingers aren't long and slender. And her ears are a different shape.

"I'm so sorry." The young woman reached out to touch Andrea's arm.

"Me too," she managed.

"*Us* too," Peter said.

Andrea stared at the youngster and suddenly thought her heart would break, not just for herself and Peter, but for the child. Where were her parents? Would anyone claim her? She looked at the two other women. "Could I give her a soft drink?"

The two women regarded one another thoughtfully, and she could almost hear Storm say, "That's not permitted." But instead her face softened. "Why not?"

"Do we know her name?" Andrea whispered to the young woman.

"No."

"Well, then," she decided, "I'm going to call you Little Girl Blue, because you're wearing such a pretty blue T-shirt." She moved close to the child and stooped to her level. "Little Girl Blue, could I buy you a root beer?"

The child looked at her warily, still sucking the T-shirt. At last she gave a tiny nod.

"Oh, good. Come on with me," Andrea said, taking her free hand.

The girl looked back at the woman who had brought her, who smiled encouragement.

Peter dropped coins into Andrea's hand and with cautious gentleness, she led the child to the soft-drink machine.

"There's lemon-lime and Coke too. And the root beer. Which would you like?" she asked.

No answer.

"Well, my daughter loves root beer. Let's have that." She dropped coins into the machine, and the can dropped with a clunk. "Here we are." She reached for it and led the child back to the reception area. Pulling the tab on the can, she handed it to the girl. She drank in noisy, greedy slurps, and Andrea smiled. When she paused and looked up at Andrea, her lips were rimmed with brown.

"Guess what? You're wearing brown lipstick." She fumbled in her purse and brought out a mirror to show her. For the first time, the girl smiled. Andrea sat down and picked her up. She seemed too absorbed in her root beer to protest. Holding her on her lap, Andrea waited while she drank. "Enough?" she asked as the child paused. She immediately drank again. And drank till it was gone.

The girl leaned against her, and Andrea rocked her gently. It wasn't Joy, but still there was a sweetness about holding a young child. She looked up to see Peter watching, an expression of deep tenderness on his face, his eyes shimmering.

She was surprised to find herself praying silently. *Oh, Lord, unite this child with her parents. Somewhere, they're grieving, yearning with empty arms, just as we are. And somewhere,* she thought, *Joy may be just as traumatized as this poor baby.* Remembering the morning's sermon, she added, *be her shepherd, Father. Lead her home.*

For the first time, the child spoke. "I want to go home!"

New tears sprang to Andrea's eyes. "I know. I know. Little Girl Blue, where *is* home? Can you remember?"

No answer.

"Dear God," she whispered, "help her to remember. Take away whatever is blocking her memory."

329

The child squirmed from her embrace and slipped to the floor. It was over.

"You leave first," Storm told the young woman. "You don't have to talk to the press, you know."

The young woman nodded, took the child's hand and slipped out the door.

Andrea saw her hold up her hand and shake her head as the newspeople rushed toward her.

She closed her eyes as devastation and despair washed over her. Another wild-goose chase. Another dead end. Would it ever, ever stop?

She felt Peter's arms around her and leaned gratefully against him.

"You all right, Mrs. Lang?" It was the first shred of concern she'd heard from Storm.

"I guess," she said to Storm, "I'm as good as you can be when you're back to square one."

34

AS ANDREA STOOD, enfolded in Peter's arms, she heard a discreet cough from somewhere behind him. Slowly, she eased her head to one side and saw Red Hawk.

"Do you folks have a return flight?" he asked.

Peter shook his head and freed his left arm to glance at his watch. "Four-fifteen. I noticed there was a five-twenty return flight. Any chance we could make it?"

"We can sure try."

Peter looked down at her. "You game?"

"I don't know," she murmured. She really didn't care.

"I'll phone," Storm called as they started outside. "Thanks," Peter said over his shoulder. "Monarch West."

Outside, the sergeant opened the squad car door.

She slid over to one side and Peter slipped in beside her. As the car pulled away, she let her head rest against the seat and felt Peter lean over to fasten the seat belt. Neither of them spoke for several minutes. At last Peter cleared his throat. "You were really good with that little girl."

She opened her eyes and turned her head toward him.

"I guess it was a way to deal with the awful frustration. Nothing we do seems to bear any fruit. We try and try and—nothing! I thought at least I could give her a tiny shred of comfort. Lord knows she needed it."

"Yeah. And you saw that need." He reached for her hand and gave it a gentle squeeze.

She let her head roll back against the seat, remembering the warmth of that little four-year-old snuggling against her. What a bittersweet moment, but how draining it all had been. Now she felt exhausted—no, more than exhausted—numb.

"Sounds ridiculous, but I think I could actually go to sleep," she murmured.

He put his arm around her. "Be my guest."

She closed her eyes and felt her head growing heavy against the seat back, sensed her jaw slackening. She saw Joy licking a chocolate ice cream cone, the brown of the chocolate outlining her mouth. How adorable she looked!

Then she was aware of nothing till she realized the car had stopped. "Are we there?" she asked drowsily.

"Not yet," Peter answered. "Traffic jam. Accident, I guess." She felt his body tense. "Took thirty-five minutes from the airport to the center. Got to be at least that long going back. It's going to be tight catching that plane."

What, she wondered, *is so important about catching that plane?* Traffic began to move, and she closed her eyes until she heard Peter. "Here's the airport. We'll have to run for it."

The squad car pulled up beside the terminal. Jumping out of the front seat, Red Hawk opened the door on Peter's side and announced, "Storm radioed to say she made your reservations. Gate six. Good luck."

"Thanks." Peter grabbed her carry-on and almost dragged her from the car, pulling her across the sidewalk and through the doorway. She felt drugged, and it was all she could do to put one foot before the other.

"Come on!" he urged. "You like to run. Exercise'll do us good."

Tugged forward by Peter, she stumbled onto the escalator. Up the moving stairs he climbed, never looking back at her. Across the terminal, through the security checkpoint, onward he towed her to gate six.

"Mr. and Mrs. Lang?" asked the uniformed woman behind the counter, handing them boarding passes. "Seats twelve A and B. Hurry."

They rushed through the door and into the plane. Andrea sank into the seat, panting, and watched Peter as he stowed her bag, his face aglow with triumph. He'd decided they'd make this plane, and he'd won. As she fastened her seat belt, she realized her numbness was gone. In its place, anger burned. Why had she allowed herself to be dragged along like baggage?

Peter sat down and buckled up. She sensed him twisting around in his seat, no doubt counting the number of rows to the nearest exit, as he always did. The plane began moving away from the terminal and without looking at him, she asked, "Was that really necessary?"

"What?" He seemed baffled. "Running? Well, sure to catch this plane."

"Was it necessary to catch *this* plane? I mean, when was the next one?"

"Oh, I don't know. An hour or so."

"Uh-huh." She could feel her cheeks burning as she turned

to face him. "You knew I was exhausted, upset. But heaven forbid we should have to wait a few minutes for the next plane. Honestly, Peter, sometimes I get up to *here* with you and your cursed goals!"

She let her angry words hang in the silence.

At last he said, "I thought after the disappointment, you'd want to get right home." He looked genuinely surprised.

"Sure," she said. What more was there to say? He didn't even understand what she was talking about. Feeling her anger wane to a depressed resignation, she turned away and looked out the window as the plane roared down the runway and rose above the gridwork of the city into a clear azure sky. Her feet hurt, and she felt sweaty and disheveled. *Thought I'd want to get right home*, she mused. Home to what? Same problems. The same empty room where Joy once played and slept. The same day-in, day-out swing from hope to hopelessness and back again. It might be better just to stay up in the sky and never come down. Circle the globe again and again. Or maybe blast off for a year or so. A space-age Flying Dutchman.

She let her mind drift with the fantasy before she sighed, her thoughts meandering back to the morning. How long ago it seemed—that rush of adrenaline, the high hopes, the dash away from the house, dropping off Tim at Connie's. Tim. She needed to get home after all, for Tim. Wanted to. She turned back her memory tapes—to finding Eric at her door after church this morning, the way he caught her when she tripped, the concern in his eyes. Would he have the report from Phoenix by now? He'd be disappointed too.

Eric. Gentle, patient Eric. Surely he'd never have put her through that two-thousand-yard dash to the plane. She closed her eyes and let her thoughts wander back to dancing with him at Dolores's party, how—"*simpatico*" they were, how she completely forgot her troubles with him. She began to picture meeting him again on the beach.

No, she broke the reverie. *I shouldn't let myself do this*, she told herself. But then she shrugged, allowing Eric's empathetic smile to play before her mind's eye.

"Something to drink?" Andrea heard the flight attendant in the aisle beside Peter.

He turned to her. "Want anything?"

She looked at the drink cart, trying to bring it into focus. "Diet Coke, I guess," she said at last. "Do you have a slice of lemon?"

The attendant nodded and looked at Peter. "Sir?"

"Same," he muttered, looking back at his magazine.

Later, when the plane started its descent, Peter said, "Funny, how it takes so much less time going this direction. Going out, I kept thinking my watch had stopped. Seemed to take forever." He glanced at his watch. "We'll land at about six-fifteen. I heard Connie say they'd barbecue after fishing, so Tim'll be fed by the time we get home. Let's call them from the airport. Then we can stop somewhere on the way home, maybe on the beach, and have a leisurely dinner."

She pursed her lips. "Did I actually hear the word, 'leisurely'? And you won't make me run from the airport to there?"

"I promise."

He's trying to make amends, she decided. *I ought to be gracious, maybe even grateful.* "Sold," she said.

From a phone booth at the airport, Peter phoned ahead for dinner reservations, and Andrea called Connie.

The outbound traffic was light, and by seven they were heading toward a window table at the Blue Dolphin. "I've heard this place is good for seafood," Peter said, pulling out her chair. As she sat down and looked out the arched window, she smiled to herself. It was the very beach where she and Eric had run.

A sinking sun burnished the breaking surf with tones of copper. In the wet sand at the water's edge a blond child with a pacifier plugging her mouth danced awkwardly while an older girl, perhaps seven, did cartwheels. Nearer to the restaurant, two lovers lay close under a beach umbrella, oblivious, perhaps, that they no longer needed it for shade. Four pelicans skimmed the sea in tight formation.

"I love this time of day," she said.

Already perusing the menu, Peter didn't reply.

She glanced at a couple at an adjoining table. The young woman's face was animated, responsive. Her eyes sparkled. He leaned toward her, gesturing as he spoke.

Second or third date, Andrea thought. So much still to say to each other. The excitement of discovery, of finding common ground. No, more than that: common feelings, responses.

I have that with Eric, she realized.

She looked across at Peter. The great stoneface. If only this was a film she was producing, and she could dissolve from Peter's face to Eric's, have his warm presence across the table, see him lean eagerly toward her. Eric would initiate conversation. With Peter, unless she opened a topic for his response, he might not speak at all.

He looked up from the menu. "What looks good to you?"

She looked down at her still-closed menu. "I haven't really looked yet."

"A number of fresh fish there, on your right." He opened her menu and pointed.

She studied the list. "I'll have the sand dabs."

"Good. I'm going for the swordfish."

She'd had so little appetite when they sat down, she was surprised how much she enjoyed the food. But they talked little, mostly about Phoenix. Part of the problem, she realized, was that before Joy's disappearance, they'd talked a lot about the future. Now, the future was on hold. How could they make long-range plans not knowing if Joy would ever return?

"May I bring you the dessert cart?" the waiter asked after the table was cleared.

She knew Peter felt desserts in restaurants weren't cost-effective. But she still felt peevish, rebellious. "Yes," she told the waiter.

Peter looked surprised. "You don't usually want dessert."

"Tonight I do."

She selected a slice of praline cheesecake, so rich that it coated her tongue with butterfat and so sweet it made her feel queasy. With the help of some black coffee, she managed all but one bite.

Peter had ordered ice cream, the least expensive dessert. "This is good," he admitted, and the unguarded small-boy expression on his face made her regret her anger. Only when they finished dessert did they speak of Joy.

"Don't give up," Peter urged. "I'm still working on some things on the computer. And you can get some more publicity out of this latest episode."

"Yep." She tried to sound energetic. "Turn this last lemon into lemonade, right? Mustn't let ourselves think that Joy—" her voice softened at her daughter's name, "might be somewhere, confused, bewildered, like that little girl in Phoenix." She stopped and bit her lip. "Oh, Peter, where *is* she?"

"I know." He swallowed the last of his water, rattling the ice in his glass. "We could drive ourselves crazy. We really, really have to commit her to the Lord."

"Easy to say. Not easy to do."

"No, and I'm not 100 percent succeeding, either," he admitted. He studied the check. "Uh-oh, they forgot to charge us for dessert." He turned to look for the waiter, and she glanced out the window at the indigo of the twilight sky. The lovers were gathering their belongings, the man tall and slender in tan shorts and the woman a voluptuous brunette wearing a very, very teeny neon-pink bikini. As they walked past the restaurant, the outside lights came on, catching them as though in a spotlight, defining the man's slender muscular legs, his sandy hair, the even-toothed smile.

She felt her face flush and thought she might be ill. No question. It was Eric. He put his arm around the woman's waist as they walked toward the public parking area just past the restaurant.

Andrea stood so suddenly she almost overturned her chair. Peter looked up at her. "I'm still trying to get our waiter, so he can fix this bill."

"I'm going to the ladies' room," she managed.

"Sure. OK, I'll meet you at the entrance."

She stumbled through the restaurant and into the rest room. Slipping into the first stall, she slammed the door, flushed the toilet, and hoped the noise would cover the unstoppable sound—half-wail, half-groan—that rose from somewhere deep within her. She leaned against the door for a moment, welcoming the cold of the metal against her flaming face. When she came out, a willowy blonde, busy applying mascara, glanced at her, then averted her eyes.

Thinks I'm crazy or drunk, Andrea realized. She ran cold water over her wrists, splashing a little on her face. Glancing in the mirror as she toweled off, she saw she needed lipstick and didn't care.

Peter was waiting outside. "Ready?" he asked.

She nodded.

All during the drive along the Coast Highway she wrestled with a sense of betrayal. Eric had seemed so sensitive to her needs. Did he dish out this same line to any pretty girl? He'd made her feel so special. But obviously there were others.

Then her embarrassment surfaced. She'd made a play for him, and he knew it. *He threw out a line, and I grabbed on like crazy, built it all up in my own mind.*

She felt as humiliated as—when was it? Ah, yes, the time she and a high school friend had a crush on a college tennis ace. After watching him play a match, they'd followed him home, just to see where he lived, only to have his friends confront them and laugh at them and call them silly babies. Eric must be amused too. How gullible she'd been. That night at Dolores's, that line that it was the first time he'd danced since his wife died. Sure it was!

As they turned up the road toward their house, she felt a huge inner void. They were returning without Joy, Peter didn't understand her, she no longer had a career, and now she didn't have Eric.

She hadn't realized how much she'd counted on him to lift the terrible heaviness, the grayness that pervaded all the rest of her life. Now that one bit of relief, of brightness was gone.

What's the point, she thought. *What's the point?*

35

❧

From Zoë's Prayer Journal

May 20: Dear Father, I had such a great time with You as I swam my laps this morning. Now I want to get it down in my prayer journal. As I prayed my way through the alphabet, when I got to "D," I had to confess I was Depressed, Discouraged, over the wild-goose chase to Phoenix. I'd hoped—You know! And frankly, I wondered why You're taking so long. And then You showed me that, just like with Lazarus (when Jesus didn't come when His friend was ill, but came after Lazarus's death and raised him), You want to do a greater thing, show us more of Yourself. Lord, my next lap was "E," and it definitely stood for Expectation. I'm not to be hopeless when You're silent but to know You're at work. I wait now in excitement and expectation. Thank You, my gracious Lord, in Jesus' name, amen.

ANDREA PULLED BACK the bedroom drapes and stared out on a dazzling May morning, the leaves mirrored with dew, the early morning coastal clouds already dissipating below to reveal a glistening, cadet-blue ocean. Ordinarily, the promise of such a brilliant day would cheer and energize her. Today, it only accentuated her despondency.

She heard Peter singing in the shower. How could he? She sighed as she dressed, trudged to the kitchen and shifted into automatic: coffee on, milk out, juice poured. Cold cereal with bananas would have to do for today.

Tim was the first to sit down at the breakfast table. He came straight to the point. "I feel bad it wasn't Joy."

"Me too." She was too tired, too numb to say more.

"Someday." He nodded confidently.

"Maybe." She was surprised how curt her voice sounded, and she put her hand on his shoulder. "Right. Someday," she murmured.

"Someday, what?" Peter asked, sliding into his chair.

"Someday Joy'll be back," Tim answered.

She saw his jaw tense. "Right." He gave the word just the proper tone of conviction. Then, pouring cereal into his bowl, he said to Tim, "So, you had a good time at the Hendrixes' yesterday?"

"Yeah. Mrs. Hendrix makes *triple* chocolate brownies. Chocolate chips in them and chocolate frosting on top."

"Paradise," Andrea agreed.

Tim poured milk on his cereal. "There's a guy in my Sunday school class, and his dad trains animals for movies, you know? We're getting to be friends, and I was thinking he might give me some ideas about Juliet."

"Maybe he could." Andrea tried not to sound too enthusiastic. "You're welcome to invite him over."

"Yeah, maybe."

Hoping with all her heart that he would, Andrea felt cheered for a moment.

But after Tim and Peter left, she stared around her. Clean up the kitchen and then what? Sit around and sulk? She didn't feel at all like writing about yesterday. Maybe she needed to go back to work. She let the idea percolate. Why not? When she quit, she'd thought she'd made a bargain with God, but obviously He'd forgotten.

She thought of Zoë and Connie and the depth of their faith. Zoë still prayed for her, she knew. And Connie kept urging her to come to the Bible study. But what was the point? She'd never have what they had.

The phone startled her. In the emptiness of the house, it seemed doubly loud. She lifted the receiver and heard Eric's smooth deep voice. "Andrea!"

Oh, no! she thought. *I can't deal with this.*

"Tried to call last night but I guess you weren't back yet," he continued.

Last night, she thought, anger flaring. *Sure you tried. When? On your way to the playmate of the month?*

He continued, his tone easy, familiar. "I'm sure sorry about Phoenix."

"Me too," she said quietly.

"You must be feeling pretty down."

"Right." What was the sense of pursuing this conversation? she wondered. She didn't even like the sound of his voice anymore. Too self-assured. Smug.

"Anything I can do?"

She longed to say, with all the sarcasm she could muster, "Sure. Take me to the beach." Instead, "No, you've done plenty," she replied.

"Well—" He hesitated. Did he sense a difference in her tone? "We'll keep in touch. Call if you need us."

After she heard him hang up she slammed the receiver down,

furious. Furious at him for his duplicity. Furious at herself for being so gullible. "Us," she muttered. "If you need *us.*" Not '*me.*'" *Face it, Andrea, she told herself, that's the way it is now. Call the sheriff's station, not Eric. But why bother to call at all? It never does any good.*

The phone rang again. "Now what?" she grumbled as she reached for it. When she heard her mother's voice, she quickly contemplated pretending to be the answering machine. "Hi, sorry I can't answer the phone right now," she could say. Just as quickly, she decided, *No, it's time to confront her, and I'm just mad enough to do it.* "Hi, Mom," she said.

"Anything new?" The voice held that familiar demanding ring.

Andrea took a deep breath and told her about Phoenix. Then, before her mother could analyze or criticize, Andrea said, "Mom, I don't want to hear one word about what we could have done or should have done. Quite honestly, I'm up to here with that after all these weeks. Why don't you try to think of some tangible way to help—like Peter's mom raising funds? Mom, I need support, not nagging."

The silence surprised Andrea. Then, "We offered to come out," her mother protested.

"That's not what I mean. Two more people in the house would be no help. Think about it. Think of a way to help us find Joy. Talk it over with Dad. I have to go now," she added firmly. "Thanks for calling. Bye."

She hung up. *Did I really say that?* she wondered. *Bet she's going to go into a tizzy, tell me what a rotten daughter I am.* She shook her head to break the thought cycle. *Well, that's her problem, not mine.*

She paced restlessly, and just as she glanced across the road at Dolores's house, the doorbell rang. She thought about not answering, but as she peeked around the corner toward the entry, she saw Dolores. She flung the door open. "Dolores! It must be ESP."

"You were thinking of me, were you? Were you also thinking of coffee and brioche?" Dolores held out a carafe and a basket lined with a Mondrian-design napkin.

"Come in." Andrea pointed toward the living room. "Let's go in here. I'll get some china."

As she returned from the kitchen with dainty flowered cups and plates, she paused by Dolores. "Guess you heard?"

"About Phoenix? Yes. On the news last night. Oh, Andrea, I am so sorry. What a disappointment!"

"Awful," Andrea agreed, gesturing toward the sofa. They sat down and she poured the steaming coffee.

"Well, I want to hear all about it. All of it."

There was something therapeutic about playing the Phoenix trip out, scene by scene. When Andrea finished, the pain of not finding Joy had eased just a little. Her anger about Eric was another matter. She wasn't ready to talk about that yet.

She bit into a brioche, fine-textured and buttery-rich. "Excellent."

Dolores nodded. "Baked this morning. Picked them up on the way home from the gym. How's that for defeating an hour's workout?"

"On the other hand, actually, you earned it."

"Right!" Dolores studied Andrea a moment before she said, "You're in a pretty deep pit, aren't you?" Her eyes were understanding, sympathetic.

"I'm right back where I was before. I feel totally empty. I'm so tired, I just want it to be over, one way or another. In other words, to know," she admitted.

"I don't blame you." Dolores pursed her lips. "Surely your God wouldn't intend for you to be so miserable."

She tilted her head dubiously. "I'm not so sure. Point A: Is He all that merciful? Point B: Maybe He does intend it, maybe He's punishing me."

Dolores wrinkled her face. "Punishment—sin. Oh, *please*, Andrea, try to get beyond that! I believe your God, if He's a God of love, would want you to use every possible means to find the answers. I mean, doesn't God help those who help themselves?" She leaned toward Andrea, her face glowing with conviction. "You deserve answers!"

Andrea's head was beginning to hurt. She sighed. "Everything's a dead end. Peter still seems to think he has some leads, but there's nothing solid."

Dolores ran a scarlet-nailed index finger lightly along Andrea's hand. "No, what I mean is, there is a way, I'm convinced, to tap into what is real and true and what is not. There's information available—but, of course, it's on a different plane than you and I, sitting in this room."

She shook her head. "Well, you must know I'm pretty skeptical after Sybil."

Dolores waved the idea away. "I know. But don't throw the baby out with the bathwater. Just because that wasn't successful for you doesn't mean there isn't another way."

"Such as?"

"Why, my women's group, of course."

She shook her head. "Mom Lang thinks your ladies are into witchcraft."

"Oh, Andrea, it isn't what you think! Have you seen me wearing a black pointy hat and stirring a cauldron?"

Andrea gave a nervous giggle, wanting to end the conversation and, at the same time, fascinated to hear more.

"You met several of the women at my party. I mean, Patty Howard, you sat with her. Did she seem weird?"

"Well, no," Andrea admitted. "But Dolores, I get the feeling that you're hostile about Christ."

"No, no, no," Dolores held up her hand. "I'm sorry if I gave that impression. We're an alternative, not a backlash to Jesus. We just believe a living, vibrant experience is superior to dogma and doctrine."

Andrea set her cup down. "I've always thought witches were connected with Satan, if there is such a person."

Dolores frowned. "You said it: 'If there is such a person.' We certainly do not believe in him—or it." She smiled. "Oh, Andrea, it is won-der-ful to feel oneness with all life. It's transforming. And," she lowered her voice, "it can be informative."

Andrea felt her heart quicken. Was it hope or fear? Andrea searched for a word "Are you talking magic?"

Dolores smiled. "You could call it that. But remember, there is good magic and bad magic. We seek the good. By the way, we spell it with a 'k.' M-a-g-i-c-k. We believe that we all have abilities, some more than others, to tap into the Life Force, to learn truth."

Andrea shook her head. "I don't think so."

Dolores leaned toward her. "But what if it works? What if you came over Wednesday night to our little ceremony. It's called 'drawing down the moon.' You'd experience such love, such insights. And very possibly, some knowledge!"

"It sounds so bizarre. The croning ceremony and all."

"Oh, but, let me explain." Dolores leaned toward her, eyes glowing with enthusiasm. "We see three primary phases of a woman's life: maiden, mother, and crone, represented by the waxing, full, and waning moon. At the croning we were celebrating the older women's maturity and wisdom."

"OK." Andrea nodded.

"Now," Dolores continued. "Because we want to help you, a mother, it's particularly appropriate that you come Wednesday, when the moon will be full." She took Andrea's hands. "Oh, my dear Andrea, I can't bear to see you go on like this. What harm could this be? Sweet friend, I believe with all my heart this could be the breakthrough you haven't found through all your work, all your prayers!"

Dolores's eyes held Andrea's, and Andrea felt herself sinking into their darkness.

Why not? she thought. *It's worth a try. Anything to end this anguish.* "All right," she heard herself say quietly.

Dolores's face came alive with delight. "Bravo!" she exclaimed. "Wednesday night. Come about eight. And," she added, "come alone."

Alone? Who else would she bring? She knew Peter would have no part of it. "Sure."

"You won't regret it," Dolores said as she stood. Andrea sat for a moment, too lightheaded to rise. Then she struggled to her feet and accepted Dolores's warm hug.

The phone rang, and Dolores said, "You get that," as she headed toward the door.

Andrea picked up the phone in the kitchen.

"Andrea," came her mother's voice. "I've been thinking, and I discussed it with your father. We'd like to hire a private detective. You know, your dad went to college with the chief of police, so he called him, and he recommended a fellow with an excellent record with missing people."

"Mom, I didn't mean . . .," she protested. It sounded expensive. She shouldn't have put her mother on the spot.

Her mother seemed to read her mind. "Yes, it's a lot of money, a stretch for us. But your dad wants to do it." She paused and her voice grew gentler. "So do I."

"Oh, Mom, this is too good to be true. Thanks." Her voice broke and tears seeped from her eyes.

"Now, Andrea. Control yourself." The brusqueness again.

Andrea grinned through her tears. Some things never changed, but her drill sergeant mother had finally come through.

"Then we'll tell Mr. Finley, Bruce Finley, to go ahead."

"Great. That's just great, Mom." She hung up, marveling at this breakthrough in their relationship. "Who'd have thought it?" she said aloud.

She looked out the window and saw Dolores crossing the road. "But maybe we won't need him," she said aloud.

36

AS ZOË UNLOADED THE GROCERIES at the Malibu house the next afternoon, Tim came out to help.

"There's my buddy!" she exclaimed, giving him a hug. "Thanks for your help."

"Sure, Gram."

They walked inside together, and she set the bag on the kitchen counter, fishing out an enormous apple. "Share it with you. Unless you can do it all."

He eyed it. "Let's split it."

Zoë washed the apple, cut it in quarters with two deft strokes and removed the core, handing two quarters to Tim.

They bit into the apple in unison and grinned at one another. "So," Zoë said at last, "I'm relieved to see you're alive and well. I was concerned about your dare, the one you told me about last time."

"Yeah, well a lot of good it did me."

Zoë grabbed a paper towel for each of them and indicated the table in the dining area. They sat and crunched their apples for a few moments. Then Zoë asked, "Did a friend let you down?"

Tim nodded. "Big time."

She put her hand on his. "Do you mind my asking? Was it Brant?"

Tim sighed. "Yeah, I might as well tell you."

When Tim finished his story, Zoë whistled. "I'm doubly glad you're alive and well! God certainly looked out for you."

"I asked Him to."

"That was smart." Zoë thought a moment. "You must feel really betrayed, Tim."

He nodded.

After a moment, Zoë looked into his brown eyes. "Tim, it's so good to see you growing in your faith. You've come such a long way. Has anyone ever mentioned to you that there's not an emotion you can feel that Jesus didn't experience during His time on earth?"

"Hadn't really thought about it."

"Well, then, think a minute about what you're feeling now. Do you suppose Jesus ever felt a friend let Him down, big time, as you put it?"

"Well," Tim frowned. Then his face came alive with under-standing. "That disciple, Judas!"

"Bingo!" Zoe said. "One of His own."

"Mega big time!"

"Yep." She waited a moment. "Tim, has it occurred to you that you already have a best friend?"

Tim's eyebrows shot up. "Who?"

"That same Jesus," she said softly.

"Ha!" Tim scoffed, sweeping his hand out before him. "He's way off, up there."

"No, He's not, darling. In the Bible He calls those who believe in Him His friends. In fact, covenant friends. Close as blood brothers. He wants to be your friend, wants to have a close, close relationship with you. You and Him. Like this." She locked her forefinger and middle finger together.

Tim frowned. "But a friend does things with you."

"So does Jesus." Zoë smiled. "Like that old song says, He walks with you and He talks with you and He tells you, you are His own."

"Yeah, I remember that."

"Tim, I know you believe Jesus is who He says He is, that He's the Savior. And that you know He died so your sins could be forgiven. We've talked about that. But have you ever asked Him to be your own personal Savior, so You could have that close friend-relationship?"

"Nah. I guess I haven't." Tim looked at his grandmother, his brown eyes wide and serious. "But I know a guy in Sunday school who said he asked Jesus into his heart. I wanted to ask him about it. Is that what you're talking about?"

Zoë nodded.

"How do I do that?"

"All you have to do is ask Him." She let him think about it before she asked, "Would you like to?"

"Yeah," Tim breathed. "I would. What do I say?"

"Just as your Sunday school buddy did, you invite Him to come into your heart. You could start by thanking Him for dying for you. Then, just *ask*."

Tim bowed his head. He was quiet a moment before he began, "Jesus, I know You died so people's sins could be forgiven." He looked up at Zoë questioningly, and she nodded encouragement. Tim closed his eyes again and added, "so my sins could be forgiven. I sure thank You. And I just want to ask You now to be my own Savior and to come into my heart and be my friend forever, amen."

They sat together for a moment, the only sound the tick of the clock in the living room. Then Tim sighed and looked up at Zoë, a broad grin spreading slowly over his face. "I felt like He said, 'Done deal!'"

Zoë smiled through her tears. "I'm sure He did." She stood and leaned over him, kissing his forehead. "Now you're my grandson and more. You're my brother in Christ."

"You're kinda old for me to be your bro', Gram."

She leaned back and saw the glint of mischief in his eye. "Now, don't get smart!" she warned, smiling as she swatted him gently.

᠅

Later that afternoon, Tim climbed up into his pine tree. He sat, breathing in the Christmas aroma, looking up at the brightness of the green needles against an unclouded blue sky. The sea breeze cooled his skin, even as the filtered sun warmed it.

He sat for a long time, thinking about his conversation with his grandmother and his prayer.

"Jesus is my friend," he said, smiling, feeling an amazing peace spread through him.

After a while, he looked toward the house and saw his grandmother and his mom talking in the kitchen. Probably about Joy.

Where *was* Joy, anyway? He stared out at the ocean and leaned against the roughness of the tree trunk, and imagined finding Joy a prisoner of kidnappers. He'd climb up the side of the building, go through the window, untie her, and carry her away to safety. Everyone would say how brave he was.

He sighed. R-i-i-ght. Maybe the best thing he could do would be to talk to his new Best Friend about finding Joy.

"Jesus," he began. But he stopped as he heard Brant's voice. "There she is! Hey, kitty, kitty! Get her!"

Tim looked down and saw Juliet begin to run, with Brant and two other boys in pursuit. One boy, blond and lean, towering over Brant, tossed his jacket over her, but she darted out from beneath it and hightailed it toward the hills.

Tim scrambled down from the tree, shouting, "Hey! You guys leave my cat alone. You hear me? *Leave my cat alone!*"

Brant shrugged and turned to a fat boy with a Mohawk cut. "We'll never find her in the brush, anyway. Let's go."

Mouth dry, heart thudding, Tim waited for them to go around the bend in the road, down the hill. Why'd they want Juliet, anyway? The image of the hacked-up rattlesnake flashed into his mind. Nah, they wouldn't, would they?

Heading toward the hills in the direction he'd seen Juliet go, he called softly, "Juuuu-liet! Kitty-cat! It's OK, Julie. You can come back now."

After awhile, he heard her leaping through the brush. Then he saw her, tail bushed out, heading straight for him. She sprang up onto his shoulder and he held her against his face. "Oh, Julie! Man, we've gotta keep you inside when those guys are around. I'm not gonna let anybody hurt you, I promise."

He went straight home and into his bedroom, lying down on his bed, holding Juliet close, listening to the comforting sounds of his mom and Gram in the kitchen.

As Zoë and Andrea worked together, chopping vegetables for soup, Zoë looked up, wiping tears away with the back of her hand. "Onions!" she exclaimed.

"It doesn't take onions to make me cry," Andrea said.

Zoë nodded. "There's a psalm that says God has all our tears in a bottle."

"He'd need more like a tank for me." Andrea thought a moment and added, "If He's there."

Zoë put her knife down. "Come here a minute, dear heart." She led Andrea to the sliding-glass door with its sweeping ocean view. "Look at that vast blue sea. I see ships and a couple of sailboats, but where's Catalina?"

"Can't see it today. Can't see it lots of days."

"But is it still there?" Zoë asked.

Andrea smiled at her mother-in-law's persistence. "I haven't read any news reports of it sinking."

"But you can't see it or hear it or feel it." She fixed her bright blue eyes on Andrea's. "The same thing's true of God. Maybe you can't see Him or hear Him or feel Him. But He's there. And He hasn't stopped loving you."

Andrea sighed. "Good analogy, Mom."

Zoë had hoped for more. *Your timing, Lord,* she prayed silently. *Thank You that it was Your time for Tim today!*

ॐ

The next morning, Peter looked thoughtfully at Andrea. "You feel better, don't you, with the detective on the case now?"

"Of course. And because Mom finally *did* something instead of just criticizing. She showed that she cares, and that's a real breakthrough. Otherwise," she hesitated, "I just hope it isn't too late."

"You've got to keep hoping. Somewhere in Hebrews it says, 'Faith is the substance of things hoped for, the evidence of things not seen.'"

"Well," she said quietly, "I don't seem to have that kind of faith. Especially after Phoenix. I keep wondering if we're not like hamsters in a cage, running and running and getting nowhere."

Tim pulled up his chair at the table. "Mom, keep Julie in today, OK? Brant and his friends were chasing her yesterday. Besides, I want her rested, so I can work with her this afternoon."

"Rested," Peter laughed. "Isn't resting what cats do best? Now, dogs—"

Andrea held up her hand. "Spare us." She turned to Tim. "Don't worry, honey, those guys won't catch her." She smiled as Juliet came in, rubbing her face against Tim's legs. Would he ever get her to walk those ropes? It would truly be a miracle.

After Peter and Tim left, she glanced across the road. Wednesday. D-Day—Dolores Day. Twelve hours and counting. Twelve hours till that "drawing down" time. She felt a strange mix of excitement and fear—a little like the first time she stepped out on a high diving board to attempt a backflip. What would this moon ceremony reveal? Probably nothing. Still, might as well go through with it, give it a try. It could take months for the detective to find anything.

The phone startled her. "I'll pick you up at nine-thirty for the Bible study," came Connie's firm voice. Andrea's mind raced. *It's Wednesday. The last thing I need is that Bible study.* "Oh, Connie, no, I'm sorry. I haven't studied."

"Andrea!" Connie's tone was unequivocal. "This is one time I'm not taking no for an answer."

"Connie," Andrea protested, trying for a light touch. "You sound downright menacing."

"Sorry, my friend. But that's the way it is. See you at nine-thirty." And Connie hung up.

Andrea stood, still holding the phone, not sure whether to be amused or angry. This was so unlike the mild Connie she knew. She replaced her phone and half-jokingly said to herself, *Connie must think she's had a word from the Lord.* She looked across the road once again. *What am I, some sort of a pawn passing between Connie and Dolores?* The thought annoyed her. *Who do they think they are, anyway? I can make up my own mind.*

37

From Zoë's Prayer Journal

May 22: Father, here I am, worrying about my time, my schedule today. After I swim my laps, I'll have to rush for my first appointment. The whole day is packed, but—listen to me. "My time." It's Your time. You gave it to me, just as You give all things. Ah, I get it: as the song says, "My time is Your time." Oh, Lord, may I give it back to You wisely and well, knowing there's all the time I need to do all You want me to do. Thank You, my Abba, in Jesus' name, amen!

STILL STANDING in the kitchen after Connie's emphatic phone call, Andrea felt her exasperation dissipate bit by bit as she considered all Connie had done for her. She headed for the shower and was dressed and ready right on time.

Connie pulled into the driveway and smiled as Andrea slipped into the car. "Hi. Guess I came on pretty strong. But I feel so clearly that you're supposed to be there this morning."

"Did the Lord tell you?" Andrea teased.

Connie glanced at her. "Not in audible words, if that's what you mean. No, He didn't say," she deepened her voice, "'Connie, get Andrea and bring her to Me.'"

"OK, just checking."

They were silent as Connie negotiated the hairpin turns in the road. Then she asked gently, "Have you seen any more of Sybil?"

"No. I decided that wasn't for me."

"Good." Connie's voice was so soft, Andrea had to lean over to hear her. "You know, just think about it. If a child's dead, her spirit wouldn't come channeling through someone to me or you. They wouldn't be restless. They'd be safe and secure with Jesus."

Andrea sighed. "You really believe that?"

"With all my heart. You know how much Jesus loves little children."

She thought a moment. "But Joy wasn't old enough to have a faith of any kind."

"Exactly. She hadn't reached—what do they call it?—the age of accountability. If by any chance she's dead, she's in Jesus' loving arms right now, and you'll see her again someday."

Andrea felt tears rise in her eyes. "In heaven." She glanced at Connie, remembering her friend's loss. "Like your son?"

"Exactly." Connie reached over and squeezed Andrea's hand.

After they turned into the church lot and parked, Connie turned toward her, hazel eyes earnest and warm. "Take a step of faith," she urged. "Trust in what you can't see or feel. Don't rely on yourself or on other people. The answers aren't within you or in others or through them. They're from God."

❧

"Well, ladies," Mary Lou smiled as she surveyed the Bible study group. "What a beautiful topic we have today!" She flashed her perfect smile. "The name of God we're studying today is Jehovah-Jireh, one of the compound names. Last week, when we studied Jehovah, we learned what?"

Connie raised her hand. "That God is self-existent, the God who always was."

Mary Lou nodded. "All right, then, if God is self-existent and all-sufficient, as we learned before, why does He need us, want us? Well, we'll get some answers today and in the following weeks. In these compounded names we'll see that His very nature is not to be all into Himself, but to reach out and love and give and meet our needs. So what does Jehovah-Jireh mean?"

"The Lord will provide," several voices chorused.

"Right. Now let's get a picture of that. Let's look at Genesis 22 and the story of Abraham and Isaac. In fact, let me run through the story."

Andrea remembered learning about Abraham and his son in Sunday school, and the revulsion she'd felt at the idea of God asking Abraham to sacrifice his son. The story had seemed so far-fetched, more like a fairy tale.

"Now," Mary Lou continued, "this man Abraham's a really important fellow. God has made a covenant with him. Even though the old boy didn't have any children, God promised him as many offspring as the stars in the heavens, and He's also promised the land between the Nile and Euphrates to his descendants. And true to His word, when Abe was ninety-nine years old and his wife, Sarah, was ninety, God gave them a son, Isaac!"

Sure, right! Andrea thought. *Childbirth at ninety.*

"Now, just think what Isaac meant to Abraham," Mary Lou went on. "He was the special son God gave him when he'd given up all hope. And God had established His covenant with Isaac as well as Abe. All of the future lay in this son. So what did God decide to do in chapter 22 of Genesis?"

"Verse 1 says He tested Abraham," Ellie offered.

"And what a test! God tells Abraham to take his only son—yes, his only son—and do what?"

"Sacrifice him on the mountain as a burnt offering," someone said.

"Right. Can you imagine what must have gone through Abraham's head? 'My only son, the one the covenant rests on. The one who's the key to descendants as numerous as the stars.' But what does Abraham do? He gets up when? *Early in the morning.* What does that show us about Abraham?"

"He's obedient?" someone offered.

More like crazy, Andrea thought. *He had no mind of his own.*

"Definitely obedient," Mary Lou agreed. "So he takes two servants with him and, of course, Isaac and the wood for the burnt offering. Now this little trip takes three days, over rough terrain. As they approach the spot on Mount Moriah that the Lord specified, Abraham says an interesting thing. Did you catch it? He tells the servant that he and the boy will go yonder and what?"

"Worship," a voice came from the back of the room.

Mary Lou nodded. "'Worship and return to you.' Very interesting. Seems like Abraham *knows* something, doesn't he?" She paused a moment, then continued, "So Abraham loads the wood on Isaac, and he takes the fire and the knife. And when Isaac asks, 'Where's the lamb?' Abraham assures him, 'God will provide for Himself the lamb for the burnt offering.'

"Sooo—they come to the place the Lord's told him about, and Abraham builds an altar." Mary Lou stacked imaginary rocks on the floor before her. "He puts the wood on it. And then he binds Isaac and lays him on the altar on the wood. Now, mind you, this kid's big enough to resist. So what do we see here once again?"

"Blind compliance. As bad as his father," Andrea muttered under her breath.

"Obedience," Connie said. "He's obedient to his father."

"Good. Now, Abraham's just taking up the knife—" Mary Lou lifted her hand, as though testing the sharpness of a blade. "And the angel of the Lord basically says *Don't*. 'For now I know that you fear God, since you have not withheld your son, your only son, from Me.' You see, Abraham hadn't kept anything from God, hadn't said, 'This is mine,' not even his most precious possession. So what happened then?"

"He saw a ram in the thicket," Carol said.

"Now, isn't that lucky?" Mary Lou shook her head. "No, it wasn't luck. Abraham knows God provided the ram. So he names that place Jehovah-Jireh—*The Lord Will Provide*. And then God gives His blessing in verse 15: 'I swear by Myself, declares the Lord, that because you have done this and have not withheld your son, your only son, I will surely bless you and make your descendants as numerous as the stars in the sky and as the sand on the seashore. Your descendants will take possession of the cities of their enemies, and through your offspring all nations on earth will be blessed, because you have obeyed Me.'"

Andrea sighed. *A pointless fable*, she decided.

Mary Lou looked directly at Andrea, as though reading her mind. "Now, we can dismiss this as a fairy tale, or we can say it's the story of blind, unthinking faith." She paused. "Or we can say it's belief based on God's Word. Abraham heard God's promises, and he believed. But he also obeyed. Obeyed to the point of being willing to offer his only son as what? As an act of *worship*. Remember, he told the servants he and the boy would go 'worship *and* return.' Did he know God would spare his son? We can't be sure. But we do see three things here: One, love, in Abraham and Isaac's relationship and also in Abraham's response to God; two, obedience; and three, worship."

Mary Lou looked around the room. "Do you see anything more in this passage? A parallel? A foreshadowing?"

As the group hesitated, the answer sprang to Andrea's mind, a shaft of light that astounded her. She started to speak and had to clear her throat to get the words out. "God and *His* only begotten Son," she managed.

Mary Lou beamed at her. "Exactly! God *loved* the world. He *gave* His Son. He *provided* the lamb without blemish. And Jesus loved the Father and was obedient, just as Isaac was. And by the way, Jesus Himself said in the Gospel of Matthew, 'Anyone who loves his son or daughter more than Me is not worthy of Me.'"

She paused and examined each face around the room, her eyes shimmering. "All right, then, here's the BIG question. If God has provided so perfectly for us, what can we hold back from Him? Can we trust God like Abraham? Can we understand that faith is the substance of things hoped for, the evidence of things not seen? Do we, like Abraham, know that everything we have comes from God?"

Mary Lou took a deep breath and slowly released it. "Then what or who is your own personal Isaac? What are you clinging to that you need to place on the altar?"

Andrea looked away quickly. *No!* she shouted in her heart. She felt sure Mary Lou was looking at her and dared not look up.

Mary Lou continued, "Did you ever build an altar, I mean literally? Last summer my husband and I were hiking in the

Sierra and we saw some piles of rocks that were probably sign-posts. But it reminded me of this lesson. I spotted this big flat rock—really a boulder—beside us and told my husband I wanted to build an altar. We knelt and I picked up a squarish rock and set it on top and said, 'This is my pride. Lord, I give You my pride.' And my husband began joining in. Together we lay selfish ambition, fear, guilt, and gossip on the altar. We don't have any children, but I did give my mom—she's an alcoholic, and I've tried for so many years to help her—to the Lord." She wiped the corners of her eyes. "It was one of those defining moments in my life, and so freeing. I recommend that you build your own altars. And let me ask you again: What do you need to place on your altar? What do you need to give completely to the Lord?"

Tears sprang to Andrea's eyes. She couldn't deny it any longer. The realization, "Joy is my Isaac!" echoed on the sounding board of her mind. She put her hands to her ears, but it wouldn't stop. She heard Mary Lou's closing prayer without discerning the words. Her senses reeling, she fled the room, hearing the murmur behind her, aware finally that Connie had followed her to the car.

"You'd like to go straight home," Connie said, opening the car door for her. It was a statement, not a question.

Andrea nodded.

Saying nothing, Connie let her weep as they drove home. "Oh God," Andrea cried at last, "it's too hard. I can't offer Joy as a sacrifice. I won't!"

As they pulled into Andrea's driveway she pushed the car door open even before they stopped. She fled, slamming the door hard behind her, running to her entrance.

Her hand shook as she tried to fit the key in the lock. At last she made the connection and heard the latch click. She flung the door open but didn't look back at Connie's car, still in the driveway, as she hurried inside and banged the door shut. She leaned against it, trembling. Offering his only son. *How could Abraham do it?* she wondered. Would Sarah, the *mother*, have been so obedient?

"Bet she wouldn't," she muttered under her breath. No, it was too much to ask of a mother, a mother who'd given birth. She thought back to the sweetness of holding Joy as a newborn, the bonding as she nursed. *It's different for men,* she thought. *Maybe Peter could give our child to the Lord. But not me! Never!*

She took a deep breath and shouted into the empty house, "No, God! No!" Her voice seemed to echo back from every room. Then the house fell silent, except for her own quick, shallow breathing. Had God heard her? Was He angry at her repeated defiance? At last she drew a breath, slowly exhaled, and forced herself down the hall toward the bedroom. She glanced at her watch. Only eleven-thirty. Whatever would she do to fill the time till Tim came home, till tonight? She felt much too agitated to work at her desk. She didn't want to think—not about Jehovah-Jireh, not about tonight at Dolores's, not about Joy, not about anything.

As she changed into jeans, the idea came, unbidden, from long years past. Bread. She'd take out all her frustrations on a huge batch of homemade bread.

"Mad bread's the best," Grandma Nickerson had once told her. "You put your whole self into the kneading."

In the kitchen she began mixing the dough, using unbleached flour, whole wheat, oatmeal, whatever she found in the pantry. A wild mixture—like her life, she realized. When the dough grew too thick to mix with the spoon, she turned it out on a floured board. There was something basic and satisfying about this huge sticky, brown-flecked mass with its yeasty, grainy aroma. *Staff of life,* she thought. *Bread of life.* Who said that? Jesus, she realized. She dusted her hands with flour and paused. *If He's the bread of life, why is my very soul so empty?* she wondered. *I suppose Connie would say because I'm not allowing Him to be the Lord of my life.*

She could feel the tension growing inside her again. "Well, too bad, Connie!" she muttered as she attacked the dough, pushing, folding, turning, pushing, folding, turning, working more flour into the dough.

"This is for Connie," she said aloud as she put her full weight into the kneading, "and for all the people who want to run my life. For Dolores. And yes, for Peter." The flour flew as she worked. "And this is for Eric. For his playing up to me. For my buying into it!" The dough was harder to work now, and she felt the perspiration forming on her upper lip. "And this," she continued, "is for all the false hopes, the dead ends, the frustrations, the unanswered prayers."

She kneaded with such fury, the dough turned smooth and elastic long before she finished her list of grievances. She wiped her lip with the back of her hand. Then, oiling the mixing bowl, she scooped the dough into it. What a satisfying, living thing! Full of promise. The only thing in her life at the moment that had any hope. Topping the bowl with a clean cloth, she placed it near a sunny window.

Rinsing and drying her hands, she pushed the sliding door open. As she stepped outside to brush the flour from her jeans, she remembered how Tim had helped her make bread when he was little. Standing on a chair beside her, he'd push and pat and taste. Afterward, he'd giggle as she vacuumed him from head to toe to de-flour him. That was before Joy.

Joy . . . the thought of her daughter drained all her energy.

She slumped against the doorframe. Finally, nudging the door shut, she shuffled into the living room and stretched out on the couch. She pulled the blue mohair afghan up over her shoulders, welcoming its light warmth, and closed her eyes. The relentless ticking of the clock on the mantel seemed amplified in the stillness, every minute drawing closer to eight o'clock tonight.

Should she cancel with Dolores? Surely going there was an exercise in futility. No, more than that. Scary. What if something horrifying about Joy surfaced? Maybe it was better not knowing. Maybe after all, she needed to trust Joy to God. She tried to relax the tension in her legs. *But it's Dolores who's offering help,* she realized. *God's demanding so much. He's way off there—maybe. Dolores is here.* Her thoughts swung back and forth, like the strokes of the clock's pendulum. Then, gradually, she became distracted by a little hiccup in the clock's cadence. Why hadn't she noticed it before? It didn't say tick-tock, but tick-ta-tock, tick-ta-tock. She listened carefully and little by little, the rhythm seemed to form into words. She strained to hear. Yes. "Have-to-*know,* have-to-*know.* You have-to-*know,*" sang the clock. She shook her head to clear away the words, but they were tenacious, mesmerizing.

It's true, she said at last, sitting up. *I have to know. Can't wait. I have to go tonight.*

38

~

"AND CATCH THAT VIEW toward the mountains," Zoë said as she showed a hilltop house to some prospective buyers. Her pager beeped, and she glanced at it. Looked like a Malibu prefix, but not Peter and Andrea's phone. While her clients were busy taking measurements in the living room, she called the number, instantly recognizing Connie's voice.

"Connie, it's Zoë. Did you beep me?"

"Oh, yes. Thanks for calling. I'm so sorry to bother you, but I believe it's crisis time for Andrea. Today's Bible study on Jehovah-Jireh really riled her."

"The Lord who provides," Zoë murmured. "Oh, Father, may You show her by Your Holy Spirit that You provide everything she needs."

"Yes, Lord!" Connie said. "But," she added, "I don't believe she's there yet. Might even be fixing to head for Dolores so she can hear stuff that's more like what she wants."

Zoë looked at her watch. Almost noon. She'd promised lunch to her clients, and she had appointments at two and four.

But, she asked herself, did I or did I not tell the Lord this morning that my time is His time? "Think I should come?" she asked.

Connie hesitated. "It's so far."

Zoë felt an inner heaviness that she'd learned through the years to recognize as a nudging from the Spirit.

"I'd better come," she said.

Connie let out a quick sigh. "Oh, good! We really need to pray," she said.

"I will, on my way. And we will when I get there."

༄

After switching her two afternoon appointments, Zoë headed for Malibu and found herself caught in stop-and-go traffic because of an oil spill on the Santa Monica Freeway. It was almost four when she started up the hill in Malibu.

She pulled into Connie's driveway and saw her pruning roses. Zoë rolled down the car window. "I'm going to head on up. Anything more I need to know?"

Connie hurried to the car and described Andrea's reaction to the Bible study.

Zoë nodded. "She's still angry and still in a hurry."

Connie placed her hand on Zoë's arm. "Oh, Lord, give Zoë wisdom. Help her to show Your truth to my friend, Andrea. We both love her so much! In Jesus' name, amen."

"Amen," Zoë agreed, giving Connie's hand a squeeze.

"Call me if you need me," Connie said, waving as Zoë shifted gears and backed out.

A moment later when Andrea answered the door, her blue eyes widened in surprise. "Mom!"

"Sorry I didn't call. Just found I needed to—" Zoë hesitated and smiled, "head out this way."

"Good. You're in time for fresh-baked bread."

Zoë sniffed appreciatively. "I smelled it before I rang the doorbell. You were ambitious." She followed Andrea to the kitchen and saw the five loaves cooling on a rack. "You were *really* ambitious!"

Andrea shrugged. "Nervous energy, I guess. Want a hunk?"

"If I can have a heel."

"Of course."

Zoë found a knife and cut a slice. "Good! Still warm. One for you?"

"Sure."

They leaned against the counters, opposite one another, nibbling the bread.

"It's delicious," Zoë said. "I feel healthier already!" She studied Andrea a moment, noting the tiny stress lines around her eyes and mouth. "How's your heart?"

Andrea bit her lip and shook her head. "This morning's Bible study on Abraham and Isaac was too much."

"Sometimes," Zoë kept her voice soft and gentle, "we struggle so against the truth, we make it harder on ourselves."

"No, it's God that makes it hard. He wants too much!" She sighed and closed her eyes. "I'm tired, Mom. I need another way, a quicker way. And," she gave Zoë a defiant stare, "I'm going to look for it tonight at Dolores's." She held up her hand. "Now, I love you, Mom, but I don't think like you do. And I'm going to trust my feelings for once, and do what I feel I need to do."

"Oh, my darling," Zoë said. "Try to trust God, not feelings! Truly, I'm worried about your going to Dolores's. It's witchcraft, Andrea. It's not of God."

"Are you saying Dolores is evil?" Andrea asked, her voice defensive.

"No, but don't you see how she ad-libs life, latches on to one thing, then another. She's restless because she has no anchor for her soul."

Zoë could see the set of Andrea's jaw. "You're very sure of yourself, aren't you?" Andrea asked.

Zoë shook her head. "Not of myself, of God's Word. Andrea, the Book of First John states very clearly that every spirit that acknowledges that Jesus Christ has come in the flesh—in other words, believes in the incarnation—is from God. But it goes on to say that every spirit that doesn't acknowledge Jesus is not from God." Andrea took a breath to break in, but Zoë continued. "It even says this is the spirit of the antichrist—"

"Dolores doesn't deny Jesus," Andrea interrupted. "She just says there are other ways,"

"But, dear heart, right there she's denied what Jesus said: 'I am the way, the truth, and the life,' and 'no man comes to the Father but by Me.'" Zoë went over to put her hand on Andrea's shoulder. "Andrea, you trusted God before. Can't you take a step of faith and do that again?"

Andrea drummed her fingers on the countertop. "You're as bad as Connie" She frowned and gave Zoë an icy glare. "Is that why you're here? Did Connie call you?"

Uh-oh, Zoë thought. *I have to be honest.* "As a matter of fact, she did. But Andrea, don't you see? It's because she loves you!"

"No, it's because she wants everybody to be just like her and believe her narrow little way."

"Andrea," Zoë kept her voice quiet but firm. "You know that is not true."

Andrea flashed a crooked smile. "No, what I know is I have work to do. If you'll excuse me, you'll find Tim in his room."

"Right," Zoë said. After Andrea had walked down the hall and shut the door to her room, Zoë said aloud, "Oh, Lord, I'm beginning to fear that Andrea has denied You. But I remember how the disciple Peter did that three times. And when he realized what he'd done, he wept. Oh, may she too experience the godly sorrow that leads to repentance and restoration."

Zoë found Tim coaxing Julie to walk over a short narrow plank between two chairs.

He looked up, saw Zoë in the doorway, said, "Hi, Gram!" and continued. "Good girl, Juliet. Come on, Julie!" Juliet sat on one chair and blinked.

"She can do it. She *can*," Tim said.

"When she's ready," Zoë said. She watched him try again and again. "You're very patient, Tim." She smiled, thinking to herself, he doesn't get that from his mother. And suddenly she blinked with the realization: In fact, his mother's walking her own tightrope right now.

After he'd finished with Juliet, Zoë and Tim went for a walk. Then Zoë tapped on Andrea's door. "I'll be leaving, Andrea."

Andrea opened the door. "You're welcome to stay for dinner."

Zoë heard the garage door open. "Ah, Peter's here." She hesitated and decided they needed to be alone. "Thanks anyway."

Andrea gave her a perfunctory peck on the cheek, and Zoë started for the front door. She met Peter in the hallway.

"Mom!" he exclaimed. "You'll stay for dinner?"

"Not tonight, darling. See you day after tomorrow." She gave him a hug and let herself out.

Peter turned toward Andrea, in the doorway of the bedroom. "What's with her?" he asked.

"Well, if you really want to know, I think she came to try to get me back on the—" Andrea drew quotation marks in the air, "'right' spiritual path."

"Oh?" He kissed her. "Do you need help?"

"Obviously she and Connie think so." She turned and he followed her into the bedroom.

"I might as well tell you." She turned to face him. "I just couldn't swallow today's Bible study on Abraham and Isaac. Peter, it's not for me! And I'm going over to Dolores's tonight."

"Yeah? What's up?"

"Her women's group is gathering."

He frowned. "You mean the designer witches?"

Andrea gave him a quizzical look.

He smiled. "Mom's term. She says they don't wear black robes. Just the latest stuff from Rodeo Drive."

"Oh, really, Peter! They are a sincere, loving group, and there's a true sisterhood there."

He sighed, closing his eyes, and she was startled to see his whole body slump. It somehow looked smaller, as though losing muscle tone. "You know, it's possible to be sincere but sincerely wrong." His brown eyes fastened on her, and they seemed infused with a deep sadness. "I wish you wouldn't," he said. "Oh, Andry, how I wish you could just trust and wait." He gestured toward Dolores's. "This really concerns me." His expression brightened. "Why not wait a little and see what the detective turns up?"

"I hear your concern, Peter, but I'm going."

He turned away from her and headed for the closet. She stared at his back. Was this all? She'd thought he'd argue, rationalize, try to change her mind. She watched him for a moment and then headed for the kitchen to begin setting the table.

The tension was palpable at dinner. She tried to make small talk with Tim, asking him about school, which worked for a short while, then began to sound like a game of twenty questions. He was picking up on the stress, too, she noted. Her own stomach felt knotted, cramped, and she ate little. The meal seemed interminable, and they lapsed into silence. She could hear the refrigerator cycle on and off, the tick of the clock in the living room. At last they finished the melon she served for dessert, and Tim asked to be excused. But Peter dawdled over his coffee forever. What a relief when he stood and she could clear the table.

She stalled for time in the kitchen after dinner, wiping out the oven and cleaning the cabinet fronts. At last the sun set into the ocean, a brilliant display of fire and smoke, and darkness began to fall. When she went into the bedroom for a sweater, she found Peter waiting. "Andrea, please don't do this. I honestly feel it's dangerous."

She pursed her lips and made no effort to hide her annoyance. "That's silly, Peter. Dolores feels that with the energy of the group, we might get some information about Joy. What's the harm?" She looked up at him, refusing to let her eyes waver. "I think you are being extremely judgmental."

She could see the muscles in his jaw tighten. "All right," he said, "but please listen just a moment, Andry." He sat on the edge of the bed and motioned for her to sit beside him.

She stood above him, eager to leave, resenting his patient, reasoning tone that made her feel like an unreasonable child. "I'm listening."

"Andrea," he said earnestly, "you used to believe the Bible is the Word of God. Do you now?"

She shrugged impatiently.

"Well," he continued, "it's very clear on the subject of witchcraft. In Deuteronomy—"

She rolled her eyes. "Oh, swell."

"God is speaking through Moses," he persisted, reaching for his Bible on the nightstand. He opened it and read, "'Let no one be found among you who sacrifices his son or daughter in the fire, who practices divination or sorcery, interprets omens, engages in witchcraft, or casts spells, or who is a medium or spiritist or who consults the dead. Anyone who does these things is detestable to the Lord'"

She couldn't resist. "Well, I'm already detestable to the Lord."

"That's not true!" he protested. "And don't you see? Witches and spells are as detestable to God as sacrificing a son or daughter! Now, that's from the Old Testament, but in the Book of Acts—"

She held up her hand. "Enough! I am out of here!"

When Peter heard the front door open and close, he picked up the phone and punched the numbers quickly. "Connie, she's gone over to Dolores's."

"Thought so," came Connie's voice. "Your mom's here with us. I think we need to get together and pray. Zoë and Jeff and I'll be right up, and I think I can get Mary Lou. She leads the Wednesday Bible study."

"Great." He hung up, sighed, and then paused to murmur quietly, "Oh, God, thanks that Mom stuck around. Isn't that just like her? And for these friends who would take the time to come and pray. But even before they get here, I have to ask You to please protect my wife."

In the hallway, he almost collided with Tim.

Tim looked up at him. "Hey, Dad, where'd Mom go in such a hurry?"

Peter thought quickly. He couldn't lie to his son. And he certainly wasn't going to send him to his bedroom or to watch TV. No. Tim needed to be a part of this, whether he understood completely or not. "Mom's going over to Dolores's."

Tim looked carefully at his dad. "Why? What's up?"

"Well, she thinks maybe she can learn something about Joy from that group of ladies meeting there tonight, and—"

"You mean the witches?" Tim interrupted.

"Yep. And I'm concerned about it."

"Gram says they're not connected with God at all."

"Right. In fact, He says in His Word not to have anything to do with them."

"That's what I thought."

"So Mr. and Mrs. Hendrix and another woman from church are going to come up and pray. Because prayer's the best weapon we have in spiritual warfare."

"Dad," Tim said, "I don't get it. She was always yelling about Brant and his heavy metal and ouija board. And now she's got herself into this."

"I know, Tim. I guess neither of us realized how desperate she is to know about Joy."

"Yeah, I guess."

"It's hard for us but probably tougher for Mom."

Tim thought a moment. "I guess she maybe kinda got sucked in with Mrs. Cooper, same as I did with Brant."

They both jumped as the doorbell rang. Peter started toward the door. "Wise observation, pal." He rumpled Tim's hair. "Come on. We need you to help us."

39

From Zoë's Prayer Journal

May 22: Dear heavenly Father, as we wait for Mary Lou to join us, I want to take this moment alone with You. Of course I'm not Andrea's genetic mother, but You know I love her as my own. And right now I have this picture in my mind of her as a baby and of me with her. I take her in my arms, and I put her in that little baby tub I used for all the kids. And I bathe her in Your living water, the water of Your Word! Oh, Lord, I have this sudden sense of breathlessness that I've learned through the years is either the enemy trying to distract me, or Your Holy Spirit showing me the gravity of the situation. It's spiritual warfare, isn't it? Time to do battle. Lead, us sovereign, all-powerful God, and please, in Jesus' name, wash Andrea clean and turn her totally, completely to You, amen.

ZOË CLOSED HER PRAYER JOURNAL as she heard Connie's call. "Zoë? Mary Lou's here."

"Good! Oh, good!" Zoë cried, grabbing her Bible and hurrying to join the others by the entryway.

Connie introduced Mary Lou, and Zoë hugged the tall, slender woman. "Feel like I know you," Zoë exclaimed. "What a sweetheart you are to come!"

"Ah," Mary Lou smiled. "The godly grandmother. What a delight to meet you."

"Grandmother, yes." Zoë said.

"Let's go, folks," Connie said impatiently.

Zoë, Mary Lou, Connie, and Jeff squeezed into Connie's car, and minutes later, pulled into Andrea and Peter's driveway.

Peter opened the front door with a sigh of relief. "Boy, am I glad to see you," he called. "Come on in, guys." He held out his hand. "You must be Mary Lou. I'm Peter, and this is Tim." They shook hands, and Peter turned to Zoë. "Mom! Bless you for sticking around!" He gave her a hug, and then grabbed Jeff's and Connie's hands. "Thanks for being available."

As he closed the door behind them, Peter said, "Let's sit around the dining room table." He led the way as Tim asked, "OK if I come too?"

"You bet!" Connie put her arm around Tim's shoulders. As they walked together, she admitted, "That Dolores really gets my goat! If only she'd stop meddling.

Zoë smiled. "I feel that way, too, Connie. But remember, our battle isn't against Dolores. In fact, it's not against flesh and blood at all."

"Oh, yeah, I know better. We're so wrapped up in ourselves and what the other guy does, we forget Satan is walkin' and stalkin'."

"Powers, rulers of the darkness, spiritual forces of evil. They're our real enemies," Jeff muttered.

Mary Lou nodded. "That's what Ephesians tells us. That and not to give the devil an opportunity."

"Yeah, and Andrea's gone and done it, right?" Connie asked. "Why, she's willingly opened the door to evil!"

"Possibly," Zoë said. "But we're all here tonight because we mustn't give up on Andrea. People may reject our message, but they're helpless against prayers!"

Connie nodded, running her fingers through her hair. "I've seen this coming, and I've been praying and praying that the Holy Spirit would ring bells and sound sirens to alert her, because she sure hasn't heard my warnings."

"Or mine," Peter added.

"Or mine," Zoë said.

"But it isn't over yet," Jeff noted, his rugged features somber and intent.

"Yes," added Mary Lou. "And when I led a study on spiritual warfare last year, I learned we don't have to just sit and wring our hands, because we're not helpless. Christ has given us power. Let's use it."

The others murmured agreement as they gathered around the circular table. Zoë looked at each member of the group. "One big way to wage warfare is with worship." She opened her Bible. "I just found this in Psalm 149. It starts, 'Praise the Lord. Sing to the Lord a new song.' It talks about how the Lord takes delight in His people. And then it says, verse 4, 'May the praise of God be in their mouths and a double-edged sword in their hands.' So I think that's saying that praise is a weapon."

Mary Lou nodded. "A double-edged sword, at that!"

"We know for sure that Satan hates it," Jeff agreed. He looked around at the group. "Let's do it!"

They took one another's hands, sitting silently a moment. Then Jeff began, "Oh, Father, we come before You with praise and thanksgiving. Praise that You are mightier than he who is in the world, praise that You are in charge, that You know the beginning from the end and that You will work all of this together for Your highest good." He continued exalting the Lord and His character.

There was a pause, and then Connie began singing, her voice soft and silvery.

"Great is Thy faithfulness, O God my Father! There is no shadow of turning with Thee."

The others joined in.

"Thou changest not; Thy compassions they fail not: As Thou hast been Thou forever wilt be."

They worked into a harmony so sweet, it brought a lump to Peter's throat. And the words—what an affirmation!

"Great is Thy faithfulness, Great is Thy faithfulness, Morning by morning new mercies I see; All I have needed Thy hand hath provided, Great is Thy faithfulness, Lord unto me!"

With the melody still lingering in the air, Peter exclaimed, "Oh, Lord! Show Andrea that You do provide all she needs. You and You alone! And dear Father, be a shield and protect her from any evil spirits across the road. Show her the truth and set her free."

ॐ

When Andrea stepped out the front door of her home, the air, dank and heavy, enveloped her like a chilled body-wrap. She shivered and buttoned her sweater.

An owl hooted mournfully above her, and she looked up at the power pole. In the waning light, she could just see the bird, perched on the crossbar, big as a cat, formidable against the deep blue sky. As she gazed at the owl, a wave of fear washed over her and she wondered for the hundredth time if she should call Dolores and make an excuse or simply run in the opposite direction. But no, she wouldn't run—not from the owl, not from Dolores and her women's group, or whatever awaited her there. She drew in a slow, deep breath. "I've got to go," she said aloud.

With each step, she could feel her pulse accelerate. Would this be a moment of truth? And if it was, could she bear it? Or would it catapult her off that thin little tightrope she'd been walking into a pit of madness? Would someone have to carry her away, a babbling idiot? "Oh, God," she heard herself breathe, "be with me tonight."

She walked past a half-dozen cars parked on the road and in Dolores's driveway and hesitated at the open gate. "Go for it!" she coached herself.

Dolores, stunning in a long black skirt and bright pink angora sweater, met Andrea in the middle of the patio. "Ah, Andrea!" she exclaimed, kissing her cheek. "I'm so glad you've come!" Andrea looked beyond her at the women gathered on the patio. Perfectly normal looking, she decided, smiling to herself as she noted an Oscar de la Renta dress and a St. John knit. Designer, yes, but that's Malibu. It'll be fine.

౩౨

In the dining room across the road, all was still. Then Mary Lou spoke. "Almighty Lord, how we praise Your Name! We know how Satan hates to hear those words, and," her voice grew stronger, more emphatic, "we do ask You, holy, righteous, omnipotent Lord, to bind Satan and his demons, in the name of Jesus. And we declare them powerless over Andrea, because she is Your child, because she has confessed You as her Savior. And even though she has, well, turned away, she still belongs to You. You have already placed a covering over her, and Lord, we believe You will give her a way to escape if she needs it.

How we praise You, Father, that You will win this spiritual battle! Satan means it for evil, but You mean it for good."

"Oh, God," Connie broke in, "I'm afraid Andrea feels safe because Dolores told her witches don't think Satan exists. But, Lord, surely witchcraft's got to be of Satan, because any sorcery or pagan ceremony is sure not from You. In fact, it denies You with its lies. And Satan is the daddy of lies. Open Andrea's eyes to see that lie! Remind her of who *You* are, that Jesus is not a way, but *the* way, the truth, the life." She paused and swallowed. "And I call upon You, God, in the Name of Jesus, to smash Satan's power, his plans against Andrea."

ॐ

Dolores smiled at Andrea. "Would you like something to drink?"

"Drink?" she asked. She'd thought she was coming to a ceremony, not a social gathering. Couldn't they just get on with it? "No, thanks."

Dolores shrugged and picked up her glass, swirled the red liquid and sipped. "Come!" she invited. "Let me introduce you."

Patty Edwards saw Andrea, smiled, and came toward them. "Andrea! Oh, I want to welcome you into this celebration of womanhood. Feel the energy already?" She gestured around the patio.

Andrea flashed a courtesy smile as Dolores led her on to a group of three. "Ah, Andrea. Blessed be!" one of them greeted her. "May you experience the divine tonight."

"Yes," another agreed. "May our Mother Luna give you knowledge and understanding."

Andrea nodded and pondered, *mother?* Following Dolores

into the kitchen, she stood awkwardly as Dolores poured a glass of wine for one of the women. When Dolores looked up, Andrea blurted, "Dolores, I have to confess. I'm a little nervous. No. A lot nervous. What is this 'mother' stuff?

"Oh, darling," Dolores soothed. "Don't be anxious. This is all very friendly. One of our principles is that we do no harm. We're practicing the craft of the wise. And you're seeking wisdom, so you've come to a good place. We'll just see what we can learn tonight. Not to worry."

Andrea nodded, but she felt an uneasiness in the pit of her stomach, and her sense of disquiet intensified. She wasn't sure if she was more worried about what might happen or the possibility that nothing at all would happen.

What if this was another frustrating "almost" time, like with Sybil's channeling? A picture of Joy, grinning out from her hiding place in the closet, flashed into her mind, like a slide projected on a screen. Then another scene: Joy riding her red Christmas tricycle, laughing. How hungry she was for a glimpse of her daughter, a sign, anything!

She glanced at her neighbor, feeling desperate for a word, a touch, some connectedness to break the silence, the tension. "Dolores," she began.

Dolores seemed to sense her anxiety. "Hush, darling. You're going to be fine," she promised, her voice deep and rich, reassuring. "Come here, love!" As Andrea moved toward her, Dolores wrapped her arms around her, increasing the pressure ever so subtly, till she enveloped her in the most incredibly calming hug.

Andrea felt the tightness in her muscles release as a sense of calm flowed from her mentor's body into her own. "It's all right," the velvet voice soothed. "You'll see." Dolores released her slowly, patting her gently, and as Andrea allowed herself to relax still more, she knew she'd been right to come.

"Just let go and let it unfold. Be open." Dolores led the way back outside.

~

The prayer group chorused agreement to Connie's call for God to rebuke Satan. Zoë continued, "Lord, You've promised if Andrea seeks You, You'll answer. May she cry out to You. Thank You that You say in Psalm 139 that we—including Andrea—can't flee from Your presence, that if she ascends to heaven You are there, and even if to hell You are also there. You're everywhere, Lord!"

She paused and lifted her hand, exclaiming, "Oh, God, of course! The moon is only a form of light. It's not the light of the world. Jesus is! You taught me that in the Gospel of John this morning. It's Jesus who enlightens every man. Dear Jesus, may You enlighten Andrea tonight."

As his mother prayed, Peter began to feel a weight, a pressure from deep inside—something wanting to be revealed, and he had no idea what, except that he felt alarmingly close to tears. But he couldn't and wouldn't cry in front of people. He tried to think when anyone last saw him cry. Probably back when he was Tim's age, when a friend told him about the dog he'd seen, dead, in the dump. And when he and his dad went to see, they'd found his own handsome collie, MacDuff, as though asleep, without a mark on him. Poisoned, they'd guessed. He tried desperately to clear away the painful image and to concentrate on his mother's prayer.

When she finished, the group waited in silence, and Peter could feel his underarms begin to sweat. *I can't cry in front of Tim and with all these people*, he thought. What, what in the world was this? Where was it coming from? It wasn't grief or even a mourning for Joy. "Lord," he prayed silently, "what *is* it?" And in a moment, he knew. Sorrow. Yes, that was it. Yet not sorrow over something he'd done, but something not done.

Connie's voice broke through his thoughts. "Lord, remind my dear friend of what she heard today in our Bible study. Take off those blinders and help her see things through Your eyes. Take away this awful need to know where Joy is. Help her to let go." She continued, but Peter heard only fragments. "Show her what Dolores offers is a counterfeit of what You have. We confess we're not always sensitive."

Now his pulse quickened, as though he were waiting to make a speech before a thousand people. Why this rising panic? It was as if there was something he needed to do. One word from all that Connie had prayed began to sound in his mind and spirit: "Confess."

Then he heard Tim. "God," he said, his voice quavering a little, "take care of Mom. Make her believe that You can," he hesitated, "handle all this stuff. Don't let anything bad happen." He swallowed audibly. "We need her."

Peter could hear someone moving close to Tim—Connie, he guessed—to comfort him. But he stayed rooted to his chair, eyes closed, knowing suddenly it was time to be honest, both before the Lord and before those who prayed with him. "Oh, Lord," he heard himself begin, "as I sit here, waiting and trusting You, I do see that I haven't been the husband I should have been through this crisis. If I'd been more, um—" he groped for the best way to say it, "accessible, more understanding, less dogmatic, Andrea might not be reaching out this way tonight. I've thought I had to be the strong one, to hold everyone together. But I've had a heart of stone, just like I read about in the Old Testament the other day. I wondered why it bothered me so when I read it, and now I see You were showing me—myself.

Oh, God, I want a heart of flesh, to be compassionate and even vulnerable. Lord, I think You've given me that heart, but I haven't allowed myself to feel it," he continued. "I've been trying to be the strong, silent rock, I guess. Now I want to break that silence. I repent of my hardness. I'm hurting, too, Lord. I'm afraid! And I need terribly to be close to my wife and my son."

Peter took a tremulous breath. "Help me, Father, to be honest, unafraid to be human, to show my love a whole lot more. Because Lord, You know how I love my family!"

Covering his face with his hands, he began to weep. And in a moment he felt each person, one by one, there with a hand on his shoulder. Their acceptance, their love, amazed and overwhelmed him.

He heard Jeff murmur. "I'm that way, too, I confess."

Tim clung to Peter and, through his own tears, whispered, "I love you, too, Dad."

*

Without preamble, the women on Dolores's patio grew quiet, turning expectantly toward a woman in a flowing white dress. A musky-sweet aroma of burning incense wafted across the patio.

"It's time," Dolores murmured. "That's Diana at the altar, our high priestess. Now, just empty your mind of everything else."

Standing at a small candlelit table in the center of the patio, the woman raised her arms toward the mountains. Then she moved toward the edge of the paving, placing each foot precisely, like a dancer. Slowly, with intense concentration, she walked a clockwise circle. The others followed, one sprinkling salt behind her.

"Diana is casting the circle," Dolores whispered, pulling Andrea into the group.

When the circle, perhaps fifteen feet in diameter, was defined, Dolores explained, "Now, she'll call the quarters. It's to protect the circle."

Andrea watched, fascinated, as the priestess picked up a goblet from the altar.

"She'll use a different implement to invite each of the elements, at the four points of the compass," Dolores noted.

Her dress flowing around her slender body, the priestess walked with slow, deliberate steps to the western edge of the circle. She held the goblet high and declared, "Blessed be the powers of water! Hosts of the water realm of the west, you are welcome to join us at this hallowed place in this sacred hour, as we honor our Mother goddess." She bent and drew with chalk on the patio, and Andrea leaned forward to see. A pentagram.

"She'll go back to the altar and get a new tool for the earth," Dolores explained. Andrea stood, engrossed as the priestess paced to the northern point, extending a dish of stones to invite the powers of earth. Then she used a twig with leaves at the east to invoke the powers of air, and a lighted candle at the south to call the powers of fire.

When she finished, the priestess returned to the western point, then to the altar and held out her arms to the group. "All who love the lady, our Mother goddess, are welcome here to share in the joy of Esbat," she declared, her voice resonant as a professional singer's. She turned toward the mountains. "Blessed be the lady moon, mother of all life. We invite your presence in our circle tonight as we stand in the light of your love to worship in the ancient way. We invoke your primal power that in our rites and petitions we may weave magick by the moon."

The group chorused, "Welcome the lady. So mote it be." Andrea looked up at the mountains and saw the sky begin to glow. In a moment, the first edge of the moon appeared, a mere wink of an eye. Little by little, the eye opened to rounded fullness. An exclamation of exultation swept through the group, and they began dancing, as one woman piped a tune on a slender wooden recorder and another beat a small drum.

This is bizarre, Andrea thought. *I want to leave. But I feel— drugged.* She put her hand to her head. *Impossible. I've had nothing to eat or drink.*

"Just let yourself relax." Dolores took Andrea's hand. "Move with it," she urged, as they merged with the circle of eleven other women.

Feeling awkward and apprehensive, alternately hot and cold, Andrea tried to blend in with the group. One woman began chanting, "Loo-nah! Loo-nah!" and the others joined in. The priestess danced alone, in the center of the circle, and Andrea marveled at how beautiful she was. She moved with fluid grace, long blond hair swirling like liquid gold about her face. The candlelight cast changing colors on her dress: pearlescent shades of lavender, aqua, rose. Then, as Diana turned, Andrea saw her face. It glowed as though lighted from within. Like an angel.

In an exquisitely controlled unfolding motion, the woman in white lifted first one arm, then the other toward the moon, moving in an attitude of supplication and expectation.

Andrea's heart seemed to swell as she felt herself on the very threshold of discovery, revelation. Surely she could trust anything so radiant, so bright, so full of light.

40

ACROSS THE ROAD, the group sat in silence around the dining room table. Then Zoë spoke. "Lord, we're all wondering what's going on at Dolores's right now, what sort of aberration might be invoked. Father, I pray that, by Your Holy Spirit, You will give Andrea a sense of unrest, a certainty that she doesn't belong there. Reveal the counterfeit. Even scare her, if that's what it takes. Then make a way of escape."

"Oh, I agree!" Connie exclaimed. "Show her she needs to get outta there, because she is Yours, and this shindig is not of You."

As Andrea stared, mesmerized, an older woman with close-cropped silver hair moved to the altar. For the first time,

Andrea noticed the accoutrements on the table: a candelabra with a pentagon base, a mirror, and a knife, together with the implements the priestess had used for calling the quarters. Now, as the priestess stood, facing the moon, she lowered her arms. The older woman picked up the knife and, positioning herself behind Diana, raised it above the priestess's head, pointing its glistening blade toward the moon.

"Blessed Luna," the older woman intoned, "your fertile light washes over our priestess, Diana, permeating her very being with vibrant life-energy." She extended the knife still higher. "Enter now this consecrated athame and prepare to merge with her. For she is your loving daughter and represents our very souls. Come into her, our Mother, and grace this sacred space."

"Grace this sacred space, oh Mother Luna," the group echoed. "We now draw down the moon."

The older woman lowered the knife, walked around the priestess and stood before her, placing the knife flat against her breastbone, declaring, "I now draw the moon into you. You are divinely incarnate. You are light."

Andrea felt her heart begin to pound an alarm. *What is it?* she wondered, closing her eyes.

Four words flashed like a neon sign into her consciousness: "Jesus is the light."

She gasped. *Jesus*, she thought. *Light of the world. Not the moon or the mother goddess. It's Jesus!*

"Now," Dolores whispered, clasping Andrea's hand. "The magick can begin. This is it, Andrea! The priestess will hold up the mirror to try to see Joy!"

"Wait!" Diana shouted, holding out her arms. The group stood, frozen like ice sculptures in the moonlight. Andrea swallowed involuntarily and held her breath. She could hear her own heartbeat.

At last Diana continued, her voice now harsh, "I sense an adverse energy. It must be expelled." She looked around the group.

"Oh, Lord, it's me!" Andrea murmured to herself, panic surging. "Oh, protect me," she murmured.

Dolores's grip tightened, her fingernails digging into Andrea's wrist, and Andrea could only cry out inwardly, "Lord, I'm sorry I turned from You."

The priestess pivoted toward Andrea, eyes so eerily white that a chill raced through Andrea's body. Then Diana reached back to the older woman. Seizing the knife, she pointed it toward Andrea. "It's you! I feel your hostile energy!"

Unbidden, a song slid into Andrea's mind, and she could hear the words, "There is strength in the name of the Lord. There is power in the name of the Lord."

"It's Jesus!" Andrea heard herself proclaim. "The One who *created* the moon."

Dolores gasped as the priestess started toward Andrea, moonlight glinting off the knife's blade. Diana's eyes glowed, twin reflections of the moon's whiteness. Her face contorted into a chilling mask of anger.

Andrea wrested her hand free from Dolores, feeling a rush of strength. But the only way out was across the patio, past the priestess. "Oh, Jesus, help me!" she cried.

The priestess stopped and sank to her knees. Opening her mouth into a broad O she shrieked like a wounded cat. The other women neither moved nor spoke.

Now! Andrea thought.

Like a sprinter exploding from a starting block, she fled, fueled by fear. Across the patio and through the gate she bolted, expecting at any moment to be pursued and caught. If she could just get to the road.

She stumbled, recovered, felt her ankle twist on the rough ground but raced on. At last, she reached the road and crossed to the foot of the stairs leading up the bank to her own house. It was only then that she looked back. Nothing. Relief flooded through her, and her knees buckled. She sank down in the dirt and the darkness. "Oh, God," she cried, looking apprehensively back toward Dolores's and then up at the warm glow of lights of her own house, "You gave me the strength to flee, I know." She felt the heat of tears on her cheeks as she prayed, "Oh, Lord, thank You for making a way!"

She drew a shaky breath. Weak and wobbly, she stood and stumbled up the stairs toward the sliding back door of her home. She could hear voices inside. Someone besides Peter and Tim. She sat on the top step for a long time, fighting a terrible sense of pressure just to the left of her breastbone. "Oh, Lord, You've delivered me, and I don't deserve it!" she cried. "I deserve to be punished for all my unbelief and—oh, God—for cursing You!" Burying her face in her hands, she groaned with pain as she wept. "God," she moaned, "I'm sorry!"

Little by little the ache eased, and she lifted her head, marveling that the fear and the weight were gone. She felt herself shaking from the cold. Fumbling in her pocket, she found tissues and wiped her face and blew her nose. *Do I dare face the group inside?* she wondered.

At last, longing to be with them, she stood and grasped the doorframe till the dizziness passed. She tugged at the door. Locked. She tapped lightly and waited. Then again, harder. In a moment, Peter appeared. His face broke into a broad grin as he slid the door open, then enfolded her in his arms.

"Oh, my darling Andry," he murmured, his face against her hair. "I'm so relieved! Oh, sweetheart, you're shaking. Are you all right?"

"I think so. Oh, Peter, it was—I—I—" She couldn't go on.

"It's OK. Come sit down. Connie and Jeff and Mom and Mary Lou are here. Man, have we been praying!"

"I know," she said. "I felt it. It was like someone was telling me what to say, like I was surrounded with, I don't know, maybe a shield or armor."

"Mom!" She felt Tim's hand on her arm. "Oh, Mom! You OK?"

"Yes, darling," she said slowly. "Maybe even better than OK."

Then Zoë was there, hugging her. Then Connie and Jeff and Mary Lou. She heard herself laughing and crying.

Peter led her into the living room, where he drew her gently onto the sofa and wrapped the blue afghan about her. Sitting beside her, he put his arm around her. Tim sat close on her other side. Someone set a cup of steaming tea on the coffee table in front of her.

She heard Connie whisper, "Should we leave?"

"Oh, no. Don't go," she pleaded. "Help me put this all together."

Zoë and the others sat on the floor by the sofa, looking up at her, waiting.

"You were right, Peter," she said quietly. "It was very definitely not from God. But at first, it was so appealing. One woman in particular, a leader or priestess or whatever, looked so beautiful, like an angel. But when she started asking the moon to enter us, I just knew it wasn't anything I wanted!" She looked down at Zoë's tender expression. "You're not going to believe this. I called out the name of Jesus. That He is the light. The One who created the moon."

"Alleluia," Zoë whispered.

"Bet that made a big hit," Connie said.

"Really!" Andrea glanced at Connie's droll smile. "Because then the priestess was coming toward me with the ceremonial knife. I thought for a minute she, and maybe the others, were going to attack me. Truly, God made a way of escape for me." Her eyes scanned the faces of the foursome on the floor, and she felt her face flush. "Oh, Mary Lou, I'm so ashamed. You've seen me shaking my head in your Bible study."

"Oh, hon, I knew you were hurting!" Mary Lou said.

"But I was so resistant, so determined not to believe. That you would come here tonight . . ." She shook her head. "And Mom! I was so ugly this afternoon. You've been so patient, so there for me."

"Of course," Zoë said with tears in her voice, "I love you."

Andrea nodded and felt tears sting her own eyes. "I know." She looked at Connie. "And my friend, I don't know how you've put up with me. You tried so hard, and with such love, to warn me, and I was so stubborn."

"Hey," Connie shrugged. "None of us are exactly overnight miracles."

New tears sprang to her eyes. "Yes, but it's more than that. You don't know what I did." Her voice broke and she pressed the tissue to her face.

"Tonight?" Peter asked gently.

"No. Way back. On Joy's birthday."

The group waited. "Do you want to tell us?" Zoë asked softly.

"Don't want to. Have to," she wept.

"Go for it," Connie urged, her voice sweet, encouraging.

Andrea took a deep breath. "It all started after Joy disappeared, and I think now that I was half-crazy. And I, um, well, Mom, you know, I made a bargain. No, I thought I could make a bargain with God." She shook her head. "I know. Who am I to try to make a deal with God, as though He were one of my clients, right? Pretty presumptuous! I see that now." She swallowed. "Anyway, my part was to quit work and stay home and be a good mom. I thought maybe God took Joy because I hadn't stayed home, got too preoccupied with work and getting that new account."

She felt Peter's arm tighten around her.

"And God's part was to bring Joy back. That's all. Just give me back my daughter. But, you see, I really expected Him to bring her back for her birthday."

Connie scooted over toward the couch to reach for her hand, and Andrea saw a tear glistening on her friend's freckled cheek. "I know, and He didn't," Connie murmured.

"Nope. And I was so ang-ry," She made two long syllables of the word. "And so I just basically—" she paused, clenching her teeth, "told God to go to hell."

Peter exhaled audibly. "You what? What did you actually say?"

"I said, 'the hell with You, God!'"

She glanced at Peter, expecting him to be shocked and instead saw softness in his brown eyes, compassion in his boyish face.

"Oh, Andry," he said, drawing her close. "I had no idea. You didn't just lose your Joy, you lost your God!" He held her closer, and she leaned against him a moment before she could look around at the others. She just knew they would hate her, be appalled, feel betrayed, never want her in the church again. Instead, she saw tears of empathy in their eyes.

"Oh, Andrea!" Connie cried. "The pain you've been through, and you were so alone. Nobody knew."

"No, nobody. Except Dolores. It happened—I said it to God—at her house."

Jeff whistled softly. "There's something about that place that is not healthy!"

Andrea nodded and glanced around the group, amazed at their reaction. "But aren't you going to stone me, or at least throw me out of the church?" she asked, her voice trembling. "I think you probably should. In fact, I think God should have zapped me right over there at Dolores's."

"That's not His style, sweetheart," Zoë said. "He loves you so much that He's been waiting for you to come back to Him, just like the father waiting for the prodigal son to return. Oh, don't you believe there's rejoicing in heaven tonight, Andrea? One big party!"

She sighed. It was too good to be true.

"Andrea," Mary Lou asked with a warm smile, "do you remember why Jesus died?"

"So we could be forgiven," she answered.

Mary Lou leaned forward, wriggling her fingers toward herself in the classic charades give-me-more gesture.

Andrea thought a moment. "So *I* could be forgiven?"

Mary Lou grinned. "Bingo! You, Andrea."

"You think so?" Andrea wiped her nose. "Will God even forgive what I did?"

The group nodded, and Tim whispered, "Hey, Gram, she's been reading the same book as you!"

Zoë smiled, "Just as I told Tim, He said He will. 'If we confess our sins, He is faithful and just and will forgive us our sins and cleanse us of all unrighteousness.'"

"I know that scripture," Andrea nodded.

"Well, it has your name on it. 'If Andrea confesses her sins . . .'"

"I did that. Tonight. And, it's true. I felt different afterward."

"I have to tell you," Zoë said, "you look different too."
She laughed. "A mess, for sure."

"No, you do look different," said Mary Lou. "When you came to Bible study, I always noticed the sadness, not just in your eyes, but your whole countenance. It's different now."

"Really?" Andrea closed her eyes as the events of the evening coursed through her mind. In some ways it all seemed like a surreal dream. But it had happened. Of that, she was sure. And she didn't want to forget one single detail. "I feel like a walking miracle," she said at last. "And as for you—Zoë and Connie and Mary Lou—you're the women I want in my life." She thought a moment. "Shouldn't we, I mean, couldn't we just thank God?"

"What a concept!" Connie grinned. She and the others hitched themselves closer to the couch, placing their hands on Andrea, Peter, and Tim.

"Oh, sovereign God," Mary Lou began, "You are our El Elyon, our God Most High, and You are in control of everything on this earth and above and beneath it. How we praise and thank You for Your victory tonight, and for watching over Andrea, for bringing her safely through and back into Your arms. And we ask You, Lord, to bind any spirits of doubt and discouragement and restrain them from attacking Andrea again and to free her from fear."

"Father," Connie added, "I want to pray for Dolores. If she's just been kinda dumb and ad-libbing her way through life and messing around with things she doesn't really understand, then use everything that went on tonight to show her Your truth, Your mercy, Your loving-kindness."

"Lord," Peter joined in, "how I thank You for faithful friends who came tonight to do spiritual battle and for the power of prayer and the fact that You hear and You act. Thank

You for protecting my Andrea and for—," he cleared his throat, "showing me how much I love her."

Andrea felt new tears on her face as the others prayed, and with those prayers, a growing need to do something specific for the Lord. But what? Something connected with Joy, she was sure. It was only as they finished that she knew just what to do. She turned to Mary Lou. "You talked this morning about building an altar, remember?"

Mary Lou nodded.

"I want to build an altar," she said. "In 'love, obedience, and worship,' right?" Mary Lou's eyes met hers in shared understanding. But she could see Peter's surprise in the lift of one eyebrow. "It won't take long," she promised. "Let's go outside." Wrapping herself in the afghan, she stood and the others followed her out the front door and into the yard. "This looks good," she said, pointing to the rock with the shell fossils that stood where the sidewalk met the driveway. It shone, damp from the dew, in the entry lights. She glanced across the road and saw the lights of Dolores's house. Never mind.

Picking up a smaller rock, she knelt. "Oh, Lord, forgive me for not trusting You, for wanting my will, not Yours. Oh, I see it now. I was being so impatient, always in a hurry, wanting answers now. Thank You for the forgiveness that is mine through Christ Jesus. I thank You for scaring me tonight, and especially for helping me get away. How gracious, how merciful You are!" She paused. "And as for Joy, who gave her to us but You? I thank you for that precious gift, as Connie says, for lending her to us."

She took a deep breath. "Now, Lord, like Abraham with Isaac—" She paused. "Oh, was it only this morning that I said I couldn't do this? Well, now I want to. I want to place this rock on this altar as a symbol of my daughter, my only daughter, my

Joy." She set the smaller rock atop the larger. "She's Yours, Lord, my Jehovah-Jireh. You are the God who provides. I thank You that You provide all I really need, and that I don't need to grasp for more. Yes, I long for Joy's return, but it's You I really need. I know that if Joy's dead, she's with You, and You are all-sufficient for her. And if she's alive, You're watching over her, providing for her. I trust her to You, Father."

She bowed her head in silence. A gentle breeze blew through the stillness, sweetly scented with wildflowers. She shook her head in wonderment, as she became aware of a sound, not audible to her ears, but discernible somehow, deep within. Speaking to my heart, she realized—a gentle laughter, an expression of great pleasure. It filled her with an oddly balanced combination of elation and peace.

She wasn't sure how long she knelt, savoring the sweetness of surrender, listening to that silent voice. Gradually she noticed the cold of the ground, the cramping in her left leg. With a long sigh of serenity, she pulled herself up and turned, seeing only Peter, and leaned into his embrace. After a while, another arm hugged her around the hips. Tim. She reached down to wrap one arm around his shoulders. Then she felt another hand on hers. Zoë's.

Somewhere, far away, it seemed, she heard a car's engine start. How sensitive it was of them, those three prayer warriors, to withdraw so discreetly.

Andrea turned toward the door. Snuggling against Peter, she pulled Tim tighter against her waist. Zoë put her arm around Tim, and together they walked back toward the house.

41

WITH A CLICK, the clock radio came to life.

"Early morning coastal clouds," the announcer intoned. Without opening her eyes, Andrea wriggled in the bed toward Peter.

"Every morning in May, 'Early morning coastal clouds,'" he murmured as he drew her close. "So what else is new?"

I'm new, she realized as the events of the previous night flooded through her mind. "Me," she murmured.

"You what?" Peter asked.

"I'm new. I mean, I feel new."

He tilted his head back to look at her thoughtfully. "Behold, the new Mrs. Lang! I like the new Mrs. Lang." He kissed her tiny nose. "Correction. I love the new Mrs. Lang." He was silent a moment. "Know what else? I'm new too. Last night was a renewal, an awakening for me too."

"And I love the new Mr. Lang!" She snuggled against him. "Wish you didn't have to go to work."

She could feel him grin. "Me too. But I do have a guy coming in from the East Coast this morning."

"Well, you're no fun," she teased. She listened for a moment. "I can hear your Mom in the kitchen. Glad she didn't try to drive home so late last night."

He nodded, and she lingered, face next to his, feeling the sandpaper of a day's growth of beard. Slowly, reluctantly, she slid out of bed and poked her head into the hallway. "Tim!" she called. "Hop to it." Back in the bedroom, she called to Peter as he headed for the shower, "Know what? I feel lighter." She shrugged. "I really do."

"Sure," he agreed. "You shed a lot of stuff last night. Stuff I had no idea you were carrying around."

"I know. I complained that you didn't communicate, but I wasn't being honest with you." She smiled and waved him into the shower.

A moment later, in the kitchen, she found the griddle heating while Zoë dipped thick slices of French bread into an egg batter.

"Hi, darling!" Zoë exclaimed, as Andrea hugged her. "I thought this morning called for something special."

"It is a special day!" Andrea nodded. "Thanks, Mom. French toast sounds perfect."

When they were all seated at breakfast, Peter cleared his throat and looked across at his mother. "I have another confession to make," he said.

"I don't know if I can handle one more thing," Zoë said, putting her hand to her heart.

Peter hesitated. "After I went to bed and thought about all the huge things that happened last night, I realized something

I'd never admitted. Not to you, Mom, or myself." He pressed his lips together.

"Yes?" Zoë prompted.

"Well, you remember when Dad left, and then you were divorced. What I realized was that I—well—I hate to say this. But a part of me as a kid—kind of blamed you."

"Oh, but Peter," Andrea broke in. "Your dad's always made it clear that he was the one who—"

He nodded. "I'm sorry, Mom. I know now it was Dad who had the problem, not you. But back then, I thought if you'd done something or said something."

"Oh, my darling, I understand," Zoë said, her eyes bright and discerning.

Peter continued. "I guess, bottom line, I just didn't want Dad to have feet of clay."

Zoë reached across the table for his hand. "So that's why you withdrew and never talked about it."

His lips parted and he tipped his head back, new insight in his eyes. "Maybe that's when I started holding in my feelings."

"Oh, Peter," Andrea murmured, grasping his arm.

"Sounds like it," Zoë murmured. She thought a moment and sighed. "Divorce is tough on so many people!"

Andrea closed her eyes and took a deep breath, feeling Peter's childhood pain, grateful for his honesty. Then her eyes snapped open. *What was I thinking of when I played up to Eric? I could have really messed up!*

"I'm glad you guys are together," Tim said softly, looking from Peter to Andrea.

Andrea nodded, feeling her eyes well. "Me too."

Zoë nodded. "Let's just thank the Lord, shall we?"

They reached for one another's hands and Zoë began, "Oh, Father, thank You for the mighty way You're working in this family! For Tim's receiving You, Jesus, as His personal Savior and friend. For Peter's honesty and tender heart. For Andrea's beautiful return to Your fold. And Lord, for showing me yesterday that I don't own my time, because without Your reminder, I'd have missed the blessing of being here. Lord, You are great, and we love You so much! We thank You for each other and for the food You've given us, in Jesus' name, amen."

They looked up, smiling at one another. Then Zoë brought out the French toast she'd kept warm in the oven.

As Tim stabbed a piece of toast, Andrea turned to him. "Are you exhausted, honey? It was a late night."

"Nah. I dreamed about angels and stuff."

She smiled. "I think there were definitely angels around last night."

"Besides," he added, "even if I was tired, I wouldn't want to miss school. Our whole grade's going on a field trip to Tapia Park. And you know what else?" He reached for the syrup. "I have a new best friend."

"You do?" she exclaimed, trying not to show too much delight.

"Yeah. His name is Jonathan. I told you about him. Met him in Sunday school. He's not in my same classroom at school." Tim balanced his fork on his forefinger. "And y'know, I said his dad trains animals for the movies? Well, he's done lots of dogs and cats. Remember the calico in *The Amazing Journey*? He trained her." He took a quick swallow of milk. "So Jonathan's gonna help me with Juliet. Can I have him over after school, Mom? Today?"

"Sure. Does he live around here?"

"Uh-huh, almost at the bottom of our hill. He could walk up after school."

"Fine. I might manage some chocolate chip cookies."

"Awright!"

Later, Andrea went outside as Zoë left. As she started out the driveway, Zoë rolled down her car window. "Ephesians 6:11!" she called. "Just thought of it."

Andrea smiled and waved, then turned to watch Peter back his car out of the garage. She blew kisses, putting her whole body into an elaborate pantomime, and saw Peter and Tim grin as they drove away.

Glancing across at Dolores's, she marveled at the events of the preceding night. Deliverance. That's what it was. She headed inside. All she knew was that she felt eager to spend time with the Lord, to thank Him, to get to know Him better. It wasn't a "have-to," but a "want-to."

She heard the phone as she opened the door and answered to hear Connie's warm voice. "Are you pooped? That was some evening you had, lady!"

"Not at all!" she exclaimed. "I'm flying high."

Connie chuckled. "I'm glad." Her voice grew more serious. "Oh, Andrea, I'm so thankful for your—well, I'd call it your deliverance. Been real worried about you."

"Deliverance is the very word I was just thinking. Oh, Connie, how can I thank you for not giving up on me?"

"Shoot, you don't have to. But I tell you, that was some powerhouse time last night. Not just for you, but for all of us. I feel such a bond now with you."

Andrea felt her heart stir in agreement, a desire to strengthen this bond. "Me too. A special closeness that's more than just friendship. Connie," she added, "I want to be here for you, instead of always taking from you. I want to be a support for you and your needs. Could we get together regularly to pray?"

"I'd love that." Connie waited a moment. "Andrea, I don't

want to be a wet blanket or look for trouble, but when I was praying this morning, I thought of something."

"What's that?"

"That maybe it's important for you to be on guard."

"How so?"

"You had such a victory last night, but you know, the enemy's a sore loser. Remember Job? The Bible calls him blameless and upright. He feared God. And Satan couldn't wait to get his hands on him."

Andrea took a deep breath. "Hadn't thought of that. Not sure I want to. I feel so protected."

"Well, you are. But I guess I'd like you to have some extra cover. So here's an idea. Wouldn't hurt to 'put on the whole armor of God.' Tells how in the sixth chapter of Ephesians."

Andrea laughed. "You and Mom! The last thing she said to me was 'Ephesians 6:11.'" She heard a blip on the phone line.

"Oh," Connie exclaimed. "It's call waiting, and I'm expecting to hear from my mom. But look at Ephesians 6, verses 10 to 18."

"Right."

Replacing the phone, Andrea headed for their living room, smiling over her two mentors. She found her Bible on the bookshelf and settled into the rocker. Locating the chapter, she read through the verses.

"Finally, be strong in the Lord and in His mighty power. Put on the whole armor of God so that you can take your stand against the devil's schemes. For our struggle is not against flesh and blood, but against the rulers, against the authorities, against the powers of this dark world and against the spiritual forces of evil in the heavenly realms."

She paused. *Right!* she thought. *I felt something more than flesh and blood last night.* She read on: "Therefore put on the full armor of God, so that you may be able to stand your ground, and after you have done everything, to stand."

Andrea read through the parts of the armor, then reread the verses and pondered them. *I know what,* she decided. *I'll pray through this whole passage.*

"Dear Lord," she began aloud, "my heart is so full of thanksgiving for last night and for being back in a relationship with You. Thank You for waiting for me. And Lord, I ask You, as verse 13 says, to help me to stand my ground against any setback or any doubts. So right now, I buckle the 'belt of truth' around my waist. Oh, thank You, for showing me last night what's true and what's not!" She paused before she continued. "And Father, I want that 'breastplate of righteousness.' I'm not sure I even understand righteousness yet, and I sure don't feel righteous. But by faith I know I can put on and wear Christ's righteousness to protect me. Thank You for that! Father, I also want to put on my feet 'the readiness' that comes from the gospel of peace. Give me those shoes, Father, so I can walk in Your will and not my own. And Lord, I need the 'shield of faith.' When I tossed that aside these past months, I was so defenseless and didn't even know it!"

She sat quietly a moment. "Next, I put on the 'helmet of salvation' and, oh, how I thank You for what Jesus did on the cross, for saving me. May this helmet cover my mind and all its stupid fears and imaginings." She thought a moment. "I see it. There was like a battle going on in my mind all these months. It's our minds the enemy wants! Thanks for that understanding, Lord." She savored her new insight before adding, "And finally, Lord, with the 'sword of the Spirit,' which is Your Word, I'm ready for battle. And I know Your Word is living and powerful. It's even sharper than a two-edged sword."

She stopped, surprised. Where had she read that? "Oh,

Lord, You're helping me recall scripture I haven't looked at in years. Thank you." She broke off at the sound of a car in the driveway. "I praise You in Jesus' name, amen," she added hastily as she hurried toward the entrance.

Through the windows flanking the front door she could see Peter's Olds. Then Eric's familiar gray Chevy pulled in behind him. Something happened on the way down the hill, she thought, pressing her hand against her chest.

She flung the door open just as the two men arrived at the entry. "What's happened?" she cried. "Tim?"

Peter reached for her hand. "No, no. Tim's on his way to school. But Eric was just heading up to our house and saw me drop Tim off."

Her mind raced. "Then it's Joy."

"We're not sure." Eric's voice was calm. "But it could be something."

Just beyond his head she saw something moving, a turkey vulture soaring in on ebony wings to land on the power pole behind their house. Head blood-red, wings still half-spread, it waited, watching. She looked away, shuddering.

As they moved into the living room, she could feel panic rising and prayed silently, "Oh, Lord, help me not to react in my old ways. Help me to trust You."

She sat on the edge of the couch, Peter beside her. Eric took the chair facing them, leaning forward. "Early yesterday evening some campers in Malibu Canyon found the body of a child."

She covered her mouth with her hand to stifle a cry.

"It took them some time to get to a place to call us," Eric continued. "Our men went in first thing this morning and are on their way back. They say it's been there awhile and is not in real good shape. They did say that the hair was reddish blond."

She closed her eyes and saw Joy on her tricycle, the sun glinting off her strawberry blond hair. For a moment, horror paralyzed her. Malibu Canyon wasn't that far from where Joy disappeared.

Is this the answer I get for trusting her to God? she wondered. She felt Peter's arm around her and took a deep breath. *Come on*, she reminded herself, *you did go looking for an answer last night.*

She inhaled sharply. "Last night I had to have an answer. Now I'm not sure I'm ready."

"Remember," Eric cautioned, "we don't know anything more than I told you. The forensic pathologist will be in this morning."

"And how much can they tell us without real sophisticated testing?" she asked.

"Mainly age and sex."

"So," Andrea said, "They might be able to say, 'Yes, it's a four-year-old girl.' But we still wouldn't know if it was Joy. So then we'd have to wait for DNA testing?"

Eric nodded.

"And that could take months?" she persisted.

"Possibly weeks."

She looked at him briefly. "Well then, we'll wait, won't we?"

Standing, Eric came and put a hand on her shoulder. "Don't try to second-guess. I'll be in touch as soon as we know something."

"Thanks," she murmured. Watching as Peter saw him to the door, she realized with surprise that her anger toward Eric had vanished. She saw him now as a man who'd worked very hard, been thorough, patient, helpful. All that a sheriff's detective should be.

She heard Peter returning and said, "You know what I'm wondering. Maybe this is a test of my commitment."

"Thought so." He waited a moment. "Mind if I point something out to you?"

"Bet it's real pragmatic."

He nodded. "Naturally. Ready? The body was found in the early evening. That was before you built your altar, before you prayed."

She smiled in spite of herself. "That's pretty pragmatic, all right, but it's true." She thought a moment. "So what does that tell me? Maybe that God was preparing me for what He already knew."

"Maybe." He sighed and pondered a moment. "I think I'll call the plant and tell them I won't be in today."

She stared at him. "With that East Coast guy coming in?"

"I think Dick Regan can handle it. They can call me with any questions."

She squeezed his hand. "I really appreciate it." She glanced at him and was surprised to see tears in his eyes. "What?" she asked softly.

"I think this could really be it," he admitted. "I mean it's pretty close to where she disappeared. And I guess after all, I'm not ready."

His tenderness, his willingness to show his feelings touched her till her own heart seemed to overflow. Putting her arms around him, she held him and felt their tears merge. "Peter," she said, "do you realize this is the first time we've truly shared our grief? No masks. It feels so good to really be one in all this."

"I agree." Peter drew back, wiping his eyes. "Wow, I've packed more emotion into this last twenty-four hours than into the last twenty-four years. Now I can't seem to stop."

She smiled. "Please don't try. This strange feeling, I think, is called having a new heart. And you know what? I love this new tender heart of yours, Peter."

She looked over his shoulder, out the window, at the dissipating cloud bank, with the blue of the ocean seeping through the white. A peace she didn't understand began to spread through her innermost being. "I'm thinking of that hymn that begins, 'When peace like a river.' Remember the chorus, 'It is well, it is well with my soul?'"

He nodded. "Wonderful words."

She closed her eyes and said, "Oh, Lord, what can we say? Nothing, it seems to me, except Your will be done!"

42

&

ANDREA SAT WITH PETER in the quiet of the living room, wondering if some alien anesthesia had pervaded the house, rendering them incapable of moving.

At last he said, "Guess it would help if we got busy with something."

"Uh-huh," she said.

Neither of them stirred. She felt her thoughts drifting to Malibu Canyon. How long had the body been there? Had the child been lost, dying gradually of exposure? Or maybe even attacked by animals? She shivered. Or perhaps killed beforehand and dumped there. Or taken there and tortured. It was almost as if she could see the thoughts zooming toward her.

"Don't," she heard Peter say.

"What?" she asked, startled.

"Don't try to figure it," he said quietly.

EVIDENCE OF THINGS UNSEEN

"How did you know?"

He flashed a wry smile. "Because I'm doing it too. I have all these pictures of what could have happened to J—" He caught himself. "To that child."

She nodded, but even as she started to speak, her earlier discovery, the battle for the mind, flashed into her awareness. "Wait!" she said. "Let's don't go on any head trips over this. Doesn't the Bible talk somewhere about 'vain imaginations'?"

Peter nodded. "We're not to have them. I think it also talks about His praise continually being in our mouths."

"OK, then, let's do that. Didn't Mom give us some praise tapes? Let's play them."

"Good. It might also help to keep our hands busy."

"Guess I could make those cookies for Tim."

"Why don't you?" he said. "I could work on that leaky faucet in the kids' bathroom."

Neither of them stirred.

"It's not easy," she said.

"Come on," he said as he pulled her to her feet.

It seemed they were moving in slow motion as they left the living room. In the kitchen she found the recipe and pulled out the ingredients. Then she remembered Connie and reached for the phone.

Connie's recorded voice told her she was out, and Andrea kept her message short. "Pray!" she concluded.

Songs of praise flowed from the stereo as she began creaming the shortening for the cookies, and she found herself singing, "To God Be the Glory."

Just as she finished mixing the dough, she heard a tap at the front door. Couldn't be Eric. He always rang the bell. She opened the door and saw Dolores.

Her hair and makeup, as always, were immaculate, and she

wore turquoise sweats, a black turtleneck, and black sneakers. But dark half-circles underlined her eyes.

"Hello, love," Dolores said, smiling easily. It was as though the night before had never happened.

"Hi," Andrea said, not wanting to ask her in.

"I just heard on the news. You poor dear, this must be agony. But I want to tell you: I don't think it's Joy."

Got a message from your Mother goddess, did you? Andrea wanted to counter. But she said, "Well, there are tests to be done." As she saw her neighbor nod, Andrea realized she had to tell it all. "But Dolores, an amazing thing has happened." Andrea looked directly at her. "I've trusted Joy to the Lord. She belongs to Him, not me. So either way, she's in His care."

"Oh," Dolores said, the tone flat, dull.

"So," Andrea continued, "that terrible desperation is gone. There are moments of fear certainly. But moments of incredible peace too."

"I see." Dolores didn't meet her gaze.

"Thanks for coming over, Dolores. I'll let you know when we hear something."

Dolores glanced at her briefly before turning to leave. "Yes, do that. Come over anytime."

Closing the door, Andrea muttered, "I—don't—think—so," just as Peter came down the hall.

"Who was it?" he asked.

"Dolores."

"You're kidding."

"No. All solicitous about the news report." She shrugged. "Weird. But I'll say this, she looked wasted."

He whistled softly. "Was it hard to see her?"

"Not really. In fact, I found myself telling her how I trusted Joy to God. Didn't plan it. It just came out."

"What'd she say?"

"'Oh.' And 'I see.'"

He put his arm around her. "Good job. I'd have answered the door, but I was on the phone with the plant. Hank Willis may have a lead on the blue car." He scratched his head. "I keep wondering if it was one of those guys from the county work gang that was up here."

She nodded. "Especially that one they can't locate." She returned to the cookies, contemplating Hank and the computer. Why did she keep feeling there was something they were missing, some piece of the puzzle?

I know I gave it to You, God, she prayed silently. *But that doesn't mean I shouldn't use the intelligence You gave me, does it?*

When the cookies were baked, filling the house with their sweet aroma, she made sandwiches and coffee. They ate little, but as they lingered over coffee, Peter said, "Remember before we were married, when we went to that retreat in Wisconsin together?"

She pictured that moonlit night when they'd both made their professions of faith. "How could I forget?"

"I felt so close to God and so close to you."

"Me too," she remembered, appalled that she could have turned away from that closeness.

"I feel like we have that back again," he said, his eyes soft and tender.

She reached for his hand across the table. "I do too. And I'm sorry for those years my priorities were so out of whack."

"I remember Mom quoting something from the Bible about the years the locust have eaten," Peter said. "That God will restore those years, I think it says."

"Oh, I hope so," she said. She glanced out the window just

as Eric's car came around the turn in the road below their house. "Peter!" she exclaimed. "Eric's coming."

They rushed to meet the detective in the driveway, and he rolled down the window, turning off the engine. "Good news—for you at least," he said. "It isn't Joy. The pathologist is sure it's a male, about five years old."

She leaned against the car, feeling the sun-warmed metal and a flood of relief. "Thank You, Lord!"

"Indeed," Eric said.

But even as Peter hugged her, she thought of the boy's parents and turned toward Eric. "Any idea who the boy is? Have you matched him with another missing child?"

"They're working on it."

"Keep us posted, won't you?" Peter said.

"I will." Eric started the engine.

"And thanks." Peter gave him a thumbs-up.

"A lot!" Andrea added.

They walked into the house, hand in hand. "Oh, Peter, obviously I'm relieved for us. But oh, those parents. My heart aches for them. They had a darling little guy with reddish-blond hair. They've been going through what we've been through. And for how long, I wonder? And what happened to that child?" She sighed. "Those parents were praying, too, I'll bet. Now they have an answer, they know where their child is. But what an answer! Oh, honey. Let's pray for them."

They joined hands in the hallway, and first Andrea prayed, then Peter. Afterward, as they hugged, she said, "Praying together, how wonderfully uniting it is."

Shortly after Tim came home from school, his "new best friend" arrived.

"You're Jonathan, right?" Andrea patted his shoulder.

"Hi, Mrs. Lang." A stocky blond with freckles dusting his nose and cheeks, Jonathan's blue eyes held an impish twinkle.

Andrea couldn't help contrasting his open-faced, all-American appeal with Brant's dark countenance. She liked Jonathan immediately. And he obviously liked her cookies.

"Mrs. Lang, these are awesome!" he declared, reaching for his third cookie. As he took a bite, Juliet landed in his lap, purring, and arranged herself comfortably against his left arm.

"She likes you," Tim said.

"Yeah," Jonathan replied, not at all surprised. He scratched beneath her chin. "Real soft fur." He looked her over. "What a crack-up. All those patches of color. And hey, get those feet. Just like you said." He spread out the six toes of one forepaw with gentle fingers.

Peter looked into the kitchen. "Hi, guys. Jonathan, right?" He gave the boys a wave, then eyed the cookies. "Do I get one now? Your mom wouldn't let me sample any till you guys got here."

"Hey, Dad," Tim said, surprised, "how come you're home so early?"

Peter glanced at Andrea, and they silently agreed now wasn't the time to explain. "Taking a little time off." He inspected the cookies. "They're kind of small."

"OK," she allowed, "take two. Oh, make it three."

He grinned and reached for the cookies. "You guys have fun," he said as he headed off down the hall.

The boys adjourned to the playroom, and she smiled at the sound of young laughter in the house once again.

She saw Peter walking toward the living room, technical magazine in hand. "Mind if I take a walk?" she asked. "Feel like I need to let off a little steam."

"Sure. I'll hold down the fort." Waving as she left, he settled into a chair by the window. He could hear the boys' excited voices from the playroom.

"OK, one chair here and one about there," Jonathan said.

"Then the two ropes between them. No, a little closer. Don't make it too hard for starters."

"How about the ropes?" Tim asked.

"Not too tight. Yeah. That's about right. OK, now where's the cat?"

"Juliet!" came Tim's voice. "Joo-leee! Come, kitty, kitty." A pause. Then, "Oh, there you are, girl."

Fascinated, Peter set the magazine on his lap. There was no doubt that Juliet was smart, eager to please and affectionate, and that Tim had a special rapport with her. If a cat was capable of love, certainly Juliet loved him. But to get her to do a trick like walking the ropes—

⟡

"OK, now, Tim, you said you have a little hand signal to get her to jump on your shoulder."

"Yeah. I kinda pat my shoulder and say, 'Hut, hut, Julie.'"

"OK, then, why don't you go over and get your shoulder right at chair level and try that?"

As Peter heard Tim positioning himself, he thought back to the night Brant had tried to help with Julie. How different from Jonathan's gentle coaxing.

"OK," said Jonathan, "now I'll start her over here, and you kinda give her the signal and maybe jiggle the cat kibble in that plastic dish so she hears it."

He heard a thump and the boys burst into laughter.

"Uh-uh, Julie, you don't jump down on the floor and then up on the other chair," Tim said, his voice soft and patient. "Let's try it again."

Peter found himself holding his breath. He heard the gentle thump once again.

"No, Juliet," Jonathan said. "Across the ropes. It's the

416

shortest way. One foot and then the other. Come on. You're a smart kitty. You can do it. You've got good equipment—those nice big feet. I know you can do it."

Peter waited. He heard Tim shake the kibble in the dish and urge, "Hut, hut, Julie!"

"Oh, Lord," Peter breathed, "it would be a miracle."

"That's the way," Jonathan encouraged. "Keep going. You're doing it. You're doing it!"

The two boys' shouts mingled. "She did it! You are one b-a-a-d cat!"

From the exultant tone, Peter concluded "bad" was good.

"Dad! Dad!" Tim called. "Juliet did it! She walked the ropes! Come here!"

He hurried into the playroom to find the two delighted boys alternately slapping each other on the back and petting Juliet, who perched nonchalantly on the chair, painstakingly cleaning her white whiskers.

"Hey, you guys are something!" Peter said, shaking each boy's hand. "Congratulations!"

"Oh, I wish you'd seen it, Dad." Tim turned to Jonathan. "Think she'd do it again?"

Jonathan shrugged. "We can try. Let's see if she'll go back the other way."

Tim picked up the plastic dish and pulled a few bits of kibble from his pocket as he hurried over to the chair opposite Juliet. He positioned himself with his shoulder just beside the chair. Jonathan gently picked up Juliet and placed her forepaws on the two ropes.

Could she possibly do it again? Peter wondered.

Tim shook the kibble in the dish and patted his shoulder. "Hut, hut, Julie. C'mon, girl."

Julie seemed to think about it a moment, as though pondering whether or not to humor these mere mortals.

"Hut, hut, Julie!" Tim repeated.

Slowly, deliberately, Juliet moved her right paw forward. She waited, as though to say, "When I'm ready, fellas."

Then she sat down.

"Hut, hut, Julie!" Tim tried again.

Jonathan picked her up once more and positioned her front paws.

Juliet closed her eyes, backed onto the chair and settled down, tucking her forepaws beneath her.

"I think she's telling us something," Jonathan whispered.

"Yeah." Tim moved over to the chair and stroked her gently. "It's OK. You'll do it again another time. You're a good kitty, Julie."

Peter could hear her purr. "Julie, you are some cat," he said, surprised at the catch in his voice.

⌁

Andrea started down the hill, taking deep breaths of the clean air. At each twist of the road, she paused to savor the changing vistas, feeling a delight she hadn't experienced since Joy disappeared. When she came to the spot where she could see the entire spread of the coastline to the west, she stopped to listen to the distant percussion of the surf and to feast on the view. It was always more beautiful than she remembered—the grace of the curving points and inlets along the coastline, the variegation of the ocean's color, the slopes of the mountains, defined by one, two, three, four canyons between.

Sometimes, she sighed to herself, *I think this is the most beautiful place in the world. Oh, Lord, You did a good job! If only the people You put here didn't do such ugly things, like abducting and brutalizing children. How You must weep over us!*

As she walked on, she considered the boy found in the canyon. Who had left him there? A phrase she'd heard in early Bible studies, "the depravity of man" ran repeatedly through her mind.

So now we know it isn't Joy, she thought, *and I'm grateful we don't have to go through months of waiting for more testing. She stopped a moment. I gave Joy to the Lord and I meant it, but I keep having the feeling there's something we're still to do.*

It was then she realized that in all these months, she'd never specifically prayed for God's direction, not even in the Joy campaign. She shook her head. Dumb!

So as she resumed walking, she began talking with God. "Lord, You know everything. You created each of us, and You know us completely. You also know where Joy is, and if we'll ever find her or learn anything more about her. I'm not going to try to snatch her out of Your hands again. But Father, haven't You said that if we call to You, You'll answer and even teach us things we don't know? I ask right now, is there anything I ought to do in the way of a contact, a news release, a promotion—whatever. And if there's some angle we haven't yet explored, would you reveal it to us? But if You just want us to wait, then help me stop trying to do and just rest and trust."

After a while, she turned and started back up the steep incline, feeling the stretch of the muscles in the backs of her legs. She began to run, welcoming the effort that made her heart pound in her ears. As she neared her home a thought zinged into her mind, and it was so alien, she stopped and blinked, hoping it would flee. But it remained. *Go see Dolores.*

"Dolores?" she exclaimed aloud. "That's crazy! I have no desire to go to that house again." She looked up. "Surely that's not from You, Lord. Don't You say to flee evil?"

She blocked out the idea as she reached the house.

As she closed the front door, Tim descended upon her, followed by Jonathan. "Mom!" Tim cried, his grin almost as broad as his face. "Juliet did it! Walked this far on the ropes." He held his arms out a yard or so. He turned and punched his friend's arm. "Jonathan's a genius!"

Jonathan looked at the floor. "Tim had done all the hard work. Especially, he'd made Juliet like him. My dad calls it bonding. Julie wanted to please him, and she was just ready to do it."

"Oh, Tim, that's wonderful!" she exclaimed, bending to hug him. Tim had needed this, and she was so grateful. "And Jonathan," she turned to him. "I've just got to hug you too! Thank you." The boy blushed and stiffened at her embrace.

"Did you tell your dad?" she asked, turning to Tim.

"Yeah. He didn't see it, but he was in the living room, and he kinda heard it happen," Tim said. "Oh, wasn't it cool that he was home?"

She smiled. "Very cool."

"I think I oughta be going now," Jonathan said. "But I'll help you with Juliet again, if you want."

"Tomorrow?" Tim asked eagerly.

"Sure. We don't want her to forget what she learned."

"Right!"

"Thanks for the cookies, Mrs. Lang," Jonathan said softly, without looking at her.

"Want one for the road?" she asked.

He hesitated. "Oh, that's all right."

"Better keep your strength up," she insisted, going to the kitchen to bring back several cookies wrapped in a paper napkin.

"Gee, thanks," said Jonathan. "See ya, Tim."

"Yeah. See ya."

"Well!" she said to Tim as she closed the door, "This has been a great day for you and Juliet."

"Yeah," he beamed. "I knew she could do it. I just knew it."

"You had a lot of faith, Tim. That faith and your loving Julie so much, and your persistence really paid off."

"Yeah," he grinned, holding Juliet against his chest as she extended one six-toed foot to touch his cheek. "What a cat!" he murmured.

"She is, indeed." Andrea gave the cat a gentle rub on the side of the head. "Tim, sit down a sec." She led the way to the couch in the living room. "I wanted to tell you about today, before you hear it someplace else." She explained about the body in the canyon and the forensic pathologist's findings.

"Whoa!" Tim exclaimed. "So you spent a bunch of hours thinking it might be Joy. I wondered why Dad was really home."

"I was so glad he was here," she said. "But Tim, even while we feel thankful it wasn't Joy, we have to think about that boy's family."

"See what you mean."

"Your Dad and I prayed for them. You might remember them in your prayers tonight."

"Good idea." He scratched his head. "So we're sorta back where we were before, huh?"

"As far as knowing where Joy is, yes."

"But," he regarded her with brown eyes so like his father's, "you don't feel as bad as you did. Before last night, I mean."

"Right. I see the whole situation in a different way."

"More the way God sees it, huh."

She felt warmed by his discernment. "You've got it."

"Is this a private party?" She felt Peter's hand on her shoulder.

"Of course not. Join us," she said. "I was just telling Tim about what happened with the sheriff and all today."

"Good." He glanced at a notepad in his hand. "Had a call a few minutes ago from Bruce Finley, the private detective your folks hired. He's been busy. Even checked the U.S. Embassy bulletin board in Mexico City to be sure Joy's picture is still there. I thought that was smart, after all these months. And yes, her picture is there—together with photos of twenty-two other Americans, mostly kids. He thinks it's quite likely she was taken to Mexico, because it's so easy to disappear there."

"Right. Could be one of the men on that county work gang. The one that blew his parole, maybe?"

"We talked about that, but he was Hispanic. A blond kid like Joy with a Hispanic would stand out. So Finley didn't see a connection there. But as you found out, a person wouldn't need papers to take Joy over the border."

"Oh, if only someone who knows would see her picture!" she exclaimed.

He nodded. "But," he held up one finger, "right after that, Eric called to say a couple of sightings were reported in North Carolina. We've had a lot of scattered reports, but these were pretty close together. I called Finley back to tell him."

"North Carolina," she pondered. "Interesting. Do we know anyone there? Do you have any business contacts there?"

"Not that I can think of. Why?"

"We could get some posters to them."

"Finley's already on it. He'll distribute them there," he said.

"Good," she murmured. "But I keep thinking there's some-one . . ."

It was only as she was fixing dinner that she remembered. "Peter!" she called toward the living room. "I remember a Carolina connection. Not sure if it's North or South. But

Dolores's daughter is in one of the two, or was the last time she wrote. It hasn't been all that long." She thought a moment, torn between the desire to check out every possibility and her hesitancy to deal with Dolores. Reluctantly she said, "Maybe she could help us."

Peter appeared in the kitchen doorway. "Long shot, but maybe worth a try," he said.

"I'll call her," she said. Reaching for the phone, she punched in the numbers and waited. After ten rings, she hung up, shaking her head. "I'll try later. Or," she said slowly, "maybe I really am supposed to go see her."

43

❧

From Zoë's Prayer Journal

May 24: Almighty God, I'm so in awe of You and all You've done in my family! You've quite literally changed Andrea's and Peter's lives, bringing them into a sweet new communion with You and with each other. You even gave them the faith to trust You in yesterday's crisis. And now Tim's called to tell me about his success with Juliet and his "new best friend." Thank You, Lord! But oh, Father, even as I thank You for these blessings, I'm so aware of the family of that little boy found in Malibu Canyon. Please, wrap Your arms of love around them. Comfort them as only You can. In Jesus' name I pray, amen.

BEFORE THE ALARM WENT OFF the next morning, Andrea padded to the window to look out on a violet dawn. The northeast sky shone with a soft pale purple glow that reflected in the clouds far toward the west. Even the corner of the house and the patio took on the tint, a delicate shade of lavender. She stood looking for a long time, catching every detail, from the dew-drenched T-shirt Tim had left outside on the chaise, to the new buds on the rosebush near the house.

She remembered Connie's lilting, "This is the day the Lord has made," and how it had rankled a few days ago. Now she repeated the verse, adding, "Yes, I do rejoice in it!"

She reached for her bathrobe and began planning the day. Prayer. That seemed not only the first priority but the first necessity.

Slipping silently into the living room she settled into a chair with her back to the window, so the view wouldn't distract her. She began with praise. "Oh, Lord, You are my Jehovah-Jireh, the God who provides. I see that more fully each day. Just look what a glorious morning You provided today. How lavish You are! You've blessed and provided for me, far above and beyond what I deserve. You provided a way of escape for me from Dolores's. You're providing for Joy right now, wherever she is, and I thank You. I thank You, too, for the comfort You've given me about her these past days. Thank You for Your love and the love of my family and Connie."

She sat quietly, meditating on God's provision.

༄

In the bedroom, Peter stirred and reached toward Andrea, feeling only the empty bed, though her warmth was still there. He stretched and lay there a moment before he rolled out of bed. From the hallway he saw her sitting in the living room, hands clasped before her.

"Andry," he exclaimed. "You look so beautiful. That soft light behind you almost gives you a halo."

She smiled and reached out toward him. He crossed the room and held her hand against his face. "Love you," he murmured. "What got you up so early?"

"I'm not sure, really. But I'm glad I didn't miss this

incredible morning. Did you see the color of the dawn?" She turned to look outside. "No, it's changed already. You missed it." She smiled. "Maybe God created it just for me." She pointed to a footstool. Drawing it near her, he sat down and reached for her hand again. She looked at him thoughtfully. "I was just praying and seeing how completely God provides, and I realized He's the one who meets my deepest needs." She cocked her head to one side. "Honey, I've expected you to do that for me. It wasn't realistic. It was impossible." Her blue eyes shimmered. "Peter, you are my rock, but you can't meet all my needs. No human being can. Can you forgive me?"

He stroked her hand and smiled. "Done!"

She sighed deeply. "Thank you, my darling Peter and thank You, Lord."

He watched her, thinking she'd never looked more beautiful, her coloring delicate in the morning light, her expression peaceful. At last he asked, "So what's on your agenda today?"

"You're going to think I'm crazy. But I got this compelling feeling yesterday that I'm supposed to go over and see Dolores. I try to blot it out, but it keeps coming back. And the weird part is, it began even before you told me about the possible sightings in North Carolina. In fact, it came to me when I was walking yesterday, after I asked God if there was something we ought to be doing."

"Doing about Joy?"

She nodded. "It doesn't make sense, does it? I mean, I think we both agree I was delivered from evil at Dolores's night before last. To go back seems stupid."

"Want to pray about it?" he asked.

"Oh, yes!" She nodded emphatically.

Together they prayed for guidance, and as they finished, a sense of confirmation startled Peter.

"Are you ready for this?" he asked. "I have a real strong sense that you're supposed to respond to this, Andrea." He saw her blink in surprise, felt her grip his hand. "But if you do go over, let's be sure you're covered with prayer."

"Oh, I agree!" she exclaimed. "I'll ask Connie."

"Good. And I'll call my men's group to pray.

"That makes me feel better." She ran her fingers over his chin. "And your sense that I should go makes me feel better too."

❧

Just after Peter and Tim left that morning, Andrea realized Peter had left his briefcase. Jumping into her minivan, she overtook them at the bottom of the hill. "Hope my new heart hasn't affected my mind," he laughed.

On her way back, she made a quick decision to stop at Connie's.

"How nice!" Connie exclaimed, wiping her hands on the checkered dishcloth she'd carried to the door. Without makeup, her freckles stood out defiantly, and her face shone with a just-washed glow. "Have time for a cup of coffee? I'll warm some cinnamon rolls."

"How can I resist?"

Connie poured the coffee, smiling pensively.

"What?" Andrea asked. "What are you thinking?"

"About you and how you handled yesterday—the body in the canyon and all. And that the Lord has sure brought you a long way in a short time from the lady who tried to play the slot machine with Him."

Andrea frowned, puzzled.

"Well," Connie explained, "when you tried to bargain with

God, told Him what you'd do and what you wanted from Him, wasn't it kinda like putting a quarter in a slot machine and waiting for God to pay off?"

She laughed. "I never thought of it that way."

As they sat down together in the sunny breakfast area, Andrea eyed the saucer-sized rolls. "Want to split one?"

Connie chuckled. "Sure. You're a good friend. You know how easily I could scarf down the whole thing. I sure would like to have more willpower about my food." She looked at Andrea earnestly. "Maybe you could hold me accountable?"

"Would you still love me?"

Connie hesitated, then grinned. "Yeah. Sure. I know I'd be better off if I got rid of some pounds."

"Then that's one thing we could pray about together. What else is on your list today?" Andrea asked.

"My mom, I guess. She's having an MRI today to see what her back problem is." Connie gave her a close look. "What about you?"

When she told her about going to Dolores's, Connie pursed her lips. "You feel up to that?"

"Not sure. The enemy seems pretty active over there. With Dolores. And I don't know about Brant, cutting up that snake and all." She shuddered. "What do you think?"

Connie pursed her lips. "Guess I'm not sure how hard-core Dolores is into witchcraft. I mean, is she dabbling and deceived or could she be a deceiver?"

"I just don't know. It does seem clear she's been trying all these months to draw me away from Jesus."

Connie nodded thoughtfully. Then she held up a forefinger, "But what we do know is that God is greater than the enemy or any of his buddies. If you think He's asking you to go, well, He protected you before, when you went in your own will.

And He'll do it again, especially if you're going in His will. We'd better pray!"

And so, for almost half an hour, the two friends prayed for one another, and Connie concluded with an "In the name of Jesus," so triumphant, it was as though what they prayed was already accomplished. Hugging Andrea, she said, "I feel good about your going."

"Me too," Andrea said, sensing a new strength that came not from any bravery of her own, but from knowing she was covered by prayer. It had been her shield and defense even when she defied God. Surely it would protect her now.

As she drove home, she decided to phone Dolores first. But as she reached the top of the hill, she saw Dolores watering the plants by her mailbox. Andrea stopped and let down the car window. "Hi! I was on my way to call you. There's something I need to ask you."

"What a coincidence, darling," Dolores exclaimed, smoothing back the profusion of hair that hung loose, shining with blue-black highlights in the sun. "I have something to ask you too. Put your car away and come have coffee. I'll make it with cinnamon, the way you like it."

Andrea nodded and drove on. She really didn't need more coffee, and her gut tightened as she remembered the first time she'd gone to Dolores's for coffee with cinnamon. It was the day she renounced God. For a moment, she could see herself with her fist held high in defiance. But that's behind me, she told herself firmly. I belong to Him now.

When she came through the gate to Dolores's patio, she could see the remnants of the chalk circle, but the altar was gone. How long ago that evening of pagan ritual and "magick" seemed.

Inside, Andrea sat down in the purple-cushioned chair at

the glass table and watched as Dolores brought two black mugs with vibrant Aztec designs.

"Here we are," Dolores announced, settling in a chair across from her. Her face looked drawn, the color sallow despite her makeup. The parenthesis of lines on either side of her mouth seemed deeper, more sharply etched. "Well, now. You said you wanted to ask me something?"

No, Andrea decided. *I'll let her ask me first. Help me, Lord.* "Yes, but you have something on your mind. You go first."

Dolores looked down and ran her index finger around the rim of her mug. "All right. It's about the other night here. I have to tell you I was positively livid with you for ruining it. Here I was, going to tremendous effort to try to help you, and ended up humiliated in front of friends." She hesitated. "But I don't know what to make of Diana. Witchcraft is a peaceable practice. She could have just asked you to leave. Now, I really don't think she'd have harmed you, but she definitely lost it." She shook her head. "Maybe she needs some counseling."

Andrea sent up a silent plea for guidance and said, "I know you wanted to help me."

"Yes. I wanted to give you answers. What's wrong with that?" Not waiting for a reply, Dolores went on, "I still don't understand what happened, where it all went wrong. I mean, everything with the coven has always been so beautiful and loving before."

She's not going to understand, Andrea thought. But Dolores's dark eyes, usually glittering and hard as blackest obsidian, seemed to be questioning, almost pleading, and she knew she had to try. "Have you ever thought that there might have been evil forces at work?" She held up her hand as she heard Dolores take a breath. "Think back. Surely what we saw in Diana was something beyond a human psychological problem. Her face changed. She made inhuman sounds." Andrea shuddered inwardly at the memory.

"Well," Dolores hesitated.

Andrea went on. "Now, I know, you say witches don't worship Satan or even believe he exists. But God's Word tells us to have no other gods or goddesses before Him. And He warns in His Word against witchcraft. I really believe Diana's 'losing it' was a demonic manifestation."

"Oh, surely not!"

"Remember when I said the name of Jesus? I think that's what Diana reacted to. I see now it must have been the Holy Spirit, reminding me that the light of the world is not your Mother goddess or the moon." She paused and added softly, "It's Jesus."

Dolores gave a quiet but derisive snort.

I'm going to go for it, even if she hates it, Andrea decided. "Surely you saw the power in the name of Jesus. Diana was headed toward me, and I am thoroughly convinced she meant me serious harm. It was when I called upon Jesus that she collapsed and screamed."

"Ah, that's true," Dolores murmured.

"After I left, I became so convinced that Jesus is the only way, as I told you, I rededicated my life to Him that night. And it feels terrific!"

Dolores didn't seem to hear. "But surely demons and Satan are a myth—scare tactics preachers dish out to panic people into believing."

She looked into Dolores's eyes. "Do you really believe that, even after Wednesday night?"

Dolores let out her breath. "Certainly that wasn't a pretty thing." She pressed her lips together. "I know you think I'm a

bit unconventional, but I certainly wouldn't choose to do business with the devil or with demons."

"Then don't!"

Dolores frowned and blinked repeatedly. "It never entered
my mind that I could be involved in anything wrong. I was
exploring, trying to expand my consciousness and yours, to
learn, to experience fully."

"I know."

"Oh, yes! I saw you as so intolerant, wanted to free you
from that narrow, crippling little box of Christianity."

"Oh, no!" Andrea interjected. "Not crippling, freeing." She
touched Dolores's hand. "What seemed intolerant, narrow, is
the confidence that Jesus was not a liar or a madman, Dolores.
He said *He* is *the* way, *the* truth, the life. Not 'a' way."

"Well, as you know, I don't agree. But so far as helping you,
I've wondered since the other night if it was more that I was
feeling a thrill to have the power to help, to change things."
She sighed. "Maybe I need help." She leaned toward Andrea.
"If there are demons—I say 'if'—do you think they're present
in my life?"

"I'm not an expert. But you might go see one of the pastors
at our church. They're very approachable." She was going to
stop there, but she saw the distress in Dolores's eyes. "I just
think it's asking for trouble when we dabble in the occult. It
creates an opportunity. I've heard that demons can enter our
lives through something as seemingly harmless as deciding to
use a ouija board or dipping into spiritualism."

Dolores twisted a strand of her curly black hair around her
finger. "Brant uses a ouija board, and he's fine."

"Do you teach him witchcraft, Dolores?"

Dolores shook her head. "No. Children have to make up
their own minds what to believe. I mainly emphasize being at
one with nature, having reverence for all life."

All life? Andrea thought. "Even snakes?" she asked.

"Of course."

"But not rattlers."

"Oh, yes," Dolores insisted. "All living things."

Did she dare tell her? Andrea hated to tattle. She cleared her throat. "Perhaps his friends haven't learned this. His club."

"What do you mean?" Dolores sat very erect.

"All I know is that Brant asked Tim to catch a rattlesnake in order to join his club. Tim did that. Then he found the snake cut into pieces."

Dolores's eyes flashed. "That's not possible. Brant wouldn't do such a thing."

They sat for what seemed a long time without talking. Andrea looked past Dolores to the bay with the window seat that faced her own house. Dolores's animosity was palpable. At last Dolores took a sip of her coffee. "So what did you want to ask me?" she asked brightly, obviously eager to change the subject.

Her about-face caught Andrea by surprise. "Me? Ask you? Oh, right. There are a couple of reports of possible sightings of Joy."

"Ah!" Dolores exclaimed. "That's wonderful!"

"In North Carolina," she continued. "I thought I remembered that your Marcy is around there. Wondered about sending her some Joy posters."

Dolores shrugged. "You know how Marcy is. The last I heard from her was a month, no, six weeks ago. She could be somewhere else by now. The note was postmarked Raleigh, North Carolina."

"Do you have an address?" Andrea pressed. "Somewhere I could contact her? Do you think she'd be willing to help?"

"She didn't give an address." Dolores frowned. "She seems determined not to have contact with me. I do worry. She was such a happy, normal girl till that stillbirth. Then everything just—" She threw up her hands.

Touched once again with kinship with Dolores, another woman who'd lost a daughter, Andrea decided to encourage her to talk about Marcy. "Did she seem in pretty bad shape the last time you saw her?"

Dolores nodded. "When she was here at Thanksgiving, she seemed very depressed. She ate so little. Just picked at my lovely pheasant and wild rice. Didn't even touch my pumpkin flan. Slept a lot. And she'd lie propped up in that window seat with a book, but she never read the book. She just looked out the window."

Andrea rose and walked toward the window. "But this is a lovely, cozy spot, Dolores. I can see why she'd like it."

"But never reading? Just staring out?"

"Maybe she was enjoying the view." Andrea sat on the seat and looked out, surprised to see there really was no ocean or hillside view. The window looked across the yard to the road.

How odd, she thought.

44

WHY DO I FEEL SO UNSETTLED? Andrea wondered as she walked home from Dolores's. *Because I'm not on the top of Dolores's popularity list?* She shrugged. *Well, the truth can be tough. Oh, Lord, help her to see what's real.*

She let herself in the front door and phoned Peter.

"Lang," he announced.

"That's my name too," she said.

He laughed. "What a coincidence!" His voice grew serious. "Did you go to Dolores's?"

"I sure did, and I lived to tell about it."

"I'm glad of that. So what happened?"

Andrea recapped the conversation. "And I did ask her about Marcy. She doesn't have an address in North Carolina. But Dolores opened up a lot about her." She thought again of

Dolores's description of Marcy's last visit. "Something odd, though. Dolores said at Thanksgiving her daughter just lounged in the window seat and stared out the window."

"So?"

"Well, there's no ocean view from that side of the house. She was just looking across the road." She caught her breath, replaying the window scene in her mind.

The thought seemed to strike Peter at the same time. "The play yard!" he exclaimed.

"Oh, dear Lord," she murmured, "is that why You had me go over today?" They were both silent for several beats. Then she said, "Peter! Could it be? I mean, I've looked out that window a half-dozen times and never noticed before. But if Marcy was looking out the window . . ."

Her thoughts flew back to Thanksgiving, a golden day, so warm she'd had the sliding glass door open.

"Thanksgiving, huh? Were we home?" Peter asked.

"Remember? Late in the afternoon we went to your Mom's in Orange County for dinner. But Joy spent most of the day outside, either with you or Tim. A lot of it in the play yard." She gasped. "Am I just grasping at straws?"

"I'm not sure," he said carefully.

Her mind raced. "But supposing. Supposing that Marcy lay there and watched Joy and thought about her own dead baby. Dolores said she was unstable and depressed."

"Uh-huh," Peter murmured.

Andrea couldn't stop. "Suppose Marcy just lay there and watched and thought and watched and thought and finally came up with a plan."

"And the plan was?" Peter asked. "Oh, wait!" he said. "Dolores was gone when Joy disappeared, wasn't she?"

"Yes. Then Marcy could have come while Dolores and Brant

436

were skiing in Mammoth. Remember? Dolores expected her there, and she didn't show."

"So your scenario is that she watched and waited," Peter began.

"And followed our housekeeper's car to the toy store. Right! Oh, I wonder what color Marcy's car is, if it's blue."

"Right. There was a report of a blue car in the parking lot at the toy store the afternoon Joy disappeared."

Andrea thought a moment. "Peter! Remember how Joy woke up screaming the night before she was taken? Maybe someone *was* at her window. It could have been Marcy!"

"That's quite a scenario," he said.

She closed her eyes and gasped at the implications. "But Peter, if I'm right, Joy could be alive and well!"

She could hear him sigh.

"Is it too far-fetched? Would it be dumb to call Eric?" Before he could answer, her mind hopscotched and she exclaimed, "Peter! I just thought of this, if Marcy wanted a child so badly, she'd take good care of her. She'd love her." She felt tears start down her cheeks.

"Right," he said, his voice husky.

"Do you think I'm crazy?"

"It's worth checking out."

"Oh, good, Peter!" she exclaimed, wishing he was there so she could kiss him. "I'll call Eric."

"Right, and I'll call Detective Finley."

Once again, the elation of hope gripped her. "Oh, Peter, down deep I feel this is what we've been waiting for."

"Now, Andrea," he began, and she heard the caution in his voice.

"No. Don't tell me not to get my hopes up," she interrupted. "They are up. Oh, Lord, please help us find Marcy!"

"I agree. I was only thinking that since Marcy seems like such a flake, she could have moved on to another place, or even just mailed the letter on her way through town."

"Oh." Her elation diminished, but only for a moment. "But you did say there were sightings in the area."

"I'll let you know what Finley says."

"Right, and I'll let you know what Eric says. Oh pray, Peter!"

"You bet."

Not taking the time to replace the phone she pressed the hang-up button, released it, and immediately punched in the number to the sheriff's station.

"Eric Jansen, please. It's Andrea Lang calling."

"He's out on a call, ma'am," the tenor voice replied. "I'll see if I can catch him."

"Oh, please. It's important." She twisted the telephone cord while she waited.

At last Eric's voice came in on a static-filled connection. "Jansen."

"Eric, it's Andrea. I think we may have come onto something." She told him the story. "What do you think?"

"Dolores was out of town when Joy disappeared, wasn't she?"

"Right, and Marcy was supposed to meet her in Mammoth. Never showed. Never explained why."

"So you're thinking Marcy could've snuck into her mother's, watched and waited, then followed your housekeeper's car to the toy shop, right?"

"That's it."

"It's worth following up. I'd better go see Dolores."

"Whoo-boy. She won't like it."

"That's OK."

After they said good-bye, Andrea remembered Connie and quickly phoned her. "Connie!" she exclaimed when she heard her voice. "The amazing thing is I really was supposed to go to Dolores's."

"What happened?"

"I'm beginning to think Dolores's daughter could have taken Joy. And I'd never have seen it if I hadn't gone to Dolores's today."

"Whoa!" Connie exclaimed. "Tell me."

After Andrea explained, Connie gave a thoughtful "I'll need to think about that one." There was a silence. Then Connie said slowly, excitement building in her voice, "You know, I have to tell you I'm getting big, fat goose bumps. It could be, it just could be!"

Andrea sank into a chair. "Oh, I'm so glad to hear you say that."

"But Andrea," Connie's voice grew serious, "think what this could mean for Dolores."

"I know."

"So," Connie hesitated, "how'd she seem today?"

Andrea described their meeting.

"Then she's been trying to put that evening with the priestess together, huh? She's been thinking."

"Yes, but this is going to blow her away!"

"We need to pray for her right now," Connie declared, and without another word, she began, "Oh, Lord, we do bring Dolores before You. Open her eyes to what's real. Help her want to help. And dear Lord, we ask You to miraculously point the way to where Marcy is—a beacon would be real nice—and to where Joy is." She closed her prayer with an exultant "Hallelujah!"

Andrea added her own prayer of thanks for this new hope

and for Connie's friendship. She hung up feeling an inexplicable serenity. No matter how protective Dolores might be, Marcy, and hopefully Joy, would be found. "But," she said aloud, "it could take time. A lot of time."

Now what? Go to Raleigh. That's what she'd like to do. Right now. No, she'd have to wait. The story of her life. Waiting. She still hated waiting!

She tried to busy herself. The clock struck twelve, but she wasn't hungry. As she walked down the hall, she saw the muddy splatters on the glass panels flanking the front door. Might as well clean them, have something to do. She assembled the window-washing supplies and headed outside. As she worked, a cold shaft of fear knifed through her elation at the morning's developments.

If Marcy had Joy, she'd tell my daughter lies about me. That I didn't want her, that I was dead. Who knows what else? She'd mess with my baby's mind! Her stomach churned and she shook her head to dispel the thoughts.

She'd finished one glass panel when she heard the crunch of gravel on the driveway. Turning, she saw Dolores. Her heart gave a jump. What now?

Dolores walked quickly up the driveway, carrying an envelope. "I apologize. Look what I found in Brant's room."

She handed the envelope to Andrea.

Lifting the flap, Andrea drew out several Polaroid pictures. The first was a closeup of a plump rattlesnake, cut into six pieces. Andrea glanced at Dolores, who gestured for her to look at the rest. The second showed a boy with a Mohawk, arm uplifted, holding a sword with the snake's head impaled at the end.

Andrea winced, turned to the third, and saw the boys marking one another's foreheads with blood from the cut pieces of rattlesnake. She shoved the pictures back in the envelope, swallowing hard.

"Even with the pictures, it's hard to believe," Dolores said, and Andrea saw the pain in her dark eyes. "What do you think?"

"Well," Andrea hesitated. "Certainly looks like some kind of ceremony or ritual."

Dolores sighed. "Guess I need to do some checking on this club." She gave a bitter laugh. "Brant told me they played chess."

Andrea put her arm around Dolores's shoulder. "I'm sorry," she said.

Dolores nodded and turned, starting back toward her house. Andrea walked with her out the driveway, wondering if she dared broach the subject of Marcy. Finally, she cleared her throat. "Dolores, what kind of car did Marcy drive when she was last here? I mean this sounds dumb, but what color was it?"

Dolores's face registered surprise as she stopped and turned toward Andrea. "Blue. A Honda Accord."

Andrea felt her heart quicken.

"Why?" Dolores asked.

Andrea swallowed. Eric would be in touch with her. Should she just wait for him to come and take Dolores by surprise? No, she couldn't. "Dolores," she said slowly, "Eric Jansen's going to be contacting you. Try to hear me out. This is hard."

As gently as she could, Andrea shared what she'd told Eric about Marcy. She could see the lines deepening in Dolores's face. "Ridiculous!" Dolores snapped.

"Eric didn't seem to think so. And you've just given me another piece that fits. Several witnesses reported a blue car in the parking lot of the toy store, a car that was gone when Joy turned up missing."

"Oh, come on now! Get real." Dolores's voice rasped with sarcasm. "That's kidnapping. No way any child of mine would do something like that!" Andrea watched Dolores stalk away and cross the road.

When she saw Dolores go through her gate, Andrea sighed and returned to her window washing. As she finished and started inside, she saw Dolores coming back. Now what? She walked out the driveway to meet her.

"I looked out the bay window and tried to put myself in Marcy's head," Dolores said. "Now, mind you, I'm not admitting anything. But it's possible."

Andrea moved closer and very gently put her arms around her. Little by little, Dolores's body begin to yield, and Andrea felt rather than heard the spasms of silent sobs.

At last Dolores murmured, "I feel sick, like the morning after some colossal binge." Andrea tightened her embrace and waited. At last Dolores drew back, tears pooling in her eyes. "I thought it was bad enough to have a problem with Brant . . ." Her voice trailed away and she stared past Andrea. Then she spoke with more confidence. "Now, of course, this theory of yours about Marcy is just conjecture. You could be wrong."

She nodded. "I agree."

Dolores swallowed with difficulty. "But it's possible." She took a shaky breath. "In fact, if I step back and try just to be an observer, it could fit together, couldn't it?"

Andrea looked away for a moment, astonished at Dolores's turnaround, praising God in her heart. "It could. Marcy might have come while you were in Mammoth."

"Yes, it's possible," Dolores admitted, her voice flat and lifeless. "Her mind was working in distorted ways, not reasonably." She thought a moment. "She knows where I hide a house key." She closed her eyes. "And there we were, waiting and waiting in Mammoth." Her voice broke and she waved the idea away before looking back at Andrea. "So Eric is coming to question me."

Andrea nodded.

"What do you think he'll want? Pictures, I suppose." She blinked back tears and looked down. "Would you come over and help me get some things together?"

"Of course."

As they walked together to Dolores's, Andrea voiced the thought that lay like a shadow beneath her hope. "Do you think it's possible Marcy was just passing through Raleigh and only mailed the letter from there?"

"Maybe." Dolores frowned. "Still, that wasn't my impression. I'll find the letter."

Inside her house, Dolores paced back and forth across the family room. "Let's see. They'll want a picture. There's that one on the end table."

"May I get it?" Assuming consent, Andrea hurried to pick up the photo of the dark-haired young woman. "She's lovely. Looks like you, with that marvelous dark hair."

"Yes," Dolores agreed. "But her eyes are different, as you can see. Blue, almost lavender. She's gorgeous." She thought a moment. "No, she was gorgeous. I should find a more recent photo. Let's see, did we take any at Thanksgiving? Yes, I'm sure we did." She moved toward the built-in desk in her kitchen and pulled open a drawer. Reaching under a catalog, she pulled out a packet of pictures. "Here." She spread them out on the counter, setting aside photos taken at her party.

Andrea stared with dismay at the photo of the woman reclining in the window seat, wearing baggy gray sweats. She'd butchered that glorious hair into a short punk style.

And perhaps it was just the picture, but the vibrant color of her eyes seemed to have faded. Even her features had changed, the nose and chin sharper, more angular. She looks ravaged, Andrea thought.

Dolores seemed to read her thought. "Looks different, doesn't she? Not my Marcy anymore." She stacked several pictures together. "Exhibit A."

Tears of gratitude sprang to Andrea's eyes. Thanks, Lord, she said silently.

"Now, what else?" Dolores resumed her pacing.

"The letter?"

"Oh, of course! I think it's in my bedroom."

As Dolores left the room, Andrea examined the pictures of Marcy. Was she too emotionally unstable to be an effective mother to a child? she wondered. Tears hazed her perspective. Oh, how confused, how bereft Joy would be!

"Here we are," Dolores said as she returned with the letter. She handed it to Andrea.

On plain paper, a tight, cramped hand had written, "Mom, I'm doing OK and will get in touch with you soon. Marcy."

"Not a lot of help, is it?" Dolores shook her head. She walked toward the bay window and back again. "What else?"

Andrea tried to calm her. "Eric will know."

"I know. But somehow I want to be ready. I don't exactly get interrogated every day, you know."

She forced herself to focus. "Let's think. What do they do in the movies? I'm kind of a fan of whodunits. Does Marcy take any medication? Anything she'd have to have a prescription for?"

"Yes. She was on—oh, now, what was it? Not a tranquilizer."

"Antidepressant?"

Dolores nodded. "I can't think of the name, but I'd know it if I heard it."

444

"I bet Eric can get a list." She thought a moment. "Does she read a lot? Would she go to a library for a certain type of book?"

"I doubt it."

"What about something she really, really likes and can't live without? Anything special? Seems to me you mentioned a cheese."

"Oh, yes! She loves havarti. I get it from that Dutch Colony cheese-shop chain when I know she's coming. We laugh about her needing a havarti fix."

"Good. That might help."

Dolores sank into one of the chairs by the glass-topped table and began to cry softly. "I'm drained. A part of me keeps saying this is all a dream and that I'm going to wake up and it won't be real. Another part says it's real. It's devastating. And I wonder where and how it's going to end?"

45

⊰⊱

From Zoë's Prayer Journal

May 24: Heavenly Father, I've concentrated for so long (with a few lapses, I confess!) on walking in the faith that "is the confidence of things hoped for, the evidence of things not seen!" Now, can it be at last, a breakthrough in finding Joy? Thank You that Andrea called with the news. And oh, Lord, I see Your hand in it all. You took her over to Dolores's. You prompted her to look out that window. And yes, You've given her the tenacity to pursue every possible clue. Now, help each of us to have unhurried spirits, trusting You as this unfolds. For You are our sovereign Lord, and we give You all the praise and glory, in Jesus' name, amen.

WHEN ANDREA HEARD Peter's car in the garage late that afternoon, she dashed out to meet him. "Peter, this is looking better and better!" she exclaimed as he opened the car door.

He eased out of the car, but before he could shut the door, she hugged him with all her might. "Everybody's digging in and helping, even Dolores," she said, as she released her embrace. "It

446

was the most amazing about-face. She admitted I could be onto something about Marcy. Actually became cooperative. She asked me to come and help her. Brought out pictures and everything. And Peter, Marcy even had a blue, late-model car."

Peter whistled softly and reached to shut the car door. Then, with his arm around her, they walked into the house.

"And," Andrea continued, stopping in the middle of the kitchen, "Dolores called Marcy's bank. It took some doing, but she found out Marcy withdrew everything, quite a large sum— seems there's a trust from her father—on January second."

She realized she was talking almost as rapidly as the fast-forward on her answering machine. But it seemed impossible to slow down. "January second," she repeated. "One day before Joy disappeared! Now does this fit together or what?"

She saw him loosen his tie. Good heavens, she realized, I've assaulted him with news before he could even recover from his commute. She took a breath and reached for his hand. "Oh, honey, I'm sorry. Let's start over." She cleared her throat. "Hi, dear. Happy Friday. How was your day?"

He grinned. "Good. Getting better steadily." He kissed her. "I don't have to ask about your day."

"And there's more too. But did you get in touch with the detective?"

"Yep."

"And?" She drew impatient circles in the air with her hand, asking for more.

"He's working on it."

"That's it?" she asked, tapping her fingers on the counter.

"He's starting by getting her photo out to doctors, hospitals, emergency-care places in the Raleigh area."

She caught her breath. "Doctors and hospitals!"

Peter put his hand on her arm. "The idea is that sooner or

later a four-year-old's going to have an earache or a sore throat."

"Right. Right. Makes sense." She relaxed for a moment. Then her publicist's mind-set clicked in, like a commercial interrupting the flow of a TV program. "But why only there? Why not a picture in the newspapers? I know! I'll put together a news release."

He shook his head. "Whoa. Think a minute. So Marcy sees the picture in the newspaper and takes off for who-knows-where."

"Oh, of course!" She shook her head in frustration. "But isn't this maddening, not to be able to let as many people as possible know to look out for Joy?" She bit her lower lip. "Well, anyway, Eric has a nationwide alert out for her car. And Dolores called Marcy's shrink to see if she's been in touch with him. But, wouldn't you know, he's deep-sea fishing off Baja till Monday."

"But things are in motion." He cocked his head. "Mind if I get out of my work clothes?"

She pretended to ponder at length. "Why not?"

She followed him back toward the bedroom. "I haven't told Tim yet, because he came home with Jonathan, and they started working right away with Juliet. They were so intent, I figured the news could wait." She smiled. "But oh, Peter, you should have seen Juliet. She knew what they wanted her to do, all right. But it was as though she was saying, 'Hey, guys, I'll do this when it pleases me, and right now, I want to play.' She was as revved up, I guess, as I am. Frisking all over the place."

Peter chuckled. "In other words, acting like a cat. Was Tim disappointed?"

"No. There was a lot of laughter. Then they decided to go down to Jonathan's and have a swim in their pool."

"Good decision." Peter emerged from the walk-in closet with cotton pants and a golf shirt. "I mean, I don't think Tim ever exactly thought he'd go pro with Juliet."

She shook her head. "No. And the main thing is, it looks like he has a great new friend. And he seems so much more like himself than he has since Joy disappeared. Oh, Peter, to hear him laughing like a normal eleven-year-old. We've all forgotten what normal is."

"Yep. This is an answer to prayer." He finished changing, sat on the edge of the bed and pulled her down beside him. "We're having a lot of answered prayers, in case you hadn't noticed."

"I have. And I've been on my knees thanking God. Peter, I really am trying to wait patiently, because I know this is all going to be on His timetable, not mine. But," she grinned, "I'd sure like him to speed up His watch a little. Oh, honey, I feel we're right on the threshold now, waiting to walk through a door."

He put his arm around her. "Meantime, you can wait for God to open that door. Because you're not the same. You said yourself you're a new person."

"I am." She thought a moment. "So you're saying I don't have to go into my perpetual-motion mode. I can rest."

"There are a lot of pros working on this now."

"I know." She sighed. "But," she raised an eyebrow, "this just struck me, Peter. 'Rest' is an active verb. I don't think it means just sit still. I mean, it's too late on the East Coast to call now. But first thing tomorrow, I'll call Dutch Colony. It couldn't hurt." She saw his puzzlement. "Oh, I didn't tell you. That's the cheese place that has shops around the country. Seems Marcy's addicted to their havarti cheese. Now, that's not exactly a best-seller. If there's a store there, it's worth checking out. Someone might remember."

He kissed her cheek. "You are not about to quit, are you? You don't think we should ask Eric to check this out?"

She was surprised at the disappointment that flooded her. "I guess I wanted to play Nancy Drew," she admitted.

Peter smiled. "I can understand that."

෴

Later, at dinner, they told Tim of the possible connection of Marcy with Joy.

"But," Peter added, "we don't know anything for sure."

"Yeah, but that's so cool!" Tim exclaimed. Then he added. "Also creepy. I mean, if Marcy was just lying there watching and planning. That's sick!"

Peter nodded. "I think you're right. She is a sick woman."

"Man, we better pray for her," Tim said.

Andrea looked across the table at Peter and knew he too was pleased with his son's discernment.

"You've got that just right, Timmer," Peter said.

"Hey, but wait." Tim pounded his fist against the side of his head. "This could be bad news for me. I mean, it could mean that before very long Joy'll be getting into all my important stuff, messing it up again."

"Hope you're right." She could visualize Joy's impish grin when she'd been caught "messing up" Tim's treasures. "Remember how Joy—" She stopped abruptly. "I'm doing it again. Getting all euphoric about finding her. It does look good, Tim, but I need to remember God doesn't always answer prayers the way we wish."

"Yeah, I guess."

෴

Though they often slept in on Saturdays, Andrea was up before seven, looking up the area code for Raleigh. She called the information operator. "In Raleigh, do you have a Dutch Colony Cheese Shop?" she asked, praying for an affirmative.

"Checkin'," came a soft drawl. And a moment later, "Here you are."

The electronic voice cut in with the number, and she jotted it down. She glanced at the clock. Five of seven. That would be five of ten in the East. They probably opened at ten.

I feel like one of Joy's windup toys, she thought, as she waited impatiently, wiping the stove burners with a sponge. At one minute past the hour she dialed.

"Dutch Colony," a nasal voice answered.

"Yes," Andrea said, suddenly nervous about how much to say. "I'm calling from California, and we're looking for a missing child. She may be with a woman in your area who—this sounds kind of crazy—but she loves your havarti cheese. Have you by any chance noticed a woman in her early thirties, maybe with a little girl, buying the havarti?"

"Oh, ma'am, this is my first day here. Let me mash the bell and get the manager."

A bell dinged and in a moment, another woman answered. "May I help you?"

"Oh, I hope so!" Andrea said fervently. "My name is Andrea Lang, and my four-year-old daughter, Joy, has been missing since the first part of January. We live in southern California We suspect a young woman took her and may be living in the Raleigh area. I'm calling you because this woman loves your havarti cheese. Can you recall a woman in her early thirties, maybe with a little girl, buying the havarti?"

The woman on the other end of the line hesitated.

"Do you feel uncomfortable talking to me?" Andrea asked.

"Would you rather I have someone from the sheriff's department call?"

"No, it's not that. Your daughter, huh? Oh, that's terrible. I'm a mother, and I want to help. Let me try to recollect. We don't get that much call for that cheese. I do remember a woman quite a few weeks ago gettin' kinda upset because we was plumb out. I told her I'd have it in a few days, but she was put out because she said she had an hour's drive to get here."

"Can you remember at all what she looked like? And was there a child with her?"

"Oh dear, it's hard to remember." There was a long pause.

"Are you there?" Andrea asked anxiously.

"Yes, ma'am. I'm thinkin'. I believe she was a young woman, yes, could have been in her early thirties, now I think on it. Thin. More like reddish hair, as I recall. I had the feelin' she had a child with her, but I couldn't see over the counter, couldn't say how big, boy or girl."

Andrea lifted her fist triumphantly. "You've been so helpful. May I have your name, please?"

"Surely. May Belle. Two words. May Belle Forrester."

"May Belle, you sound like a caring woman," she said. "If this person should come in again, would you call the police and tell them you think there may be some connection with the kidnapping of Joy Lang from Malibu, California?"

"Let me write that down. Joy Lang. Where?"

"Malibu." She spelled it out. "California."

"I've got it. And yes, I surely will! Now wouldn't that be excitin'?"

"Thank you so much, May Belle."

She was ready to hang up when the voice interjected, "Ma'am? I just now thought. I might have that woman's name.

She asked me to save the havarti when it came in. It'd take some time to look back."

"Oh, if you would, I'd be so grateful. Let me give you my phone number. Would you call me collect if you find it?"

"Yes ma'am, I will."

Andrea told her the number and May Belle repeated it. Then she added, "I'll be praying for you, Miz Lang."

Tears sprang to her eyes. "Thank you. Thank you, and God bless you, May Belle."

Oh, Lord, she thought gratefully, *you do bring prayer support from the most unexpected places.*

She went to the living room bookshelves and pulled out the atlas. Locating the detailed map of the southeastern United States, she knelt on the floor to study North Carolina. The map was black with town names all around Raleigh. How far would an hour's drive be? As far as Greensboro, to the west, probably. Or maybe off in the other direction. She sighed. "Lotsa luck," she muttered.

"Whatcha doin'? Geography?"

She turned as she heard Tim's voice in the hallway. "Looking up North Carolina. Breakfast is on the table, honey. I'm coming."

She brought the book with her to the kitchen and set it down, open, on the end of the breakfast table. When Peter came in, she told him about her call. "So," she added, "maybe the detective needs to fan out from Raleigh." She anticipated his response. "I know. We don't know it's Marcy, but it could be. She stopped. "Oh, I just thought, I should have asked her where other Dutch Colony shops are in North Carolina. I mean, if there's one within an hour's drive to the west, for instance, that would eliminate coming from that direction." She glanced around the table at the juice, granola, fruit, milk.

"I think everything's here that you need. Be with you in a minute."

Hurrying to the phone, she redialed the cheese shop and asked for May Belle. "May Belle, I'm sorry to bother you again. But it would help to know what other Dutch Colony shops there are in North Carolina."

"Surely. I have a list right here. Let's see. There's one in Durham. And Fayetteville. And Greensboro. Am I goin' too fast?"

She made quick notes. "No, it's fine."

"New Bern and Winston-Salem. That's it."

"Thanks a million, May Belle!"

Andrea said good-bye and brought her notes over to the table. She studied the map. "OK, if there's a shop in Winston-Salem and another in Greensboro, she probably didn't come from the west."

Tim looked across at the map. "Fayetteville is straight south."

"You're right. So she wouldn't come from the south."

"And Durham is north and a little west," Tim noted and thought a moment. "Most likely she comes from the northeast, east, or southeast."

"I agree!" She turned to Peter. "See what a smart son you have. Well, what do you think, Peter?"

"A long shot. But I'll pass it on to Detective Finley."

She stood and leaned across to kiss him. "You'd better! Because you know me. I'm ready to head for North Carolina!"

෴

Midmorning, Eric called. "We traced Marcy and her car to Las Vegas. She sold it there, January fifteenth, for cash. Didn't buy another, OK? At least not from that dealer. No records of sales to her at any other dealership in Vegas."

"But she'd need transportation. Unless she flew out or took a bus or train," she thought out loud.

"Right, we're checking. But listen, the car dealer thought she had a little girl with her."

"Hallelujah!" Andrea exulted. "Oh, Eric, I just know Marcy's the key."

"We'll find her," he said confidently.

"I think so too. And Eric, here's something else, not as substantial, but it could be something."

She told him about her call to the cheese shop and her thoughts about where Marcy might be, then realized how nebulous it must sound to him. "Never mind."

"No. It could be something," he assured her. "I'll keep in touch."

She hung up thinking about what she'd do if she were Marcy, if she wanted to hide. Change identity, certainly, but how would a person assume a new name? She couldn't use her old driver's license.

She decided to give Dolores a call. "Anything new, darling?" Dolores asked, her deep voice edged with anxiety.

"Eric says Marcy sold her car in Las Vegas. Of course, it's been almost five months now, but the dealer thought she had a little girl with her."

"Oh, my!" Dolores breathed. "Your greatest hope and my greatest fear."

"I know." Andrea's voice caught as she thought of the emotional dichotomy: hope and joy for her, fear and despair for Dolores. She waited a moment before saying, "Dolores, I was thinking that if Marcy did take off and wanted to cover her tracks, how would she go about taking up a new identity? I know Marcy's a bright young woman. Do you have any ideas how she might do it?"

"Hmm," Dolores considered the question. "That's not easy,

455

is it? I guess she could give herself any name. But would that be a problem?"

"I was thinking how people always want to see your driver's license for an ID." She frowned. "How would you change your name on that?"

A blip in the phone line told Andrea she had another call coming in. "Hold on just a sec. I'll be right back." She clicked the second call in. "Hello?"

"We have a collect call from May Belle Forrester in Raleigh, North Carolina," a woman's voice said.

"I'll accept it," she said, taking an anxious breath.

"Miz Lang? It's May Belle. I looked back at the orders and seems like the lady's name is Laura. The last name's a little blurry. Looks like Clinton."

"Laura Clinton," Andrea wrote the name on a notepad. "Thanks a million, May Belle. God bless you!"

"'Welcome, ma'am. The Lord bless you too."

She waited for May Belle to hang up, then clicked in Dolores. "Sorry to keep you waiting, but I've been in touch with a lady from Dutch Colony cheeses in North Carolina."

"How clever of you," Dolores said. Was there a tinge of sarcasm?

Never mind. Andrea pressed on. "Dolores, does the name Laura Clinton mean anything to you?"

"Clinton? No."

Andrea felt her hopes plummet. "Oh. That seems to be the name a young woman was using. Asking for havarti."

"No," Dolores repeated. "Doesn't ring any bells for me."

Another dead end, Andrea mourned as she told Dolores good-bye.

46

~

From Zoë's Prayer Journal

May 25: Oh, Father, thank You for taking me to the Psalms for my Bible reading this morning and for showing me Psalm 103:17. It is so perfect: "But from everlasting to everlasting the Lord's love is with those who fear Him, and His righteousness with their children's children." Oh, Lord, what a beautiful promise, and what exquisite timing! I claim right now Your righteousness for my little angel, Joy. Bring her home safely now, dear Lord, in Jesus' name, amen.

LAURA CLINTON—*Laura Clinton—Laura Clinton.* The name repeated rhythmically in Andrea's mind as she finished her phone conversation with Dolores. *There has to be some connection. Isn't there, Lord?* she pleaded.

Without hanging up, she pressed and released the off button and called Eric to tell him about Laura Clinton.

"Clinton, huh?" he pondered. "Let me look at my notes from talking with Dolores.

She heard papers rustling. Then, "Yeah, here it is. When I

asked her about the family, she mentioned a stepdaughter. Her husband's child by a first marriage. Lived with the mother. Thought I remembered her first name was Laura. She died a year ago."

Andrea caught her breath. "And her last name?"

"Married name was Blanton." He spelled it. There was a pause. "Not that far from Clinton, is it?"

"No!" Andrea exclaimed. "And Eric, the clerk did have trouble making out the last name. Said it was blurred on the order." Her mind rushed ahead. "So Marcy could know all the pertinent stuff about Laura Blanton, like her birthdate. She could become Laura."

"Possible. I'll alert the Raleigh area."

"Oh, thanks, Eric!" She replaced the phone and hurried to the garage where Peter and Tim were working on the Olds.

"Listen to this!" she cried and told them about Laura Blanton.

"Hey-hey!" Tim exclaimed.

"Let's hear it for our Nancy Drew!" Peter gave her a hug. "I'll call Finley back." He started for the house.

Andrea walked with him. "And Peter, the fact that the car dealer in Vegas thought she had a little girl with her. Isn't that encouraging? Oh, and I forgot to tell you, Marcy didn't buy another car."

"So you think she wanted to cover her tracks—maybe changed her name after that?" he asked.

"A good possibility." She could hear the lilt of optimism in her own voice as she added, "If she's taken a new name, maybe it'll turn up in a bank or on a new driver's license."

Peter grinned and nodded. "This is starting to roll!" He gave her a quick kiss. "Sure glad you made that cheese-shop connection."

They went inside together, and after Peter called the detective, he phoned Zoë. "Answering machine," he told Andrea. "Oh, right; it's Saturday. She's out selling houses." He left a detailed message.

The day lapsed into slow motion for Andrea, as she waited for something, anything to develop. The waiting reminded her of childhood summers, when her mother wouldn't let her swim for an hour after a meal. She remembered all the days she'd thought the time was up, but found there was still fifty minutes to go.

She called Connie, hoping to talk with her, but only a recorded message responded. "All we do is talk to answering machines," she grumbled.

Each time the phone rang, a charge of hope coursed through her. Each time, she answered eagerly only to hear a bottled-water salesman, a request for a donation to save an endangered spotted owl, and a wrong number.

At four, Dolores called. "Talked with Brant," she began without preamble.

Startled, Andrea exclaimed, "What? Oh, about the pictures?"

"Right. At first, he denied it all. Then became defiant. Bragged about the ceremony, the brotherhood. I don't like it, Andrea. I don't like it one bit. I especially don't like his rebellious attitude."

"I don't blame you."

"I think he needs help." Dolores sighed.

Andrea struggled for words of reassurance, but none came. "Dolores, why don't you get in touch with the youth minister at our church? He's really good with this age group, I understand." Ignoring a disdainful "Pff!" from Dolores, she gave her the name and number. Then she added, "Do you suppose it would help to get Brant away from Malibu for a while? I mean, it's only two weeks till school's out."

"I thought of that," Dolores said slowly. "There's a place, a house in Carlsbad where we could go. But I have to see what happens with Marcy." She sighed again. "Is there anything new?"

"Well," Andrea hesitated. "Do you think Marcy could be using the name, not Laura Clinton, but Laura Blanton?"

She heard Dolores gasp. "It's possible," she said at last. "For Marcy to become Laura," she mused, "oh, what an irony that would be!"

"How so?"

"She hated her half-sister's guts!" Another pause. "Keep me posted."

"Thanks, Dolores. Of course I will."

A moment later, Zoë called. "Oh, my darling," she exclaimed, "God is at work. I know it." She told Andrea of the promise she'd found in the Psalms.

Andrea felt her eyes brim. "God is good!" she exclaimed. "Oh, Mom, keep praying! Pray like crazy!"

"I am! I am!" Zoë assured her.

꒰꒱

It was almost five when Eric called. "News from Raleigh," he announced.

"Oh, yes! What?" Andrea pressed the phone against her ear.

"Your cheese lady in Raleigh called the police. The woman she told you about was there, buying that weird cheese. And she had a little girl with her."

Andrea gasped. "Are you serious?" she asked.

"I am," he replied. "The manager did her best to stall her,

but the woman took off before the police got there. So the cheese lady tried to follow her, OK? Seems the shop's in a mall, and she tried so hard not to be obvious, she lost her."

"Oh," Andrea moaned. "So May Belle didn't see her car or get a license or anything."

"I'm afraid not. But listen to this." She could hear a new lilt in his voice. "The police showed her Joy's picture. She said the hairstyle was different, but she was pretty sure. And she was also pretty certain about Marcy when she saw her picture."

"Oh, Eric, then this could mean Joy's alive, well, safe." Suddenly, her legs turned mushy, and with her back against the wall, she slid down onto the smooth coolness of the kitchen floor. "Oh, thank You, Lord!" she whispered.

"Now, we can't be absolutely certain, so hang in there till we actually find her, OK?"

"Don't tell me that!" She couldn't hide her irritation. They were so close now. It was all fitting together. She felt so sure. She wanted to be in Raleigh now! Why was he being so like Peter?

"Hang in there," he repeated.

"Right," she said, suddenly too choked to say more. She heard Eric sign off and dropped the phone on her lap as tears flooded her face. Her heart felt as full to overflowing as her eyes, and she repeated again and again, "Thank You, Jesus. You are so good! Thank You, Jesus."

Dimly, she heard the message from the phone, "If you'd like to make a call, please hang up and try again. If you need help, hang up and dial your operator." When the repeated beep began, she pressed the off button and sat, clutching the phone 'til she heard Tim come in.

"Mom!" he cried. "You OK?"

Nodding, she handed him the phone to hang up.

He took it, then knelt beside her, concern creasing his forehead. "Bad news?"

She shook her head and wiped her eyes with both hands. "No, good. Oh, Tim, go get your dad! Is he inside? Peter!" she called.

She could hear his deliberate steps in the hall.

"Hurry!" she shouted.

"Andry!" he exclaimed when he saw her.

She held up her hands so he could help her stand. Leaning against the counter, she said, "Oh, Peter! Tim!" Her voice broke and it was a moment before she could continue. "The woman in Raleigh in the cheese shop thinks she's seen Joy. And Marcy too. With Joy. It's a miracle that she came in so soon after I called. Oh, Peter, if only we can find her and make sure! Oh, maybe we'd better go to North Carolina right now!"

Peter hugged her tight, and she could feel the quick beat of his heart.

Tim lifted a fist. "Yes-s-s!" He grinned. "So didn't the lady at the cheese shop tie Marcy up or hit her over the head with a cheese and get the police?"

She laughed. "Not quite. She did call the police but they didn't make it in time. But the fact that we're pretty sure they're together—Oh, dear Lord, if it's Joy, please find them soon!"

"In Jesus' name," Peter added. He thought a moment, one eyebrow raised. "I think we should call your folks and my dad."

"You do?" she asked, surprised. "You don't think it's premature?"

"No, I don't."

Andrea reached her parents immediately and updated them. "Oh, Mom, isn't this great? Your hiring Finley and your support has brought a break in the case! Thank you both so much! I'll let you know the moment we hear something more."

Peter placed his call, listened, and shook his head. "His answering machine." He waited a moment, then said, "Dad, Peter. We're getting close. Looks like Joy is in the Raleigh, North Carolina area, and our neighbor's daughter has her. We'll call when we know more."

They reached Zoë's answering machine once again and Connie's as well.

"You'd think," Andrea said with mock indignation, "that people could stay home on an important day like this!"

47

WITH ONE FOOT in her pantyhose, Andrea caught the phone on the second ring.

"Can you meet before church to pray?" came Connie's exultant voice. "Oh, Andrea, I got your message, and all the pieces of the puzzle are falling into place. We just have to thank Him."

Andrea smiled at her friend's exuberance. "I couldn't agree more. What time were you thinking?"

"How about, oh, twenty of?"

Andrea glanced at her watch. If they hurried . . . "We'll be there."

"I'll get others," Connie promised. "Meet you in the front of the sanctuary."

An hour later, Peter, Andrea, and Tim walked into the church to find at least twenty people waiting.

"Can you believe it?" Peter said, as they walked down the aisle. "My whole men's prayer group."

"Yes, and oh, look at the women from the Bible study," Andrea added.

"And Jonathan and his folks!" Tim exclaimed.

As they reached the front of the church, Andrea looked around the group at Mary Lou, Connie, the woman who'd warned her so gently about Sybil, the one who'd lost so many babies. *Friends*, she thought. *I wouldn't let myself see them as friends before.* The love in their faces brought tears to her eyes.

How different, Andrea thought, *from the witches.* Mom's right. When we all love the Lord, there's a very special kind of love that spreads out to one another. Makes me sad for what Dolores's friends are missing.

They formed a circle, holding hands, and Jeff began, "Oh, Lord, how good You are! It seems You may be bringing resolution to this nightmare, and we praise and thank You. And we thank You for the privilege of praying for the Langs through these months, for it's surely brought each of us closer to You. And oh, Lord, thank You for their growth in You and renewed love for You."

When he finished his prayer, others joined in, with Connie praying for Andrea's trust and patience and quoting, "'Now, faith is the substance of things hoped for—'"

"'The evidence of things not seen,'" Andrea finished the verse. "Thank You, thank You for teaching me that, dear Lord."

As they concluded, one by one the women hugged Andrea and whispered personal, tender prayers. The last to come was Connie, her own face tear-streaked.

As she released her hug, Connie reached into her pocket and pulled out a fresh tissue. With a flourish, she tore it in half to share with Andrea, just as she'd done almost five months earlier, the first time they'd cried together.

They laughed together now through their tears and hugged once again.

Tim and Jonathan went off to Sunday school, and the adults took seats together as the service began. The morning's message, "God's faithfulness to all generations," echoed perfectly the scripture Zoë had found, and Andrea felt her throat tighten and tears threaten once again. When they sang the closing song, unable to trust her voice, she could only lip-sync the words: "To every generation. To every generation."

Later, as they headed home, Peter remarked, "Don't we have a great family Tim?"

"You and me and Mom and Joy? Oh yeah."

"More than that. Our church family," Peter said.

"Oh, yeah. It is like a family, 'cause we care about each other and help each other." Tim nodded.

"You've got it," Peter smiled.

~

The next morning, as Andrea pondered what to do with her day, Connie called. "How you doin'?" she asked.

"I feel peaceful, but the time does drag."

"I think you should pack your bag," Connie declared.

"You do?" she asked, surprised.

"Yep. You're gonna want to take off in a hurry when they find Joy."

"That's true," she said, elated to have something to do. "And I'll pack for Peter and Tim. I think he should go too. This has been tough for him."

"Definitely." Connie said. "It's been a lot for a kid his age. But hasn't he grown with it? Haven't we all?"

~

466

That afternoon, Zoë called. "I'm too excited to work," she confessed. "What if I come out and we could do some cooking—things Joy really loves. You make a list of what you need. I'll shop on my way, and if you don't mind my staying over, we'll cook up a storm tomorrow." Andrea could hear the smile in her voice. "If you take off for North Carolina before that, I'll cook alone."

"Oh, Mom, what a wonderful idea. So practical." Instantly, Andrea knew what to fix. "Gingerbread. We'll make gingerbread. And fried chicken."

Midmorning the next day, with the gingerbread in the oven, Andrea glanced out the kitchen window and saw Eric's car heading up the hill. "Oh, Mom! Do you suppose . . ." she cried as she ran to the front door. She met Eric in the driveway.

His grin told her everything. "I wanted to tell you in person," he began. "It's what we've been waiting for." He glanced at his watch. "Waiting, I figure, for four months, three weeks, five days."

"They found Joy!"

He nodded. "She's fine."

"Oh!" she exclaimed and flung her arms around him. They hugged briefly and she asked, "Where?"

"Town named Goldsboro. About an hour from Raleigh. A little south and east. You were right about the general location."

She saw Zoë at the door, gave her a thumbs-up and motioned her to come out. As Zoë joined them, she put her arm around Andrea and breathed, "Thank You, Father." Then she grabbed Eric in a tight hug.

He returned the hug, laughing, then looked toward Andrea as she asked, "Tell me what happened."

"It was totally routine. Tracked Marcy—or actually, like we figured, she had a license under the name of Laura Blanton through the North Carolina motor vehicle department. And the rest, as they say, is history."

She shook her head, feeling giddy. "Does Peter know?"

"Not yet."

"I've got to call him!" She turned toward the house.

"Right. But first, Marcy's in jail and they're taking Joy to a shelter till you get there," he explained. He handed her a piece of paper. "Here's the shelter number."

She glanced at it. "Good. Oh, and now we've got to get there quickly." She looked at her watch. "Ten after ten. There's a three-hour time difference. That's tough."

"I'll make some calls about flights." Zoë started toward the house.

"Thank you! Thank you for everything," Andrea said to Eric, clasping his hand, feeling enormous gratitude. Nothing more, she realized.

"My pleasure," he grinned. "Especially when a case ends like this." His smile faded. "Now the hard part: breaking the news to Dolores."

She gasped. "Oh, she'll be devastated. What will happen to Marcy?"

"It's a federal case. There'll probably be an extradition hearing, unless she waives extradition. In any case, since it happened in California, they'll send her back here for trial."

"I feel so sorry . . ." she began.

He shook his head. "No, don't go soft. It's a major crime. A kidnapper takes a big chunk out of a child's life. And it costs weeks and months and sometimes a lifetime of anguish." He turned and got into the car, starting the engine. "I'll come around to meet that girl of yours in a few days. I've only seen her pictures."

"That's right! We'll have a party!" She waved and watched him head out the driveway and across the road to Dolores's.

There would have been no solution without Dolores, she realized. *If she hadn't pulled me into her stuff. There was a reason for my relationship with her from the very beginning. It's really true what the Bible says about things that are meant for evil, that God uses them for good.* Oh, help Dolores now, Lord, she prayed.

She ran into the house and found Zoë in the kitchen, poring over the phone book. Zoë turned to give her a long, warm hug and she could feel Zoë's tears against her face. "Thank You, Lord!" Zoë exclaimed.

"Yes. And thank you, dear Mom, for everything," Andrea said. "You've done so, so much." As she released her hug, she looked over Zoë's shoulder and smiled at the view. "Come here, Mom, I want to show you something." She led Zoë to the window and pointed. All the mountainous contours of Catalina Island stood green and clear in a sea of blue-gray. "See!" Andrea exclaimed. "Catalina is there!"

Zoë laughed. "Told you so!"

"Now," Zoë bustled as they moved apart, "I'll see what's available flight-wise. After you call Peter."

"Oh, Mom, it's the call I've been waiting to make all these months!" she cried.

The line rang several times before Peter answered.

"Let's go get our daughter!" she said.

She could hear him suck in his breath. "Really?" The old tone of caution.

"Really! She's safe, in Goldsboro, southeast of Raleigh. Like we figured. Marcy's in jail."

"No! Andrea, you're absolutely certain?"

She crossed her heart. "Absolutely. Eric just left."

"I'll be right home. Ya-hoo!" he bellowed.

She held the phone away from her ear and echoed his cry. It took a moment before she could force herself back to the details of getting away. "Now, if we can both come down to earth for a minute, your mom's working on airline reservations. How soon can you get home?"

"Well," he laughed. "I just threw two hundred pages of system proposal up in the air. But oh, hey, everybody heard me, and someone's picking them up. So I just left!"

"Oh, good. And Peter, I do want Tim to come with us. I'll have to pick him up at school." She saw Zoë pointing to herself. "Mom's saying she'll do it."

By eleven, the plane reservations were made, and both Tim and Peter were home.

"Bless Mom for getting us so organized," Andrea said.

"Now," Peter pondered. "We leave at 2:40 this afternoon, change planes in Dallas, and get into Raleigh at 12:50 A.M. Probably no point in going on to Goldsboro then. I'll book a hotel room at the airport."

"Couldn't we just go straight to the shelter and sit on the doorstep till daylight?" she asked. "I know I won't sleep a wink."

"We can be at the door of the shelter first thing in the morning," he said.

"Peter!" she protested.

He gave her a gentle smile. "Tell you what, let's call the shelter and tell them we're on our way."

"Oh, yes." She clapped her hands together. "Maybe we can talk with Joy!"

Peter placed the call and connected with the shelter's psychologist.

"Ask if we can come tonight. Just to see her," Andrea prompted.

Peter introduced himself and gave their flight plans. "My wife wants to know if we can see Joy tonight." He listened. "I understand. Of course. So what time can we come in the morning? Eight. Fine." He hesitated. "How does she seem, Dr. Adamson? Uh-huh. Pretty quiet, huh? Yes. Confused. Sure." He listened.

"What? What's the matter?" Andrea cried.

"Just a moment," he said to the psychologist. "Marcy told Joy she was her real mother. Had her call her Mamá, like the French, with the accent on the last syllable."

She leaned against him, hand covering her mouth. "I was afraid of something like that."

"I understand," he said to the psychologist. "Can we bring her back tomorrow? Good. And how do we find the shelter?" He pulled out his DayTimer and made notes. "Yes. A brick building. Good."

She whispered, "See if we can talk to her!"

"Right. Could we speak with Joy?" he asked. "We'd like her to hear from us that we'll be there tomorrow." He nodded. "You bet I'll wait!" He handed the phone to Andrea. "He's getting her."

She grabbed the phone and with the other hand nervously polished the sink faucet with a towel as she waited. At last a woman's voice said, "Mr. Lang?"

"No, it's Mrs. Lang on the phone now."

"Fine. Here's Joy." There was a silence and the woman whispered, "Say hello to your mommy."

"Hello?" came a hesitant little voice.

"Joy!" Andrea could barely get the word out and tried again. "Joy! Darling, it's Mommy. I'm at home, in our house on the hill in Malibu. Oh, sweetheart, how are you?"

A pause. "Okay."

"Honey, we're going to come and get you, but it's a long way away. We'll be there tomorrow, and we'll bring you back home that very day."

Joy didn't respond.

"Did you hear me, darling?"

"Yes."

She ached for more reaction. "I can't wait to hug you," she said. She glanced at Peter. "Want to talk to Daddy?" She felt Tim beside her. "And Tim?"

"OK."

"Is this Daddy's little girl?" Peter asked, one eyebrow cocked expectantly. "Good! You understand we'll be there tomorrow?" He listened. "Oh, they did? A stuffed doggy? How nice. So you can take him to bed with you tonight, eh? You'll be sleeping there, where you are now, Joy. But we'll come to get you in the morning. Joy, how much does Daddy love you? This much?"

He listened, grinning.

"This much?" He laughed at her response. "You're right. Much more than that! Here's Tim."

"Hi, pest," Tim said and listened. "Hey, I've missed you gettin' into my stuff. And guess what? We have a new cat. Her name's Juliet. You'll like her." He was quiet a moment. "See ya tomorrow." He handed the phone back to Peter.

"That's right, honey, we'll see you tomorrow—all three of us. And you know something? We can't wait!" Peter looked at Andrea and whispered, "Want to say anything more?"

She shook her head.

He listened a moment. "Oh, wait," he said to Andrea. "Dr. Adamson, the psychologist, is on the line. He wants to speak with you."

She took the phone again. "Yes?"

"Mrs. Lang, I wanted to explain. If Joy seemed a little quiet, or, well, wary, that's entirely normal. Remember, she's been with this other woman almost five months, a woman who claimed to be her mother. Joy was told you'd gone away and wouldn't be back. She doesn't know yet what's really true. Don't be surprised if she's a little slow to trust, perhaps doesn't respond immediately to you. Five months is a long, long time in the life of a four-year-old. But she's been well cared for. Physically, she's fine. The woman even managed to get the phenobarbital for Joy. Evidently heard on TV that she needed it."

"Oh, good." She breathed a sigh of relief. "Would you recommend we take her for some counseling here?" she asked.

"I think it would be a good idea."

"Thank you. We'll see you tomorrow." She hung up, turning to Peter. "Funny how you develop this scenario in your mind about how it'll be when we're reunited. And you see a rainbow shining and Joy just falling into our arms and everyone saying, 'I love you,' and picking up where we left off. But this isn't 'happily ever after.'"

"There are wounds," he said softly. He put his arms around her.

"Oh, Lord," she prayed, "heal them quickly!"

48

From Zoe's Prayer Journal

May 28: Dear Lord, every morning I pick up my newspaper and read so many stories with unhappy endings. There are still other parents with missing children. We're not one tiny bit better or more worthy than they. Yet now You're giving us a happy ending. And we know Joy's return isn't because of anything we've done to earn or deserve Your mercy. It's strictly Your grace, Lord, Your unmerited favor that's returning our Joy to us. And I bow down before You now, once again amazed at that grace, and humbly, tearfully grateful. Thank You for finding my little angel, our Joy. Thank You for keeping her safe and well. Oh, how I praise You for Your faithfulness to all generations, in Jesus' name, amen.

ZOË CLOSED HER PRAYER JOURNAL as she heard Peter come into the kitchen.

He smiled. "You don't go anywhere without that, do you?"

She shook her head. "Never know when I might need it!"

Peter stood combing his fingers through his hair as Andrea and Tim joined them. "Let's see now. Are we forgetting anything?" He ran through his predeparture checklist with the thoroughness of NASA preparing for a space launch. "Tickets ready to pick up from that agency on Pacific Coast Highway. Right on our way. Tim, did you check your bag to be sure you have everything you need?"

"Yes sir." Andrea thought for a moment Tim might salute.

"My bag's ready and thanks for doing that, Andry," Peter said.

She nodded. "And I'm all set. I even crammed 'Mr. Bear' into my bag."

"And I'll stay here till you're back," Zoë said. She feigned a pout. "Someone has to hold down the fort, finish cooking, put Juliet out, let Juliet in, put Juliet out—"

"Let Juliet in," Tim added. "Gram, you're the greatest!"

"I know," she said, all modesty.

Peter nodded. "Thanks, Mom." He looked at the clock and back at Zoë. "Could we have a prayer?"

"Let's!" Andrea said.

They joined hands and after a moment, Andrea spoke. "Oh, heavenly Father, our hearts are so full! How can we praise and thank You enough? Please, enfold Joy in Your arms. Heal her. Restore her to trust and wellness. May the reunion be sweet. I can't wait to hug her! Then bring us all back swiftly to this grandmother's arms. And may others see Your love and power and goodness in all this, in Jesus' name, amen."

"Beautiful prayer, darling," Zoë said, as they all hugged.

Peter glanced at his watch. "OK, we'll use the airport parking. It'll be faster than going in a lot outside LAX and taking a shuttle." He snapped his fingers. "Mom! The reward. Doesn't the cheese-shop lady qualify?"

"Absolutely!" Zoë exclaimed. "What a smart son I have!"

"Is there any way we can get the check?" Andrea wondered. "It'd be nice to give it to her in person."

"Sure. Bank's on our way. I'll call and alert them." Peter picked up the phone.

"While you're doing that, I'll slip over to Dolores's just for a minute. I won't be long," Andrea promised.

She hurried across the road. When Dolores opened the door, Andrea embraced her immediately, realizing once again what an imposing figure she was.

"Oh, Dolores, I'm so sorry. This is so hard for you."

Dolores returned the hug, and Andrea could see the effort it took for her to smile. "But for you," Dolores said, " I'm so glad it's over."

"Me too," she admitted. "I just didn't want to go to Goldsboro without seeing you. Have you talked with Marcy?"

Dolores nodded. "She insists Joy is her child, that a terrible mistake was made in the hospital. Calls it a hideous conspiracy."

"She really believes that, doesn't she? Poor girl! From what I hear, Dolores, she cared for Joy as if she was her very own. They tell me our daughter's in fine shape physically. That should help Marcy's case. And surely her mental state would be a—what do they call it?—mitigating circumstance."

"I hope so. And I'm glad she took good care of Joy. When she was first married, Marcy would have made a wonderful mother. I think she wanted something or somebody to love so much, she flipped out." She shook her head. "She's going to need therapy." She leaned against the wall. "Therapy sounds good to me right now."

"You must feel absolutely overwhelmed."

"I do." Dolores rubbed her eyes. "I've called an attorney for Marcy."

"Good." She clasped Dolores's arm.

"Otherwise, where to begin?" Dolores's voice sounded dull, exhausted. "I feel like I've stepped into quicksand and don't have a thing to hang on to."

Andrea studied her, debating whether to express what to her was the obvious. What did she have to lose? "You might try God."

"I did," Dolores snapped.

Andrea cocked her head. "You tried the true God, the everlasting God of the Bible? Jesus? You looked at God's Word?"

"Well . . . "

"I'd like to make a suggestion."

Dolores eyed her warily. "Yes?"

"Get your calendar."

Dolores raised a skeptical eyebrow, but turned and brought her calendar from the desk.

"OK, next Wednesday at ten o'clock. Write down 'Bible Study.'"

Dolores threw back her head and laughed, that same deep, throaty laugh that had beguiled Andrea in the very beginning. "Surely you jest!"

Andrea smiled but didn't reply. As she stood watching her flamboyant neighbor, she felt a supernatural love for her and quickly prayed that Dolores would sense it too.

"Well . . . " Dolores relented and scribbled a note on her calendar. "I'm not promising anything, mind you."

"I understand," Andrea said, starting out the open door. "We'll be back tomorrow night, and I'll be praying for you and Marcy and Brant."

"I could use your good thoughts and that energy flow," Dolores said.

Andrea held up a cautionary finger. "Uh-uh. Not good

thoughts, not energy flow. Prayers, Dolores. Communication with God. Prayers for you and your family, going up from me to an almighty, sovereign God."

Dolores smiled, or was it a smirk? "I'll keep an eye on things," she promised.

"God, You're going to win her yet," Andrea murmured as she hurried home.

Peter greeted her at the door. "I talked with the bank, and I called my dad." He laughed. "He sang the first phrase of the Hallelujah Chorus."

Andrea smiled. "He would! I'd better phone my folks." She saw Peter consult his watch. "I'll be quick." She headed for the kitchen and placed the call. "Daddy," she cried when he answered, "Good news! Joy's been found in North Carolina."

She heard him shout to her mother. "They found Joy! Thank God," he breathed.

"Oh, I do too!" she agreed. "We're going right now to the airport, but I wanted you to know. Finley helped break this case, and Joy's fine."

"That's great, punkin. We can hardly wait to see her."

"Andrea!" It was her mother's harsh voice. It modulated quickly. "You give that little girl a big hug from Grandmom."

꒲

It was well after one-thirty in the morning when they settled into their hotel room in Raleigh. Tim went straight to bed and to sleep.

"He's dead to the world," Andrea said. "I'm exhausted and wired all at the same time."

"Me too. What time do you want to get up this morning?" Peter asked.

She groaned. "That's right. It's tomorrow already." She considered the question. "It's an hour from here to Goldsboro? Do we have to have breakfast? I'd say no later than six. Want to make it earlier?"

"Five-thirty?" he suggested.

She hugged him. "You're as eager as I am."

"You're right." He picked up the phone and sat down, waiting for an answer. "I need a five-thirty wake-up call, please," he said.

Andrea sat on his lap, relaxing against him as he held her. After a while, she said, "Could we stay right here? I feel very content. I might actually go to sleep." She pretended to snore. When he didn't answer, she added, "Well, I might, but you might not. Let's try the bed."

∼

The next morning, they dressed quickly and had breakfast in a coffee shop adjacent to the hotel. As they left, Tim said, "Hey, check that newspaper!"

She looked at the news rack. "Missing California child found," the headline read. Peter pressed a coin into the slot. Grabbing the paper, she scanned the article as they headed for the car. "It's real!" she exulted. "It's in the paper and it's real!"

"You publicists think anything in the paper is real," Peter laughed, "but this time you're right."

As they headed toward Goldsboro, she glanced over at the speedometer of their rental car. Peter was driving at the legal speed limit, but to her the car was barely moving. She grasped Joy's koala bear, twisting its fur.

She saw Peter smile.

"What?" she asked.

"I was remembering a psalm that says joy comes in the morning."

"And this is our Joy with a capital J!" She patted his knee.

"Boy, Dad, this is real different from California," Tim said.

"Right. And we don't see crops like these growing in California. I'm pretty sure that's tobacco."

"Yuck!" Tim exclaimed. "Those shiny big green leaves turn into cigarettes?"

"Yep, and pipe tobacco, chewing tobacco, snuff," Peter explained.

"Aack!" Tim clutched his throat.

A bit later, Andrea warned, "We're getting close now." She'd read and reread the directions given by the shelter till she knew them by heart. Still, she glanced back at them repeatedly, anxious not to take a single wrong turn.

At last she cried out, "There it is—the brick building!" She saw the mobile TV trucks as they pulled into the parking lot. "Like Phoenix," she said. "No, not like Phoenix. This time it's for real."

As they got out of the car, reporters and cameras clustered around them. As the questions came all at once, she answered, "Yes, we feel terrific. We'll feel even better when we see Joy."

"Excuse us," Peter said firmly, pressing through the group, leading Andrea and Tim. "We want to get to our daughter."

Inside the shelter, Dr. Adamson came out immediately to greet them, and though Andrea thought he'd sounded at least fifty on the phone, he looked as though he'd just started to shave.

He led them into the director's office. "When you're finished, we'll take you to Joy," he promised. "Oh, and one thing more. The policeman who went to the house and brought Joy in. He wants to see you all."

"Fine," Peter said.

Andrea sat twisting her purse strap as they went through the necessary paperwork. At last Dr. Adamson reappeared and led them to a small reception area with a couch and two chairs.

"Remember, Mrs. Lang, that woman told your daughter she was her mother, that you'd gone away, that you weren't coming back," he warned. "Don't expect too much. And by the way, once you're home, feel free to contact me at any time."

He pointed toward a couch, but Andrea, Peter, and Tim stood, waiting. She could hear her heart thud.

At last the door opened, and a tall auburn-haired woman urged a reluctant small girl into the room. Joy's hair, still glistening strawberry blond, was much longer. It elongated her face making her look older. And her wine-colored T-shirt drained the color from her peaches-and-cream complexion.

Andrea stooped down and held out her arms, trying hard not to cry. "Joy!" she exclaimed.

Joy drew back behind the attendant.

"Here's Daddy's little girl!" Peter said softly.

Joy peeked around the attendant and looked first at Peter, then Tim.

"Dad-dee! Tim-mer!" she cried.

And then she was in their arms. Andrea waited, watching, aching to hold her child. Dr. Adamson caught her eye. "It'll come," he whispered. "I'll be right in the next room. Knock when you're ready to go."

She nodded. I've waited five months. I can wait awhile longer, she told herself, and the pain eased, but only a little.

As Peter sat down on the couch with Joy in his arms, Tim beside him, she joined them and pressed the koala bear against Joy's arm. Joy turned, saw the toy, and clutched him tight. "Oh, there you are, Mr. Bear!" she sighed.

Ecstasy, Andrea thought.

Peeking over the bear, Joy regarded Andrea with sober, thoughtful eyes.

Tim played finger games with Joy, and Peter stroked her hair as they sat, savoring the moment. He looked at Andrea. "Mom missed you terribly, Joy."

"Mamá said she wasn't coming back," Joy murmured.

"Well, she was wrong, honey," Peter said. "Mom is your real mother, and she wants to be with you more than anything."

Joy didn't respond, and when Peter glanced at Andrea, she mouthed, "Thanks, honey."

After a while, Tim looked around the room. "This place is a major downer."

"It is," Peter agreed. "How about it, little Miss Lang? You ready to go home?"

Joy nodded emphatically.

Andrea stood, went over to the door, and knocked. Dr. Adamson appeared with a uniformed policeman, an awesome figure, at least six-foot-six, she judged.

"This is Officer Manchester," Dr. Adamson said.

"Mr. and Mrs. Lang and Tim. And you know Joy."

He crossed the room and knelt to touch Joy's hand. "Remember me? I'm the one who found you."

She nodded shyly, clinging to her dad. "He gave me the doggy," she whispered to Peter.

Manchester snuffled and wiped his forefinger beneath his nose. "Well, I just, uh, somehow I wanted to see y'all together. I see a lot of sadness, and this is a real happy ending. You're a good-lookin' family."

"Thank you, Officer." Andrea took his hand. "And thank you for helping bring our Joy back to us."

When at last they were on their way to the car, Andrea

whispered to Peter. "We need to give the press a statement. They've been very good to us."

Outside, they posed for the cameras and spoke into the microphones. Squinting into the sun, Peter said, "Well, obviously, this is the day we've been waiting for. We are so grateful that Joy is safe, and we thank everyone who's supported us and brought us to this great day of reunion. And we thank God. We could never have made it without our strong faith. Correction—our faith wasn't always strong, but it was faith in a strong God. That and the faithful prayers of family and friends."

"Mrs. Lang? Mrs. Lang?" several voices called.

"Yes," she said. "God is faithful to all generations." She paused. "As you can imagine, this is a mother's dream come true. I really want to thank you and all the media for all the help you've given us."

A reporter pushed a microphone in front of Tim. "How do you feel, young man?"

"Good," he said simply.

"And you, little lady?" he held the mike up to Joy. She turned her face away, against Peter's jacket.

"I'd like to announce," Andrea added, "that we're going now to deliver the reward check to the woman who first positively identified Joy. May Belle Forrester in the Dutch Colony Cheese Shop in Raleigh."

The reporters made notes and scurried to leave.

As they came to the car, Andrea reached out to take Joy so Peter could unlock the door. Joy clung to him, burying her head in the crook of his neck. Andrea sighed inwardly. How she longed to hold her daughter. "I'll drive. You navigate, Peter," she said.

As they drove toward the cheese shop, she could hear Joy

chattering to Peter in the backseat. Then Peter said, "We're making good time. Say, fifty minutes to the cheese shop. Maybe fifteen minutes there. Then twenty to the airport, including dropping off the car. That still gets us there in plenty of time."

She smiled. Got to get to that plane, as always.

"Good," she said.

She felt Peter leaning forward, his head by her right ear. "It's hard, not having Joy come right to you."

"Yes. Awful."

"She will."

"I know," she said, wiping her eyes.

When they reached the cheese shop, the press had already arrived, and May Belle, a pudgy woman with her dull blond hair in tightly permed ringlets, fidgeted with her cheeses, her face flushed with excitement, upper lip beaded with perspiration.

Andrea introduced herself and her family. "Thank you so, so much, May Belle."

May Belle grabbed her in a damp hug. "Oh, it's wonderful that you and your l'il darlin' are back together!" she exclaimed. "I just praise God and how He used me!"

"And I thank Him for you and for your prayers and everything!" Andrea said.

"You'd do the same for me," May Belle said. She saw Joy and stooped to look at her. "Oh, and here she is! Oh, she's a sweetheart!"

"Ready for TV, Mrs. Forrester?" a man called.

"Oh," May Belle fussed, "I do declare, I'm so discombobulated. Is my hair all right? Wish I'd washed it last night. Shall I leave my apron on, you think?"

"Your hair is perfect," Andrea assured her, "and I'd leave the apron on. Brings out the blue in your eyes."

May Belle smiled, and her cheeks formed into round little apples of flesh.

The reporters tried to coax Joy to hug May Belle, but Joy refused to leave Peter. He presented the check three times, to satisfy all the print and broadcast media. Each time, May Belle beamed and repeated, "Praise God and how He used me to get this beautiful baby girl back with her family!"

As they finished, Peter said to Joy, "Now we can go get on the airplane. We're going to take a plane ride back to California. And Gram's waiting at our house, waiting to hug you."

جى

When they were finally settled on the plane, Andrea breathed a sigh of relief. "Whew! Wasn't sure we'd make it." She looked wistfully across the aisle, and a sense of separation washed over her. She felt so outside of the family, as she saw Peter, Joy, and Tim seated together. *Oh, Lord,* she moaned inwardly, *it's so hard!*

Tim had given Joy the window seat, and now she heard him singing to her, "Goin' home, Joy, goin' home."

"Goin' home," Joy echoed, "Joy goin' home."

Quickly Andrea's feelings of isolation dissipated. *How grateful I am, Lord to see all three of them together, all that You've given me that I love most in this life. How I thank You for all You did during these past five months.*

After the plane took off and the seat-belt signs went off, a flight attendant came to Peter. "Mr. Lang, we have seats in first class. We know this is a very special day for you. Why don't you and your family move on forward?"

The attendant helped them settle into the spacious new

seats, Joy again at the window with Peter beside her, Andrea across the aisle from Peter, with Tim beside her at the window.

"This is too good to be true," Andrea said, tilting her seat back. "This whole day and yesterday are too wonderful for words."

"Right," Peter said.

She closed her eyes. *Wonderful*, she thought. *But realistically, there are those wounds. This is a different little girl than I left at home that morning way back in January. Will the Joy I remember come back to us? Will that lively little spirit of hers return? And how long will it take for her to trust me again?*

"Andrea?" She looked up to see Peter pointing at the phone in the seat back before him. "Shall we call Mom?"

"Great idea!" she said.

He turned to Joy. "Want to talk to Gram?"

Joy nodded.

"All right, let's see if we can get her." He picked up the phone, and after several attempts, made the connection. "Mom!" he exclaimed. "We're on the way home!" He listened to her. "Yep. Four of us! There's someone here who wants to talk to you." He handed the phone to Joy.

"Hi, Gram. Uh-huh. Uh-huh." Joy grew silent, but she smiled and nodded.

Peter handed the phone to Andrea. "Hi, Mom."

"Oh, darling, it's so sweet of you to call. Joy sounds a little subdued," Zoë said.

"Especially with me," Andrea murmured.

"This is a major adjustment, love. She's probably not quite sure about you yet."

"Right."

"It'll just take some time. I'll be praying."

"Thanks, Mom. We should be home about—" Andrea

looked across the aisle at Peter. He held up five fingers. "About five. Love you."

Tim grabbed the phone from her. "Love ya too Gram!"

As Andrea took the phone from Tim and handed it to Peter, she leaned out to look at Joy. Their eyes met briefly, but Joy looked away. Andrea sighed and settled back in her seat.

Tim put his hand on her arm. "You going back to work, now that we have Joy back?"

She twisted in her seat to look at him. "No, honey. I don't think so. I only get one chance at being a mom to you and to Joy." She thought a moment. "Oh, I might do some consulting from home. But I have plenty of time to go back to work when you're both older."

"Good," he said. He relaxed a moment, then looked across the aisle at Joy. Unbuckling his seat belt, he slipped past Andrea into the aisle, wriggling his hand to catch Joy's attention. Then he leaned over Andrea. "Let's play 'owl,'" he said.

What in the world? she thought. He was a bit old for that little game. It was Joy that . . . tears stung her eyes. Her sensitive son wanted Joy to remember. "Right," she said, and they locked foreheads together.

"Eyes closed?" he asked.

"Yes."

"One, two, three—owl!" he said.

They opened their eyes and both laughed at each other's 'owl eyes.'

She heard Joy's voice. "Down, Daddy." Peter unbuckled her seat belt, and she pushed Tim away so she could stand beside Andrea in the aisle. "Want to play 'owl,'" she said. Her forehead and tiny nose met Andrea's, and Andrea smelled Ivory soap. "Close your eyes," Joy ordered. "OK. One, two, three—owl!"

Andrea's eyes misted as she opened them, and she could barely see her daughter's owl eyes. But she could hear Joy's infectious giggle, and Andrea found herself laughing through her tears. She gently drew Joy into her arms and felt the sturdy little body yield to her embrace. "My precious little owlet!" Andrea whispered. "Welcome back!"